PRAISE FOR MELANIE DOBSON

The Curator's Daughter

"Melanie Dobson is a master. With great insight into racism in the past and in the present, the novel brings up deep questions about what risks we would take to stand up for what's right. Exceptional research shines on each page, but the intertwined stories of Hanna, Lilly, and Ember are what kept me flipping those pages. A gem of a novel."

SARAH SUNDIN, bestselling and Carol Award–winning author of *When Twilight Breaks* and the Sunrise at Normandy series

"Set in a world coming apart at the seams, this story will sweep you up in life-and-death struggles but ultimately fill you with love and hope. A haunting, totally immersive novel."

CHRIS FABRY, bestselling author of *Under a Cloudless Sky*

"Intriguing, multilayered, and suspenseful, *The Curator's Daughter* winds through generations like the labyrinth it portrays. . . . I started this book late one morning and could not put it down. Melanie Dobson's historical research alone is astounding, but the story is also brilliant and masterfully told. Readers of time-split fiction will love this."

CATHY GOHLKE, Christy Award–winning author of *Night Bird Calling* and *The Medallion*

"[A]n unforgettable saga. With her vivid description, well-crafted characters, and rich historical detail, Melanie Dobson transports readers to Nuremberg, Germany, during World War II, telling what might seem at first a familiar tale of the Nazi regime, yet leaving us with a new, deeper understanding of the legacy of evil left in its wake decades later. The history at the heart of this story should never be forgotten."

MICHELLE SHOCKLEE, author of *Under the Tulip Tree*

Memories of Glass

"*Memories of Glass* is a remarkable, multilayered novel that weaves stories of friendship and faith in wartime Holland together with a modern-day orphanage in Africa. Memorable characters portray the complexity of human relationships and reveal the lasting consequences of our choices, whether cowardly or courageous, and the mysteries kept me turning pages, leaving me with much to ponder."

LYNN AUSTIN, bestselling author of *If I Were You* and *Legacy of Mercy*

"Like colored shards in sunlight, Melanie Dobson once again shines her light of truth in this elegantly complex and gripping tale of the hidden terrors of the Netherlands during WWII. *Memories of Glass* is a remarkable story and one that will linger in the hearts of readers long after the last page."

KATE BRESLIN, bestselling author of *For Such a Time*

"Heart-wrenching history combines with gripping characters and Melanie Dobson's signature gorgeous writing to create a tale you won't be able to put down—and won't want to. *Memories of Glass* is an amazing, intricately woven story of finding light in the least likely of places."

ROSEANNA M. WHITE, bestselling author of the Shadows over England series

"Breathtaking, heartbreaking, and ultimately uplifting, *Memories of Glass* shows the beauty of helping others, the ugliness of people helping only themselves, and the destructive power of secrets through the generations. . . . This novel will stay with you."

SARAH SUNDIN, bestselling and Carol Award–winning author of *When Twilight Breaks* and the Sunrise at Normandy seriess

"I couldn't stop turning the pages of Melanie Dobson's *Memories of Glass*. . . . Peopled with characters heroic, flawed, and unforgettable, *Memories of Glass* is sure to please longtime fans of Melanie Dobson's books as well as readers new to her novels."

LORI BENTON, author of *Mountain Laurel* and *The King's Mercy*

Hidden Among the Stars

"This exciting tale will please fans of time-jump inspirational fiction."

Publishers Weekly

"A romantic tale of castles, lost dreams, and hidden treasures wrapped inside a captivating and suspenseful mystery complete with an unpredictable, unforeseen, and unexpected ending. Not a book to miss!"

Midwest Book Reviews

"Star-crossed, forbidden love and the disappearance of family members and hidden treasure make a compelling WWII story and set the stage for modern-day detective work in Dobson's latest time-slip novel. . . . *Hidden Among the Stars* is Dobson at her best."

CATHY GOHLKE, Christy Award–winning author of *Night Bird Calling* and *The Medallion*

"*Hidden Among the Stars* is a glorious treasure hunt, uniting past and present with each delightful revelation. It's must-read historical fiction that left me pondering well-crafted twists for days."

MESU ANDREWS, award-winning author of *Isaiah's Daughter*

Catching the Wind

"Dobson creates a labyrinth of intrigue, expertly weaving a World War II drama with a present-day mystery to create an unforgettable story. This is a must-read for fans of historical time-slip fiction."

Publishers Weekly, starred review

"Dobson skillfully interweaves three separate lives as she joins the past and present in an uplifting tale of courage, love, and enduring hope."

Library Journal

"A beautiful and captivating novel with compelling characters, intriguing mystery, and true friendship.."

Romantic Times

"Readers will delight in this story that illustrates how the past can change the present."

LISA WINGATE, national bestselling author of *Before We Were Yours*

A NOVEL

THE CURATOR'S DAUGHTER

MELANIE DOBSON

Tyndale House Publishers
Carol Stream, Illinois

Visit Tyndale online at tyndale.com.

Visit Melanie Dobson's website at melaniedobson.com.

TYNDALE and Tyndale's quill logo are registered trademarks of Tyndale House Ministries.

The Curator's Daughter

Designed by Jennifer Phelps

Edited by Kathryn S. Olson

Published in association with the literary agency of Natasha Kern Literary Agency, Inc., P.O. Box 1069, White Salmon, WA 98672.

For information about special discounts for bulk purchases, please contact Tyndale House Publishers at csresponse@tyndale.com, or call 1-800-323-9400.

Library of Congress Cataloging-in-Publication Data
Names: Dobson, Melanie, author.
Title: The curator's daughter / Melanie Dobson.
Description: Carol Stream, Illinois : Tyndale House Publishers, [2021]
Identifiers: LCCN 2020037007 (print) | LCCN 2020037008 (ebook) | ISBN 9781496444165 (hardcover) | ISBN 9781496444172 (trade paperback) | ISBN 9781496444189 (kindle edition) | ISBN 9781496444196 (epub) | ISBN 9781496444202 (epub)
Subjects: LCSH: World War, 1939-1945--Fiction. | GSAFD: Historical fiction. | Christian fiction.
Classification: LCC PS3604.O25 C87 2021 (print) | LCC PS3604.O25 (ebook) | DDC 813/.6--dc23
LC record available at https://lccn.loc.gov/2020037007
LC ebook record available at https://lccn.loc.gov/2020037008

Printed in the United States of America

27 26 25 24 23 22 21
7   6   5   4   3   2   1

AUNT JANET WACKER

MARCH 29, 1946–JUNE 13, 2018

I'm forever grateful that you shared your stories,

Wacker-strength, love of people, and friendships formed

while teaching in a segregated all-black school.

KIKI

My beautiful explorer and encourager.

Thank you for partnering with your mama

on every book.

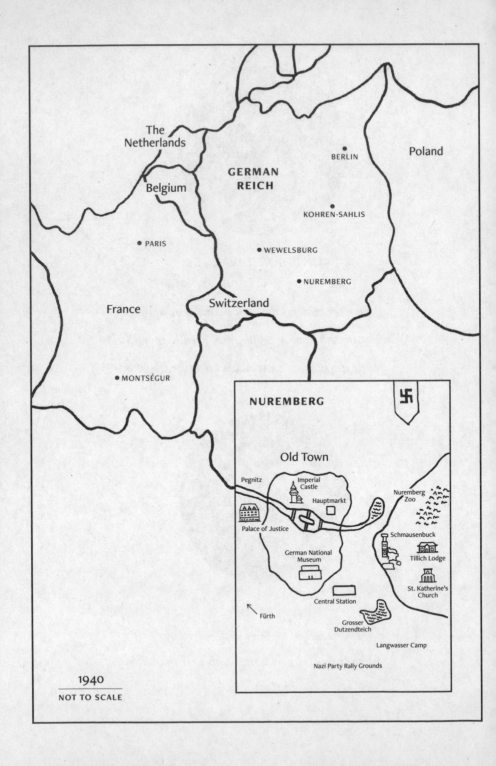

The Netherlands

Belgium

GERMAN REICH

• BERLIN

Poland

• KOHREN-SAHLIS

• PARIS

• WEWELSBURG

• NUREMBERG

France

Switzerland

• MONTSÉGUR

NUREMBERG

Old Town

Pegnitz

Imperial Castle

Hauptmarkt

Nuremberg Zoo

Palace of Justice

Schmausenbuck

Tillich Lodge

German National Museum

St. Katherine's Church

Central Station

← Fürth

Grosser Dutzendteich

Langwasser Camp

Nazi Party Rally Grounds

1940
NOT TO SCALE

PROLOGUE

The moon gazed across Eagle Lake through a veil of mist, watching over this valley of lofty white pines and locked gates that welcomed only those with the purest of blood. Those who fought boldly for the strength of their humanity.

Fresh snowmelt lapped against the muddy bank, its sting icing Sarah's toes, blasting up her ivory skin like the storms that thundered through these rocky canyons each spring. In this early morning hour, dressed in a cotton nightie, she didn't feel the noble strength of her Aryan blood. Didn't feel it at any hour really. Her blood seemed to fail her whenever she needed it most.

These nights alone on the lakeshore, she wasn't even certain what she believed, but Lukas stockpiled enough passion in his heart for both her and their baby. Before they'd married, Lukas had assured her that he would erase any doubts lingering in her mind, but she was fifteen now and the doubts only swelled with age.

The bright eye of the moon blinked—or had it winked at her? Perhaps it was mocking her like those who didn't want them in this valley.

Town was just twenty minutes away. She'd attended public school in Coeur d'Alene for a short time until Father found out she was required to pledge that every citizen in their nation was under God. He pulled her out of second grade but not before a classmate—a black friend—told her that God was love and He had the audacity to love everyone, no matter the color of their skin. Her school friend told her about this love and so did her brother, before Father banned her from speaking with both of them.

The glazed surface disappeared for a moment, black and then a white sheen frosting the lake. Two colors that haunted her both day and night.

As the black and white melded into gray before her, it seemed, in the strangest sense, that they needed each other.

If God created mankind and a world full of color, why would He love only those with the lightest of skin? Why were those who reflected the variety of nature's palette seemingly less in His eyes?

These questions burned like the icy water on her toes, but she didn't dare ask them. The Aryan Council, led by her father, didn't appreciate questions. Their nation was supposed to be of one mind. Always. The lesser races, Father had explained, were spawn of Satan's alliance with Eve, after she'd been banned from the Garden.

Sarah was supposed to believe that anyone stained brown was marked as an enemy of God, but out here her mind could go rogue. She could be who God created her to be, far beneath her layers of skin. Ask the questions churning inside her. Out here all the colors of night, the sweet smell of pine, replenished her soul.

Lukas and their sweet daughter, three months on this earth, were asleep in the cabin behind her. Fifty other members of their esteemed council, including her parents, were also sleeping in the cluster of cabins.

She'd found no peace in this remote enclave, its chapel rumbling with hatred, the armory stocked with enough weapons to take out the entire town and a good chunk of Idaho along with it.

But a different God seemed to reign along the shores of Eagle Lake. One that embraced peace instead.

Lukas and Father had tried to erase her doubts, but neither had succeeded. When her soul cried out in desperation, she could find a glimpse of God here and feel, for the briefest of moments, as if she were truly alive. On nights like this, when her heart longed for answers, she desperately needed this glimpse.

A smooth stone glimmered by her foot, and she plucked it from the mud, tossing it back into the water. Then she listened to its gentle splash before it disappeared.

What would it be like to untie one of the boats along the dock and drift away? Or wander into the cold water, let it swallow her up in depths that dropped hundreds of feet, mirroring the height of snow-swept mountains around them?

What would it feel like to just be *gone*?

A coyote howled in the distance, mimicking a baby's cry. And the cry brought her back. No matter how much she wanted to leave this compound, this life, she couldn't leave Elsie behind.

The mist shivered as if it knew the sunlight would chase it away soon. That everything was about to change.

She should return to bed before Lukas awakened, but she couldn't think inside their cabin—couldn't worry or even wonder what would happen if she tried to step outside the gates, the barbed wire, alone. Inside the cabin, she tried not to feel at all.

All she did was hold her daughter and wish they could steal away together in the night. A wish she could never tell another soul, not even whisper to Elsie. Others in the Aryan Council had longed for an escape, but they never ran far. Her father wouldn't allow it.

Often they never ran at all—those people simply disappeared like the sinking stone.

The lake lapped over her toes again, delivering its chill from a long journey down the mountains. Then a light flickered through the fog, a tiny spark on the water. A lone star in this galaxy of night.

She stared at the spark until a flame, as sharp as her husband's sword, dipped and curled itself in the black space, piercing the edge of the veil, its glow burning through her mind.

A nightmare, she thought, of fire and screaming and people trying to scale the barbs and spikes on their property's fence. She must still be asleep in the cottage above the lake, Lukas at her side, Elsie rocking in her cradle beside them.

Only a dream—

A siren shattered the silence, rippling across her skin, slicing through the mist in her mind.

This was no dream. Nor was it a drill. Her father wouldn't allow the guards in their gatehouse to train without warning. A siren meant the men must fight. The women and children run.

She knew exactly what she was supposed to do if the enemy attacked. Father had boats waiting to transport the women and children and eventually the men to the opposite shore. Deep in the mountains, far from town, was another compound called Eagle's Nest, a fortress stockpiled with weapons and enough food to last a decade if necessary.

A hiding place their enemy would never find.

She was supposed to run, but her feet froze in the mud.

The flames lapped against her parents' cottage, like the water across her feet, and in a blink, the fire devoured the pine.

People poured out of their homes now, screaming with the blare of sirens.

Was Lukas still in their cottage? He'd been asleep when she crept down to the shore, but sometimes he left during the night as well.

Had he—had they—left Elsie alone?

Fear swept through her, igniting her feet. Instead of climbing into a boat, Sarah raced up the hill until another young woman—Aimee—grabbed her arm, tried to pull her toward the water. "You can't go back, Sarah."

A second cottage succumbed to the blaze, then one beside it. Her cabin was next.

"Elsie!" she cried out, shaking off the woman's hold.

Not that her daughter could respond, but she must know her mom was coming. That she would never leave her baby alone to face this fire.

She coughed as she ran, the smoke burning its way into her lungs, stinging her eyes.

"Sarah—" Lukas's voice roared over the chaos. "I've got her."

The fire licked against the cottage as she squinted through the haze, searching for her husband and the girl in his arms.

A glimpse was all she needed. Then she would know.

"We'll meet at Eagle's Nest," he shouted.

Sarah pushed through the crowd, her arms outstretched as she pressed toward his voice. "Give her to me."

"No." The sound was fainter now, as if the fire was swallowing him. "I'll carry her to the mountain."

Aimee took her arm again, tugging toward the dock. "We have to go."

"Get into the boat," Lukas commanded from behind, his face lost in the blur of smoke and haze. Others climbed into the old pontoon, but her wet toes hung on the edge of the slippery dock, refusing to move.

"Not without Elsie—"

"We're on the next boat."

Always, she did what Lukas said, but defiance blazed through her now with the swirl of light. Red laced with black and the heat of white, the stench of charring wood and—her heart dropped— gunpowder in the shed.

A push, and she fell into the pontoon as an explosion ricocheted across the shore, rocking the boat. The driver didn't wait for their entire stockpile to catch fire. He pulled back the throttle and raced through the smoke to the opposite shore.

The Aryan Council never made the climb to Eagle's Nest. On the other side of the lake an army of camouflage surrounded them. Sarah, they swept to one side before corralling the adults into the waiting vans.

She searched the water's edge for another boat, through the curtain of mist that glowed orange. The others couldn't be far behind. In minutes—seconds—Lukas's boat would join them.

These camouflaged men couldn't keep her from her baby.

"My daughter," she pleaded when a man directed her to his car, grasping her arm so she couldn't run back to the lake.

He shook his head, told her he was sorry.

A new name, he said. A new name for her and a new life.

But he couldn't tell her what happened to Elsie.

PART ONE

National Socialism is . . . the care and leadership
of a people defined by a common blood-
relationship. . . . We thus serve the maintenance
of a divine work and fulfill a divine will—
not in the secret twilight of a new house of worship,
but openly before the face of the Lord.

ADOLF HITLER
FINAL NUREMBERG RALLY
SEPTEMBER 1938

HANNA

MONTSÉGUR, FRANCE
SPRING 1940

Secret keepers—that was what Hanna Tillich called the sect of Cathars who once hid in this cavern. And she respected anyone who could keep a secret, especially one this big, to their death.

A breeze drummed against the rock walls, whispering stories from this old passage. Secrets that Hanna was determined to find.

If only she could decipher the cadence of the wind.

While her fellow archaeologists worked to excavate the cave's front room, she'd stolen back into this tunnel. Candlelight flickered across the wall, illuminating the charcoal etchings of three shields, each one marked by a rust-colored symbol that looked like an Iron Cross, the carvings well-preserved in the darkness of this grotto.

Hanna shivered in spite of the fur-lined jacket issued to her by Heinrich Himmler, the trowel in her other hand clanging against the metal lantern. Hundreds of Cathars had gathered in the ruined castle above this cavern in the thirteenth century, most of them killed by Catholic crusaders for refusing to renounce their faith.

Had some of the members been murdered inside this cave? Perhaps they'd left these symbols behind as a warning. Or a clue as to where they'd hidden their secrets.

She studied the crosses on the shields, so like the cross that had decorated her father's military coat when he fought against France. Like the cross the Führer awarded men today who were fighting for the *Vaterland*.

Hanna wasn't fighting, but her service for Germany, Reichsführer Himmler had said, was just as important as their soldiers. He'd hand-selected her and each archaeologist in his Ahnenerbe team to unearth evidence that would prove to the entire world that the German people had descended from the Aryan Nordic race. The Noble Ones.

But her team of archaeologists had traveled to Montségur for another reason. Seven hundred years had passed since the massacre here, but no one had discovered where the Cathars had hidden the Emerald Cup—the Holy Grail—that once pressed against Christ's lips at the Last Supper, later collecting drops of His blood. Three years ago, German explorer Otto Rahn had stolen secretly into this region and climbed the treacherous cliff up to this cavern, convinced that the Cathars had buried the jeweled cup in one of its passages.

Rahn had been the only German, to Hanna's knowledge, to ever excavate this cave, but no one knew exactly what he found. Rahn had died last year, taking yet another secret to the grave.

As strong as Himmler's drive was to unearth the Aryan roots of Germany, the man was also obsessed with finding this Holy Grail. A Christian artifact with mystical powers, he said, that could win the current war.

Hanna didn't obsess over power like Himmler and the Nazi leadership. Stories were her lifeblood, especially those from the past that could root a generation struggling to find its identity. After the devastation—the humiliation—of losing the *Weltkrieg* in 1918, the German people were desperate to pour a new foundation.

In the past months, Germany had finally begun to overcome the defeat of this World War by expanding their *Lebensraum*—living space—into France. Now Himmler had commissioned Hanna's team to find the Grail. They could search this entire region without government interference.

He'd promised to keep the Holy Grail safe under the mantle of the home forces and his SS officers so it wouldn't be destroyed like so many of the artifacts of Germanic roots, just like he'd promised to protect every German who'd rooted themselves in a Christian heritage. Their team still needed to keep the work quiet, though, as many who lived along the Pyrenees weren't fond of the new government or its interest in holy relics.

Another light bridged the chain of shields, and Hanna swiveled in her military boots, almost stabbing her superior, Kolman Strauss, with her trowel.

He knocked the blade away swiftly with the handle of his tripod as if it were a sword. She'd learned plenty in her four years at the University of Berlin, but fencing was not a required class for her studies in anthropology.

"These were carved by the Knights Templar," Kolman said, his easy smile excusing her ineptness.

She picked her trowel off the dirt floor and turned back to examine the sharp lines of each shield beside him. "One of the many mysteries in this place."

"She'll share her secrets with us."

The Brylcreem in Kolman's hair defied even the temperament of the wind, and his Aryan blue eyes had secured him a lifelong membership as regiment leader in Himmler's *Schutzstaffel*. His gray sleeves were rolled up to his elbows as if he were warm inside this frigid cavern, ready to capture on motion-picture film whatever this medieval religious sect had left behind.

Some historians thought the Knights Templar had collaborated with the Cathars to guard the holiest relics, but these etchings might not be artwork from the Cathars or Templars. It was quite possible that others, like Rahn and Hanna's team, had scaled the mountainside in recent years to seek treasure or simply to commemorate the six hundred thousand Cathars who'd been massacred during the Crusades.

"Kill them all for the Lord knows them that are His."

That's what the abbot supposedly said to validate the bloodshed of Cathars and Catholics alike in 1209. Let God sort it out in the end.

How exactly, she wondered, did God sort those who'd vowed to serve Him?

Despite Kolman's confidence about finding the Grail, the contents of this cavern were a mystery to all of them, shrouded in centuries of legend and literature. No amount of threatening or even coaxing would force her to give up her secrets if she wasn't willing to share.

But Hanna and Kolman and two other archaeologists could work here for days or weeks if necessary, however long it took to unearth any artifacts left by the Cathars. They would spend their nights at a vineyard, and each morning, they'd use ropes and the mountain's footholds to bring their gear up into the cavern while German soldiers guarded the cliffside entrance and waited in the surrounding forest below, in case the local residents decided to rebel.

Hanna prayed no one would threaten them or the soldiers. It would be senseless for any more blood to be shed here while she and her team were trying to protect the holy relics from harm.

She pointed with her lantern toward the narrow corridor. "I'm going farther in."

The feet on Kolman's tripod punctured the ground. "I'll retrieve my camera."

He had hauled his motion-picture camera up to this cavern with all of their supplies, just like he'd taken his camera with them to film their work across the continents, but she didn't want the camera peering over her shoulder this morning. The flood of Kolman's lights. He had plenty of earlier film to prove her worth, but if she didn't find anything today, all Himmler would see when they returned home was her failure.

"No," she insisted. "This is something I want to do alone."

A defiant strand of straw-blonde hair escaped from its prison of pins, and she set her lantern and trowel on the ground to remove a glove and return the strand to its messy chignon.

As her superior, Kolman could insist on accompanying her, but he stepped back. "You're a brave soul, Hanna."

"More curious than brave, I'm afraid."

"Both are important to the Ahnenerbe. It's unfortunate you're not a . . ." He stopped himself, but the unspoken word still dangled between them.

A man.

It truly was unfortunate. The few professional women in Germany were slowly being reassigned to other jobs. Hanna was the only female archaeologist still working in the field, but she suspected that would not last much longer. Himmler had recently moved the department of the Ahnenerbe under the umbrella of the powerful Schutzstaffel. As a woman, she would never qualify to become an SS officer.

But if the Holy Grail was hidden in this cave, if Hanna was the one to excavate it, surely Himmler would keep her employed. More than anything, she wanted to continue her work of preserving the history, the stories, of her people before their heritage was completely lost, but if she didn't prove her worth, her dedication, Himmler would reassign her to type, file, and transfer reports for one of his men.

"If I find it," she assured Kolman, "then I'll bury it again so you can film our discovery."

His sharp nod was one of respect for a colleague who was equally as focused on this task. "We're going to find it."

The other archaeologists had stopped in the front room to dig under a stalagmite, a fixture that French literature had deemed the Altar. A worthy location for a religious sect to bury their relics or bones, but it was too close to the entrance, she thought, for a powerful treasure like the Holy Grail. If the Cathars were willing to die for their secrets, they'd have taken great care about where they buried them.

Another gust shuddered through the entrance, loosened hair from her knot, and the strands folded themselves over her eyes, blinding her from the light. Kolman brushed the hair away from her eyes, and her skin flickered at his touch. Had he felt it too, the spark that passed between them?

"Hanna—"

"We have to find this cup," she said, hoping to dampen the flicker.

He smiled again. "I know."

"We can't lose our focus now."

He wrapped the hair over her ear, the flame sparking again.

Her first—her only—love now was digging for artifacts. She had to extinguish these schoolgirl notions before she made another choice she'd regret.

The trail of lamplight led her away from Kolman, into the unknown. A place where she thrived. She followed the wind and light through the narrow entrance, into a chamber with a ceiling that soared far beyond the range of her lantern. Like the nave of Lorenzkirche back home, the church she'd attended with Luisa each Sunday.

How she missed Luisa, her cousin who'd come to live with Hanna's family after she lost both parents in an accident. Only a few years older than Hanna, her cousin had become a tutor, sister, and friend, teaching her to search for answers to questions others didn't even know to ask.

Hanna smoothed her gloved hand over the ridges on the limestone wall, trekking over the hard-packed dirt embedded with stones, into an underground cathedral. Here the air was still and damp on her skin, the smell musty like the attic where she'd once played. Like the old graphite mine on her family's property.

The Cathars wouldn't have buried their treasure in a grand chamber like this, but they might have hidden it nearby.

The cave's ridges bowed into alcoves and tiny rooms notched into the sides. Cupboards, she thought, as she stepped into one. Or a cellar.

Hanna dropped her rucksack along a wall and then crawled with her lantern and steel trowel into a jug-sized room that spilled into an even smaller chamber. Lantern light danced across shells embedded in the walls and then something else—

The faintest sketching on *dem Stein*, a line—two lines—drawn in a white ochre faded with time, parallel in their fall to the ground.

She followed the stripes down to her knees and at the bottom of the wall was a triangular tip, stained a faint red like the Iron Crosses. A lance. Or a blood-tipped arrow.

Hanna swept her trowel across the surface as if it were a brush before edging out a neat square with the blade. This was what she lived for. The possibility of finding answers if only she chose the right place. Digging deep enough to locate whatever her team was searching for.

The utmost care was necessary when excavating, but she worked swiftly this morning, her heart pounding as she shaved away the dirt. When they were looking for remnants of Atlantis, the archaeologists used sifters so they wouldn't miss the smallest pieces that hinted toward the greater story. Here, though, they weren't looking for the pieces. Himmler wanted the entire cup. Intact. As if it were a white rabbit to pull out of their magician's hat.

He wanted the impossible really, but it was her job to either deliver it or produce enough evidence to continue their search.

Since receiving her degree in Berlin, Hanna had been trekking across Sweden and Tibet with the Ahnenerbe to discover where the Aryan people had originated and how Himmler could replicate their strength today. Power and proof of the Germanic heritage—the two things that Himmler seemed to crave more than anything.

They hadn't found conclusive evidence about Aryans in Tibet or Sweden, but they'd found dozens of shards in Sweden that pointed to an advanced civilization. Whatever Kolman reported back seemed to satisfy the Reichsführer.

In the light of a new candle, Hanna started to dig, willing the dirt to reveal its secrets. Square by square, meter by meter, she would search this room until she found either the cup or another clue.

An hour passed as she carved through the pressed soil, finding fragments of bone and pottery. Her trowel hit a stone, and she pushed her way around it, the rounded edges of this rock reminding her of home. The stones in the nearby labyrinth where her mother used to pray.

The steel blade clanked against something, and her heart lurched as the candlelight caught a glimmer of green.

She removed her pocketknife and had just begun to ease away the dirt when she heard Kolman's voice, shouting her name from another room.

Quickly she dumped the dirt back into the hole, smoothing it over, and then turned, lantern in hand, to crawl back into the chamber.

She wanted to film her discovery and then carry the treasured cup out in triumph so the entire team could see what she'd found hidden. So word would trickle back that Hanna Tillich had discovered this holy relic on her own.

If Kolman found it, he and his camera would take full credit.

Tossing her trowel beside her rucksack, she rushed back toward the cathedral chamber, the shadows from her lantern rocking across the walls.

"What is it?" she asked when she reemerged in the main hall.

Kolman grasped her wrist. "We have to leave."

"But—"

"Now," he said, his rank as an officer punctuating this word.

She shook off his hand. "I'll gather my things."

"We don't have time."

But her pocketknife and trowel, her pack with its notebook and pencils and extra candles were inside. She couldn't just leave them all behind.

"Time for wh—?"

A distant thunder echoed through the grotto, and she stared at the arc of light leading to the entrance, confused. The skies had been clear when they climbed to the cave.

"Someone doesn't want us in France." He was pulling her now into the passage, away from her things.

"I need my pack." And a glimpse at whatever was buried in the dirt.

"The others have already started down." It was his job to guide their team in and then out of this cave safely, but surely she had time to fetch her rucksack.

The sound of another explosion placed her firmly on Kolman's side.

She clipped into the mountainside hold before rappelling back into the forest.

In the morning, she'd retrieve her pack, after the soldiers had calmed this storm.

2

HANNA

LIMOUX, FRANCE

Burgundy and green dappled the slope as Hanna nursed a goblet of wine harvested, pressed, and aged in the valley below. Every blossom, it seemed, was trumpeting this season of spring, but even with the solace of wine, Hanna's forehead pounded after she'd hammered it against the dashboard of the military truck that had whisked her team away from the cavern, into the protection of the French police.

The team around her was laughing now, but they hadn't done much laughing in their hours along the rock-strewn path that would never be mistaken for a road.

She took another sip of the dry wine while her fellow archaeologists and the six soldiers who'd accompanied them recalled their afternoon's adventure as if they'd been sent into combat, overcoming the enemy instead of fleeing from resistance fighters who'd blown up a nearby railway. Fighters who probably wouldn't have even known the archaeologists were in the cavern until the Wehrmacht trucks roared through the forest.

How long would their team have to wait now to return to the cave?

After the other men staggered off to their beds, she'd speak with Kolman alone. If he knew about the arrow engraving, the metal buried beneath it, he'd find a way for them to continue their work. She could travel back secretly with him and his camera, tonight even, and this discovery would secure her a lifetime position in the Ahnenerbe. Himmler could easily make an exception, overlook her gender, and she could continue searching for significant artifacts, using history to build a new kingdom.

The sun lingered above the vineyard's ridge, dangling like a marionette over an extravagant theater, as the wine slowly pressed the ache from her head. A man in denim overalls, the owner of this vineyard, refilled their goblets; then he placed a red-stamped *Telegramm* into Kolman's hands.

While many Germans thought the Nazi Party was uniting their land, some saw only the divisions. But Himmler and the others were pursuing history and science and things like homeopathy that her mother had once prized. The World War had demoralized their country, fracturing it into pieces, but Adolf Hitler was reuniting them. Germans were finally moving forward again with dreams and ideas that brought them together. A holy pursuit to bring their world back into order, increase their living space to the east and west, and fight off the Russians who threatened their land.

Once again, Germany was strong, but at what cost? Hanna wrestled with this daily, hearing rumors about animosity in the Nazi ranks. A dangerous undercurrent flowed below the greater good, Jewish people leaving in droves because they could no longer work or even shop in a country they once called home.

Her only weapons, a trowel and pocketknife, could do nothing to stop the current. She had to keep her eyes on preserving the past, not trying to control the future.

In the lull of conversation, Kolman read the telegram before placing his empty glass back on the table. "Walk with me," he said to Hanna, offering his hand as if she were the marionette, waiting for him to pull her strings.

Heat flooded her cheeks as the gazes of their colleagues dropped to their goblets, suddenly fascinated by their crystal rims. It was one thing for Kolman to hint at his interest when they were alone, quite another to advertise it. He would blow up their entire team if he propositioned her here.

She didn't take his hand. Instead she straightened the scarf over the collar of her blouse and stood. Her profession as an archaeologist was hard-won. She wouldn't lose this job because Kolman Strauss crossed a line.

He reached for the bottle of wine and two empty glasses before following her down the slope. While she'd changed into another blouse, she still wore her work trousers and boots on their descent between the grapevines.

Hanna stopped walking halfway down the hill, in plain sight of the team. While her racing heart might fail her, she must keep her head firmly about her in the presence of this man. She'd speak to him about the excavation and then they'd return to their wine.

Arms crossed over her chest, Hanna turned to face him. "We need to return to the grotto."

Instead of answering, he scanned the vineyard with its posts and vines and sheds knotted on the hill. Then he directed her toward a stone outbuilding. "Let's talk in there."

She glanced up at the patio, her team looking back down over the vineyard, and decided that plain sight wasn't the best place for this discussion after all.

Kolman put down the wine bottle long enough to open the door, and she stepped into a room filled with dozens of barrels, a bitter smell permeating the wood.

"Hanna . . ." With the bottle and glasses resting on an oak lid, he pulled the telegram out of his pocket, and she stared down as if it were soaked in venom.

"What does it say?"

He tapped the envelope on one of the barrels. "Your father owns a house in Nuremberg, yes?"

She blinked, the question far from what she'd anticipated. "My father is no longer alive."

"But the property is yours?"

Hanna's mother had died when she was three, and her father had passed away seven years back, before she left for the university. The Tillich home, a restored hunting lodge, was being cared for now by Luisa and her husband, Paul. Hanna could return at any time, but home, for as long as she proved her worth, was wherever Himmler sent her and her trowel.

"It's being leased," she told Kolman.

He tucked the telegram into his front pocket, looking relieved at her words. "You can break a lease."

"I'm not breaking this one."

"You will do what the Reich requires of you."

Her shoulders clenched. What interest did the Reich have in her property?

He poured red wine into the glasses and lifted one as if he were about to offer a toast, but she had no interest in celebrating. They needed to stay focused on the matter at hand. "At the cavern today—"

"Hanna." He lowered his glass, reaching out his hand to her again. "I'm afraid you won't be going back to Montségur."

Whether it was the wine or because she was desperate for answers, she didn't know, but this time she took his hand.

Kolman squeezed it gently, as if he might pass along the strength inside him. No matter what happened, no matter what he said, she wouldn't gasp or cry or give him any reason to accuse her of weakness, because she *would* return to the cave, once she told him about the Grail. They'd need her.

He looped his fingers through hers. "The Germanic National Museum has requested your services."

She yanked her hand away from his tangle of fingers. "A museum?"

"In Nuremberg," he said as if she didn't know the location. "It's time for you to go home."

She'd known it wouldn't be long before they pulled her off the field, but the reality still pierced like an arrow straight into her heart. She couldn't sit in a sterile museum office, no matter how renowned its collection, when they were on the cusp of discovering this relic. She wanted to be the one searching for artifacts to display, not filing paperwork.

The female curse of tears, a swift current of them, threatened to flood across the banks, and she blinked back the surge before it ruined her.

She was stronger than the tears.

"What if I found something, Kolman? Something of significance."

His smile was one of amusement. Pity, even, as if she were a child with one more excuse to suspend her bedtime. "Like the Grail?"

She didn't dare tell him what she thought was in that chamber. Not yet. "Any artifact important to Himmler."

"He'd be thrilled with the find."

"But it wouldn't influence this reassignment . . . ?"

"I'm afraid that decision has already been made."

A chill swept across her skin. "I need to find the Holy Grail, before I return to Nuremberg."

"The Ahnenerbe needs to find it, Hanna." He took a sip of the wine. "This is a good position waiting for you."

"A good position for a woman . . ."

"For anyone," he countered. "You'll be an excellent archivist."

The cave, the dirt, her pack lying in that hidden corridor. The possibilities that rested under the soil.

"Did Himmler say why he wanted me to do this job?"

"The telegram wasn't from Himmler. It was from the director of the museum."

"So Himmler has stepped away . . ."

"All the archaeologists are required to be members of the Schutzstaffel," he said.

"For which I'll never qualify." She moved toward the window. She needed to find strength inside herself, not siphon it from him.

A hundred shades of sunset swept across the sky, but all she wanted right now was to surround herself again with the darkness of the cave, the pile of dirt swelling beside her.

"It's not just you." Kolman curled his arm over one of the barrels. "Eventually Himmler will call all of us back to Germany."

"For another dig."

"For whatever he sees fit."

How was she going to tell their team that she wasn't returning to dig? Even worse—what if they already knew?

They all could have known except her.

Tears spilled out now, flowing beyond her control. She grabbed the wine bottle and rushed from the building, not caring if any of the men above saw her.

The chamber was a secret that she'd keep. One day she would return to the cavern by herself.

"Hanna!" he called as he trailed behind her. She gulped the wine as she ran, the liquid warming her throat and head, dribbling down her chin. If they were in Berlin, she'd sweep down into the U-Bahn station, take the next train out. And she'd stay on board until the end of the line.

Kolman was no longer her superior. She didn't have to answer to him.

Her feet delivered her to the bottom of the hillside, to a stream she wished would carry her away like a train.

"Hanna," he said again, stepping up behind her.

She threw the bottle into the river, the glass shattering on a rock, and wiped the stream of tears with her scarf. Why must she cry in the face of this man who always remained strong? "Leave me alone."

He was beside her now, his breath warm on her neck. She didn't dare breathe, angry at her heart for betraying her. Racing when she willed it to be still.

The dirt, she could control. The digging. But not the pounding inside her.

When he turned her around, she began backing into the grass. Leave—she needed to run again before she did something she'd regret for a lifetime.

But Kolman didn't waver. Her eyes on him, she didn't see the stone in the grass until her heel stubbed the edge of it, and she stumbled. Her arms flailing, she grasped for a branch, a wall, a boulder, a strong arm to catch her.

Kolman reached out, and with his arms around her, she rested against his chest. A rock in human form.

"Kolman—" Her breath seemed to escape her as he straightened her scarf, the fabric brushing against her skin.

"There's a silver lining in this," he said.

"What possible good could come of it?" Finding things was her dream, not curating them. She was no good at the keeping.

"Marry me," he whispered.

"What?"

"Marry me, Hanna."

"Why would I want to marry you?" she asked, trying to lighten the weight in her voice, the heaviness in her heart.

"Because you like relics," he said, his blue eyes fading into gray with the setting sun.

"You're not a relic."

Kolman was ten years older than her twenty-six, but they'd been colleagues on three digs now. She'd almost forgotten their age difference.

But to marry him?

"We're good together, Hanna." He took both her hands. "We can change this world."

Kolman had been married once before; he'd told their team about his former wife on their expedition in Nepal. The travel, he'd said, had been the demise of their union.

Her obsession with the past, her quest to change the world, would ruin their relationship as well.

"This doesn't have to end," he said.

"You can't be serious." She shook her head, tried to step away. "I'm being sent back to Nuremberg."

He held her hands. "I will go to Nuremberg with you."

Her head felt as if it were sinking with the sun.

"Himmler needs you here."

"I'll return the moment we're done in France."

A picture flashed in her mind of impeccably dressed women who'd attended Berlin's *Reichsbräuteschule* before they married SS officers, learning how to polish buttons and daggers, cook German meals, raise Aryan heroes to take over the world.

"I'm not going to the Reich bridal—bride's school." Her words slurred as she tried to speak.

What was wrong with her? She knew exactly what she wanted for her life, had spent a lifetime preparing for it. Kolman was a worthy suitor for another woman, but marriage itself didn't suit her. Would never suit her.

"You already have enough education," he said, a smile on his lips, but there was nothing amusing about this. Instead of condemning her tears, he wiped them away. "Please, Hanna."

She dug her heel into the stone so she wouldn't stumble again. "I can't give up my work." Even if she was caged inside a museum.

"Of course not."

"You don't want to marry me, Kolman."

But he swore that he did.

3

EMBER

A stumbling stone.

Ember Ellis stared at the photograph on her laptop. At the glitter of brass cemented between Nuremberg's gray cobblestones.

Some German towns had allowed residents to replace sidewalk stones with tiny plaques. *Stolpersteine*, they called these memorials. As if someone might—as if they *should*—stumble over this reminder of where a Jewish man or woman had lived before World War II. One of the six million who never returned home.

Her fellowship with the Mandel Center, an extension of the United States Holocaust Memorial Museum, came with a shared office in the heart of the district and a vast collection of off- and online resources, papers, and photographs. She'd almost finished the dissertation that would add a *P*, *H*, and *D* after her name. Letters that meant after years of trying, she had finally made something of her late-blooming self.

Ember smoothed her fingers over the screen as if she could feel the cool brass, the ridges of engraving.

> Here lived Paul Gruenewald
> Born 1898, Deported 1938
> Murdered in Auschwitz 1942

This short tribute was similar to those recorded in Jewish *Memorbücher*, a tradition started in Nuremberg when entire Jewish communities were being destroyed. These rituals of memory were as important now as they had been for seven hundred years.

> Nuremberg shines throughout Germany like a sun among
> the moon and stars.

Martin Luther had written those words in the sixteenth century, after Nuremberg embraced the Reformation. This was a city, he'd written, that moved others to follow. Good or bad, Luther's words had echoed through the centuries, rays from that renaissance city sparking fire across Germany.

Yet the cycle of sun rising each morning, the darkness that followed when it fell, cast long shadows in Nuremberg, hurtling across time. For almost a year now, Ember had been searching for the reasons, the patterns, as to why the history of persecution continued to repeat itself in that city. Searching to expose the lies people believed.

The information was hard to find—most of Nuremberg's records had been destroyed in 1945 when the Royal Air Force unleashed its bombs. In fact, it was a miracle that anything, or anyone, survived.

She wanted to find more than stumbling stones in this city where Hitler once held his party rallies, where SS officials and other Nazi leaders were held and tried. Before she completed her dissertation, she wanted to find a hero. A German man or woman who'd snubbed

National Socialism and remained strong in the storm of persecution and propaganda. Held on to what was good and right while many of their neighbors had succumbed.

Ember downloaded the archived photograph, then closed the lid to her computer. Next week she was flying to Nuremberg to interview several people, including the assistant director of the Germanic National Museum. She'd roam inside the ancient walls of this city that occupied a significant space in her head, perhaps even stumble herself over one of these stones that remembered the names of so many Jewish people.

If she and other researchers did their jobs well, their stories wouldn't be forgotten either.

She slipped her laptop into an oversized handbag and slung it over her shoulder. In exactly fifty-eight minutes, Noah would knock on the front door of her condo in Georgetown, and he'd expect her to open it. A minute or two late and her phone would start blasting "Never Give Up." Over and over until she finally returned his call.

If she hurried to the Metro, she would make it home a few minutes before Noah arrived.

"Do you have a minute?" Rebekah May, the head of security, stood outside her office with an iPad and small stack of mail. Her short hair reflected an orange tint like rust rimming this woman of steel.

"I have to be home by 3:40."

Rebekah didn't waste time. She turned her screen so Ember could see a scan of the vile letter addressed to her, typed in a faded Courier font as if the printer had been forced, under duress, to comply.

Ember looked away. "Any return address this time?"

"None. It was postmarked from Boise."

She shivered. Whoever wrote her these letters always sent them from the state where she'd lived two decades ago. The state that she'd spent a lifetime trying to forget.

The letters started coming ten months ago when she'd taken this fellowship. Someone, Rebekah suspected, had picked her name off the Internet listing of fellows.

"It's another empty threat."

"Probably." Rebekah turned off the screen. "But I want you to be careful. Let me know if anyone harasses you outside the mail."

"I will." She checked her phone. Noah would be at her door in forty minutes. Last time she was late, he'd started texting at 3:41. Every thirty seconds, for a full hour while she was stuck on the Metro without cell service. "Thanks for keeping watch over me."

Rebekah handed her a newspaper and two journals from the mail room. "Unfortunately it's getting worse. For everyone."

The hostilities were increasing across their country. She'd seen the recent photographs of fraternity men lifting their hands in faux salutes, heiling Hitler decades after the dictator was gone. Of American children wearing swastikas and mothers teaching their toddlers how to salute. Of adult men attacking their Jewish neighbors.

The side entrance emptied employees into a private alley, but Ember preferred using the museum's main entrance. The long lines of visitors strengthened her hope in humanity, knowing she wasn't the only one who wanted to stop this madness.

A glass elevator delivered her down to the lobby, where hundreds of people waited to remember the terror of all that happened across Europe eighty years ago. And honor those who'd died by remembering their stories.

Parents often brought their kids to remember alongside them, and that, to Ember, was the greatest tribute of all. These children would learn, she prayed, and not repeat the horror, this knowledge defeating any hatred in their hearts.

As she moved through the lobby, toward the front entrance, she heard someone shout. While tourists might yell on the Mall or even the steps at the Lincoln Memorial, this museum was a reverent space to remember. Rarely did anyone, young or old, shout inside these somber walls.

She paused, listening, but the sound had dissipated.

Ahead was a string of doors, but when she reached out to open one, a policewoman stopped her. "Sorry, miss, you don't want to go out there."

"But I—" Then she saw them through the windows. Men built like tanks marching down Fourteenth Street, their raised arms locked into fists, tongues loaded with hatred. They chanted in rapid fire, hurling verbal ammunition at the museum.

Placards pumped up and down, the volley fire of mortars to reiterate their words. A protest against anyone who wasn't like them.

History, she feared, was on the verge of repeating itself.

The policewoman eyed the badge around Ember's neck. "You better use the side door."

The safe exit.

But this was a public place, a memorial, for anyone to enter or exit as they pleased. She'd cowered plenty at the threats of a bully long ago. She wouldn't cower anymore.

Ember pushed open the door.

"Don't go—"

But she was already outside. The men marched past her and the helmeted police, faces protected by shields, who'd gathered on the empty sidewalk to keep the protestors off the museum's property.

Anger blazed inside her. This was exactly what these men were trying to spark, she knew, but in the height of emotion, her voice demanded to be heard.

One of the men shouted another obscenity, one directed at Ember. And she yelled back.

A policeman turned and glared at Ember as if *she* were the problem. As if she were spewing hatred across this district.

Her hands balled into fists as she stared back at the silver badge, the bulky Kevlar vest, of this man whose impossible job was to protect freedom, including the freedom of speech.

These protestors were trying to fuel anger with their words. They wanted her and others to retaliate with their fists. They wanted to be the victims in this war of words.

With the return fire of her own voice, she'd stepped up to play their game.

Hands in her pockets, despair washed over her. Hopelessness. She wanted to stop the hostility, but how could she, in all of her research, stop those whose very identity was grounded in hate?

She couldn't fight on this sidewalk, with words or fists, but she wouldn't flee either.

Noah would have to wait this afternoon. Just a minute or two.

She stood vigilantly like the police officers as the supremacists marched by. On guard.

She wouldn't confront nor would she cower. Like a rock that wouldn't move, a stone to stumble over, she would continue digging up the stories.

And she'd force all of them to remember.

HANNA

The skeleton of a stone spire rose above the eastern hills as if its ghostly bell might toll out across Nuremberg this afternoon, calling them all to prayer. Hanna's taxi was about three kilometers away from the spire now, its tower a beacon to guide her home from the train station.

Home.

Four years had passed since she'd returned to this city that cradled her childhood memories. The hills that had stolen away her mother's breath and eventually the life of her father as well.

At least she still had her cousin to welcome her back. Every letter she'd received over the years from Luisa had begged Hanna to come home.

A hastily packed suitcase was resting on the taxi seat beside her; the contents of trousers, blouses, and work boots had been all she'd needed for the past four years of fieldwork. And her journal and trowel—items she'd left in the cave before Kolman Strauss proposed.

She remembered quite clearly the revelation that she was no longer employed with the Ahnenerbe, but the other details of that night were blurry from the bottle of wine—or was it two?—that she consumed in the aftermath. She had said no to him—hadn't she?

She'd meant to reiterate her refusal the next morning, after the haze of wine cleared from her head, but Kolman and the others were already gone. Only a driver had remained to escort her to Paris, and the man insisted that he didn't know where her team had been sent.

She'd written Kolman a letter on her train ride into Germany, declining his offer of marriage. Then she'd delivered it straight to the headquarters office in Berlin, so they could forward her message to him. The sparks between them were just a distraction. She'd had sparks before, with an American man, and that relationship ended in disaster.

The taxi driver turned sharply onto Bayernstrasse, each windowsill underscored with boxes of spring flowers. But the medieval structures ebbed quickly into modern office buildings, the walls poured from cement. The softness of window blossoms hardened into a crisp red that dripped from the lanky buildings like blood, each flag stamped with a swastika.

In all of her travels, she'd never seen so many flags lined up like this except those that striped the sky red on Unter den Linden, the parade route in Berlin.

She leaned her head back, closing her eyes for a moment, rubbing her hands together as if her trowel might reappear.

What had the Cathars buried in that chamber?

The question had haunted her for the last week. She'd tried to return to Montségur without Kolman and the others, but the one soldier remaining at the vineyard had refused to take her anyplace except Paris.

Had Kolman returned to the cave without her? He'd fling safety off a sinking ship if he must to unearth the find of the century, give Himmler the power he craved. If Kolman fanned his supervisor's fame, he would secure a top position with the SS as well. And Kolman would do just about anything to please Himmler.

At least Hanna no longer had to concern herself with Himmler or the SS.

Paul and Luisa should have received her telegram yesterday. Tonight she'd settle into her old room, and tomorrow she'd begin her work at the museum.

Ahead was Grosser Dutzendteich—the great pond—and beyond it, a forest of branches that seemed to extend all the way to the former Czechoslovakia and into Poland. At the sight, her childhood memories with Luisa flooded back, the two of them paddling across Grosser Dutzendteich on rented boats whenever they visited the Nuremberg Zoo. On the other side of the lake were her favorite animals—the sea elephants and kangaroos and a monkey named Charlie.

Funny, how she'd later met a real Charlie at the university. *Affe*—monkey—she'd called him in their earlier months as friends, before her heart had gone rogue.

Her nose smudged the window as she remembered those years gone by when it was just her and Luisa watching the animals they'd loved. Soon she would see the wall around the zoo with the sign announcing their newest tenant—a gorilla or ostrich or elephant—to draw residents back for a visit.

But the wall never appeared nor the famous billboard. Instead the entire zoo had been cleared into a huge field like the nearby Nazi Party Rally Grounds, and in the distance was a giant stadium.

"What happened to the zoo?" she asked, her nose pressed firmly against the window as if, by remembering, she could make all of the animals and their cages reappear.

The driver glanced curiously in the rearview mirror, pockmarks knobbed across his thin face. He was probably twenty, not much younger than she'd been when she first met Charlie Ward. "How long has it been since you've visited?"

"Four years."

"A lot has changed in four years," he said.

A lot had certainly changed for her and for Germany as a whole. A tornado had roared through their parliament, breaking apart the concrete blocks of their society, sending the pieces flying in different directions.

No one knew when or where it was all going to land.

Just for one moment, why couldn't they settle the winds? Cherish their heritage together instead of launching each piece back into the storm? For just a moment, she wished everything would be still again.

"Did Nuremberg close its zoo?"

The driver straightened his cap. "Apparently the Nazis needed the space more than the animals, but the mayor wouldn't let them close it altogether."

Disdain pierced his explanation, but these days, no one dared to critique Hitler or his hierarchy. Once-vocal criticism had burrowed far under the weight of National Socialism.

But the Nazis' obsession with Nuremberg made sense. Most politicians were fond of the city's former position in the First Reich—the Holy Roman Empire—and the richness from the German Renaissance. The history of its independence and elite culture.

"Where did they send the animals?" she asked.

He nodded ahead to the ghostly tower. "The mayor built a new Tiergarten on Schmausenbuck for everyone to enjoy. Even Hitler made an appearance for the grand opening."

Hanna's father had begun supporting Hitler after one of his Jewish employees embezzled thousands of *Reichsmarks* from the toy factory's accounts. Vater also thought Deutschland needed a leader who could fight back against the disparaging terms of the Treaty of Versailles, and it seemed as if Hitler was the only politician willing to do it.

Luisa, on the other hand, had deemed the man crazy for his hateful rhetoric about the enemy who he said lived among them. Many thought the Nazi Party was uniting their land, but her cousin only saw the divisions.

While Hanna wasn't fond of Hitler's forceful entry into politics or his cruel words, she was pleased that he and Himmler wanted to revive their nation, putting all the broken pieces back together again on the strength of their shared heritage.

"I'm surprised Hitler came back to Nuremberg for a zoo."

"It seems he is fond of our town."

"Indeed." Her mind flashed again to the crevices and mossy trees across the Schmausenbuck, to the abandoned mine shafts in the hills. The place was beautiful but hardly safe for children and animals to be frolicking about. Not even the town youth ventured out that far unless they were camping, and then they pitched their tents up by the abandoned abbey, not by the quarry or old hunting lodge now owned by the Tillich family. "The mountain doesn't seem to be the best place for animals or their visitors."

"The zoo is actually at the bottom of the mountain. Mayor Liebel thought the animals would be protected there."

"Protected from what?"

The driver shrugged.

As they drove farther east, the city's modern buildings turned into neat cottages and eventually the cottages faded into a grove of alder trees. A new sign hung at the base of the mountain, one that announced the grand opening of the zoo with the toothy grin of a billboard gorilla waving at her.

Perhaps she and Luisa could visit this new zoo together.

The driver rounded a corner, heading into the hills, and she saw another sign for the zoo's entrance. The lane on their right led to a ridge of sandstone that overlooked the city.

She leaned forward. "Turn after the sign."

An arbor of gnarled vines arched over the dirt lane. Wind and rain had partnered with a host of ancient miners to etch steep cliffs into this forest, the crevices carved into stone from a quarry that dated back to the Middle Ages.

If only she could roam as she'd done as a child, digging up roots in search of buried treasure and crawling with her lamp into the mine shafts. When Luisa arrived, they'd explored every meter of the abbey's ruins above the lodge and then the surrounding hills. The land had evolved over the centuries, roots sprouting up into a raging green to overtake all that had been stripped away. But the chasms still ran deep in these ragged hills. Nothing except a drastic act of God would ever fill those in.

The taxi driver slowed at the intersection and glanced up the winding road built for wagons and carriages. It was hardly wide enough for an automobile, but her dad used to drive his roadster under this mantle of leaves, the top rolled back so she could bat the low-lying branches.

She took a deep breath. "Left please."

He glanced at her in the mirror. "Are you certain?"

"Of course."

The driver slowed his car as if he were afraid a gorilla might spring from the underwood. "I used to think these hills were haunted."

"No haunts out here," she said. At least none they could see.

He accelerated the taxicab. "I've lived in Nuremberg my entire life, but I never knew about a house in these hills . . ."

Perhaps she shouldn't guide this man all the way to her home. Not that she was frightened of him—she knew how to defend herself—but an undercurrent rumbled beneath the newly formed unity in their country. She didn't know many Jewish people, but she'd been warned that the Jews were trying to rise up and overthrow the state. She didn't need anyone trying to organize a coup back here, especially if they thought she lived alone.

The driver paused beside an ancient water fountain, the stone sculpted into the face of a lion. When she was a girl, she'd been terrified of the trees and mystical monsters and even this fountain, pedaling her bicycle like a pinwheel whenever she passed. Luisa used to laugh at her, thinking it was all a game, but Hanna never thought it was funny.

As the driver crept forward again, she glimpsed the convent's tower before it vanished behind the trees.

"Actually—" she tapped the man's shoulder—"I'll get out here."

The sun was falling behind the hills, but it didn't worry her. She opened the door and lugged her suitcase onto the packed dirt.

"I can't leave you alone out here," he said. "It will be dark soon."

She flashed a smile. "I thrive in the dark."

He gave her a strange look before glancing over her shoulder. "Where exactly do you live?"

"In a cave." She pressed ten *Reichsmarks* into his hand. "With the other gorillas."

A nervous laugh escaped his lips. "Ma'am—"

"That's a secret, just between us."

Instead of responding, he locked his door.

"We all live in a castle." She smiled. "With a scientist named Frankenstein."

He reversed the car so quickly that his fender bumped into one of the trees, trimming the metal with moss. Then dust trailed him as he sped from the hauntings in this place, leaving her alone. He'd be too frightened, she hoped, to return.

Cool water puddled in her hand as she cupped it below the lion's mouth. A long sip of water, the sweet essence of spring. Perhaps she wouldn't have been afraid of this lion if she'd realized it was offering her life.

The dirt lane hooked around a coppice of trees before climbing to the top of this old mining road. Rising above the trees, a hundred meters up into the forest, was the former bell tower that would have trilled its song grandly before the Reformation.

Instead of taking the road, she chose a shorter route, lugging her suitcase up a root-strewn path until the forest opened up again into a meadow with tall grasses as high as her knee. The meadow tumbled down an embankment, a welcome mat for the former timber-framed convent turned *Jagdhütte*—a royal hunting lodge.

Hanna dropped her suitcase on the drive and scanned the windows for light, but the curtains were all closed. Two chimneys anchored the three-storied home, and leaded windows adorned the steep pitch of roof. She knew every corner of this lodge with its restored kitchen and great hall on the ground floor, the four large bedrooms on the next level. Her grandfather's attic workshop that crowned the remaining books and portraits from medieval years. To the right of the house were a bicycle shed and an empty garage that once housed her father's car.

Before she left for university, she'd peeled back the layers of history for this house, savoring each one. In the fifteenth century, the building had been a residence for Saint Katharine's cloister, the meadow outside a peaceful place for grazing and gardening. In the dark hours, when she was younger, Hanna thought she could hear the swish of skirts in the corridors, the voices of nuns chanting their songs, praying for her after her mother died.

Before the Reformation, Nuremberg's elite would pilgrimage up past this convent, to the hillside abbey named after Saint Katharine of Alexandria, and light candles, their prayers penetrating the thin veil that separated heaven from earth. Then men like Luther and Philipp Melanchthon began speaking out against the abuses in the Catholic church in the 1500s, and monasteries across Germany closed their doors. After the nuns finally left this place, a local patrician with the extravagant name of Hieronymus restored their residence into a lodge so he and his parties could hunt red deer, wolves, and wild boar in the surrounding forest.

After another century of neglect, her grandfather purchased the property in 1890 and renovated the lodge into a home. The place, Vater once said, reminded her grandfather of the dollhouses that Tillich Toy Factory designed, the antique furniture similar to what his carpenters would have built. The lodge and meadow and treed hills beyond had been a retreat from the factory noise and wood dust and smell of turpentine.

Hanna searched the front windows one more time before picking up her suitcase. The telegram should have arrived by this morning, but when she pounded on the knocker, no one answered.

In the hours that she'd contemplated her homecoming, she'd never considered that the Gruenewalds wouldn't be here. Even with the world changing around them, in her mind, this lodge and its occupants always stayed the same.

"Luisa?" she called as she walked around the building, to the garden out back. "Schatzi?"

Neither her cousin nor the golden cat they'd found a decade ago responded, and the garden patch that Luisa had tended for most of Hanna's life was riddled with weeds.

The last letter she'd received from Luisa said all was well, but by the state of the yard, all was not well now.

A bird fluttered into a nearby tree, the branch bowing toward Hanna as if it was the only creature left to welcome her home.

She shuddered, turning away as the sun dipped behind the trees.

Had Luisa and Paul gone into town for the evening? Or had they decided to leave Nuremberg?

She prayed not. Luisa was the only family Hanna had left. She'd never move away without sending a letter. Or leaving a note, at the very least, inside the house.

She checked the back door, but it was locked like the front.

As night swelled between the trees, a coolness latched itself to the breeze. Hanna snagged her cashmere sweater from the suitcase, then secured her suitcase in the shed.

She had hidden a spare key after her father's death, in a place no intruder would ever look. She had to retrieve the key before it got dark. Tomorrow she'd find Luisa.

5

EMBER

Ember pressed through a wall of tourists to catch the blue line headed west, her hands trembling as she fell into an open seat. She wouldn't let that rally ruin her afternoon. The hatred of those people, the animosity of whoever had decided to write another angry letter, drove her to succeed. Before history circled again to lure those in search of finding significance in the worst possible way. Preserving their culture by hurting other people.

She fidgeted with the clasp of her handbag and slipped out her phone. It was already after three.

She'd stood on that sidewalk for too long, her blood boiling at the barrage of words. Usually she walked twenty minutes from the Metro station at Foggy Bottom to her condominium in Georgetown, but if she walked this afternoon, she'd be too late to answer Noah's knock. When she reached the station, she'd forgo the walk and use one of her rideshare apps. It was the optimist in her, but if the driver hurried, she could still be inside her condo door by 3:40, maybe even a minute or two before Noah knocked.

As the subway rumbled through a tunnel, she checked email and found one from Brooke.

> Mom sent me this story from the *Vineyard Gazette*. Hate me as much as you want for forwarding it but thought it might help with your paper. You're only allowed to be mad at me for a day!

How could she possibly hate Brooke for forwarding an article? They'd been friends for twenty years now, bonding for life after they'd twinned their junior year in art history with matching pink blouses, their collars popped up to their ears.

Much later they both confessed to despising pink as well as their desire to fit into the well-established pecking order at their high school. Ember had been the new kid without any money and with enough emotional baggage to down a fleet of planes. Brooke's family didn't have much money either, but she'd managed to secure a foothold among their fellow students. Not only had she thrown Ember a rope, she'd belayed her to the same platform until Ember fled from the island, seven months before graduation.

Even though they'd gone on to climb different mountains— Brooke working as a nurse at Children's Minnesota and Ember on a winding trek as an educator and researcher—they still talked at least once a week.

The article was a feature on Mrs. Kiehl, the social studies teacher who'd inspired Ember to dig deeper into the history of Nuremberg. The woman who'd told her that no one else could establish her identity, no matter what they said about her. It was her choice who she was, who she would become. Her choice to let the past define her. Or not.

Ember had loved Mrs. Kiehl, but she'd been head over heels for the woman's grandson.

That's why Brooke was nervous. Dakota was the one boundary they'd drawn between them long ago, setting it deeply in cement after Ember left the island. The Dakota Ban, they called it. Any news that Brooke had about him, she was supposed to share with someone else.

Ember shook her head, declining the invitation for Dakota to step back into her mind. There was no space left in her head for that man.

She refocused on the article, and in the photograph, Mrs. Kiehl was sitting on the front porch of her family's farmhouse, a cat nestled in her lap. This story was published last week, after Mrs. Kiehl finally agreed, at age eighty-five, to retire her part-time position. According to the reporter, three generations of islanders, about ten thousand students, had taken one of her classes.

The class of 2002 had 114 students. Ember had wondered about some of her classmates fondly over the years, checking their profiles on social media. Others, like Dakota, she refused to display on any of her screens, but they still swept into her mind uninvited. An invitation that would never come.

Dakota was the sole reason why she hadn't contacted Mrs. Kiehl for an interview. The logic was irrational, she'd told herself this repeatedly, but it was her irrationality. No one, she'd decided long ago, needed to pity her.

Mrs. Kiehl had been born in Nuremberg right after the war. When she'd talked about this city during history class, the plight of the Jewish people there for five centuries, Mrs. Kiehl had deposited those stories straight into Ember's memory bank, inspiring her to learn more.

Over the years, Ember began verifying the woman's stories and found they were true. Anti-Semitism had new faces in each century, but the hatred remained. During her fellowship, this extension of time and resources to write her dissertation, she was trying to identify the cycle of hate in places where it had not only repeated but had grown into a Nazi stronghold until it capsized in 1945.

How did an entire society fall victim to the deception, the madness, of one man?

It was a question she'd spent a lifetime trying to answer.

The subway stopped and more people crowded around Ember, heavy shoulders and worn heels carrying their own stories.

Much of the information in the article was familiar. Mrs. Kiehl had spoken freely about Germany, proud of her heritage. In hindsight, Mrs. Kiehl hadn't really talked about her parents, but according to the article, Charlie Ward—Mrs. Kiehl's father—had been an American investigator for the military tribunals, and her mother— a German woman named Hanna—had been an archaeologist.

Ember read the line again.

A female archaeologist?

If Mrs. Kiehl had mentioned that piece, she would have remembered.

Intrigued, she signed into the museum archives. While she didn't find information about Hanna Ward, she found a short listing for Hanna Strauss, a former archaeologist with the Nazis' Ahnenerbe Forschungs und Lehrgemeinschaft. The Ancestral Heritage Research and Teaching Society.

The Ahnenerbe was an umbrella organization for about fifty research branches that Heinrich Himmler termed institutes to study everything from the Nordic symbols called runes to ancient Gregorian chants. With Himmler at the helm, the organization became increasingly focused on proving, under the Institute for Germanic Archaeology, that German people descended from a mysterious group of people called Aryans.

Ember cringed at this word, tapping both legs to clear it out of her head as she refocused on the crowded train, on the diversity that could either strengthen or destroy. Each person in this railcar, the smallest of samples, had chosen to work together on this journey. If only others could choose this kind of peace across their nation. The world. Choose to embrace love instead of hate.

They didn't have to keep grinding through the cycles from the past.

Her past.

A snake of a memory crept into her mind, tempting her to dwell, but she wouldn't linger here. Like she'd done with Dakota, she'd banned these memories for life.

In 1940, when the world finally confronted Hitler's evil force, the Ahnenerbe changed as well. Every member was required to join the notorious Schutzstaffel, an organization only open to men. Nothing she could find online mentioned what happened to its female staff.

No wonder Mrs. Kiehl had talked so much about finding one's own identity outside the definition of others, the shadows of a family and past. Whether or not Hanna had supported Hitler's rule, Mrs. Kiehl had been raised by a woman who'd partnered at one time with the Nazis.

How had Hanna managed to immigrate to the United States? The US government wouldn't have welcomed a former Nazi employee in the 1940s, even if she was married to an American. Hanna had probably changed her name and the pieces of her story to start a new life with Charlie on the island. Like Ember had done when she moved back to Martha's Vineyard to live with her brother.

She read Hanna's short biography one more time, as a crowd under McPherson Square boarded the subway car. Only a few words to describe what must have been a remarkable life. Perhaps not a sympathetic figure, but a fascinating one nonetheless.

She swiped back to the newspaper article.

"Hanna was a friend to the Jewish people," Mrs. Kiehl said. "And the best of mothers to me."

That's what Ember wanted to find. Someone who had taken a

stand in Nuremberg after the Nazi Party had brought that city to its knees. A German man or woman who'd tried to stop the cycle.

If only Mrs. Kiehl could tell her how an intelligent, educated German woman decided to partner with a maniac like Hitler. And how her mother had befriended the Jewish people when everything was stacked against her. Ember wanted to understand how the animosity had swept across Germany and how someone who'd lived in the bowels of Nazism helped others in the midst.

As the car neared her station, she slipped her phone back into her handbag. Eighty years had passed since the Holocaust and still, so many stories to be found. To be told.

In spite of her desire to avoid Dakota Kiehl, she had to pursue his grandmother's story.

Ember raced out of the Foggy Bottom station, summoning a car to rush up the hill to her condo that overlooked the Potomac River. At exactly 3:38, she unlocked the door and hurried into the kitchen, yanking the ice cream that Ben & Jerry had deemed Phish Food out of her freezer and plopping it on the counter.

Just in time for the knock.

"Surprise!" Noah said, a gold-plated soupspoon in his hand when she swung open the door.

"What a pleasant surprise." Ember smiled, the rhetoric as familiar as the ten-year-old's ripped jeans and cherry-red Converse that he wore to school every day.

It was their ritual. Their way of reminding each other in a world of bullies and busyness, someone still cared to stop and remember.

"What brings you by today?" Ember asked, the door's edge balanced against her hip.

Noah tried to glance around her at the kitchen counter, but Ember didn't budge. The ice cream would have to wait.

"I can't figure out how to divide," he said.

The irony, Ember thought. Division came so naturally to much of this district, especially for kids like Noah. "There's no need to rush division."

Noah tilted his head, sweat beaded on his brown skin from the run between his bus stop and her front door. "That's not what Mrs. Worthington says."

She tapped her fingernails on the doorframe. "I much prefer multiplication and addition."

The boy shrugged. Math wasn't usually part of their banter. "I'm hungry."

"I have plenty to eat," she said. "Trout. Salmon. Mahi-mahi even."

He grinned. "I prefer Phish Food."

She propped open the door, and Noah ducked under her arm, those red high-tops carrying him across the hardwood floor in record time. Within seconds he was digging out a scoop of ice cream that might have been perfectly rounded if it weren't for the lumps of chocolate fish swimming in caramel pools.

"What did you remember today?" Ember asked, sitting on a stool.

Instead of asking what he'd learned, they always remembered his day together. Some things they remembered quickly and then decided to forget.

He hooked a fish with his teeth and reeled it in. "I remembered that our government is a tree."

Ember scooped out swirls of chocolate and marshmallow with her matching golden spoon. "A tree?"

"With three branches. Executive. Legislative. And . . ." He tapped the spoon against his forehead, trying to remember.

She made a branch with one of her arms, the spoon dangling off the end. "Judicial?"

"Right." He clicked their spoons together. "Lots and lots of branches grow from that one."

She sighed. "Multiplication *and* division."

"What did you remember today?" he asked.

She thought for a moment, of the marchers who hated those different from them. Of people around the world who had stood up against the hatred. "I remembered the life of my history teacher from high school. They're celebrating her eighty-fifth birthday."

Noah leaned forward. "Too bad she didn't teach you math."

It was too bad. Ember might have learned something.

She showed Noah the picture of Mrs. Kiehl when she was much younger, marrying a local man named Albert Kiehl. Underneath was a photo of Mrs. Kiehl with Titus, her only son.

Noah skimmed the first paragraphs before looking back up. "Are you going to call your old teacher?"

"Former teacher," Ember corrected. "She was born in 1945, but she probably doesn't want to be called old."

Noah shrugged before retrieving a notepad and pencil from his backpack. Then he began scribbling on the paper, hiding his work with his hand.

"What are you doing?" she asked.

He turned his paper around. "You said your teacher was born in 1945."

"She was."

"Then your story said it wrong."

"Said what wrong?"

"Her age."

She stared down at Noah's numbers, the proof scribbled onto his paper.

She smoothed her fingers over the edge of her iPad as she read the article again. The reporter had said that Mrs. Kiehl was eighty-five. If that were true, according to Noah's numbers, the woman would have been born around 1936. Nine years before her American father came to Nuremberg.

"My memory must have failed me."

Noah eyed her curiously. "Your memory never fails."

"Then the reporter must be wrong." She turned off the screen.

"Why don't you text your teacher? She can tell you when she was born."

She lidded their ice cream. "I don't have her number."

"But you can find it."

"Maybe I will. After you're done with your homework." Ember tousled his hair. "There's nothing wrong with your subtraction skills."

Noah pulled out the binder with his math sheets, and they worked on dividing the numbers until one very important professor, Jack Matthews, knocked on her door. Noah's dad taught mathematics at Georgetown, but he rarely bothered with the basics at home.

Not that she minded. Noah's daily knock was the highlight of her day. That and the Phish Food.

"Thanks for keeping him out of trouble." Jack lifted the Star Wars backpack off the floor, his light-blue shirt still perfectly pressed after a full day of teaching. The dry cleaner must use an entire can of starch to bar his wrinkles.

"We got into loads of trouble." She handed Noah his golden spoon. "Almost cleaned out an entire tub of ice cream."

Jack didn't reply, but he lingered by the door as if she might ask them to stay for dinner. While she was thrilled to spend an hour with Noah each day, she had no interest in pursuing a relationship with a wrinkle-free man too pompous to help his ten-year-old son with division, even if Noah saw the world a little differently than the man who'd fathered him.

Noah dragged his feet down the hall, waving to her one last time before Jack unlocked the door to their condo.

After another bite—okay, *two* bites—of the melted Phish Food, she returned the remaining ice cream to its hold in the freezer. Then she logged into her computer and searched across social media for Mrs. Kiehl.

But Ember couldn't find information about her former teacher online. Instead she found another short biography about an archaeologist named Hanna Strauss who'd worked at the Germanic National Museum during World War II.

A woman who, according to this writer, had disappeared.

6

HANNA

Hanna followed the familiar path up the hill and around the abbey's sacred ruins to retrieve her house key. The roof of Saint Katharine's abbey had collapsed centuries ago, the stained glass shattered, but a stone shell and ribbing of columns remained, a rickety bell tower and open door leading out to a labyrinth that curled like a caterpillar through the bramble and grass, each stone clothed in a mossy stole.

This labyrinth was a place to pray. A place to remember.

A place to hide one's treasure.

Pushing aside a shrub, Hanna could almost see her mother again, smiling and circling this walk as she prayed. Sharing the ancient stories as Hanna trailed behind her.

Hanna's favorite story had been about an orphaned postulant from the Middle Ages. After an uncle brought her to the convent, Cristyne resigned herself to becoming a nun. Legend claimed that a man named Emrich, son of Nuremberg's burgrave, dismounted his horse to pray at a wooden cross built here while his party was hunting in the forest. Cristyne was kneeling in prayer that day, at the foot of the cross, and Emrich's heart was forever changed.

As the months passed, he continued to ride up the mountain to pray, and when he saw Cristyne, he'd beg her to leave the convent. But even with her growing love, she'd devoted herself to the service of the Lord. Nothing he said would persuade her to leave.

Then a terrible plague swept across Nuremberg, along with rumors that local Jews had poisoned their wells. No one in town seemed to care when Jewish men and women also began dying.

The next time Emrich visited, he knocked on the convent door below the abbey, the son of his Jewish teacher in his arms.

God urged Cristyne and the sisters to help, not just this child but others, young and old, whom Emrich began transporting up the hill. And for each person who died, she and Emrich would place a rock at the cross. Namestones, they called them, carving the initials for each person who'd died. To remember.

The mound of namestones turned into a path, several hundred stones circling around the cross. They partnered together for months, nursing the sick, building the path for prayer, until Cristyne caught the pestilence. Emrich never left her side until her life slipped away. Then he continued his work until the plague was defeated, the labyrinth of namestones complete.

The prayers of the nuns, Hanna's mother once told her, lingered in this space.

Hanna counted the namestones as she walked around the labyrinth—*Eins, Zwei, Drei*—all the way up to *Fünfzehn*. Number fifteen was the stone that she pried out of the soil, and hidden underneath, in the sunken crevice caked with mud, was a slender sardine tin. Holding her breath, she opened the tin, and relief flooded out of her lips when she saw the key inside.

She refilled the hole with soil and moved the slippery stone back into place before scraping away the tiniest piece of moss with the trowel of her fingernail, sifting gently until a letter peeked out from its covering. The bottom of an *A*.

Not even the rain, five centuries' worth, could wash these letters away. The memories of those lost to the plague withstood even the storms.

Hanna replaced the moss sliver to preserve the carving, and as she stood, her gaze looped around the circumference of stones. Her mother had circled this memorial while Hanna was still in her womb. Praying consistently, Vater once said.

She had been named Hanna in memory of her grandmother, but instead of choosing another ancestor for the middle name, her mother had chosen Cristyne.

Hanna Cristyne Tillich, after the postulant who'd given her life to rescue others.

Long ago, Hanna decided that she also wanted to become a nun.

Before she'd left for the university, Hanna often walked this labyrinth alone, remembering her mother here since her actual memories at home were few. Confusing. In this place, when Hanna was a child, her mother had seemed close, but even those memories were fading.

A bat reeled past her, its wings clipping the breeze.

Darkness was turning this forest into a cavern, and while she could quip about Victor Frankenstein with the cabdriver, locals talked more about mystical creatures like the *Wolpertinger* haunting these woods, a rabbitlike animal with antlers, wings, and fangs that came out of hiding after dark. A bat, she could handle, but she didn't want to meet any other creatures of the night.

Another day, early in the morning, she'd walk the entire labyrinth again. And she'd remember her own past as she stepped into her new role as a curator. For one must never forget where one came from. It was the foundation to building a life.

The key in hand, Hanna rushed down the hill through the fading light. Perhaps when she emerged from the trees, she would see Paul or Luisa in the distance. This hike into the forest would be for naught.

The sky cradled a half-moon, splashing light across the cornflowers in her meadow, but the house remained unlit. Neither Luisa nor Paul, it seemed, had returned.

She retrieved her suitcase from the shed and unlocked the front door. The heavy door groaned when she pushed it open, as if she'd awakened it from sleep. She called for Luisa, but no one responded.

Beside the door was an electric switch, but the entry lamp didn't respond when she flipped it. Had Luisa and Paul neglected to pay the electricity bill?

Luisa knew—she should have known—that Hanna would help her if they were struggling with money. She and Paul could have as much time as necessary before paying their rent. For that matter, they didn't have to pay at all. Luisa had moved into the lodge more than twenty years ago, before Hanna's mother died. She belonged in this place.

Hanna swept back drapes that covered the front window, and with the moonlight as her lantern, she slipped through the dining room and into the kitchen. She searched the pantry first, the shelves filled with tins of cookies and crackers, jars of pears, applesauce, and tomatoes, their lids coated with a fine dust. A taper candle, she found on the bottom shelf. Matches were in the alcove beside the pantry with its small desk and one telephone that her father had installed.

She melted the base of the candle, cooling the wax in a silver stand to keep it from teetering. With the flickering light, she moved back through the dining room and a corridor, into the former banquet hall, where the count's hunting parties were once entertained.

When her grandfather bought the lodge, the walls in this great hall had still displayed the trophy heads of a stag, moose, and wolves, all of them facing a series of arched windows that climbed up both the ground level and first story. Thank goodness, her grandfather had removed the mounts and repapered the walls with a navy-and-gold damask. And these days, one had to travel all the way into Poland to locate a gray wolf.

Her grandfather had left the exposed rafters from the Middle Ages, along with the green ceramic stove and shelves to house the many old books. The banquet table, he'd replaced with clusters of chairs, couches, and small tables on a worn carpet.

A portrait of Saint Katharine was the one original art piece that remained in the great hall, above her father's corner desk. Hanna could see it in the glow of her candlelight—the young woman dressed in an elegant gown, her hands folded in prayer as the wheel meant for her demise splintered into a thousand pieces behind her. The emperor, his scepter raised like a sword, looked as if he might hit her after she'd refused his proposal of marriage in order to be fully committed to God.

But an angel held the emperor back until the time God had chosen for Katharine to surrender her life for His sake.

Portraits of Hanna's family had replaced the animal trophies, but they were mounted too high to see now. Once the electricity was restored, an iron chandelier would light this room.

Several frames occupied Vater's desk. One of him with Hanna, and one of Luisa and Hanna, their legs dangling over one of the docks on Grosser Dutzendteich, laughing together. Luisa with a porcelain brooch pinned on her scarf, pretending to push Hanna over the side. She glanced across the desk's surface, looking for a letter from Luisa, but all that remained was a ledger resting below the desk lamp and a slab of sandstone her father had used as a paperweight. In perfect Tillich order.

Worry roped its tethers around her mind, and she chided herself for it. Fear like this benefited no one. Perhaps Luisa had left a letter in her bedroom upstairs.

On the far side of the hall were wooden steps that Cristyne and her sisters would have solemnly climbed after chasing God in their prayers. Steps that, centuries later, hunters stomped up after a long day chasing prey through the forest. Steps she once raced up as a child, afraid a ghost might be chasing her.

Until now, she'd spent her adult life running toward something instead of away, but it seemed that Himmler had been chasing her as well, all the way back home.

Four bedrooms were located on the next floor, two on each side of the corridor. Luisa and Paul had used the one across from Hanna's old room.

Clothes were stacked neatly in their dresser, the oak top sprinkled with dust like the jars below, their twin beds equally tidy with matching blue duvets, but she saw no letter.

They'd been gone for longer than the day or even a week, it seemed. Months, perhaps. Had they left to visit relatives now that their country was changing at such a rapid pace? Paul's family lived in the nearby town of Fürth, just west of Nuremberg.

If they'd gone for an extended visit, why had they left so many of their things behind?

She dropped her suitcase inside her old bedroom and stepped back into the hall with her candle.

If Kolman were here, he'd point to her logic. The Gruenewalds didn't have to tell her they were leaving. They could have simply moved while Hanna was traveling. Any letter from Luisa might have gotten lost while the Berlin office tried to find her location.

But something was wrong; she could feel it now in the marrow of her bones. Luisa wasn't only a tenant. She was family. She wouldn't leave without notice.

Hanna hurried back downstairs to place a call. The upright telephone was ancient compared to the ones in Berlin, but change was slow to arrive in these hills. And this one worked just fine.

Lifting the clunky receiver, she held it up to her ear before asking the operator to connect her with Frau Weber, one of her mother's closest friends. A woman who'd also befriended Hanna and Luisa.

"I'm sorry," Frau Weber said when the operator connected their lines. "I didn't hear your name."

"It's Hanna Tillich," she explained.

"You've come home . . ." Perhaps it was a bad connection, but no welcome enveloped these words.

Then a line clicked in the background, the operator listening. Due diligence, she supposed, to report anything suspect to the Gestapo. But Hanna didn't have anything to hide. She was simply trying to locate her cousin.

"I'm only home for a season," Hanna said. "I'll be working at the National Museum."

"Luisa would have been pleased to know you've returned."

Would have been?

Hanna pressed her palm against the wall. "Where exactly is Luisa?"

A long pause before Frau Weber responded. "Is she missing?"

But her question didn't ring true. "You must have known she left."

"Come visit me, dear. When you have time."

"But—"

"I've missed you too."

An answer, that's all she wanted. And she didn't want to wait until morning. Luisa, of all people, wasn't suspect. "Where is—?"

"Auf Wiedersehen." Another click and the woman was gone, Hanna's question dangling with the telephone cord.

A series of possibilities, none of them good, swirled in her mind, but she couldn't sort through them tonight. Not without answers to her questions. Even if she managed to ride a bicycle into town, she wouldn't get far. Curfew was one of the immovable columns in their theater of law and order, enforceable with a stint in prison. She had no pass or even a decent excuse to be out after dark.

At first light, she'd search for a bicycle and ride it back down the hill to Frau Weber's.

She eyed the narrow bed in her former room, the marigold-yellow duvet unchanged. In the past two years, since she'd graduated from the university, she'd spent the night in some perilous places across Europe and Nepal, but always with her team. And usually accompanied by soldiers.

In her travels she rarely felt afraid, but tonight, alone in her own home, Luisa gone, the old childhood fears reared.

But she'd always been stronger than her fears. Had to be.

Vater had taught her how to use both a knife and a hunting rifle, but if he'd kept the gun, she didn't know where he'd hidden it. A knife would have to do, in case the taxi driver told a friend that he'd dropped off a madwoman near the ruined chapel. She feared men less than she feared the mystical, but Vater would tell her a smart woman was always prepared.

The kitchen knives were dull, so she sharpened one with a stone before wrapping it in an apron to transport upstairs. Her hand cupped behind the flame, Hanna blew out her candle before stepping back into her bedroom. Then she locked the door.

Branches batted the window as she slipped the house key and knife into the top drawer of her nightstand. In the moonlight, she changed into her nightgown and crawled under the familiar flannel duvet.

The last time she'd been home was for Luisa and Paul's wedding. She and Charlie had come together on their break from the university. Instead of pursuing a monastic life, she'd begun to dream for the first time about her own wedding.

In that week, everything changed for her and Charlie. She'd never planned to sleep with him, not unless they married, but she who once snubbed romance had been swept away by her handsome escort, the easy camaraderie between them. The last night of their trip, when Charlie was supposed to stay in town with a friend, she'd asked him to stay in the empty lodge with her instead. A mistake that cost her dearly.

She'd traded their friendship for a bumbling romance that ended when Charlie returned to America. Traded the truest of love for a broken heart.

And she decided again that while marriage was a fine proposition for Luisa and other women, it wasn't for her.

The warmth of the flannel began luring her to sleep, the memories of Charlie fading.

In the morning, she would find out what happened to Luisa. And in the morning she would write to Kolman again. While the Berlin office might have misplaced a letter from Luisa, she wanted to make sure that Kolman was clear about her rescinding any promise of marriage.

But Kolman wouldn't wait until morning. He smashed right into her dreams.

With his gray eyes, pressed lips, he hovered near her bed, his forehead broken with sweat, and his voice—he growled like a wolf.

There were no wolves left in Germany. Only in Poland. She tried to tell herself this, in the fog of her nightmare. As if it mattered.

This ghost of a man tugged open the nightstand drawer and found her knife. Then he turned toward her, and she could see the fangs of folklore. Another monster created in a German lab.

When he lifted the knife, she screamed, the word *no* ripping from her lips as she awoke in the stillness.

No Kolman. No wolf. No fangs.

No creature wanting to hurt those who could help him.

Her *no* had meant something.

She elbowed herself up on the pillows and relit the candle. Her body was covered in sweat as she stepped toward the window, the flicker of light chasing the shadows of this monster outside, to the meadow beyond.

The candlestick trembling in her hand, she knew for certain that she couldn't marry Kolman. Not now or next month or next year. Not even when the war was over.

Kolman was attractive, strong, but marriage to him wouldn't console her loss. Nor did she need a man to take care of her. She could change the world on her own.

Germany had needed her to excavate its past so the German people knew exactly where they'd come from. Now she would do her best to curate this past as her country forged into the future.

She returned to bed, and the next time she woke, someone was ringing the doorbell.

Luisa and Paul, she prayed, had come home.

7

EMBER

Ember chewed on the end of a pencil, staring at her forlorn Facebook profile instead of the river below her loft. She rarely posted on social media, and the only reason she kept her accounts was to connect with friends who liked to unfold the pages of their lives online.

She wasn't opposed to sharing one's life, but the digital world seemed to favor those who didn't want to talk to each other. Only *at* each other. Talk or shout, like those men on the streets who were spewing their anger, refusing to consider the opinions of others. The constant talking, never listening, did no one any good.

The screen blinked back as if it sensed her dilemma.

Years ago she'd promised herself that she would never, ever look up Dakota Kiehl, a promise soldered by the memories of him discarding her like a rotten apple their senior year.

But she'd also promised herself that she'd never again hide from him or any man.

She switched on the lamp beside her desk. The sun wouldn't set for another three hours or so, but the evening light cast shadows through her condo and she couldn't stand the dark.

Instead of obsessing over the past, she had to keep her gaze focused on the future. If not, she would paralyze herself.

Today she'd tried to track down a phone number to interview Mrs. Kiehl, but no one at the high school or any of the businesses that she'd called on Martha's Vineyard or even the postmaster could help her. The only number she found online was outdated, belonging to a man in Cape Cod who'd never heard of the Vineyard teacher.

Typing quickly, she searched for Dakota's name before she changed her mind. It wasn't like she was planning to stalk the man. This was a professional search to inquire about his grandmother. To ask Mrs. Kiehl to share her mother's story.

A brief search brought up an article about Dakota's marriage to a former Miss Massachusetts. She hoped for his wife's sake, for the sake of their children, that he had changed, but there wasn't much else to see online. Most of his social media settings were private, so no family pictures or selfies of the man who'd busted open her heart long ago. He might have posted his photos privately, but she'd have to send a request to see them and she'd never extend an invitation to restore even an online friendship with this man.

She typed out a message, edited it twice. Then she deleted it. With their lack of Facebook friendship, he'd probably never get it anyway.

While she shouldn't spend another moment this evening on Dakota's profile, she continued to scroll. The few pictures he'd posted publicly were mostly of mountains. Grand, snow-covered peaks, one with purple wildflowers bursting through the fresh powder.

Other photos on Dakota's profile were from Martha's Vineyard, taken years ago. The rolling waves at sunset. A boiled lobster, probably caught right offshore. A picture of Captain Kiehl with his high school varsity football team.

That's the Dakota she remembered. The teenager she would have done anything to please.

She shivered. How pathetic she'd been back then, thinking that caring for a man meant you did whatever he wanted. That worship somehow equaled affection.

A printed copy of the *Vineyard Gazette* article lay beside her keyboard, and she studied the photograph again of the woman on the front porch. The Kiehl family had owned the same farm on Martha's Vineyard for more than a century, a picturesque place tucked back in hills that insulated them from the tourist crowds.

She could find their address and overnight a letter, asking if she could visit, but this was ridiculous, stalling her research because Dakota hurt her twenty years ago. What mattered now was asking Mrs. Kiehl about her mother before Ember boarded the plane to Nuremberg. Perhaps she could still find one hero whose story survived.

Picking up her phone, she breeched the Dakota Ban. **Thanks for the article. I only brooded for half a day.**

Brooke texted back in seconds. **I hoped you wouldn't stay mad for long.**

She tapped her phone several times before replying. **Do you happen to have a phone number for Mrs. Kiehl?**

A wide-eyed emoticon fired off Brooke's response. **Which one?**

Very funny . . . Ember started chewing again on the metal ribbing around her pencil. **Definitely not Dakota's wife.**

Ember took a sip of LaCroix, looking out over the treetops and the glimmer of the Potomac below as she waited for Brooke to text back.

I didn't even know Mrs. Kiehl was still alive until Mom sent me that article.

Me either.

You should call Dakota.

No!!! Just his grandmother.

Sorry, Em. You'll probably have to go through him.

Ember fell back against the seat. It was a reasonable statement but not a reasonable situation. She would not call Dakota.

Her phone in hand, she slipped down the stairs and out the door of this historical home that had been turned into condos, locking it behind her. She needed to move.

If she texted Dakota, he might gloat for the rest of his pitiful life, in the lie that she was still pining for him.

Wait. She started another text to Brooke on her walk down the hill.

You have Dakota's number?

No, but I have one for Alecia.

Dakota's ex-girlfriend. The second-to-last person Ember wanted to contact.

I won't ask how you acquired that . . .

People change, Em. Punctuated with a goblin and haloed smile.

Some people, but not all, Ember thought. Some people never changed.

She swept down the old Georgetown street, her mind reeling back to her senior year when she'd thought the captain of the school's football team had cared for her as well. It was ridiculous, thinking about it now. She'd been an awkward, bumbling eighteen-year-old who'd been wounded deeply. And only her books, those very best of friends, would have declared her popular.

She didn't understand this disparity when Dakota turned his eyes toward her, but their history no longer mattered. She'd grown up in the past twenty years and surely he had as well. All she wanted to do was find out about Hanna.

Her phone vibrated, and she looked down to see another text from Brooke with Dakota's contact information. **Tell me what he says.**

Will you text him for me?

A long pause before Brooke wrote: **Nope . . .**

Ember drummed out the next words. **I. Can't. Do. This.**

Yes, you can. You're no longer THAT girl.

The reminder bolstered her. Brooke was right. If she could stand on the sidewalk this afternoon, face off with those white supremacists, she could communicate with Dakota Kiehl by text. It wasn't like she had to talk to him.

Dakota's area code placed him in Denver, and it was only five o'clock, Mountain Time. She'd simply ask him for his grandmother's phone number and be done with it. In the morning, she'd call Mrs. Kiehl.

She revised her request to him three times before hitting Send.

This is Ember Ellis, and I'm hoping to connect with your grandmother. Could I please get her phone number from you?

Dakota would know which grandmother. His mother's mom had died while they were in high school. He'd started crying in geometry their junior year, a burly, rugged football player broken from grief. When Mrs. Kiehl had escorted him from their classroom, Ember's heart had broken as well.

It wasn't until the next year that Ember realized a person's tears didn't equal kindness. One could cry and still be cruel.

Brick steps led her down past a row of shops where locals and tourists alike could buy some of the best coffee and cupcakes in the whole metro area. Then across a steel bridge that overlooked the grassy towpath along an old canal.

To her right was a paved prayer labyrinth, a quiet space along the water for her to reflect, but she turned left, rushing south along the riverfront as if someone were chasing her. All she'd done was ask the man for a phone number, but it felt like she'd exposed her heart once again.

Her phone in hand, she refused to look down as she waited for a response that might not come for hours. Might not come at all. It was entirely possible that Alecia had an old number for her ex.

Her mind ached from the second-guessing. She'd worked her entire life to maintain sanity, and if she didn't stop this, she was going to drive herself crazy.

Twenty minutes passed and then thirty. Still her phone didn't chime, and the emotions of her seventeen-year-old self reared. Desperation. Fear. A teenager whose life had turned upside down.

Ringer off, she stuffed her phone into her back pocket. The fragrance of cherry blossoms swept up the Potomac, and a crowd of tourists pressed against her as Ember neared the Lincoln Memorial, this monument a testament to freedom for all in their country.

A half mile later, she came to the ring of cherry trees that circled the Tidal Basin. A gift, those flowering trees had been, from Japan to the United States. A symbol of friendship in 1912, an offering of peace that the Americans had displayed for people around the world to see. Crazy how friendships, how family, could deteriorate in just a few years. Blossoms of affection decaying, blistering into hate.

Less than thirty years later, their former friends had dropped bombs on a harbor known for its pearls. More than two million people died in the subsequent years of a friendship gone terribly wrong.

The relationship had once again been restored, but the wounds were still there.

Ember sat down on a bench and saw a missed call on her screen, from the Denver number. And a text.

She glanced up at the pink blossoms dangling over the bench, her hands trembling. She didn't want to remember the bad in her past. Only the good.

And yet the bad kept circling back.

Taking a deep breath, she opened the text, determined not to read between any lines.

Good to hear from you, Em. It's been too long. Gram rarely answers her phone, but you can call her housekeeper.

He listed out the woman's name—Kayla Mann—and a phone number. Thankfully, there were no lines to read between.

She ignored the pleasantries—it hadn't been nearly long enough in her mind—and typed her response quickly, ready to be done. **Thanks. I'll contact Kayla.**

The phone chimed when she put it back in her pocket, and she dug it out again.

I'm glad to ask Gram for whatever you need.

Not in a million years did she want to work through Dakota.

I'll just give Kayla a call.

And so she did, before Dakota tried to convince her to speak with him.

8

HANNA

Below Hanna's window, a black Mercedes-Benz waited in her drive, a newer sedan built for the Nazi elite. She'd already resigned her job without a fight, relocated back home where they'd sent her. What could Himmler want from her now?

When the doorbell rang again, she tied the belt of her dressing gown around her waist. No time to find a pair of slippers, Hanna pinned back her hair as she rushed toward the steps. Perhaps a messenger was ringing the bell, under orders of the Reichsführer, to return her directly to the cavern at Montségur. Perhaps they needed her in the field after all.

As the visitor pounded on the brass knocker, she checked for loose pieces of hair one last time. Oversleeping was not a respectable practice in the eyes of her superiors, no matter what kind of monster plagued one's dreams.

A stocky middle-aged man stood on her stoop, wearing a plain black suit in lieu of a uniform, his lips chiseled into the grim mold of Himmler's secret police.

His arm planked forward, nicking her sleeve. "Heil Hitler."

"Heil Hitler," she muttered, her outstretched arm wobbling like gelatin.

A messenger, she'd welcome or a fellow member of the Ahnenerbe. But not the Gestapo. Under Himmler, these men had risen above German law to create their own rules, no courts necessary to enforce their judgment. And no steps to appeal.

She waited for the agent to speak, knowing her every word, every emotion, would be weighed for dissension. He could judge her as he liked, right here on her doorstep.

The man drew out a pocket notebook, reviewing a page as if remembering the basics of this mission was beneath his rank. Then his head rose, his gaze as stalwart as a soldier stepping into battle. "Are you Luisa Gruenewald?"

She flinched at his question, then regretted it. What could the Gestapo want with her cousin?

"I am not," she replied, staring at him, refusing to blink. As an opponent, she must match the coolness of his glare.

He blinked first. "Do you know where she is?"

"No, but I would like to find out."

He drew a pen from his pocket. "Why are you searching for Frau Gruenewald?"

If only she could ask this same question of him. What had Luisa done to warrant the attention of the Gestapo? And why hadn't this agent asked about Paul?

"Luisa is my tenant, and she seems to have disappeared. I am concerned about her well-being."

He made a note in the book. "What is your name?"

She stood taller. "Hanna Tillich, the owner of this house."

"Frau Tillich?"

"Fräulein."

Something shifted in his eyes. A spark of curiosity that she needed to douse.

He flipped his palm. "Your identification card."

"Of course," she said. "It's inside."

He eyed the space above her head. "You won't mind if I look around while you retrieve it."

"Does it matter what I mind?"

"Not particularly."

With no recourse, she opened the door, assuming he would begin his search on the ground floor, but the man trailed her up to the first story, right to the doorway that opened into her room.

Perhaps he feared she was going to warn Luisa.

The ID card was under the house key in her nightstand, beside the apron. She retrieved her identification but left the drawer open. When she turned back, the agent was standing behind her, a wicked smile fired on his lips. Then his gaze fell to the crumpled duvet on her bed.

She equaled the man in height, but she'd never be able to overpower him without a weapon. Nor would he care that she'd worked as an esteemed archaeologist for Himmler or was employed now as a curator for Germany's National Museum. All he saw was an opportunity to wield his authority, and the Gestapo gorged themselves on morsels of power.

Her hand dipped behind her, fingers creeping under the gingham material of Luisa's apron. If she killed a member of the Gestapo, the organization would retaliate in kind, no matter what this man did to her. Not even Kolman would be able to save her from a swift penalty.

But if Kolman killed this man, to defend her honor, no one would question an SS officer.

"Do you know my fiancé?" she asked, feeling for the kitchen knife in the folds of gingham.

The bloated smile grew, as if she'd offered him a challenge.

"He's a regiment leader," she said. "With the Schutzstaffel."

His smile froze.

"You must know him." She checked her watch, diverting his attention as she wrapped her other hand around the knife's handle. "Standartenführer Strauss."

She would not let him rape her and perhaps leave her for dead. If he didn't relent, she'd have to take justice out of the Gestapo's hands. His car, she could transfer, if necessary, to the opposite side of Nuremberg.

"I've yet to have the honor," he replied.

"Well, you will meet him soon." She glanced out the window. "I'm expecting him at any moment."

His smile faded, leather soles screeching against hardwood as he swiveled toward the door.

Relieved, she dropped the ID card back into the drawer but not the knife. She slipped it into the pocket of her housecoat, still wrapped in the apron.

The agent searched the four rooms along the corridor, and in the last one, her father's bedroom, he opened the closet and found the separate, smaller door to the attic. Her grandfather's workshop.

Kneeling down, he jostled the locked handle. "Open this for me."

She steadied her voice. "I'm afraid I don't have the key."

"You're the owner of this house!"

"I have just recently returned home," she said. "Sadly my father is deceased, and I don't know where he kept this key."

He stood, brushing off his trousers. "What's behind the door?"

"Dollhouses," she said. "My grandfather was a toymaker."

"I will return with a locksmith."

Her entire body trembled as she watched him drive away from the kitchen window. Just last night, she'd promised herself that no man would stop her from pursuing the goals she'd had since childhood.

This weakness, she hated herself for it. One man's display of power shaking up all that was inside her.

How long would it take the Gestapo to procure a locksmith to open her attic door? She searched Vater's desk for the attic key, but all she found in the drawers were unpaid bills. Would he or Luisa have hidden it away like she'd done with the extra house key?

Almost two hundred stones lined the former prayer walk, all of them set deeply into the soil. It would take days for her to search under each one, and she was supposed to report to the director of the museum by noon. The attic would have to wait. Before she started her new position, she had to find Luisa and warn her cousin, if possible, that the Gestapo was looking for her.

She scooped coffee grounds from a tin and dumped them into the percolator basket. Not until she pressed the button did she remember that the electricity had been shut off.

Jarred pears, that's what Hanna ate for breakfast. Then she dressed quickly in a pine-colored cardigan to accompany the tweed trousers that she refused to give up after wearing them every day in the field. With her hair pinned neatly back, she retrieved her bicycle from the shed and pumped air into the tires.

While much had changed since she left Germany, the road into town had not. She knew every rock embedded along the path, every hole that led past the new zoo, down to the city streets. A bicycle rack stretched along the sidewalk beside the tram stop, and she snapped her steel lock on the rear wheel before stepping onto the waiting tramcar.

Ten minutes later, the tram delivered her to a stop outside the medieval wall that encircled Nuremberg's Old Town. The sandstone wall had been built centuries ago to keep Hussites out of this imperial city, and on the other side of the entrance, perched high on a cliff, the Imperial Castle crowned the twisting passages and waterways, the Gothic churches and houses chiseled from stone. Hanna knew every bridge and half-timbered building, the cobbled paths that people had walked for more than five hundred years.

Frau Weber's apartment was on the third floor of a half-timbered house once owned by a patrician family. Geraniums bloomed under her window, the colors cascading over its box, blossoms sprinkling onto the shops below.

Within moments the older woman opened her door, latching on to Hanna's arm, yanking her into a cramped formal room. Two antique chairs and a couch huddled together in front of the windows and a jungle of houseplants lined the far wall, framing both sides of a closed door.

"Heil Hitler," Hanna said.

The woman's blue eyes narrowed. "A good morning to you as well."

Her chestnut hair coiled into a chignon, Frau Weber held her shoulders with the confidence and beauty of a patrician's daughter, as if she'd lived in this house since the Middle Ages.

Frau Weber had been friends with Hanna's mother since grade school. After Ruth Tillich died, she'd adopted both Luisa and Hanna as her own, visiting often when Hanna was a girl, bringing scraps of fabric for them to stitch together, leftovers from her work as a seamstress. She'd written multiple letters while Hanna was at the university, but she'd stopped when Hanna began traveling with the Ahnenerbe.

Frau Weber offered her a seat on the worn sofa. "I'm glad you've come."

Hanna remained standing. "What happened to Luisa?"

The woman clasped her hands together as she paced toward the window, her voice silent.

"Please," Hanna begged. "I had a visitor this morning. He was . . ."

"Concerned?" Frau Weber asked, her thin eyebrows arched.

"Very much."

She looked down at the burgundy-stained timbers on the cobbler's shop, then scanned the street as if she were its queen. As if no one could pry the information about Luisa from her lips until she was ready. "People are disappearing from Nuremberg, Hanna, but no one knows exactly where they are going."

Hanna's heart skipped, her mind slipping back to the faces of Parisians she'd seen lined up in France, the soldiers with their guns trying to manage the queue. Rebels, the driver explained. Those who'd resisted the occupation of the Germans were being taken away.

But Luisa wasn't a rebel. She was a carefree woman who loved to garden and hike up to an abbey no one visited anymore.

"Why are the Gestapo looking for Luisa?"

"You've been gone too long." Thin fingers slid down a lacy curtain edge before she turned back, her voice somber. "Hitler's determined to get revenge on anyone who is Jewish."

Hitler was quite outspoken about this prejudice, one of many who blamed the Jewish population for anything that went wrong. Even Albert Einstein, with his Jewish ancestry, had left Berlin when the Nazis came into power.

But hateful words weren't the same as vengeance.

"Luisa isn't Jewish," Hanna said.

"No, but her husband is."

Hanna's mouth dropped open. Paul and Luisa's wedding had been an outdoor event, a Christian ceremony in the shadow of the abandoned abbey with chairs lined up along the meadow. Paul had been working as a vice president at the Tillich Toy Factory when he'd met Luisa. Jewish men weren't allowed to even date an Aryan; they certainly weren't allowed to marry one. That law had been passed here in 1935, during the annual rally of the Nazi Party in Nuremberg. Just months before their wedding.

It seemed that Luisa had rebelled against the Nazis in her own way.

Frau Weber reached over and nudged Hanna's mouth closed. "You didn't know . . ."

Hanna collapsed on the couch. She'd hoped this visit would bring clarity, but her mind was more muddled than when she arrived. "The Nuremberg laws forbid marriage between an Aryan and Jew."

"Love doesn't always fit neatly into our laws." Frau Weber sat on a chair across the room, her back poised like an arrow intent on a target. "Paul's family wasn't observant, but the Gestapo knew about their background."

"The Gestapo keeps a record of everything."

"A record of everyone else's life perhaps. They wouldn't dare track their own crimes."

The agent who'd searched Hanna's home this morning. He wouldn't have left a trail.

"Why did you come home?" Frau Weber asked.

"Himmler no longer wants women working in the field."

"*Kinder, Küche, und Kirche,*" the familiar phrase spilled off Frau Weber's lips. Children, kitchen, and church—the mission of German woman today.

Hanna forced a smile. "No *Kinder* for me."

Frau Weber stood. "I have coffee waiting in the kitchen."

Kinder, Küche, Kirche. The words jumbled in her mind as Frau Weber slipped through the side door, closing it carefully behind her so she didn't knock over any of her houseplants.

Hanna had never been much good in the kitchen, and while she'd attended church on most Sundays, she felt God's presence more in the labyrinth or in those books transcribed by nuns who'd once lived in her home. And children—she had never really considered having them. If one didn't marry, one didn't have this hassle even if the Nazis thought rearing them was critical to building their new Reich.

If she'd agreed to marry Kolman, she would have married the entire Nazi organization and their philosophy on women. They probably wouldn't even let her work at the museum.

Frau Weber returned with two cups of black coffee. After setting them on the table, she stepped back to close the door.

But something shifted on the other side of it. A mouse or—

It was a cat, with bright-golden fur.

Hanna stood. "Schatzi?"

Frau Weber quickly closed the door.

Hanna leaned forward, her voice but a whisper. "Luisa's here . . ."

Frau Weber's face blanched. "I don't know what you mean."

"She hasn't left Nuremberg."

"I couldn't say." Frau Weber glanced back at the window. "But it will soon be too dangerous for anyone from a Jewish family to remain in this town."

"Luisa can come back home with me. I will—"

Frau Weber stopped her. "The Gestapo was searching your house!"

"I'll find a way to hide her."

"A way to get us all killed, I'm afraid."

The woman was right, though Hanna didn't want to admit it. The Gestapo agent would return, and other than the attic, the only place to hide someone on her property was the abandoned graphite mine on the hillside, between the lodge and abbey. No one could last long in that cold space.

"Tell her that I miss her," Hanna said. "That she is always welcome to come home."

Frau Weber checked her watch. "You must have to report to the museum soon."

"The Gestapo will return." Hanna wrung her hands together, wanting to open that side door to see if Luisa was hiding. "To search my attic. I want to make sure they don't find anything up there."

Frau Weber glanced at her garden of houseplants as if to consult with friends. Then she moved back toward the door. "Wait here."

When she returned, Frau Weber pressed something cold into

Hanna's hand. "There are some papers in the attic, under the labyrinth. Burn them."

"But the labyrinth is up on the hill . . ."

"Burn them, Hanna, before the agent finds out what she did."

"What did Luisa do?"

A door slammed in the corridor outside. "You must leave now. The museum will wonder."

"Please, Frau Weber. Why is she in trouble?"

"The less you know, the safer you'll be."

She knew little now, but she didn't feel safe at all.

EMBER

Tourists crowded the ferry deck in front of Ember, anxious to catch a glimpse of an island where celebrity sightings blossomed, but oddly enough, grapes did not. While legend had it that someone named Martha—or Martin—inspired the island's name, the only vineyard ever planted here had struggled to survive. But wild vines flourished in this New England climate, the rogue, tangled kind that could weather any storm.

The sole commercial vineyard was long gone and only a backbone of locals weathered the snow, wind, and torrential rain. Unless islanders embraced the tourists or decided to maintain a family farm, work was hard to find. And considering that the value of farm property would buy a home equal in size to those owned by celebrities, it was perfectly understandable why many had decided to leave the island.

Each fall, after the threat of a nor'easter blew the crowds away, islanders tucked themselves away in cabins and cottages that spanned the Vineyard's hundred square miles. And legends continued to grow like wild vines, the Hollywood stars and their gazers giving locals plenty of fodder.

Stars and tourists and families like hers.

A line of waves headed toward the ferry, the water churning in the wind. Ember was safe behind the glass, but the thought of tumbling up and down, the water their captain, cinched the already tightly woven knot inside her.

She'd been born on this island, on the west side, where her father had pastored a small nondenominational church. She didn't remember much about those early years, but her brother, Alex, twelve years her senior, had told her that it was as close to normal as it would ever be for their family.

At some point before her sixth birthday, their father stopped praying to God . . . because he thought he *was* God. And it became his calling to purify their nation.

When he began protesting against the island's Hebrew Center— their Jewish neighbors—people started to leave the church. Her mother had cried at the departure of her closest friend. Ember remembered crying too, but her father only wanted those he considered "faithful" to remain in his flock. Those he considered to be true soldiers of Christ.

According to Alex, the whole island had begun to talk about the strange church that displayed a swastika behind the lectern. By the time their family and half the church membership left this island in search of a more accommodating community, her father and his twisted rhetoric were legend.

The Heywood family, along with her father's ardent followers, had relocated to Idaho, but Alex, eighteen at the time, chose to stay on Martha's Vineyard. Titus Kiehl—Dakota's dad—offered Alex a job and a cabin at the family's farm.

Her brother decided to change his last name to Ellis. Start a new life. No one except the Kiehl family, he'd said, remembered his past.

A decade later Ember returned to the island, her heart shattered like broken shells along the shore. Her brother was the only relative she had left in the world.

She and Alex had brought in the new millennium in his cabin, but neither of them celebrated. On that icy lakeshore in Idaho, everything had changed for both of them.

Ember took a long sip of the Sprite she'd bought back by the ferry dock in Woods Hole, hoping it would settle the rocking, but her anxiety stemmed from a place much deeper than the ocean. A seagull circled the ferry before cresting up with the breeze, and she tried to focus on the bird rather than the rise and fall of the waves.

In lieu of arranging a phone call, Kayla Mann had invited her to visit Mrs. Kiehl this evening. They'd talk over dinner, and then Ember would stay in the Kiehls' gingerbread cottage in the town of Oak Bluffs, one of those built for the Methodist camp meeting more than a century ago. It was a second homecoming of sorts after being away for so long.

Now she needed to embrace this coming home.

The boat rocked again, and she tucked her suitcase under a bench before slipping out of her seat. The stuffy air wasn't helping her stomach or clearing her mind.

Wind blew through the door as she moved out to the bow, ruffling the skirt of her white sundress. The island's bluffs were in view now, large homes perched on the edge. Even though she'd been born on this island, attended school here for several years, she was more stranger than local. She and Alex had moved to Pennsylvania during her senior year of high school. Then Brooke attended college in Minnesota and opted to stay. There'd been no reason for her to return until now.

Happier memories spilled over in her mind with the choppy waves, of riding the carousel with Brooke when they were in high school, hooking the brass rings. Camping out along the cliffs at Aquinnah, a million stars melded into the sky.

The ridicule on homecoming night ended those few years that she'd tried to embrace being a teenager. Laughter had echoed behind her as she escaped down to the shore that evening, wading through the foamy water in her gown while her classmates danced among construction-papered coral in the gym.

Dark-blonde hair tangled around her face as the ferry neared the port, and she tried to hold it back in the wind. She'd left DC before daybreak, taking the train to Boston and then a bus down to the ferry terminal. Dakota never texted again, and she was relieved. Back when she was an awkward teen trying to find herself in a strange new world, she'd practically declared her love for him, days before he humiliated her in front of the school.

She'd since learned to keep her feelings close to her heart.

In the distance, a line of clouds was ballooning into gray, rustling up the waves as they prepped for a grand production on this theater of sea. The clouds could blow over the island with just a sprinkle of rain or they might dump buckets across the crowded towns and quiet farms.

When the ferry docked, Ember tied her hair back in a ponytail and pulled out her phone to check the time. In a half hour, Noah would return home, but she'd told both him and his VIP dad that she would be traveling today and tomorrow. No matter how many times Noah texted, she couldn't return home any faster, but she had given Jack a tub of Phish Food and homework instructions. Hopefully, the man would put both to good use.

Her phone chimed as she descended the narrow staircase with the crowd. A Denver number appeared on the screen before she reached the platform, the one she hadn't assigned a name.

A missed call and then a message.

I'll meet you by the ticket office.

A man ran smack into Ember, sending her down two steps into a blessedly large woman who stopped her fall.

"I'm sorry," Ember blurted, shaken more from the text than the near miss of landing on the vehicle deck below.

At the bottom of the stairs, she turned left to the pedestrian walk and waited while the remaining cars rattled off the boat. She didn't want to see Dakota. Couldn't see him.

He was supposed to be in *Denver*, not on this island.

What was she going to do now? She wasn't stepping off this ferry, not until her racing heart began to calm. It was one thing to remember the humiliation from high school. It was quite another to be confronted with it.

The last car rolled onto the island, and an attendant looked over at her. The gangway was clear now, all the passengers gone. And a lineup of new vehicles were waiting to cross the waters into Woods Hole. Back and forth, rain or shine, a steady rhythm of delivering people as if they were packages.

Right now, she wanted to take the train back to her condo in Georgetown, dig her golden spoon into a bowl of ice cream with Noah. If she refused to disembark, they'd have to take her back to the mainland.

The attendant stepped up beside her. "Are you afraid of the gangway?"

She stuffed her phone into purse. "I'm afraid of what's on the other side."

"Martha's Vineyard is one of the safest places on earth."

But it wasn't safe for her heart.

When she still didn't move, the man pointed at a yellow building at the end of the dock. "If you're going back with us, you'll need a return ticket. And with this storm coming, we might be leaving early."

She tilted her head. "Can I just buy a ticket from you?"

"Sorry." He smiled. "The ticket office will get you set up though, and you can walk right back on the ferry."

She wanted to study the past, the centuries before, but the realities of her own story were overwhelming. Then again, she was no longer that teenager thrown into a strange new world, struggling to stand on legs so shaky that she once clung to whoever supplied what she'd deemed worthy. No man had control over her anymore—except this attendant, she supposed. He wasn't going to let her stay on the boat without a ticket. "I'll be returning first thing in the morning," she said as if he cared about her plans.

He tipped his hat, and she stepped onto the gangway, her suitcase rolling behind her to the ticket office. Then she walked right past it.

Hopefully Dakota was so madly in love with his wife and a houseful of children that he barely remembered anything from their high school years. Hopefully he would respect her decision to leave their past in the past.

A sidewalk on her left pointed toward the rumble of ocean waves. Dark clouds bruised the afternoon sky, a bully threatening to unleash its power.

Ahead was a parking lot where taxis usually waited for the island guests and a grassy plaza with a gazebo for events. To her right was the village of Oak Bluffs, where she and Alex had moved after a few months in Titus's cabin.

Perhaps Dakota had returned home to work at the farm like his father and then Alex had done for a season. He'd probably exchanged his football uniform for overalls and a straw hat, a dirty handkerchief around his neck.

If she hurried, she could stick to her original plan of taking a taxi to Mrs. Kiehl's house. The thirty-minute ride would give her time to process seeing Dakota, perhaps meeting his wife.

"Ember?"

Her stomach rolled again, but it wasn't the waves that plagued her. She pretended that she didn't hear, that the buzz of tourists, the engines from waiting cars, blocked his voice.

She waved her hand at a Prius with *Martha's Vineyard Taxi* displayed on its side. The cab moved toward her.

Dakota called her name again, louder, and this fear—she had to stop being afraid. She dug her heels into the cement, then turned slowly.

In front of her was one of the men that she'd never wanted to see again. The man who was supposed to be living in Denver.

The hem of his beach shorts fell almost to his knees, and he wore flip-flops and a sweatshirt as if he'd spent the day surfing at Squibnocket before picking her up. She'd been so hoping for the denim overalls. Or the sprouting of horns. Anything to detract from the curly brown hair that splayed to one side, a smile that had once made her heart cartwheel.

But Dakota Kiehl was just as attractive as she remembered, perhaps even more so with his shadow of a beard.

He was the primary reason why she'd received a C in Algebra II, something that would haunt her months later when she applied for an honors scholarship at Georgetown. She never did explain to the college administrator that the captain of her high school's football team had ruined her ability to ace the class, just that she was in the process of overcoming her aversion to numbers.

Her lack of attentiveness almost cost her the scholarship, and she'd determined that this man would never cause her to lose anything important again.

Dakota smiled at her. "Hello, Ember."

She forced her lips into what she hoped was a smile. "Hello."

The salty tang of sea rolled over the bluff, threatening to take her back again to those high school years.

"Gram said you took the train."

"A train and bus." She nodded toward the water. "And the ferry, of course. A taxi ride is what I need to complete my journey."

He reached for the handle of her suitcase, but she waved him away, picking it up instead.

"You still get seasick?" he asked, studying her face.

If he remembered that, he'd never forget how she'd groveled in her admiration for him. "Nothing wrong with your memory."

. "Or my vehicle." He pointed at a muddy black 4Runner with roll bars parked above the beach, a later model of the one he'd driven their senior year. "No reason for you to ride in a taxi."

But she could think of a hundred good reasons. A thousand even.

"I'm still taking one," she said, scanning the parking lot again, but the Prius was gone.

"I'll just be following you home."

When she looked back, she saw the questioning in his gaze. Was he taunting her like he'd done long ago? While she could remember facts well, she'd always struggled to read people. A memory of steel, that's what she had, but her discernment . . . it was more like Jell-O.

But he must understand why she couldn't get in his car.

"You do what you want, Dakota. I'm here to see your grandmother." She didn't want to be mean, not like how he'd treated her, but she wasn't going to spend a half hour with him. Alone.

"What if you can't catch another taxi?" he asked.

The island shuttle pulled up by the plaza to distribute tourists to the towns and remote beaches across the island.

Without another word, she rushed across the street and hopped on it, locking her heart tight again. And she didn't look back, not until the shuttle pulled into the parking lot of West Tisbury's town hall.

But she hadn't locked her heart tight enough. At the sight of the black 4Runner, of the man who stepped out into the rain, her heart felt exposed. Raw and tender.

And she had no place to hide.

10

HANNA

The director of the Germanic National Museum was middle-aged, but he looked like one of the museum's artifacts, with cheeks so taut they could have been chiseled from sandstone. This building and the thousands of artifacts inside were Heinrich Kohlhaussen's kingdom, and Grete Cohn, the secretary who'd greeted Hanna at the front door, explained clearly that the director wouldn't let any of the staff undermine his work.

Director Kohlhaussen stood in the stark-white lobby, silently critiquing Hanna's trousers before shaking her hand. "Welcome to the National Museum."

"I'm pleased to be here," she said, praying that God would forgive her recurring lies.

"With all of our recent acquisitions, our collection is on the way to becoming the best in Europe." He waved her through a gallery of historical artwork, each piece hung in a gilded frame. "We're preserving the German heritage, but we're also a safe house for valuables from across the Continent."

At the end of the corridor, they passed through the arched cloister of a former Carthusian monastery, the monks' cells now used as exhibit rooms for the twelve wooden panels of an altarpiece, each depicting a different scene from the life of Christ.

"Lunch is provided for all our employees in the cafeteria," the director said as they neared a staircase. "You will leave your personal belongings in a locker outside the front door so none of your things are stolen."

And so nothing was taken from their collection, she surmised. Too many museum workers would be tempted to walk out the door with artifacts stuffed into their handbags.

"Your work is waiting for you downstairs."

He directed her through a dimly lit basement, the ceiling a gray cloud socking them into this space, a variety of posters lining the walls. Some promoted the ideal of a perfect German family, several blond children with their parents, a baby in the mother's arms. Some reminded Germans about the dangers of an air raid. Others displayed frightening creatures, crossed with skulls, to warn them about typhus, the infection that would afflict any Aryan who associated with their Jewish neighbors.

The face of Paul Gruenewald swept into her mind, the sharp eyes that understood the internal workings at Tillich Toy Factory, the warm smile that rested on Luisa whenever he visited their home.

Paul didn't look anything like the dirty, disease-infested caricatures on these posters. Nor did Albert Einstein or the Jewish professors and students she'd met in Berlin.

She reached in her pocket, felt the key that Frau Weber had given her to the attic. Her cousin had loved Paul for years. Was the Gestapo planning to punish her now for their marriage?

Director Kohlhaussen opened a door to show her their storehouse of extinguishers for an air attack, gas masks, and buckets of sand if necessary to extinguish a fire before it burned their collection. She'd heard the war reports, seen the prisoners in France, but the fighting was outside Germany. No one would ever penetrate their defenses here, even by air.

Farther down the hall, the aroma of cardboard and worn leather seeped from a second storage room. Inside were two filing cabinets and a regiment of box-filled shelves.

The director handed her a clipboard with lined paper. "You must catalog everything in these boxes and then repackage the items in crates so not even a British bomb will shatter them."

She looked at him as if he'd lost his mind. "No amount of paper and wood will stop a bomb."

"Our bunker will soften any blow."

She blinked. "What bunker?"

"That I can't tell you."

Her hands ran over one of the boxes. "So I'm burying your treasure."

"In a way, I suppose."

She wanted to learn the stories, find the pieces that nodded to their past, not create an inventory. But if she couldn't dig in the field, she'd do her best to curate the artifacts here, saving them from the bombs. Each piece had a story. A creator and an owner and probably a family who'd ushered it carefully through the years.

Director Kohlhaussen lifted a bolt of fabric off the top of a cabinet, slipping it onto one of the shelves so she could use it to wrap the artifacts. "I understand you are to be married soon."

Startled, she didn't reply. Had the secret police reported this information to her supervisor? In her statement to the Gestapo agent, a lie to save her life, she feared that she'd lynched herself.

Instead of responding, Hanna lifted a bronze *Glocke* from a box and examined the beehive-shaped bell from a much earlier century.

Thirteenth or fourteenth, back when these bells were used to signal danger or death.

"Fräulein?"

She glanced back up at the director, a flickering light bulb reflecting off his balding head. He was waiting for some sort of response about her impending marriage.

She placed the bell on an empty shelf. "We haven't set a wedding date."

His eyes clouded with confusion and then cleared. "When is Standartenführer Strauss expected to arrive in Nuremberg?"

"Soon" was all she offered, hoping she wouldn't see Kolman soon at all. That he would receive her letter of refusal and become so immersed in wherever Himmler sent him that he'd forget about her completely.

"I look forward to meeting him."

She gave a brusque nod. She was here to do a job, and she'd do it to the best of her ability. If the director wanted to speak with Kolman, he needed to contact the SS.

"We work from nine until five, every weekday," he said. "You'll have time off, of course, for your wedding."

"I'm not getting married."

He patted her shoulder as if he was more concerned about her future as a wife than her work at the museum. "These storage rooms double as bomb shelters for all our employees, so if the air siren goes off, you'll have a crowd."

While she longed to feel the dirt on her hands instead of cloth, she unfolded the paper from another box, removing a circular wooden panel. The center was gerated with pieces of iron, leather, and parchment, and on the top of the panel was a helmet with red-glazed wings, the bottom a silvered coat of arms.

A memorial shield, made to remember the dead.

Where had the museum secured such a treasure?

It didn't matter, she supposed. She'd do whatever she could to protect it from the Royal Air Force and its bombs.

For hours, she sorted through the boxes, recording porcelain figurines, paintings, and engraved glass from the House of Habsburg. Treasure, all of it, to further prove their Nordic past. She noted the items on the clipboard and wrapped them with cloth before placing them in crates. Most of the artifacts were passed down, she suspected, from the patriciate in Nuremberg, before their city was swallowed up in 1806 by the federal state of Bavaria.

"Fräulein Tillich?" someone called from the corridor.

"I'm in here." She reached into a new box and pulled out an egg-shaped watch hooked to a silver chain. One that appeared to be from the 1500s.

Grete walked into the room, a cup in her hand, eyeglasses dangling around her neck with a beaded strap. Early twenties, if Hanna had to guess her age, but she held a firm air of authority as if she could run this museum on her own. "I thought you might want some coffee."

Hanna took a sip of the warm drink. No sugar but fresh cream. "Thank you."

"You can come upstairs whenever you'd like more."

"I lost track of time," Hanna said, holding up the old watch as if it concurred.

"Director Kohlhaussen always stays until eight. He can write you a curfew pass if you'd like to work late."

Hanna glanced at her wrist. It was almost four, and she was eager to explore the attic before the Gestapo returned. "I have to leave right at five."

"These boxes, and perhaps a few more, will all be waiting for you in the morning." Grete glanced down at Hanna's trousers. "I wish I could wear a pair of those to work."

"It makes lifting these boxes much easier." Hanna swept her hand over the display of artifacts that she'd lined up on a shelf. "Where did the museum get all of these things?"

"From different homes across Germany."

"People donated them?"

Grete hesitated. "Not exactly."

"But how—?"

Grete moved toward the door. "I must get back upstairs before the director starts looking for me."

Hanna swathed the watch in linen and carefully packed it into a crate. Had the museum purchased these items from local dealers? Perhaps their brokers weren't as reputable as the museum would like to admit.

Or had the museum taken these things from those who'd rebelled against the regime? Himmler was notorious for picking and choosing whatever he pleased, even antiquities that belonged to others. In his mind, the Aryans owned everything, and no one dared to defy him, not if they wanted to keep their life.

In the next box she found a fragile book made with parchment and a worn leather cover. Turning the pages carefully, she marveled at the calligraphy, the ink artwork of leaves and vines, wishing she could read the Hebrew lettering. This wasn't an artifact to prove the German's ancestral heritage. It was a *Memorbuch*, once owned by a Jewish family.

She'd read about these *Memorbücher* but had never seen one before. The Jewish population in Nuremberg began keeping these memory books in the thirteenth century to remember those who'd been killed in pogroms.

The Nazis wouldn't protect Jewish people like Paul and his family; it was strange that they would care for their things.

Her mind wandered back to the letters on the labyrinth stones beside the abbey. Each person who'd died had a story, but to her knowledge, no one had written them down. And according to her mother, the Torah said it was imperative to remember the stories, reminding readers—169 times—of this decree.

Rachel. Benjamin. Mary. She and Luisa had picked biblical names for all the letters in the labyrinth so these people wouldn't be forgotten. It was another game for them, which name matched which number of stone.

Her stomach curled again at the memory.

If only she could visit Frau Weber one more time, try and help Luisa, but if the Gestapo began to track her, she feared she might lead them right to Luisa's hiding place.

At five, she hurried back upstairs, anxious to return home with the attic key.

Director Kohlhaussen stood by the front door, wishing his employees a good evening, scanning their clothing to make sure nothing left this building that was supposed to remain. That no employees would plunder what they'd already taken and stored.

One woman was motioned to the side. Random selection, Grete had explained. All of them were subject to a personal search.

The director shook Hanna's hand, deftly searching for any bulges in her cardigan. "Thank you for your work today."

"It was my pleasure."

"Take the next week off," he said when he released her hand. "Spend it with your husband."

"I'm not getting—"

But the man had already turned his back, shaking the next hand.

11

EMBER

"The house is still two miles from here," Dakota said after Ember stepped off the bus. The shuttle pulled away from the parking lot, returning to the ferry terminal in Oak Bluffs, but it had delivered her a good fifteen miles into the heart of the island.

"I'll head up when the storm stops." She ducked under an awning on the town hall as rain dripped off the shingles onto her open toes. Two miles was an easy walk after living in DC.

"I can't blame you for not wanting a ride, but my grandmother is expecting us at four, and it's almost 3:40."

With those words, her cell phone chimed.

While Noah knew she'd be gone, that information never stopped him from checking in.

Where are you?

Ember shot the boy a quick text back, reminding him that she was only gone for two days.

When it chimed again, Dakota glanced at her screen. "Who misses you?"

She flipped the phone over. "His name's Noah."

"Your husband?"

"No, I've never been married." That's what the FBI told her, at least, after they'd rushed her away from Eagle Lake. Nothing about her arrangement with Lukas had been legal.

"Well, this Noah is a blessed man to have found you."

Lifting the phone, she keyed in one more response.

I miss you too. Now back to your homework!

And Phish Food, Noah said.

After muting the volume, she slipped the phone into her handbag. No sense trying to explain Phish Food to the man in front of her.

Dakota held out his hand beyond the awning and the raindrops sprang off his palm, diving into the puddle below. "You're going to get soaked."

"It will let up soon."

"Not according to the National Weather Service. We've got a thunderstorm blowing in this afternoon that's supposed to last all night."

If she continued this, her stubbornness would end up in an unexplainable tardiness for her meeting with Mrs. Kiehl, not to mention a nasty cold. She was supposed to be ambivalent, but once again she'd let Dakota get under her skin.

"I guess I'll have to ride up with you." Two miles would go by quickly. She wouldn't even have to talk until she saw Mrs. Kiehl.

"You want me to put your suitcase in the 4Runner?" he asked, his hands in his pockets.

She slowly released her grasp on the handle. "That would be fine."

Dakota thought she had a boyfriend. A blessed man, he'd said. Noah really was the only guy in her life at the moment, and she didn't see any reason to correct Dakota's flawed assumption. A phantom boyfriend would help her make it through dinner at the Kiehls'. All she wanted was to hear the stories about Hanna and Nuremberg, and then she'd be gone.

After depositing her luggage in the back, Dakota cleaned a stack of papers from the passenger seat. Lightning flashed in the distance, and she hopped into the SUV as he started the engine. Then he turned onto a farm road built for locals and lost tourists, limestone walls fencing both sides.

"The cottage in Oak Bluffs is ready for you. You can have it for a whole week if you'd like."

"I'm only spending the night." The reverse order of transportation, from ferry to Lyft, would whisk her back to her condo in Georgetown tomorrow. By Friday morning, she would be inside the safe walls of her office at the Mandel Center, pulling files from the shelves, enjoying ice cream with her favorite fourth grader that afternoon. "How long has your family owned one of the gingerbread cottages?"

"Since 1872," he said. "We used to rent it out, but now I—"

She sucked in air so quickly that it felt like a hit of helium to her brain. "You live in it?"

Leaves shuddered around them, a thousand sails in the wake of this storm. "Not tonight, of course. I'll stay at the farm with Gram."

The fading light flecked his brown eyes with gold as he adjusted the rearview mirror. She looked away.

"You keep in touch with anyone from school?" He slowed the truck to dodge a fallen branch.

"A few."

"A couple of our classmates are still on the island," he said over the rhythm of the wiper blades. "But only Beatty and I keep in touch. You remember Beatty?"

She remembered the names of everyone in their class. "He was the skateboarder with the Rugrats collection."

"That's him."

She glanced back at him, surprised. "You and Beatty were friends in high school?"

"A lot has changed, Em. For me in particular." She flinched at the familiar name, but he didn't seem to notice. "Hard to believe we're almost at the twenty-year mark."

"I don't want to talk about high school."

A gray sheet of rain blew across the pond on their right, its corners rippling in the storm, and a rogue drum, the distant bellow of thunder, joined the chorus of wind.

"I still feel like a teenager some days," he said. "I just don't want to make the same miserable choices over again."

Which choices? That's what she wanted to ask, but she didn't want him to think her interest had in any way returned. Men like Lukas and Dakota might learn how to charm, but they never really changed.

Branches bobbed overhead as if trying to hook their vehicle, and she watched a yellow patch creep across her weather app, the warning about a thunderstorm churning offshore. She wanted to go straight to the ferry terminal, return to the safety of the mainland, but the ferry would remain docked until the winds calmed again. No one in their right mind would cross the sound in this weather.

Then again, she wasn't exactly in her right mind.

Dakota was hunched over the steering wheel, squinting to see the asphalt in the onslaught of rain. The wiper blades ticked like the hands of a broken clock across his windshield. Stuck in time.

He glanced at her as they climbed the hill. "We're almost there."

"Good."

He jerked the wheel to the left, avoiding another fallen branch. "Maybe five more minutes with this storm."

The last time she had been in a nor'easter, she'd been sixteen. A mesocyclone ripped across the shore before a tornado touched down outside Oak Bluffs. The winds had flipped boats and stirred up the ocean floor, covering the beach with debris.

She and her brother had battened down their own hatches that night, filling the garage with the car parts he'd strewn across the yard and then locking the shutters in the house. Alex had—

A deafening crack and she watched in horror as an oak tree teetered ahead of them before falling across the road. Dakota slammed on the brakes, and the 4Runner slipped to the right, toward the stone wall. As she clenched the handle, a picture flashed through her mind of the SUV slamming against the wall, rolling back down the street on its bars.

The 4Runner spun instead, the tail end thudding against the tree, halting their slide. Then all was still as if they'd stopped this moment in time.

Like the gate on a drawbridge, the oak cut off their access to Mrs. Kiehl.

Dakota didn't move, his hands clutching the wheel. "I'm afraid it's going to take a few more minutes to get home."

"Okay," she said, her voice small, the image of their truck tumbling downhill on replay in her head. Thank God, they hadn't flipped over.

He shifted to park and hopped out, examining the tree before he returned to his seat. "I'll need to bring back a chain saw to clear the road."

She nodded toward the muddy path between the tree and wall. "Can we walk up to the house?"

A flash of lightning answered her question.

"I'm afraid we'll have to reschedule until tomorrow," he said.

She nodded slowly, trying to let go of her plans like she'd asked Noah to do with his plans today. "Tomorrow would be fine."

She could still take the ferry back in the afternoon. Maybe she could even stop in Pennsylvania and spend the night with her brother.

In the morning, she prayed, the storm would be gone.

12

LILLY

SONNENWIESE CHILDREN'S HOME

Lightning stabbed the village below, and the little girl, her nose pressed against the glass, waited until the thunder rolled across town and up the hill, shaking this big house.

They had thunder at her home too, back in the trees. Perhaps Mama had heard it.

This big house with its endless rooms, all the children crowded inside, was nothing like home. She missed the fields and stream behind her cottage. Missed her brothers and how they'd bring her sweet *pączki* when they returned from work.

Most of all, she missed her mother.

"Lilly?"

The girl didn't move, her nose squished against the cold as she waited for another light, a second roll of thunder. Was Mama thinking about her?

"Lilly," the woman called again.

This time the girl turned. Lilly was her name now; she'd forgotten.

The matron was standing before her, a white apron wrapped tightly around ribbons of flesh, a towel in her thick hands.

Was it time to be measured again? She hated the doctors with their rulers who made notes about her face, her arms. Picked through her hair. Hated the nurses who smacked her bottom like they were giant bats, she the ball.

When her brothers played *palant*, they would drop their bat—after they'd hit the ball—and race between *niebo* and *piekło*. Heaven and hell.

Some days it felt like she was between heaven and hell here, searching for a safe place to hide.

Sonnenwiese, they called this house. Sun Meadow. A happy name, but still she felt so very sad.

She followed the matron into the kitchen.

"Where are we, Lilly?" the woman asked, taking a silver tray off the counter, filling it with peppernut cookies for the children.

"*Kuchnia,*" she replied softly, knowing the word wasn't right, but she couldn't remember all these new words.

"*Nein*. Try again."

"*Ku—*"

"*Küche,*" the woman said. "You have to learn these words if you ever want a family."

Family.

That word made her smile, but she didn't want a new family. She already had one.

"Come along," the woman said.

She followed the matron through the stark hall, into a room unlike any other in this place. The brown walls reminded her of a forest, the seat cushions like autumn leaves. A pretty woman sat on a chair, wearing a bright-green dress as if she were budding on the branches.

When Lilly walked in, the green lady wrote something on her notepad.

"She's about three," the matron told her. "But she's not ready yet."

"When will she be ready?"

"In six months, maybe sooner."

The green lady's eyes narrowed. "We have hundreds more children waiting for a decent bed."

"She's a slow learner."

"Then you must encourage her to learn faster."

The matron nodded briskly before shuffling Lilly into the next room. Instead of forest browns, this room was gray and silver. Like the storm.

New children were lined up against a wall, waiting for the doctors and nurses. The matron guided her to the opposite end of the room, where they made her climb up on a metal step, lower a bar onto the top of her head. To see if she measured up.

That's one word she learned early.

Messen.

Everything here was measured.

Were they measuring Mama in another room? Or another house?

They couldn't measure Papa—he'd left home a long time ago—but her brothers would measure up.

Once she'd asked the matron about her family, and she received a slap in return. She had no family, the matron said. Not yet.

But she did have a family. And they would be looking for her.

Questions were not permitted here—she'd learned that quickly—but they bubbled up inside her like apple soda, no place to spill.

The matron pushed her along and then handed her a dolly. She was supposed to pretend like she was the mama, taking care of this baby, but she couldn't shake the questions out of her head.

Why had the soldiers taken her from Mama?

And if she didn't measure right, why couldn't she just go home?

13

HANNA

Hanna jimmied the key in the attic lock. When she was a child, she'd often sneak into Vater's room, testing this door. Never once had she found it unlatched, but it became a ritual, a crusade of her own to explore the world of dollhouses that her grandfather had created. A world she'd explored with her brother before the war.

After Jonny's death, Vater had locked the door for good. She'd desperately wanted to play among the dollhouses again, discover the secrets they must contain, but then she'd grown up and decided to uncover secrets in other places around the world.

If Luisa had hidden something incriminating here, if the Gestapo agent found it, he'd implicate both women. She had to find this piece—the labyrinth that Frau Weber described—before the agent returned.

If only her muscles were stronger than her mind. Instead of wriggling this old key in the lock, she'd force the door open with her shoulder, like the men in the movies.

A click from the lock, and her breath skipped. Tentatively she pressed down on the latch, and the hinges groaned in response.

The haze of afternoon light pressed through splotches on the weathered windows, pinholes of light illuminating the vast space. Like a cavern, she thought, without a dirt floor for her to dig.

A flashlight in hand, she trailed the sunlight under low timbers and then the room opened up into a magical space, even grander than her childhood memories.

Opa's workshop was a wonderland.

Dollhouses encircled the room. The kind that wealthy people of old would purchase—not for their children but as a collection to impress their aristocratic neighbors. Oversized *Puppenhäuser* normally found in museums across Nuremberg, not hidden away.

Mesmerized, Hanna shone her flashlight on one of the dust-coated houses to study the details. Each room was meticulously designed with colorful chintz drapes and polished tables and tiny pewter candlesticks and tableware. One of the bedrooms had a canopy bed with carved posts and a miniature hobbyhorse for the little girl who was tucked into bed, a pink stocking cap to match her gown and a shelf on her wall filled with books.

The next house was fashioned after a home from the early 1800s, it seemed, with an attached stable and carriage house. The carriage inside rolled seamlessly when she nudged it forward.

Her grandfather must have worked up in the attic religiously, creating samples to replicate in the Tillich Toy Factory. Or was he commissioned by local families to build these? The workmanship seemed too precise to be a sample, unless potential customers came to view these models.

She would have been about three when she and Jonny had talked Vater into letting them see this place. Perhaps she'd forgotten all these marvelous details, but it seemed they would have been seared into her young mind.

Had Vater worked up here as well, after Jonny died?

The third dollhouse stretched almost a meter above her head, the rooms a mirror of the former hunting lodge, the downstairs hall mounted with trophies of faux animal heads. At the base of the house was a wooden stool, and Hanna stepped on it, looking into the miniature attic. Inside were tiny dollhouses and a male doll bent over a workbench, his graying hair a mantle above the tools.

She moved to the next house, brushing dust off a tea service in the parlor.

Perhaps her grandfather had simply enjoyed building these as a hobby for himself. Or as a gift for his children. Instead of daughters, Opa had two sons. The oldest died in 1887 from typhoid when it swept through the factory. The younger one, Hanna's father, inherited a toy factory that he had never wanted to run.

Why hadn't her father allowed her to enjoy this legacy of toys instead of hiding them away? She would have loved nothing more as a girl than to slip up here and create stories of her own.

It was possible that her father, like her, wanted to preserve the past, but it was probably something deeper. Vater had never wanted her to be a child, at least not a girl. He'd loved her in his own way, but he didn't want her enamored by dolls or the other playthings that parents bought from his factory. He'd wanted her to be well-versed in books so she didn't have to focus solely on *Kinder, Küche, und Kirche*.

She circled the far end with her flashlight, searching for a labyrinth. Tools rested on the former workbench and beside it was a container with an assortment of fabric scraps and threads. Had her grandfather stitched the curtains and clothing himself? Forged the pewter? The factory, perhaps, had fired the porcelain for the dolls, but he might have painted some of the faces here.

The stories he would have been able to tell about creating these pieces, perhaps he did tell, but Vater never passed them along. Her father didn't like talking about the past. One of the many reasons why history had intrigued her so.

She had no plans for children, but if she ever had a daughter, she wouldn't lock doors to an attic or bury keys or hide the past away. She'd leave her daughter a legacy of stories, like her mother had left for her.

A picture flashed in her mind, one of her pragmatic father up here as a boy, learning the trade. Was it possible that her father had worked in this attic alongside Opa, stitching or painting or carving as an apprentice? Perhaps, decades ago, he had been happy, before he was sent off to the war. Perhaps, in this place, he had escaped into his own world later in life, adding to Opa's collection.

There were an endless number of hiding places here for papers, folded into a neat square—trunks and cabinets and armoires. What had Luisa meant about hiding them under a labyrinth?

Light was fading outside, and she didn't want to alert anyone, especially another unwelcome visitor, to her presence with the flashlight. But what if the Gestapo agent returned first thing in the morning? He might find the papers that Frau Weber asked her to burn.

She stepped back to the dollhouse that resembled the lodge, opening the small cabinets and a miniature steamer trunk, lifting the beds and furniture to look underneath.

Outside one of the dollhouse windows, paned with glass, was a meadow of sorts, like the one behind her real home. Hanna shuffled behind the play house and shone her light on the ground.

A block of green fabric stretched across a small square of floor, decorated with ceramic flowers that had been stained blue and yellow. At the far end of the meadow was a cropping of rocks on a gray circle of fabric, markings etched on each one. Like her labyrinth on the hill.

Hanna lifted up the edge of the fabric and saw two pieces of paper stashed underneath. One was typed, then edited with a blue pen. The second was a sheet covered with names—some of them checked, others crossed off in pen. She didn't recognize any of the names, but the addresses were all in Nuremberg.

She locked the door and carried the papers downstairs, placing the key in the back of one of Vater's desk drawers. If the Gestapo found it, she would claim ignorance. Her father had left it, and she'd yet to go through his things.

On a pantry stool, hidden away from the windows, Hanna shone her light across the typed sheet. Paul's name was at the top in bold letters, and the following paragraphs described the man who'd been born in Nuremberg and employed in management at various toy factories until he'd been asked to take over Herr Tillich's role. No one at the Tillich Toy Factory, according to this report, had known that Paul's parents were Jewish.

The biography continued on the back of the sheet. As the new president, Paul had been determined to create toys to calm children's fears about a possible war. He was successful at his work and the Nazis allowed him to continue running the factory until 1937, three years after Hanna's father died. Then the Nazis requisitioned Tillich Toy Factory to build compasses for soldiers. Much more important than toys, management was told, their children needed the promise of a safe homeland where they could thrive.

Numbers stacked themselves up in Hanna's head: 1937 would have been two years after the Reichstag passed the Nuremberg Race Laws to prevent race pollution, prohibiting Germans and Jews to marry. A full year after Hitler hosted the Olympics so the world could see that, in spite of the rumors, all was well in Germany.

According to this biography, Paul and Luisa annulled their marriage months after the wedding, but they continued to live as husband and wife. When Paul was forced to resign his job, Luisa supported their family by caring for invalids, some of them Jewish, inside the lodge.

A year ago, the Gestapo showed up at the Gruenewalds' front door. They beat Paul until he could no longer walk and hauled him and their guests away in a truck. Then they shaved Luisa's head and marched her through the heart of Old Town, a placard around her neck stating that she'd sullied the honor of German women. For the next three months, they'd imprisoned her for racial defilement, an atrocity among the Nazi leadership.

Hanna's stomach turned. Her cousin had gone to prison for loving her husband and helping those who required medical care. Her purported enemies.

Hanna had spent a lifetime learning about purity, her education steeped in the Aryan traditions. A Germanic race to rule the world. Searching for one's identity was one thing, but the thought of this, what happened to her cousin, made her nauseous.

And Paul—how could the Nazis convict this kind man, a good leader, for the blood running through his veins? As if he'd committed a crime. He could change his behavior, but he couldn't aryanize his blood.

Now she understood why Frau Weber wanted her to burn Paul and Luisa's story. The museum could curate Jewish artifacts, but the Gestapo would imprison, kill even, anyone who dared to record the oppression against Jewish people today. If the outside world found out the rumors of persecution were true, they might intervene.

But Hanna couldn't burn these papers. She'd dedicated her life to discovering and preserving artifacts, wishing the stories behind those pieces hadn't been lost to time. What if she could preserve the stories now? Hide this biography away like the Cathars had done with their relics?

Their society, thank God, had advanced past the massacres of earlier centuries—when they'd tried to exterminate a whole population—but Hitler and the others had made it quite clear that people like Paul were no longer welcome in Germany. They were already being repressed by impossible laws, but if they didn't leave voluntarily, it seemed they were being forced to move away.

Someday the world would want to know what happened when the Nazis were in power. If she saved just one story, salvaged this record of two innocent people who'd been criminalized, others inside and outside Germany might learn the truth.

She'd carry the story of Paul and Luisa up to the prayer labyrinth tonight, bury it under stone number *Vierzig*—forty—to commemorate the year.

The doorbell rang, and her heart skipped. She hadn't expected the Gestapo to drive up the mountain after dark, but the agent was probably keen to find her home alone, especially if he discovered she'd lied about her engagement to Kolman.

Folding the papers quickly, she hid them inside a cookie tin, placing it right back up on the pantry shelf with the other food.

She could pretend she wasn't home, hide in one of the bedrooms. But if the agent had brought a locksmith, it wouldn't take them long to enter the lodge. And the repercussions would be swift.

The bell rang again as she retrieved the knife from the kitchen drawer and wrapped it in a dish towel, holding the towel at her side as if the agent had interrupted her dinner preparations. If he dared to threaten her, she'd threaten back.

Through the windows, she saw the headlamps of a car and slowly opened the front door, the knife secure in her hand. But instead of the agent, a much younger man stood at her door, his cap tucked under one arm.

"Telegram delivery for Fräulein Tillich."

She thanked him as she took the offered envelope, glancing both directions to see if there was a Gestapo agent nearby.

He thrust the cap back on his head. *"Guten Abend."*

She wished him a good evening as well; then she relocked the door.

Had Kolman sent her a note from the field? If she knew where he was located, she would write him tomorrow.

But the message wasn't from Kolman. It was an official notice from Himmler, stamped *Reich Leader of the SS*.

Your presence is required at Wewelsburg Castle the morning of 10 June for your marriage to Standartenführer Strauss. Arrive in wedding attire. Only invited guests permitted to attend.

Her marriage? Hanna flipped the envelope, thinking for a moment this telegram must be meant for someone else, but the message was addressed to her.

Sinking to the floor, she read Himmler's words again. There was no congratulations in them. No invitation. This was a summons to her own wedding on Monday, with a man she didn't want to marry.

And then she knew. That's why Director Kohlhaussen had congratulated her. Himmler had told her supervisor about the wedding before he'd bothered to tell Hanna. Grete probably knew about the ceremony too.

No one defied Himmler without consequence. He'd think nothing of taking down a woman who no longer aided his research, imprisoning her like Luisa or worse.

There was no way out of this marriage, not if Himmler had personally ordained it. She could try to hide, but if they found her . . .

She bundled her legs against her chest.

It would be impossible to refuse Kolman now.

PART TWO

Whatever is available to us in good blood of our type, we will take for ourselves, that is, we will steal their children and bring them up with us, if necessary....

We have carried out this most difficult task [of Jewish extermination] out of love for our own people. And we have suffered no harm to our inner self, our soul, our character in so doing.

HEINRICH HIMMLER
SS GROUP LEADER MEETING IN POLAND
OCTOBER 1943

14

EMBER

Rain pelted the windshield as Dakota drove up to the former grove called the Campground. Storybook cottages, with all their trimmings, had been built on tent platforms here in the nineteenth century, each one displaying brightly colored paint and a whimsical name over its front door.

Dakota parked along the perimeter since the lanes traversing the old camp were only wide enough to accommodate a carriage. Then he yanked an umbrella out from under the seat. "We'll have to run for it."

The umbrella, she feared, might take them on a ride like Mary Poppins, straight out to the Atlantic. "I think we should leave the umbrella behind."

He looked skeptical. "You'll get drenched."

"I'll be drenched either way."

Dakota tossed the umbrella into the back seat and zipped up his jacket. "I'll grab your suitcase. We're the seventh house on the right, the blue one trimmed with white."

She glanced out at the theater of rain, the house colors blending into gray. A flag on a nearby cottage flapped as if it might sweep the entire house into the air.

"It's number fifteen," he said. "Just follow me."

He rounded the car to grab her bag while she tugged on the hood of her coat, checking the zipper again, hoping the marketing claim about water resistance was closer to waterproof.

"You ready?" he called from the back.

"No."

"I'm afraid it's only going to get worse."

She hopped out of the truck and the two of them raced through the cold, the storm soaking through her dress and coat, pelting her cheeks and hands, drenching her sandaled feet.

The Kiehls' cottage overlooked a grassy plaza and the open-air Tabernacle that still held church services and events. Dakota stepped up on the veranda, fiddling with his keys, the rope from a hammock flogging his arm. One of the rocking chairs had tipped over by the picture window, and the second hung over the wooden banister, about to take wing.

When Dakota opened the door, she hurried into a tiny living space, cascading water onto the rug. He set the suitcase beside her. "I have to bring in the porch furniture."

"I'll help you."

He started to refuse, but she scooted around him, ready to work like she'd done with Alex before the tornado.

As she unlatched the hammock, Dakota lifted a rocking chair and pointed it toward the side of the house. "We'll put this stuff in the shed."

They battled the wind together, securing the furniture and retrieving his chain saw so he could clear the fallen tree from the road.

Back inside the house, Dakota took her jacket and rushed through the small living room, hanging both of their coats on pegs at the far end of the room. Beside their dripping jackets was a bathroom, and she stepped inside, changing into shorts and a ribbed T-shirt. After hanging her wet dress with the coats, she collapsed onto the couch, exhausted from her day of travel. Dakota sat beside her. "This morning the weatherman said light rain."

"Chalk one up for the Atlantic." She studied the gingerbread trim along the built-in shelves, the white wicker chair and couch crammed into this cozy room that housed both a living room and kitchen. No electronics muddied the Victorian decor. "It's like a dollhouse."

"You've never been in one of these?"

"I used to walk through the grove at night and look in the windows." At the families sitting around tables, parents eating or playing games with their children. A fairy tale in her mind.

"My ancestors erected a tent here each summer for the Methodist camp meetings until everyone decided to build cottages. I don't think anyone imagined that these summer homes would last more than a hundred years."

"It's wonderful that you've kept it in your family."

"Gram spends her winters here, attending events at the church and ordering lobster rolls, delivered straight to her door. Sometimes she even comes for a day or two in the summer to enjoy a concert in the Tabernacle."

He turned toward the picture window, watching the rain blow across the porch. The clock said it was almost five, but the steel-gray clouds, along with her long day of travel, made it feel as if it were later.

"It seems like a lovely place to winter. And safe for her."

Turning back, he stretched out his legs on the rug. "I wish she valued safety a little more."

Ember ran her fingers over the frame of a photograph on the coffee table. It was Wartburg Castle, where Martin Luther and his ink drove the devil away. "Where do you and your wife live in the winter?"

He crossed his legs, leaning back against the cushions. "Unfortunately my marriage ended in 2014, but I lived in Colorado until a few months ago. I decided to move back here when the principal asked me to coach the football team."

She chose to ignore the sad revelation about his marriage. "Were you coaching in Colorado?"

"Part-time."

"And the other part?"

"Flying."

"You're a pilot?" Her voice was laced with doubt, as if he'd straight up lied to her.

"Shocking, huh." He grinned. "I didn't want to stay in one place for long."

"That I can believe." She paused. "You're not a captain, are you?"

He shrugged. "It's not like a football team."

"Captain Kiehl," she muttered. "You couldn't leave it behind."

"I started flight school the summer after graduation."

"Did you really do it for the title?" she asked.

"I did it because I couldn't keep my feet on the ground," he said. "I fly out of Boston now so I can help Gram when I'm home."

Since when did Dakota start caring about someone other than himself?

"And you're working for the Holocaust museum," he said.

"I taught for eight years in Virginia and decided to return to school myself for my doctorate. When I began writing my dissertation on anti-Semitism, the museum offered me a research fellowship."

Something banged into the front window, making both of them jump.

"I better head back with that chain saw," he said. "Let me give you a quick tour."

Every inch of the cottage was utilized, from the corner break-fast table between the kitchen and living room to the closet laundry beside the refrigerator. A steep staircase led up to two bedrooms and a modern bathroom with a clawfoot tub.

"You're welcome to sleep in the master," he said, pointing to the front room. "Everything's clean, and you'll have a nice view of the Tabernacle when the storm clears."

There was no way that she was sleeping in Dakota's bed. "I'll take the guest room."

He set her suitcase on a chair and turned on a stained-glass lamp while she studied the watercolor paintings on the clapboard walls, each frame mounted with white rope. The bedspread looked as if it had been splashed with pastels.

She stepped up to a watercolor of an oystercatcher pecking its orange beak in a mirror of bay water. A stone labyrinth hung on a separate canvas beside the oystercatcher, its circle of mossy rocks crowned by autumn leaves. "Who did these?"

"Gram painted them a few years back."

The colors on the stained glass flickered with the lamp, but the electricity stayed on.

Dakota waved her back toward the door. "I'll show you where the flashlights are, just in case."

That's all she needed, to spend the night alone on this island without electricity. And without a cell phone if she didn't plug it in soon.

Back downstairs, he moved the couch forward and opened a door underneath the staircase, pulling out two flashlights and an extra blanket. "Unfortunately we don't have a fireplace. This place is a tinderbox."

"I'll be fine."

He hesitated as if he might suggest that he stay.

"You should get back to your grandmother."

"I'll call you in a bit, just to check in."

"Don't worry about me."

"Please, Ember," he said.

She took a deep breath. It was ridiculous, this war inside herself. He'd done nothing since they left the ferry to remind her of his betrayal in their teen years. "If it will make you feel better."

"It would," he said. "Please call me if—"

"I'll be fine."

He tied his shoes, zipped up his jacket again, and then she locked the door behind him.

Ember clutched her phone to her side as she sat back on the couch, staring at the channels of water streaking down the window. And she felt alone. As if Dakota had abandoned her to this storm.

He hadn't, of course. She'd asked him to go. This she knew in her mind, but the thought continued to war with her heart.

She hated this feeling. The heart cry of people leaving her, *rejecting* her, as if it were personal. As if she had to clutch on to them, beg them to stay.

As if, if she held on tightly enough, Elsie might still be alive.

She tapped her legs, trying to clear the memories. Desensitization, her therapist had called it. Replacing the flashbacks with something else.

But no amount of therapy could completely overcome her trauma.

The wind blew the memories back again as it battered the walls, breaking down her will to forget. That cold night on Eagle Lake had shattered her life. In hours, she had no home, no husband, no daughter. And no other family except Alex.

She tossed her phone onto the coffee table and grabbed a pillow, holding it to her chest.

In the days after the FBI raid, the hours after the TV crews turned off cameras and packed away their microphones, the world had moved on. But not her. Like an autumn leaf fallen from its branch, frozen to the ground, all she remembered was blurred by a thousand other leaves blowing over her. Members of the council being taken away in transport vans. An airplane flight back to this island alone, to the only family member she had left and a corner chair where she'd curled up, wishing she could die in the storm.

The Aryan Council, she'd wanted to leave behind, but not Elsie. Not her beautiful girl.

A door inched open in her mind, the path into a dark place that wanted to trap her once again.

She began to pace the floor, tapping her fingers together, a desperate prayer slipping from her lips. A familiar one from Philippians.

Help me forget what's in my past, Lord. Help me to press on.

The truth—that's what she needed to focus on. Her identity wasn't shackled to the hatred of her father. She'd been freed from the chains, redeemed by love. She had a new life. A new name. And a deep desire to keep others from stumbling into places that would wound their souls. A desire to exhume the past in order to stop the hatred today.

Remember everyone's stories, except her own.

She plugged in her phone to text Brooke, but the table lamp flickered. Then all the lights went out.

She waited in the silence, hoping the lamp would flicker back on, but darkness reigned. With the remaining light on her phone, she retrieved the flashlight that Dakota had left on the kitchen table and bundled herself up on the couch, the wind blowing under the door, chilling the room.

What if a tornado swept across the island again, uprooting buildings and boats alike? She had no basement to hide in. No way to even tell if a tornado was coming.

With her dwindling cell phone power, she tried to call her brother, but it didn't go through. The tower must have gone down with the electricity.

If only she could listen to a radio, hear the local weather. For no other reason than to know that she wasn't alone.

Ember pressed her nose against the cold picture window, her fingers drumming against her legs. A light glowed across the plaza, another flashlight in another house.

At least she wasn't completely alone.

Thunder echoed through the room and a chair hurtled across the plaza.

What if the storm picked this old cottage off its platform and splintered it into pieces? Even if she had a radio, if the announcer told her to take cover, she had no place to go. The storage closet, if she holed up there, would collapse with the rest of the house.

The wind swept the memories back again, stealing her breath away.

She never should have come back to the island. Never would have come if she'd known Dakota was here.

She reached for her jacket. Perhaps it wasn't safe to go out, but it sure didn't feel safe to stay.

The front door inched open, and she whirled around at the sound of her name.

In that blessed moment, air reclaimed her lungs.

Dakota hadn't called. He simply returned home.

15

HANNA

Few outside the elite world of Schutzstaffel were invited through the doors of the renovated Wewelsburg Castle, and women were rarely welcomed inside. The only ladies here today were Himmler's secretary and six brides, including Hanna, waiting for their wedding ceremonies.

Hanna wished that she could run back to Nuremberg and hide.

A Black Sun was emblazoned on the tower floor of this Black Camelot, the mosaic pieces of a wheel glowing in sacred flames. Twelve pillars around the tower represented King Arthur's Knights of the Round Table.

If only she could escape the darkness that danced with the flames along the wall, but with all the guards, she'd never make it out the front door. This hilltop castle was as secure as the legendary Camelot with the stone walls, moat, and drawbridge to block out any intruder. Or allow their prisoners to run.

It was the flames, the Norse runes engraved on the walls, that frightened her even more than the guards. Rumors filtered through the SS about Himmler's brew of occult rituals held in this castle. The Reichsführer bowed to religion when necessary, but he certainly didn't bow to the Christian God. The State was his Higher Power.

Because of this, the Schutzstaffel refused church wedding traditions. Instead a man and woman married the State first on their wedding day, then married the history of the German people. Lastly they married one another.

Hanna shivered. In this one way, as the wife of an officer, she would be welcomed into the SS.

Himmler had sent a car for her at dawn to ensure her attendance. She'd been up most of the night, trying to concoct an alternative plan. She'd even thought about returning to Frau Weber's with a plea to be allowed to hide alongside Luisa.

But the Gestapo would only have to interview the telephone operator to find Hanna's one phone call to Frau Weber's home. She couldn't put Frau Weber in even greater danger.

So she dressed in a simple blue frock with a sash, an outfit approved by Kolman's commander when she'd arrived this morning, no veil on her head. The SS didn't allow its brides to wear such finery on their wedding days.

Then she'd waited for hours in a back room with the other women.

Himmler took special interest in the weddings of his officers, presiding over them himself. In lieu of family and friends, a crowd of steely SS officers, each one alloyed with iron and silver, encircled the altar. All of them reminding her of the monster in her dream.

A monster who had beaten Paul Gruenewald, harassed his wife, and then escaped back out into the night. A monster who'd hurt anyone daring to help the Jewish people.

She'd yet to see Kolman among the silver-and-black coats, but he must be here. Had he told Himmler that she'd agreed to marry him?

She'd been vetted completely before she became an archaeologist, so Himmler knew she was of Aryan stock, but did these men know that she'd once loved an American? A man who'd now be considered an enemy of their State. How different her life would be if Charlie had whisked her away to his island as she'd hoped. It was good, perhaps, that she had no childhood dreams about her wedding because only shadows would accompany her walk across the mosaic tiles this afternoon.

The officers waited in silence, but she heard a voice beside her. One she recognized.

"It's good to see you, Hanna."

She turned slowly toward Kolman. His hair was combed neatly back and coated with stiff Brylcreem. He looked handsome enough to make a host of German girls swoon, but her heart didn't belong to him. It never would.

"I sent you a letter, Kolman."

His forehead wrinkled with confusion, so different from his pressed uniform. "What letter?"

"The one to clarify that I didn't want to marry you."

He tilted his head. "But you accepted my proposal."

She shook her head. "I didn't—"

"In the vineyard, I asked, and you agreed." He looked heartbroken at her response. "I didn't know the Reichsführer would arrange our wedding so quickly."

Her eyes narrowed. "How did Himmler know that you proposed?"

"The man knows everything."

"It's not too late to stop this," she said.

Kolman's eyes saddened. "Why would we want to stop it? We're made for each other, Hanna."

"Later, perhaps. After the war."

He took her hand, held it to his heart. "Let's have a glimmer of happiness in the midst of it."

The monster began to recede in her mind. The crazy dream. In actuality, perhaps her fears were the monster. The longing for a man like Charlie Ward.

Himmler motioned them forward, and she took a step toward the flames.

She wanted to be as strong as Saint Katharine, who'd refused her marriage proposal, even under the threat of death, but Katharine's story wasn't the same as hers. While she'd had the terrible nightmare about a monster, Hanna had never had a vision of marrying God. And Kolman wasn't royalty like the man Katharine had been commanded to marry.

But Himmler acted like an emperor, relegating her to a marriage with this man he considered to be a son, and if she refused, they'd kill her, like the emperor had done with Katharine. No one confined to this inner circle was allowed to step outside the lines.

But if she stayed in the inner circle—with Kolman as her husband—the Gestapo would never threaten her again. Perhaps, in time, she would learn to love this man beside her. If she couldn't refuse this marriage, she would have to navigate being his wife.

Kolman's eyes were focused on Himmler, his superior officer who stood between two bowls of fire. The man had a toothbrush mustache like Hitler's, a grim mouth and glasses that pinched his nose. And in Hanna's opinion, he took too much of an interest in the personal lives of his SS officers.

But no one—at least, no one in their right mind—went up against Himmler.

The two remaining brides waited in the hall, and the only other woman in the room was Hedwig Potthast, Himmler's devoted secretary, who stood near the edge in case he required her attention.

If he was such a proponent of matrimony, why didn't Himmler bring his wife to the SS weddings? Or had she been forced into marrying him as well? Most of Germany knew the man spent his leisure time with his secretary instead of his wife anyway, discounting the whole entity of marriage.

Himmler nodded at Hanna, but the respect that he'd shown her long ago, when he'd first offered her a position in the Almenerbe, was gone. Now she was just a woman in a plain dress, one of thousands commissioned to carry their quest forward by conceiving the next generation.

"Our strength is in your blood," Himmler proclaimed in the dull tone of a rhetoric overused. "Your marriage will bring hope for the future of Germany. Your children will stand strong for the Aryan world."

I don't want children.

The words rang in her head, but she didn't dare speak them.

"You will do your duty to preserve our German race."

She heard a voice, swearing to preserve it, and wondered, for a moment, who sounded like her.

"Your duty is to the Schutzstaffel," Himmler commanded Kolman. "If you remain faithful, your brothers will protect you with their lives, and you, Hanna Strauss, have been accepted into the Schutzstaffel as an officer's wife. You and your husband are duty bound to protect the cause of Germany."

He'd already taken away her role as an archaeologist, but with these words, he stripped her identity as a German woman who'd thrived on her own. Given her a future that she didn't want as a wife in his SS.

Was that what the Nazis had done to the Jewish people? With their regulations, their duties bound, cut out their very core?

Himmler listed out each of Kolman's duties to the Reich, a long list of obligations, and Hanna had no doubt her husband would perform every one, his utter allegiance devoted to this kingdom.

"Heil Hitler," Himmler said to complete the ceremony.

"Heil Hitler," both she and Kolman concurred with their lips.

But in her heart, she heiled the strength rising inside her.

Men like Hitler and Himmler only ruled because of the secrets they kept, dark ones like beating up innocent men and divining through the ancient runes. She had no admiration for those kinds of secrets.

Stories were the lifeblood of the Nazis. Propaganda, they called it. Promoting their own interests to the public by extolling the fruit of the Aryan, degrading the Jews. But they also knew how dangerous a story could be.

Himmler and the others wanted to write their own history, but she would write the truth.

She'd already buried Paul and Luisa's story in the labyrinth. What if Frau Weber could help her collect more stories? Even as she cataloged artifacts for the museum, she could help preserve the heritage of her neighbors. Be a secret keeper, like the Cathars. A guardian of the stories that no one was supposed to hear.

Together they could create a *Memorbuch* for those who were being persecuted today.

16

EMBER

"The road's flooded," Dakota said sheepishly, as if Ember might turn him away. When she stepped to the side, he rushed through the front door, a backpack hanging from one shoulder.

"What about your grandmother?" she asked, both hands resting on the couch.

"Gram's ridden out many storms on her own, but Kayla is still spending the night in case Gram needs anything. Her husband manages the farm, so they live nearby."

Did that mean Dakota was sleeping in the cottage? In all of her craziest, wild dreams, she'd never imagined herself seeing this man again, much less trapped overnight with him.

"My emergency supplies." He unzipped the backpack and pulled out a battery-powered radio. "I carry this around in my car."

"Did your radio say anything about a tornado?"

"Nothing's been sighted. The weatherman said the winds should settle by midnight, but no one knows when the roads will be passable." He patted the arm of the couch. "You mind if I sleep here?"

"Of course not." This was his home, and she wasn't afraid of him, only what he might do to her heart.

"I also have . . ." He dug around in his backpack until he retrieved a bulky mug and two packets of Ghirardelli hot chocolate. "These."

"If only we had something to heat the water . . ."

"They call this an Ember." He flipped over the mug. "It's battery operated."

She waited for some sort of quip about her name, slow to warm up or something, but he didn't pursue it. "You're quite prepared."

He grinned, the stubble on his cheeks glistening like sand in the wash of her light. "Learned my lesson the third time the lights went off."

"It took three times?"

"All those knocks in high school dimmed some of my thinking."

"Your poor passengers!"

He laughed. "The flight deck computers make up for it."

She'd wanted to knock his head off in those years, but she didn't mention that. "I'll make the chocolate."

Another bang outside and her heart leapt, but not quite as high this time. "The wind sounds like it's about to shred this house."

He patted the white wall as if it were a faithful friend. "She's been standing for a hundred and seventy years, through ten hurricanes and countless storms. To my knowledge, we've never even lost a shingle."

She lifted the Ember mug. "Then here's to one more night of holding it together." For her and the house.

But she didn't need to use the heated mug. Her hands trembling, she filled two ceramic mugs with hot water from the kitchen tap.

She'd spent more than a decade angry at this man for humiliating her. And yet something had changed.

The flashlight secured under her arm, she dumped chocolate packets into the water, but she didn't walk back into the living room.

The homecoming game their senior year had sealed her fate with Dakota, but in the hours before, she'd suspected nothing. He had been her Mr. Darcy, a boy who'd shown her around the farm when she'd first moved back, who was friendly enough at home but ignored her at school. By their senior year, she thought he'd begun to care for her. At eighteen she imagined herself as Lizzy Bennet, but really she was more like Lydia. Silly and naive and completely broken when it came to men.

Dakota had brought a wrist corsage with two roses he'd picked up before homecoming. Purple and white. Their school colors, so different and yet beautiful together. She'd thought she was about to step into a fairy tale.

And it was a tale, one as tall as the mountains in Idaho.

Hours later she was the laughingstock of the high school. Nice, she'd learned, was sometimes a prelude to nasty.

"Ember?"

She turned quickly, blinding him with the flashlight before she put it down. Then she held out one of the mugs. "Your lukewarm chocolate."

"Thank you." He dug two candles out of the storage closet, both of them powered by batteries, and set them on the coffee table beside her phone before sinking into one of the chairs.

She stretched her legs out on the couch, the mug folded between her hands. "This wasn't exactly how I saw today going."

He nodded toward her phone. "It might be a day or two before the tower's working again."

"And the ferry?"

"They should resume service by Friday."

Groaning, she let her head fall back against the cushion. Another full day on this island, whether or not she wanted to be here.

He leaned forward, his fingers wrapped around the mug. "Ember—"

A storm raged within her, worse than the winds outdoors. He wanted to talk about the past, and she didn't want to relive it.

She swung her feet back onto the wool rug. "I'm heading up to bed."

"I was a jerk in high school," he rushed on, undeterred. "Especially to you."

She willed her legs to move, but her toes seemed trapped in the yarn.

"I'm sorry," he said. "Words don't suffice, but I wanted you to know."

She looked down at the mug, the ceramic warm in her hands. "It doesn't matter anymore."

"But it does. You didn't deserve what we—what I—did to you."

"No one could possibly deserve that . . ."

He nodded. "You're right."

"I didn't come here to reconcile, Dakota. I just wanted to see your grandmother."

"Fair enough." He paused. "But I needed to apologize."

The window rattled behind her, but she didn't even glance at it since Dakota didn't seem to be ruffled by the storm.

She didn't want to discuss the past and yet . . .

Perhaps finally putting words to it would help her understand.

"Why did you do it?" The question cranked out of her, rusty and cold.

He rubbed his hands over the stubble on his cheeks as if he could sandpaper his answer, smooth away the rough edges of the truth, but she wanted to know.

"You invited me to homecoming," she said as if he'd forgotten. "You pursued me."

"I know."

Not that he had to be relentless in his pursuit. She'd mushed like putty in his hands. "It had all been a ruse, hadn't it? Some sort of sick joke for your friends."

"I'm not proud of it . . ."

"That first time you called and asked me out to dinner, Alex said you would hurt me, but I didn't believe him." Her words spilled out now like rain. "I knew you were cocky at school, but you were always nice to me on the farm. I thought in some weird way that I could help you find yourself under all that pride. See what I saw in you."

"It was rotten, Em. All of it."

"Ember, please." Fire, not ash.

"I was wrong, Ember. Terribly wrong. You have no reason to forgive me, but I wanted you to know I never should have done it. About ten years later, I realized how cruel I'd been."

"It took you ten years?"

"God finally woke me up."

She stared at the man beside her, dumbfounded. "Since when did you start caring about God?"

"When He rescued me from myself."

A relationship with God required humility, and pride had been Dakota's crutch. But he did seem different now. Kind, even.

If he hadn't been so kind to her, right before he'd crushed her, she might believe it true. How could she possibly trust him now?

Yet he sounded broken, exactly what she had hoped for in the moments after she'd crossed the football field in front of the entire school body, ready to accompany him as he accepted his royal crown. She'd stepped out when the announcer said his name, just like Dakota had instructed, his corsage decorating her wrist.

She hadn't been selected queen, but the homecoming king was allowed to choose his escort. Dakota had asked, if he was elected, that she accompany him, and she'd been elated that Dakota Kiehl wanted her!

In the months they'd dated, they had kept their budding relationship a secret. He hadn't kissed her or even held her hand, but she'd slopped admiration all over him, telling the man he was *beguiling*. Even now, her face flushed red with the memory. The humiliation from beginning to end.

She should have suspected something when he drove her all the way to Aquinnah for their pizza dates. And when he didn't run the moment she'd tried to channel Shakespeare. Not until much later did she realize that the scenario was a whole lot like several movies from the nineties. If only she'd seen them before homecoming, she just might have realized why Dakota was inviting her.

"It was a dare, wasn't it?" She crossed her arms, a shield between them. "From your friends."

"Yes."

"Why did they pick me?"

He started to speak, and she stopped him. "Never mind. I was weird and ugly and naive." The perfect target for bullies.

"You weren't any of those things, Ember. Except naive. It only worked because you trusted me."

"A life lesson learned."

"It was a pathetic attempt to show how cool we were. As if we could prove this by stomping all over the—"

"Underdog, I get it. You all ruled the sandhill."

"And then fell promptly off, right on our faces."

She barely heard his words, the rawness of her heart bleeding out. The exhalation and the fallout. The laughter that had rippled across the bleachers.

She'd stood on the field alone that night, stunned by his betrayal, her mind flashing back three years earlier when she couldn't even save her own child, memories she'd desperately tried to repress in order to be normal. In order to find love.

"Glen Hammond waited until I was halfway across the field to name Alecia as your escort." Over the loudspeaker so everyone could hear.

"I talked him into it," he said, and she tried to ignore the sadness in his voice.

"So half the school was trying to humiliate me?"

"It was my fault." He turned on one of the candles, its warm light flickering across the table, but it didn't help. "I instigated it."

"And Alecia helped you."

"No," he said. "I'd already asked her to escort me if I won."

Ember groaned. "They all thought I was crazy, Dakota. The poor library mouse, chasing after the almighty Captain Kiehl. And then you called me a—"

She didn't say the word, but she knew he remembered. A name that propelled her right back to the council of Aryans who'd misused her. The man who had called her his wife but treated her like a slave. She hadn't known the difference when she was fifteen, but by eighteen she'd become keenly aware.

Dakota slouched in his chair, no words left in his defense.

Still she didn't stop. "I know it was stupid in hindsight, but I thought you liked me. Instead you took advantage of me for a laugh."

"I was the stupid one. Not that it helps, but the laugh was ultimately on me. My own pride took me down."

She closed her eyes for a moment, listened to the rain on the window. She wouldn't, *couldn't*, empathize with this man who'd demeaned her, rubbed her heart raw. Dakota didn't know that her life had been crushed in Idaho, that she'd lost the baby girl she loved, but he'd known that she didn't fit in with the other high schoolers. That everything about her screamed *weird*.

"You were gone," Dakota said, flinching as if the memory was a hard one for him, "before I could apologize."

Her eyes flashed. "You were going to apologize?"

"I'd like to think so."

She had been behind in school when she arrived on the island, halfway through her sophomore year, but for the next two years, she studied morning and night and all summer long until she collected enough high school credits to graduate early. And she'd done just that after homecoming, fleeing the island with her brother on the winds of that nor'easter, finishing up the last of her schooling in Pennsylvania.

Dakota leaned back in his chair, taking a slow sip of his chocolate, watching the candle flicker. "My pride came full circle when my wife left me to marry the man who was supposed to be my best friend."

The words dropped like nails between them, hammering out the worst of his life. In spite of everything in the past, what he'd done to her, she still felt a pang of compassion for his loss. "Humiliating?"

"Terribly," he said, his voice quiet. "She tore my life apart and didn't seem to care. For the next two years, I felt like I was staring at a mirror of myself. She wounded me like I'd wounded you and so many others."

Her heart quaked with the storm-shaken walls as they talked like old friends instead of enemies. As two people who sought truth from the past.

How could she criticize those who hated when she'd carried hatred in her heart for so long? She had to release it or she was no different from the supremacists who thronged to the streets. Or the Aryan Council.

Justified or not, hatred would kill her on the inside.

She pulled one of the pillows over her chest, strapping it to her. "Do you have kids?"

"No. I'd say I was disappointed except if we'd had children . . . the outcome would have been devastating for all of us." Dakota nodded at her phone on the coffee table. "So tell me about your guy."

"I don't think so."

"Why not?"

Because he'd realize that she was just as pathetic as she'd been her senior year.

Because Noah was the only barrier left between them.

"Even if I forgive you, it doesn't mean that we're friends," she said.

Instead of responding to her edict, he slowly sipped the last of his drink. "I have more of these packets stashed in the kitchen."

The rain pattering against the glass, the yellow candlelight along the wall, the man in the shadows warming more chocolate. Her eyes closed as she rested on the couch, in sweet surrender as the pangs of bitterness began bleeding out.

She was on safe ground, with a man who knew better than her how to fight a storm. Not even the wind bothered her anymore.

At some point during the night, Dakota draped several blankets over her, but she was too tired to thank him. As the rain continued, in the warmth of the blankets, she dreamed of a lake. A light. A net catching her when she fell.

17

HANNA

Kolman didn't seem to care about hiding his kerosene lantern behind curtains as he explored the Tillich lodge. Hanna followed him into the great hall, none of the windows covered by drapes, and she was stunned by what she saw. Spring flowers spilled over clusters of vases, infusing the room with a candied fragrance. Icing spread across centuries of dust and decor.

Kolman held his lantern over her father's former desk. The face of Adolf Hitler had replaced Saint Katharine's portrait. "Looks like we're not the only one celebrating."

Hanna didn't want to think about who had been in her home today, arranging bouquets on the dining table and hanging pictures on her walls while she was at the Wewelsburg Castle. Still the grim face of a certain Gestapo agent reemerged.

Had he returned with the bouquets and a locksmith? If so, he would have found nothing upstairs except the dollhouses.

An exotic honeymoon had been delayed by the war, and that was perfectly fine for Hanna. She'd wanted to delay the inevitable this evening but hadn't been able to suspend it for any longer than the drive back to Nuremberg with its various checkpoints along the way. When the soldiers saw the silvery skull on Kolman's cap, the lightning bolt on his collar, they waved him through. A shiny uniform seemed to blind everyone these days.

Kolman straightened the portrait of Hitler before examining a picture of her family, taken more than twenty years ago in a local studio. Her mother was seated, her cheeks sagging as if she'd used every last ounce of her energy to birth the baby girl held in her arms.

"I didn't realize you had a brother," he said, picking up the frame, studying the confident young man who'd been fourteen years her senior.

She remembered only glimpses of Jonny. How he'd made her laugh. How she'd cried after he left home.

The military had conscripted him on his seventeenth birthday.

"Jonny died at Amiens." Three months before the World War ended.

"Your father," he said, still looking at the picture. "He was in the war as well."

She nodded slowly. Her father had also fought at Amiens, but he never spoke about his time in the military. Or about the son he'd lost. By not speaking, it was almost as if the loss had never happened. He'd remained quiet while Hanna longed for the stories.

"A colonel," she said. "He injured his leg in battle."

"My father died in France."

She glanced over, surprised. While he'd told her he was from Hanover, he never talked about his family. Did his mother, his siblings, regret not being at their wedding? "When will I meet your family?" she asked.

Instead of answering, he picked up the picture of her and Luisa. "You also had a sister?"

"No." She took the photograph from him. "My cousin. Luisa."

"Your tenant?"

"Yes, she moved here when I was a child and then stayed to care for the place in my absence."

"She was Jewish—"

"She was German."

Kolman strolled to the desk at the corner of the room, flipped through some of the papers. The list of names, thankfully, was buried in the labyrinth. "Where is Luisa?"

"I don't know."

He turned slowly. "She's gone?"

"Apparently. She and her husband left without even a letter to say goodbye." If Kolman didn't already know, she wouldn't be the one to explain that Paul had been taken because of his Jewish heritage. And Luisa was hiding away from men like him.

"I wonder where they went."

She shrugged as if she'd never been to Frau Weber's home. Never read Paul's story.

But Frau Weber was right. She could never hide Luisa here.

"People are spreading terrible lies about this regime," he said. "You must not believe them."

"I've heard the Jews are being sent away if they don't leave on their own."

"They are going east to find work."

"In Poland?" she asked. The new living space.

Irritation flashed in his eyes. "A place where they can provide for their families."

"At least they're not being forced to marry," she said.

He stepped back, taking her hand. "I know you're not thrilled about our arrangement, but we're going to make it work. For the sake of the—"

"Please don't say that." She shook off his hand to rub her temples.

While she wished this day would end, she didn't want to be pressed into another duty for the sake of their Reich.

"You're tired."

"Tired and confused," she said. "I hate the confusion most of all."

He nodded toward the steps. "Show me the upper floors."

They climbed the stairs and he turned once to look from the balcony at the raftered ceiling and stone fireplace below. Then they moved into the dark corridor.

The lantern spilled light across the bedroom doors, and he opened the door to Luisa and Paul's room first, scanning the decor before closing it. Then he opened her bedroom door.

Flowers packed this space as well, the petals sprinkled across the rug and duvet on her narrow bed and a second bed hauled over from Luisa and Paul's room. As if someone had uprooted a tulip farm and replanted the stems in her private garden.

Kolman eyed the two beds, pressed tightly together, in the kerosene light. They were married now, and he had a right to her body as much as he had a right to this house.

"Your duty is to the Schutzstaffel."

Himmler's words rang in her head, but she hadn't married the SS. She had married one of its officers, and she would make it work. Not because Himmler forced her into this wedding, but because marriage was a sacred union before God.

Kolman turned off the kerosene, the house tour over for tonight. He crossed the room, but he didn't kiss her, instead brushing away the strands of hair that had fallen from their pins, twirling one of them against her neck.

When she stiffened at his touch, recoiling, he stepped away. "I'll return when you're ready."

She sat on the edge of the bed in her wedding dress, knowing what she must do, wishing there were another way. If she fought him, would he fight back? No one would care about a man who'd hurt the wife who denied him the most base of privileges extended in marriage.

Her virginity, she'd lost to Charlie Ward, and they never recovered their friendship after they crossed that irremeable line. While she'd longed to marry Charlie, he'd taken a ship back to America alone, and she'd poured herself into the work she loved. The hostilities began in Germany soon after—if he had tried to send a letter, she had never received it.

She'd never given herself to another man. It was a gift, she thought, this giving of one's self. A gift that was expected with the flowers and ceremony and SS ring.

When he returned, Kolman set one of the bottles of French wine on her nightstand, two goblets beside it. Then he poured them each a glass, and she drank until her mind was fuzzy, her fight gone.

Turning, he sat on the bed behind her, unbuttoning the pearl beads on the back of her dress. Any spark between them had disappeared, his charm gone, but maybe this man beside her would be her husband first. His covenant with the SS a step behind the one he'd made with her.

The monster, she prayed, would remain in her dreams.

18

EMBER

Music pulled Ember from her sleep. Someone was playing the piano, the melody trickling through the glass instead of pounding rain. She bolted up on the couch and glanced around the room. Dakota must have slept upstairs.

A quick test, the flip of a switch, but their electricity hadn't returned.

She rinsed her face off in the bathroom sink and brushed her teeth before tying her hair back into a messy sort of bun. Then she tucked her cell phone into her back pocket and slipped on wet sandals, stepping out under the blissfully sunny sky.

"Don't Let the Sun Go Down on Me" was the song streaming out of the Tabernacle, and she stepped over a graveyard of fallen branches to reach the open-air building in the center of the plaza. Sitting on a bench, she listened to an elderly man play Elton John.

When the piece ended, she clapped, the sole audience member.

The pianist waved back before launching into a passionate rendition of "Blessed Assurance," the notes pouring out from his fingers. In that moment, she could envision Mrs. Kiehl on the front porch of her little cottage, listening to a hymn like this one, foretasting the glory divine. Music could transport them all into the next life, at least for a glimpse of what was to come.

Someone sat down beside her, and she looked over at Dakota, a Red Sox ball cap pulled over his messy hair, the Ember mug in his hand. "You want some coffee?"

"Did the electricity come back?"

He shook his head. "It's instant and just barely warm, but I added a little milk and sugar to make it tolerable."

She took a long sip from the heated mug, the caffeine surging through her veins.

Dakota nodded toward the stage. "Mr. Talbot is out here every Thursday, no matter the weather."

"That song makes me want to run straight through heaven's gates."

"I suspect that's exactly what he was hoping for." He pointed at the phone in her hands. "Is your cell service working yet?"

"I don't know," she said. "I'll need electricity first to revive it."

The man began playing "How Great Is Our God," and Dakota leaned back on the bench, stretching his legs out.

She let the music thunder over her, marveling at the power of one man over his ivory keys. Marveling that Dakota was here beside her, that some of the anger in her heart seemed to have washed away in the rain.

What was happening inside her? She'd clung to her anger for so long, her nails digging in as if she could punish Dakota for all that he did, just by remembering. How foolish of her to think that she had the mind power to make him pay. She'd given the teenage ghost of this man control over her.

It sounded like he'd paid plenty already, but not because of her anger. His own struggles, his past, had crash-landed his life, and God, it seemed, had been putting the pieces back together.

Almost two decades ago she'd sworn never to come back on this island. Yet here she was, having coffee with the same man who'd driven her away. Perhaps it truly was a foretaste of heaven, righting what had gone wrong.

"He wraps Himself in light and darkness tries to hide."

These beautiful lyrics she knew from the church she attended now, one so different from the church where she was raised. Darkness, she'd learned, couldn't hide in the light of God's splendor. The lies would be exposed.

She'd been angry at Dakota, but the light slowly turned this morning, shining brightly on her and the anger she'd been clenching inside. For twenty years, she'd been trying to make herself pay. For being stupid enough to stay with the Aryan Council. For losing her child.

She hadn't allowed herself to be angry at those who'd led her down that path, for the abuse of her parents and then Lukas. She'd pushed those memories into the darkness.

The pianist covered the keyboard and tipped his classic brown fedora toward them and their applause. Then he retrieved the cane that he'd stretched over the lid and shuffled down the steps, exiting the stage on the opposite side.

Dakota turned toward her. "What's your name?"

She looked at him, slightly alarmed.

He held out the peace offering of his hand. "I'd like to start over, if we could."

"I'm Ember Ellis," she finally said, shaking it. "Used to live on this island."

"My name is Dakota." He let go of her hand. "I've made a winding journey across our country, but the Vineyard is home for me now."

"It's nice to meet you, Captain Kiehl."

"Very funny."

"I don't know you well enough to call you by your first name."

He grinned at her, and she saw a flash of the man that she'd hoped he would grow up to be. The sculpture under plaster casting. "Just Captain works."

And she laughed, genuinely laughed, with Dakota at her side.

He folded his arms over his chest. "Why did you decide to spend this season of your life researching the Holocaust?"

"I have a deep affinity for people who've faced persecution."

His face fell. "Because of high school?"

"No," she started. "Well, maybe that was part of it. A nudge toward finding out why people hurt others. But my search began years before that homecoming game."

He knew a glimpse of her story perhaps, about the church her father led and the demise of the Aryan Council in Idaho, but he didn't know about Elsie. No one on this island knew.

She took another sip of the coffee. "Do you remember the stories your grandmother used to tell us in school?"

"I remember more of her stories from home."

"I wrote one of my high school papers based on those stories," she said. "Nuremberg was a Nazi stronghold, but the persecution started there long before the war. In the fifteenth century, residents thought the Jewish people had poisoned their wells, so they massacred hundreds of them during the Black Plague and expelled the rest to places like Poland. Then, during the Holocaust, the Nazis expanded their territory right into Poland, exterminating the descendants of those Jewish people who had fled."

"Gram said she doesn't remember much about living in Nuremberg," he said. "Good or bad."

Ember swirled the last of the coffee in the mug. "The article said her mother helped the Jewish people during the war."

"Gram rarely mentions Hanna, but my great-grandfather attended college for a year in Germany before the war and then he was an inspector during the military tribunals. The Great Atlantic Hurricane hit our farm, and he had to leave Germany before the trials were finished so he could help restore it."

She sorted through the little she knew of his family's history. If Charlie and Hanna had moved to the island after the war, they would have brought Lilly with them as a baby.

But the Americans didn't even enter Nuremberg until April 1945. Plenty of soldiers fathered children in Germany, but the math still didn't work for Charlie to have a child before he returned to Martha's Vineyard.

"When did Hanna bring your grandmother to the States?"

"Actually, my great-grandfather brought her here by himself when he returned home." Someone rumbled down the path nearby with a wheelbarrow. "Charlie was already married to my great-grandmother by then. A woman named Arlene."

Ember tucked a loose piece of hair back into her bun. That must have been an emotional scenario for Charlie to return home with a child from another woman. A girl who'd been scarred from the war.

"Did your grandmother keep in contact with her biological mother?"

"I don't know," Dakota said. "She doesn't talk about Hanna out of respect for the woman who raised her, I think, and because she doesn't remember much. I'm told Arlene loved my grandmother very much. She just refused to let Gram speak German in their home."

"She was probably afraid that someone might hurt her because of her German heritage."

"A valid fear, I would think, right after the war."

Ember nodded. A lot of American Germans tried to hide their heritage. "Mrs. Kiehl used to speak German in class."

"She said that she never stopped speaking it in her head or with the German boyfriend who became her husband. My grandparents used to speak German at home when Dad was a kid." Dakota glanced over at her. "Do you remember my father?"

Titus Kiehl had knocked on their cabin door often for Alex in the late hours with something he deemed to be an emergency, long after her brother's shift on the farm had ended. Alex had put up with the man's anger for years, but after Ember arrived back on the island, her brother found a new job so they could move into Oak Bluffs.

She remembered Titus from those late-night outbursts and from sidelines of their high school football games. He was the parent who stood right behind the coaches, an equal opportunist when it came to yelling at the refs, the coaches, the opposing team. Most of all, at his son. Sometimes he even turned around and yelled at the home crowd, as if they were the enemy.

Dakota's mother was quite different. Instead of yelling at the students, she was volunteering on the PTA. At least, until Dakota's senior year. Those autumn weeks before Ember left school, when she'd thought that Dakota and she were a thing, he'd told her that his parents were getting a divorce.

After the disastrous homecoming game, Dakota's mom left flowers on the patio when Ember refused to answer the door. There'd been a Bible verse on the card from the book of 1 John, about how God had lavished His love on her.

She hadn't felt lavished on at the time.

"It would be impossible to forget your dad," Ember said.

"He doesn't like for Gram to talk about the past, and right now she wants peace in our family. It's a bit of a mess."

"Is your father still on the island?" Ember asked.

He shook his head. "Both my parents moved away after graduation. Dad went west and my mother lives near Boston. My sister has three young kids, and Mom thinks her job is to spoil them properly."

"A worthy calling."

"She and Gram are still close. According to Gram, my mom will always be a Kiehl."

So different from Ember's family—she didn't want anyone to know that she'd once been a Heywood.

"How is your brother?" Dakota asked. Everyone in her class knew that she no longer had parents. An accident, she and Alex had told the high school principal when she moved back. No other explanation was needed.

"He's doing great." The happiest, in fact, that she'd ever seen him. "He and his wife live in the Poconos with their two kids."

Maggie and Saul. Twins who were a year younger than Noah.

A crew with yellow vests began circling the Tabernacle, collecting branches from the storm.

"Why the Poconos?"

"He met a lovely woman whose family owns an inn there. Alex helps run it now."

"I always liked your brother," Dakota said. "He was nice until—"

"I can't say he was very fond of you."

"Understandable."

Dakota drummed his cell phone against his hand before piloting their conversation back to Germany. "Surely there must have been someone besides Hanna who helped the people in Nuremberg."

"I haven't found a record of anyone yet," she said. "And now the same kind of hatred is brewing again in our country that's supposed to be welcoming for all."

He looked back at the stage. "People hurt other people so they can feel better about themselves."

The way Dakota's father used to berate him in public. She'd never really thought about it before. Perhaps Dakota decided, at seventeen, to turn that anger on someone else. Hurt her like he'd been hurt.

"Does it work?" she asked, genuinely curious as to what he thought.

"For a while, until they realize the damage they've done. If they ever realize it." He stood up. "And now I have another pressing question."

"What is it?" she asked. Her official defense wasn't until September, but she was prepared to defend for her dissertation on the spot if she must.

"Are you hungry?"

She laughed. "Starving."

He pointed back toward the cottage. "We could attempt to grill pancakes."

"Barbecued pancakes?"

He shrugged. "Why not."

"I suppose we can try it on aluminum foil."

His phone rang, and she trailed behind him back to the house until he finished the call. "Gram's electricity is back on. She's wondering if we can come for brunch."

"And give up our barbecue . . ."

His brown eyes sparked when he smiled. "Perhaps in another storm."

"Is the road passable?"

He held up his keys. "Only one way to find out."

"If we can get through, I'd love to visit her this morning."

When Dakota stepped onto the porch, he picked up several branches and dumped them into a pile beside the cottage.

Second Chance.

That was the name she'd missed in the storm last night, the plaque nailed above Dakota's front door. And she liked the promise in it.

A Second Chance for all of them.

HANNA

19

Hanna opened the front door, a pail in her hands to harvest the forest's bounty. The summer morning was warm, sunshine to offset the gloom settling over this mountain.

During their first week as husband and wife, Kolman had awakened early almost every day, leaving the house for a hike while she pretended to sleep. This morning she watched him cross the meadow again, vanish up into the trees.

Was it merely exercise or was this man who'd become her husband searching for something? Everyone seemed to be hiding things these days, and she feared he would find the labyrinth on the hill, the freshly turned soil where she'd buried Paul's story. But he never told her where he'd been nor had she dared to ask.

Today she was returning to her work at the museum, but before she took her bicycle down to the tram, she decided to follow Kolman into the forest.

With her pail in hand, she stole through the meadow, and as she climbed the rugged hill, she passed the entrance to the old mine that Opa had blocked with an iron grate. A grate that had long since tumbled over.

There were multiple entrances across the hills, most of them sealed up to keep curious parties from injuring themselves. Only a foolish person, Vater once said, would go into an old mine, so he never bothered to restore the gate.

She'd been known to be foolish a time or two.

Her footfalls were as light as leaves dropping onto the padded floor so she wouldn't startle Kolman if she found him, in case he'd holstered his Luger.

Wild blueberries clustered on the bushes, and she swiped up handfuls of them, fruit pinging against tin as she filled her pail. Then she topped the blue with a fresh cropping of raspberries. Kolman had encouraged her to pursue her housewifery skills, and if he found her in these woods, she'd show off her harvest so he wouldn't suspect curiosity had forced her out of the house.

They'd had the oddest honeymoon, but one that suited her fine. Kolman had been kind enough in the days after their wedding, leaving only once in a hired car to visit the Gestapo station. They'd visited Old Town together and the newly remodeled zoo.

In the past week, she'd given him a complete tour of the house including the attic, but he wasn't the least bit interested in dollhouses. They'd draped black fabric over the windows and painted the edges of glass so the house wouldn't fall victim to a night bombing.

Once the electricity had been restored, they spent their evenings in the great hall. Kolman read through the collection of books and wrote religiously every night, sitting at her father's desk. As if he'd already made the lodge his home.

At the top of the hill, the abbey ruins stood empty except for a red fox that watched her closely, ready to steal any berries she dropped from her pail. The moss-covered labyrinth curled beyond the church, and she circled the trail once to pray, stopping by the stone where she'd hidden Paul's story, praying like her mother had once done. Like the nuns who remembered those who'd died after the plague.

When she returned home, Kolman was already dressed in his uniform. He stopped by the mirror to shine the lightning bolt on his collar with his sleeve. Except for the one time that he'd gone to town alone, he hadn't donned his uniform for an entire week. And he'd seemed more like the man she'd known from the Ahnenerbe.

He turned slowly toward her. "Where were you?"

"Picking berries." She held up the pail. "Would you like muesli for breakfast?"

He hesitated as if he wanted to ask something but wasn't certain of the words. "Muesli would be fine. Will you be ready by eight?"

"I have to leave a bit earlier to catch the tram."

Kolman shook his head, his blue eyes firing. "It's silly for you to take the tram when I drive past the museum in a perfectly good automobile."

She had no argument for that except that she wanted to be alone for the hour. "Are you inviting me to ride with you?"

"A car will be here by eight for both of us."

Kolman would never understand that she enjoyed the freedom of riding a bicycle down the hill, especially on these summer days. The German people had traded most of their freedom for security, the power of the Reich, but this one small freedom remained for her.

She would take her bicycle down to the tram tomorrow.

"Where were you this morning?" she asked, removing a pan of soaked oats from the refrigerator to mix with her freshly picked berries.

"Right here."

"But you left—"

"I was in the great hall, Hanna. You must have missed me."

But she'd seen him crossing the meadow. Why was he lying to her?

The driver didn't speak to either of them beyond his greeting, and Kolman was silent as well on their drive into town. When they stopped along the sidewalk, several meters from the museum entrance, he patted her hand. "I'll meet you back here at a quarter after five."

She eyed the driver, but the man's gaze had settled on two young women across the street, staring at the mannequins in a clothing shop. "I'm taking the tram home."

"A quarter after—"

She slammed the door. While she might have been strong-armed into marrying Kolman, she did not require an escort, especially since she wanted to visit Frau Weber's flat after work.

Grete met her at the front door with a cup of black coffee. "Congratulations, Frau Strauss."

It was the first time anyone had called her by her married name, and it sounded strange. "Please call me Hanna."

"Dozens of new inventory boxes are waiting for you downstairs."

She took the cup of coffee. "Where did the boxes come from?"

"I'm not allowed to tell you that."

Hanna sipped the strong drink, as if it were the French wine that Kolman brought home. "Did someone take the other crates away?"

Grete nodded. "Everything you've cataloged has been stored."

"But you won't tell me where . . ."

"We're all just cogs in the wheel, Hanna. Only the director knows how it all works."

This storage place couldn't be far from the museum. Somehow they would have to transport the artifacts during the night, to a place that looters wouldn't suspect. A place strong enough to protect the crates.

Downstairs the clipboard was waiting for her beside a collection of Pelikan fountain pens, the shelves towering with new items. Boxes pooled in her mind. Shifting side to side. Rearranging themselves and replicating like bunnies, hopping up and down.

It would take weeks to catalog all of it for the next transport, but no matter how fast she recorded and wrapped, she suspected the director would keep adding more.

First was a cache of heirloom jewelry; then she began listing vintage clothing and porcelain figurines, packing them for a bombing she hoped would never happen. She pulled out candlesticks from one box and then a block of stone with a lion head centered inside a star, a Hebrew inscription below it. She studied the heavy piece, not knowing what to call it. A plaque. A nameplate. A memorial from a shuttered synagogue. She could read Latin, but she'd never learned Hebrew or Yiddish.

Someone had taped a piece of paper with an address on the back side, and she ripped off the address to tape onto the back of her clipboard. Instead of packing the stone away, she left it on a shelf.

Hours later, Grete brought down a second cup of coffee, this time with a cube of sugar. Hanna reached for the stone.

"Have you ever seen anything like this?"

Grete picked up the piece, examining the back like Hanna had done for markings. "Only once, in a book."

"What is it?" Hanna asked.

"A wedding stone. They were built into synagogue walls centuries ago. The groom would smash a glass on it during their wedding ceremony to chase away the demons." Grete pointed at the letters. "'Mazel tov.'"

"You read Hebrew?"

Grete cringed as if it was an accusation. "Most of these stones say the same thing."

"I wonder how this one made its way into the museum."

"I don't know, but the wedding stones are only found around Nuremberg."

Hanna took a sip of the coffee and then started wrapping the block of stone. "And the museum wants to store it."

"It's an important piece of history."

A menace—that's what Hitler had called the Jewish people. A parasite in the body of other nations. How strange that the Germans would be keeping their artifacts even as they warned against the threat of their owners.

She finished the coffee, thanking Grete as she handed back her cup.

After wrapping the wedding stone, Hanna memorized the address taped to her clipboard. It was only a ten-minute detour between Kaiserstrasse and Frau Weber's house. Perhaps she could find out what happened to the people who'd owned this artifact.

Right at five, the director shook her hand, thanked her for her work even as he scanned her frame, like she might have stuffed the wedding stone under her blouse. Instead of walking through the center of Old Town, she turned left to follow the perimeter of the city wall. Then she turned onto another passage between buildings, losing herself in the pedestrians and bicyclists before she crossed a bridge over the Pegnitz River, out to a cobblestoned plaza.

The Hauptmarkt was framed by the gothic Church of Our Lady with its medieval Männleinlaufen clock, Town Hall, and a gilded fountain called Schöner Brunnen. Before the war, this plaza had hosted an annual Christmas market with its lights and concerts and cinnamon-spiced wine. Along with the zoo, it had been one of her favorite places as a child.

Kaiserstrasse was stitched like a hemline along the tranquil river, the hill beyond it skirting straight up to Kaiserburg Castle. An archway off the street led into a courtyard of bicycles and garden of herbs. The medieval houses were boxed together around the yard, each one sharing the warmth of walls, many of their windows overlooking the water. The owners of the wedding stone must have been quite wealthy to live here.

The door of Number 18 was locked, so Hanna rang the bell. A uniformed man in his early twenties answered. His widowed mother had just signed a lease for the upper floors, he explained, the opportunity of a lifetime for her and his siblings since he was preparing to leave for the eastern front. No, he didn't know the name of the previous occupants. They'd left nothing behind in the rooms.

Hanna waited on the front steps until another tenant returned home, a lady with impossibly high heels and a shopping bag.

Hanna stood. "I'm searching for the family who used to live here."

The woman glanced over Hanna's shoulder, scanning the empty courtyard. "I didn't know them well."

"Do you know what happened to them?"

"I heard they received an invitation to relocate. To a better place for work." The woman slipped a cigarette into her mouth and lit a match, her hands trembling as she took a long draw. "What do you want with them?"

"I found something of theirs."

"They owned a bakery, over on Adlerstrasse, but they were *Itzige*."

Hanna cringed at the slur. The government must have shut their store down.

"They had two children who used to play hopscotch right here." She pointed at the paved walk. "Back when children played."

Back before they had to march across Nuremberg like troops with their bandannas and flags. Before they had to memorize large portions of *Mein Kampf* and diagram the treachery of their Jewish enemies.

"The Dreydel family, that was their surname," the woman said quietly. "Richard and Josefine."

Hanna caught her breath. Josefine Dreydel was a name she knew. It was on Luisa's list.

Did Luisa know what happened to the Dreydel family? And why the museum was now the keeper of their things?

She had to find—*keep*—their story.

No one answered her knock on Frau Weber's door, so she wandered down to Lorenzkirche, settling onto a bench to hear the organ play. She no longer felt welcome in her own home, and these summer nights were long, the sun staying up until ten. Kolman could eat the leftover muesli for dinner if he was hungry.

"I was supposed to retrieve you after work," Kolman said when she finally returned home by tram and the long walk up past the zoo, a loaf of fresh bread and bottle of milk in her hands. "We were meeting by the curb."

"I told you that I was taking the tram."

"It's not necessary—"

She placed the bottle of milk into the refrigerator. "Himmler secured this position for me, Kolman. If I can't be in the field, I intend to do this job to the best of my ability, even if it means working late."

"What exactly are you doing at the museum?" He reached for a kitchen knife and began to cut the rye bread. It would be a simple meal tonight. Sausages with bread and the tomatoes she'd found growing in Luisa's garden.

"Cataloging the new items they are bringing in."

"Perhaps it's not good for you to work," he said. It was a threat, hardly veiled. He knew that she needed this job, much more than she needed a marriage. If she was required to spend her whole day in this lodge alone, she'd waste away.

"Himmler said . . ." But she didn't know exactly what Himmler had said about this position. Kolman had received the telegram.

"The car will pick us up at eight in the morning."

She'd done everything the Reich had asked of her and yet they continued to siphon off more, as if they owned her. As if she were one of the caged animals at the zoo, a lioness in all of her glory, unable to fight because she was trapped behind steel bars. The zookeeper would shoot this creature in a heartbeat if she became a threat.

Hanna couldn't threaten, not now. She had to embrace the walls of her cage and wait until someone opened the door to an animal they thought tamed. A lioness who purred in public, swallowing her roar until the time was right. Until the women of Germany could speak out again.

The Nazi Party might suppress her voice for now, but she wouldn't let them take her paper and pen. If Frau Weber would help her, she'd find out what was happening to people like the Dreydel family. She would write inside this cage, bury the Dreydels' story with Paul's biography in the labyrinth, when Kolman wasn't home.

The Gestapo would never find out what she had done.

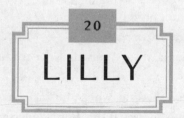

20
LILLY

SONNENWIESE CHILDREN'S HOME

The matron wrapped Lilly and three other girls up in pretty blue dresses, red bows in their hair. Then she paraded them in front of the lady who'd visited before except this time the woman was wearing a dark-brown dress instead of green. A branch instead of a leaf in this forest room.

Sitting beside the brown lady was another woman and a man—a mother and father—both of them drinking from white cups. Both watching the children.

Lilly squirmed in her shiny black shoes. What was she supposed to do now?

Adoption, the matron had said, that's why these people were here, but Lilly hadn't learned that word.

The mother studied Lilly's braided hair, her tight shoes. She muttered words that Lilly didn't understand.

Mama had always bent down to speak with her, in a voice that made her heart sing. Never rushed like this.

The mother stared at Lilly as if waiting for her to speak.

Had she asked a question?

"Lilly," the matron prompted.

"Don't wrap the truth in cotton."

That's what Mama always said. Tell the truth, even when Lilly was scared.

"Nie rozumiem," she said when the matron nudged her. Very polite. Like Mama would say if she didn't understand the words.

The mother's eyes flashed with surprise, black liquid splashing over the side of her cup, adding polka dots to her dress. "What is she speaking?"

"German, of course," the matron said. "She's garbling it."

The mother's eyes turned dark. "That's not German."

"To a three-year-old it is."

The brown lady glared. "Get her out of here."

The matron shuffled Lilly away as the lady introduced the next girl in line.

Lilly sat on a cold metal chair for what seemed like hours, the nurses in their white uniforms passing by as if they didn't see her. What did she do wrong? She'd spoken the truth, but the truth made the women angry.

Was she supposed to lie?

She wasn't allowed to move, not even to use the toilet, not even when her insides felt as if they might explode.

The bow slipped off her braid, falling into her lap, and she crushed the ribbon in her hands, trying to pretend she was back home, running through the forest and farmlands with her brothers, hunting mushrooms for Mama to pickle. How she'd loved eating those mushrooms. Loved everything about their little home that always smelled like *bigos*—her mother's stew.

They had a toilet at home, in a small shed out back. Her mama wanted her to use it, whenever she needed to. And Mama never made her wear bows or tight shoes or sit in a chair for saying she didn't understand.

Always, she was supposed to tell the truth, especially when she didn't understand.

The potty wouldn't stop, no matter how she tried. It dribbled down her legs, soaking her tights, and she wanted to curl up under the chair before anyone could see.

The nurses noticed her then, the puddle underneath the seat. And she knew it was wrong.

A dog, one of the women called her. Another just laughed, making her flush warm. She should have been able to hold it for longer, and now she was wet. A wet, dirty dog.

If only she could go home.

The matron was angry. Sweeping into the hall, she grabbed Lilly's arm, and the woman's fingers hurt worse than the man who'd taken her from Mama.

"I'm sorry," Lilly pleaded, but the matron held up a stick, the wood punctured with holes. A bat ready to swing.

"Beat the Polish out of you," that's what the matron said.

She cried out for her mama after the first hit. And the second one.

"You have no mother now."

Lilly whimpered at the next swing, the pain rippling down her bare legs. The thought that her mama might be forever gone.

The matron stopped to wipe the sweat off her forehead. "You are German, Lilly."

She didn't reply.

"Ich bin Deutsche." Another swing. "Say it."

"Ich bin Deutsche," she whispered. If only this terrible game would end.

"Louder."

"Ich bin Deutsche," Lilly repeated, wishing she could run away.

Over and over, the German words, the beating, as if the matron were nailing every word to her skin.

The woman finally stopped. "From now on, you only speak German or I will bruise every *Zoll* of your body."

She understood enough. *"Ja."*

"You are German," the matron repeated. "And you should be proud."

A black web crawled up the top of her legs. To be German meant everything hurt. To be German meant she could never again speak her mama's words.

The matron left her then, and a nurse scooted her off to a bath.

The woman tsked as she peeled off Lilly's dress and undergarments. "She shouldn't have done this to you."

"Ich bin Deutsche," Lilly said, the water burning her skin.

"What?"

Lilly spoke louder now. *"Ich bin Deutsche."*

The nurse patted her head. "Of course you are."

21

EMBER

Water and debris covered the back roads as Ember trekked inland with Dakota, her cell phone charging in his console. The 4Runner cleared all the storm's damage, including the split pieces of fallen oak.

Sheep ambled behind the limestone walls, grazing peacefully on the hills as if they'd slept through the storm. In the distance she saw a glint of blue, a panorama of ocean for the sheep and their caregivers to enjoy. Alex once said he'd learned more about God in his years shepherding these animals then he'd ever learned in church.

A wide porch wrapped around the front of the Kiehl family farmhouse with several rocking chairs turned on their sides, a string of display lights beaming over the hill. Ember had spent only a few months living on this property, but for a moment she felt as if she'd come home.

Dakota picked up the chairs before opening the front door. "Gram?"

"We're in the kitchen."

Ember followed him to a long dining room table set with fine china and several pitchers, bowls of fresh berries and whipped cream on each plate.

"Hello," Ember said, sitting beside the woman who'd opened up the world to her in high school. Mrs. Kiehl's hair was short, a stylish pixie of gray, and her green eyes glowed like the light from a firefly. Around her neck, she wore a polished white stone on a silver chain.

"Ember." She reached forward, taking her hand. "My eyes are a bit blurry, but my ears are as clear as the day I was born. I'm glad you've come back."

"It's been a bit of a journey."

"How's the cottage?" Mrs. Kiehl asked.

Dakota sat on the other side of the table. "Not a bit of damage that I can see. All we lost were a few branches."

"That place has more lives than a cat," Mrs. Kiehl said. "It should have crumbled years ago, but there's a whole lot of strength under that gingerbread roof."

Dakota grinned. "Sort of like you, Gram. Strong and beautiful."

"And old."

Ember suppressed her laugh. She'd told Noah very clearly that her former teacher wouldn't want to be called *old*.

"I didn't say that."

Mrs. Kiehl smiled, playfully tapping his hand. Clearly she loved Dakota as much as he loved her. "One more chance for all of us."

"Where's Kayla?" Dakota asked.

"Right here." The young woman breezed into the room with a teapot. The mismatched squares on her brightly colored apron were sprinkled with flour, and her dark-brown hair tumbled over her shoulders as she poured black tea for each of them. "We were up half the night, praying for you."

Dakota kissed her cheek. "Thank you."

"Eat some fruit," Kayla said before turning back to the kitchen. "I'll get the casserole out of the oven."

"That's a lovely necklace." Ember pointed at the stone resting on Mrs. Kiehl's collar.

"It's my *Schatzi*," Mrs. Kiehl said. "A treasure from Germany."

"Did you bring it with you from Nuremberg?"

"My father gave it to me with a reminder," Mrs. Kiehl said, fingering the piece. "All King David needed was the stone that God gave him to kill Goliath, and I need to use whatever gifts that God gives me to defeat the giants in my world."

"A wise dad."

Mrs. Kiehl took a slow sip of her tea. "Dakota says that you are working in Washington, DC."

"I'm researching and writing my dissertation about the pattern of persecution in Nuremberg."

Mrs. Kiehl turned toward the window, looking at a weathered barn and meadows that rolled behind it, all the way to the ocean. The cabin where Ember and Alex once lived was no longer there. "What do you plan to do with this research?"

"Publish it," she replied. "And then I'll return to teaching. The more people know about the past, the more we can work together to expose and end this cycle of hatred."

"I'm afraid it will never end, Ember. Not if people continue to turn their backs on the love of God for all of His creation."

The thought seeped into Ember like the bitter leaves in her tea. "But I have to do something before history repeats itself."

Mrs. Kiehl placed her teacup back on its saucer. "You think words can stop hatred?"

"Words can help curb it."

Mrs. Kiehl sighed. "I once thought the same thing."

"Why don't you think so now?"

"Words will never penetrate a hardened heart," she said. "The persecution won't end until people are willing to humble themselves and love their neighbors."

Ember eyed the white stone. "This research is the only rock I have to throw."

Mrs. Kiehl smoothed her hand over the necklace again. "Then I hope you aim well."

"You were the one who inspired all of this," Ember said.

"All of what?"

"My interest in the history of Nuremberg."

Another smile flickered on Mrs. Kiehl's lips. "It makes me immeasurably proud that you are doing this. No matter how people react, it's a story that needs to be told." Her voice fluttered away, as if she'd gone to Nuremberg in her mind. "Have you been there?"

"I'm going next week."

"I never went back after the bombings, but I've seen photographs of Old Town."

Ember had seen the pictures too, the mountains of rubble. It took seven years, she'd read, to clear it all out on what they'd deemed the Rubble Express. Thirteen million cubic meters—enough to fill more than four Egyptian pyramids—relocated with their shovels.

Mrs. Kiehl scooped more sweetener into her tea. "The reporters said they restored the town exactly how it was before the war."

"Perhaps your home is still there," Dakota said.

"If it is, I'll send pictures."

"It was an old lodge, above the zoo," Mrs. Kiehl explained. "I don't remember the address, but we lived near an abandoned quarry. The rust-colored cliffs reminded me of giant chalkboards."

Ember tapped her fingers together, trying to balance the arithmetic in her head, but the mental gymnast fell flat off the beam. If she'd been exploring the cliffs, Mrs. Kiehl must have been born long before Charlie Ward arrived for the Nuremberg trials. Perhaps

Hanna and Charlie had known each other while he attended college in Germany. "I'm glad you had some space to play during the war."

"The war seemed far away when I was young. I remember visiting the zoo in those years and a crumbling church on the hill by our house. I used to wander around the columns while my mother was praying."

"Why did she go up to an abandoned church to pray?" Ember asked.

"There was a labyrinth nearby." Mrs. Kiehl's voice traveled away, as if she was just rediscovering this memory. "My mother would walk in circles, like the sisters might have done long ago. Sometimes she would kneel on the path as if she couldn't carry her burdens all the way to the end."

"Her load must have been quite heavy."

"I wish I could remember more . . ."

"It's okay," Ember said. "It was a long time ago."

"Dakota, could you help Kayla with the casserole?" Mrs. Kiehl asked, taking over as captain.

He ringed the handle of his cup to take with him. "Are you trying to get rid of me?"

"Only for a moment."

He kissed his grandmother's forehead and walked into the other room. Mrs. Kiehl tipped forward, folding translucent hands with lavender-painted nails. "He used to like you a lot, Ember. When you were in school."

She froze. "I don't think—"

"Had a rough upbringing, but he's come around just fine. Unlike his dad."

"Mrs. Kiehl—"

"I don't want to meddle, but . . ." Mrs. Kiehl took a sip of tea.

"I believe this would be considered meddling."

"Dakota's a good man. My hero."

She quickly changed the subject. "I'm trying to find a hero in Nuremberg, Mrs. Kiehl. One man or woman who stood up against the anti-Semitism. One person who swam solely against the tide."

"Anyone who swam against the tide there was sent east," Mrs. Kiehl said. "If they survived the war, they would have had to float along with the surface tide and then double back underneath the current so the Nazis wouldn't know."

"Was your mother an archaeologist?"

Mrs. Kiehl glanced toward the kitchen door. "After I was born, she worked as a curator at the German National Museum."

"But before your birth?"

"She never spoke much about her past." Mrs. Kiehl steepled her fingers as if to breathe a prayer. "It was a complicated time, Ember. My mother loved history and she loved telling me the stories about the nuns who lived in the convent. She did not love the Nazi Party, but I was raised to be a model of the German people in my early years. Certain people . . . they were cruel to my mother and me."

"I wish we could mend all the wounds in our past." Make the memories go away. None of them should define themselves by their childhood. "Dakota said your father left Nuremberg at the end of 1945."

"That's correct."

She didn't want to insult the woman and her memories, but no matter which way Ember tried to maneuver the facts, it didn't make sense. Mrs. Kiehl would have been much too young to remember anything about Nuremberg if she'd been born after the war.

"So you would have just been born before Charlie returned to America."

"I was born a few years before the war began," she said. "My certificate was lost in the aftermath, I'm afraid, but my mother said I was born in 1936. The Germans were meticulous with their paperwork, but their storage was no match for the Allied bombs or the subsequent fires."

Ember took a long sip of tea before she asked the inevitable, the same question that had been pressing down on her. "Was Charlie Ward your biological father?"

Mrs. Kiehl lifted the tea bag from her cup and wrapped it over her spoon, wringing out the last drops of tea. "I believe so. He attended Columbia University and did an academic exchange for a year at the University of Berlin. But my mother never told him about me until the end of the war."

"So Charlie brought you back to the States . . . ," she said, confirming what Dakota had been told.

"Yes. After my mother disappeared."

Ember could smell baked cheese and ham wafting out of the kitchen door. "You don't know what happened to her?"

Mrs. Kiehl shook her head. "I've searched for information over the years to no avail."

She'd traveled here to sort out the knots in this story, but they seemed to be tightening. "I can ask about her while I'm in Nuremberg."

Mrs. Kiehl lowered her hands. "Anything you can find would be a gift to my family."

"You once told me that no one could force their identity on me," Ember said.

"And I still believe that. You must choose—we all must choose—how we are going to live our lives. No matter what someone else did in our past, with God's help, we choose how to move forward."

"I'll try to find out what happened," Ember agreed. "In the article, you said your mother was a friend to the Jewish people."

"I shouldn't have said that to the reporter." Mrs. Kiehl blinked. "You understand how complicated family can be."

"A bit."

"I thought you might, because of what your husband did . . ."

Ember fell back against the chair, the word *husband* ringing in her ears. "I'm not married."

"Your ex-hu—"

"Gram!" Dakota set the bubbling casserole dish on the table, a reprimand in this word.

But Ember barely heard him, her vision shriveling. "You know about Lukas?"

Mrs. Kiehl shook her head, the stone wobbling across her neck. "No—"

Then Dakota was beside Ember, reaching for her arm. "Let me show you the farm."

She didn't move. "What do you know about Lukas?"

"I'm sorry." Mrs. Kiehl waved both hands in front of her. "I shouldn't have said anything. It was a long time ago."

No one on Martha's Vineyard was supposed to know about Lukas. He belonged to a different life, one she'd put far behind her.

The trembling in Ember's legs traveled up to her voice. "Please, Mrs. Kiehl . . ."

The woman shook her head again. "These lips of mine, sometimes they speak out of turn."

Dakota was tugging on Ember's arm now, pointing her toward the back door.

"I'm sorry," Mrs. Kiehl said again as Ember stepped out into the sunshine, her shoes sinking in the muddy grass.

She'd spent all this time searching for information about others, even as she'd tried desperately to forget what was behind her, especially this man who'd been her husband in the eyes of the Aryan Council, if not the state—

Lukas was supposed to be in prison now, locked away for life.

How did this woman know him?

HANNA

22

"You never told me the Gestapo searched the house," Kolman said, slamming the car door.

She was too exhausted to fight. Another shipment had arrived at the museum last night, and Director Kohlhaussen said she must work faster in order to secure the items immediately, as if Great Britain might be dropping bombs on Nuremberg before the summer's end.

She needed to work longer hours, but oddly enough she might lose her job if she worked overtime. If she wasn't finished by five each day, Kolman, she feared, would pull this position from her, snapping closed the door on her cage. Director Kohlhaussen would have no choice but to bow to the Reich's oversight, and she'd be reassigned to *Kinder* and *Küche*—Kolman would never allow her to attend church.

Dust billowed in the dry air as the driver backed away.

"I assumed they told you weeks ago," she said. "They haven't returned."

Red dirt clouded around Kolman, making it look like he'd just crawled out of a furnace. "The Gestapo is not permitted in our home."

"I wasn't in a position to refuse them."

"This is important, Hanna." His boots clipped as he stepped closer. "You need to tell me what they said."

She suspected that Kolman already knew every word of that conversation. He was probably testing her to see if she would be honest with him.

"They were searching for Paul and Luisa." She glanced up at the second floor as if she might see their faces in the window.

"And what did they find?"

"Nothing. Paul and Luisa were already gone when I returned home."

"The agent said you refused to open a door."

"I didn't refuse," she said. "He wanted to see the attic, and I couldn't find the key."

"But you have a key—"

"I discovered it later." She could never tell him or anyone that Luisa had given it to her.

"Why was the attic locked?"

"I don't know, Kolman. Until Himmler ordered me back home, I hadn't been here in four years."

He pointed toward the front door. "I'd like to see the attic again."

She retrieved the key from the desk and handed it over to him. When she'd given him the tour before, he had merely glanced at the dollhouses and returned to the lower floors, but this time he scanned the room like he was searching for something.

"My grandfather made some of the finest dollhouses across Germany," she said, tracing her hands across the polished roof of one that was almost her height.

He moved to one of the finer houses and picked up a silver

candlestick, rolling it between his fingers. "I almost want the agent to come back with his locksmith. See what he missed."

"There's nothing for him up here."

Kolman examined her grandfather's workbench. Then he knelt on the ground and chimed two pans together in the kitchen of the building that resembled the lodge. Outside the dollhouse window was the stone ribbing of the labyrinth, but he didn't seem to notice it as he opened and closed the oven.

He looked back up at her. "This is perfect for a girl."

"I suppose," she concurred, not wanting to talk about children again. It would have certainly been a good place for her to play when she was younger, if her father had given her the choice.

He stood slowly, then scooted a miniature tricycle across the floor of another dollhouse. "We will have children soon, won't we?"

"I don't know—"

"At least four of them."

"Four?" she gasped.

"Himmler is requiring all of his men to revitalize the Aryan race in Germany first and then around the world."

"It's not like I can order a child from the store!"

"I'm quite aware of what it takes to make a baby." He stood up and reached for a strand of her hair, twirling it slowly, and a torrent of nausea flooded over her at his touch, so different from the sparks she'd felt back in France.

She was supposed to be researching their heritage, proving the strength of their roots, not contributing to a new generation of Aryans. How could he ask her to birth and then raise four children while he was out working for the Reich? Even one child, she feared, would break her, just like she'd broken her mother.

Kolman didn't understand this. Motherhood was supposed to come naturally to women, he thought, even more so than digging in the dirt. But no matter the motto of Deutschland, she'd never make a good one.

Sleep evaded her most of the night as she tried to devise a plan to convince Kolman that she lacked the necessary skills to mother a nest full of Aryans.

The next morning, she awoke a few minutes after six and saw her husband already dressed in his uniform. She scooted up quickly in bed, confused. When he began working in Nuremberg, he seemed to have stopped his morning walks into the forest.

Kolman stuffed a jar of hair cream into his razor bag before glancing out the window. "If the Gestapo agent returns, tell him by the orders of Himmler himself, he must stay away from our house."

"You tell him." She inched up against the headboard, pulling a pillow in front of her. Beside the door was a leather suitcase, and he heaved it onto the bed, clasping the brass buckles to close it.

She stared at the suitcase. "Where are you going?"

"Himmler has reassigned me to a location up north."

She flung her legs over the side of the bed, blood waking every vein. She could almost feel the trowel in her hands, the packed dirt under her feet. The mystery in the air as their team wondered what was underneath the curtain of soil. All they had to do was draw back history, one layer at a time, to see what nature would reveal. And just maybe find something like the Holy Grail.

Outside the window, in the first light of day, she could see a Volkswagen waiting for him in their drive. "You're traveling alone . . ."

He lifted his suitcase off the bed. "I spoke with Director Kohlhaussen, and he said that he can't spare you right now."

She pulled her feet back off the floor, curling them under her legs. How long had Kolman been planning to leave? As much as she wanted to be back in the field, she didn't want to be there as his wife, waiting at the hotel or inn while the team excavated. The men would never respect her again for her expertise.

Still Kolman should have told her that he was going away.

"There is much to be done at the museum," she said.

He kissed her cheek. "And you will do it better than anyone."

For the first time in weeks, she felt a ray of hope. As if this new life of hers could finally begin. As if she might be able to flutter free from this cage after all.

"Hanna?"

Her mind was racing so fast with possibilities that she thought Kolman had already left. Instead he was still standing beside the door. "What is it?"

"The driver will take you to work at eight every morning and pick you up at five."

"I don't need a driver."

"He will keep you safe." His eyebrows narrowed with the clap of his heels. "And help you stay away from Kaiserstrasse."

Then he was gone.

She shivered against the pillows. How did Kolman know she'd tried to find the Dreydel family in Old Town?

She watched him climb into the Volkswagen and speed away.

His driver might keep watch over her outside, but he couldn't control what she did inside this house.

23

EMBER

"We weren't really married." Ember sank onto the damp bale of hay, as if the storm had opened up a hole, sending her tumbling into the sea. The light, she needed it to catch her before she drowned.

"It doesn't matter—"

"No one told me until much later that Lukas and I were supposed to have a license. I was so young—in order to marry, I needed the approval of a court."

"I'm sorry, Em."

She shook her head. "Please stop calling me Em."

"Gram wasn't trying to hurt you."

"I know." She looked through the barn door, at the sheep salting the hill outside, the thread of blue sky and sea beyond. The clouds had reached a truce, but a new storm was raging in her heart. "I was only fourteen when we had the ceremony. Lukas was supposed to be the next—"

But how could she explain to him, explain to anyone, about the

Aryan Council? How their fierce religion wasn't to be questioned. How she'd been trapped in the web until the FBI broke her free. She'd gained her freedom then, but her sweet daughter . . .

She tapped her hands against her legs again, reminding herself that she was strong. That God had replaced her weakness, her loss, with an outpouring of love.

"Did you know what happened to my family in Idaho?"

He sat down on the bale beside her. "Only a little. Dad had attended your father's church a few times on the island, and I heard him talking to Gram about the compound in Idaho when you moved back. Arguing, really, about Lukas and something that happened when he lived near here."

Ember flinched. "Lukas never lived on Martha's Vineyard." Her first memories of him were on Eagle Lake, working with her dad to repair the cabins at the former church camp.

Dakota leaned back, chewing on a piece of straw. "He had moved here from Germany; I remember Gram saying that. She and Dad fought about Lukas before my dad moved off the island. I thought it was odd since your father's church had been disbanded for at least ten years."

The tapping on her legs slowed. "What did Lukas do to your grandmother?"

"I don't know," he said. "Truly. But I do know that Gram cares about you, Ember. She would never want to hurt you, not like I did . . ."

"You hurt me, Dakota, but the humiliation started long before you. For most of my childhood, I was made to feel . . ." She took a deep breath. "Worthless."

Her only redeeming value, she'd been told, was her Aryan blood, to create a new generation, but she couldn't tell Dakota that. He'd think she was crazy.

"No one should have made you feel like that, especially not me. If I hadn't been so stupid, I would have told you that you were a treasure, Ember. Worth more than gold."

She dug her phone out of her pocket. "I need to call my brother."

"Of course." He stood. "You want me to take you back to the cottage?"

"No," she said. "I'll call him from here."

Dakota wandered off, giving her space.

Mrs. Kiehl was right. Nothing she wrote in her dissertation would stop the ballooning hatred in their country, but she could remind those willing to listen that the pride of any race, pitted against another, led only to another kind of fire, burning people up from the inside.

She couldn't bury this desire that God had given her, this passion to share the truth. Her readers, her students, didn't have to respond, but they would be given the opportunity to make a change. Ember and others were responsible, before God, to share what they had been given, and she desperately wanted others to know the history of how persecution began and what they could do to stop it.

Her words, sprinkled on the raging fire, might not help, but if others joined her in looking solidly into the past and its reflection on their future, perhaps they could extinguish this persecution together.

Alex's familiar voicemail greeting was short, the same one he'd recorded years ago when he bought his phone. Her brother was a fixer, and a cell phone interrupted his work of resurrecting broken things for the guests at his inn. He celebrated every revived motor, each plumbing feat, the wires that sparked at his touch. Material things. He'd always been good to her, but relationships he struggled to mend.

After the entire student body had laughed at her ridiculous walk onto the homecoming field, Alex made a strawberry milkshake for the two of them to share, as if that was all it took to wash away her tears.

Sort of like the Phish Food she kept for Noah.

"I'm coming through Philadelphia tomorrow and wondered if you'd have time for a late lunch. I wanted to talk to you about . . ." She couldn't very well explain over voicemail why she wanted to speak with him. "I had a couple of questions that I wanted to ask."

Then she called another number in her list of contacts, one that she'd called often over the years. She gave the penitentiary officer at Atwater the familiar ID number, and in return, he gave her the same information that he'd given her the last four times she'd called.

Lukas Tillich was the prisoner's name, convicted of second-degree murder, age forty-eight, six feet and one inch, 210 pounds. His next parole hearing—what she wanted to know most of all—was September 13.

The charges were second-degree only because the prosecutor hadn't been able to prove that Lukas intended to kill her parents and five other members of the Aryan Council who'd died when he started the fire. According to the news articles that she read, he'd planned to confuse the federal agents so council members could flee.

To Eagle's Nest. The reporters didn't write this, but she knew, like the others, where they were supposed to run.

The FBI agent had whisked her away from the scene, but they never found Elsie. When they arrested Lukas, he was empty-handed. Her baby, Alex told her later, had drowned in the lake and Lukas had been locked away for thirty years.

She and Alex had mourned this loss together when she arrived on the island. They'd given their family—her mother, father, and Elsie—a private memorial service, then they pressed on into the new millennium. She'd immersed herself in high school, trying to find value in fitting in, while Alex worked to support both of them. When she turned sixteen, she began serving buttered lobster rolls at a tourist stand to help pay bills and rent for their new house in town. Between school and work and the books she loved, she tried to fight off the ghosts from Idaho on her own. Another five years passed before she found a therapist able to help her face them.

It was a delicate balance now, trying to forget the past even as the past kept haunting her.

Dakota was beside the stone wall, stacking a mound of branches.

Quietly she joined him, sweeping up the branches and trees that dangled from the limestone, tossing them in with the others.

"You okay?" he asked.

"Yeah." Her cell phone chimed, and she looked down to see a text from Alex. **Where are you?**

Dakota nodded at her phone. "Is it Noah?"

"It's my brother." **On Martha's Vineyard,** she typed.

She loaded up another armful of branches before he texted back. **You swore you'd never go back there.**

I needed to meet with Mrs. Kiehl.

His next note came back in rapid fire. **I can be in Philadelphia by noon.**

She looked at Dakota. "The ferry will be running tomorrow, won't it?"

"I'm afraid not. They've postponed the next departure until Saturday afternoon."

She groaned, but the news wasn't nearly as bad as it would have been last night. "I'll have to reschedule with my brother."

"If you want, I can take you to Woods Hole in the morning so you can catch a bus to the Boston train station."

"You have a plane on this island?"

"No, but I have a boat stored near the marina."

"If I get seasick on the ferry, I'll never survive your boat."

Several sheep ambled up beside him, and he petted the fur of one as if it were a pet. "As long as another storm doesn't come through, it should be a calm trip, but if you want to wait, you're welcome to stay at the cottage. Either way, I have to take the boat over tomorrow morning. I'm scheduled to fly out of Logan in the afternoon."

She began to scroll through the Amtrak schedules to Philadelphia. "I'll need to be at South Station by nine."

"If you're ready to leave the cottage by six, we should get there in plenty of time."

She closed the app. "I'll be ready."

"Tell you what." He eyed the house. "Why don't we say goodbye to Gram, and then I'll take you out to eat?"

She studied his face. "Where did you want to go?"

"I know a decent place in Aquinnah."

She took a step back, cringing at the memory. "That pizza place?"

"Please," he said. "Give me one more chance at being your friend."

She thought for a moment. She wouldn't mind a redo of that terrible night, when she wasn't fawning over the man in front of her, but he'd only taken her to Aquinnah because he didn't want anyone seeing them together.

"I'm not hiding out on the other side of the island."

He patted the head of the sheep again. "Then how about lobster in Oak Bluffs?"

"Locals will talk, Dakota."

He smiled. "I hope they do."

It was a risk, having another meal alone with this man, but he was only trying to be kind. Make up for what he'd done in the past. She was a strong believer in repentance and restitution. "Lobster sounds good."

He picked up another branch and threw it onto the pile. "Thank you, Em—Ember."

As if she was doing him a favor.

"Do you think your grandmother would let me borrow some hot water for a shower before we leave?"

"I suspect she's going to want to apologize again."

"She only asked a question," Ember said. "No need to apologize."

"Gram always apologizes, even when she hasn't done anything wrong."

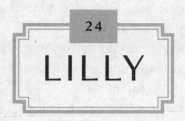

LILLY

24

The adoption lady was dressed in red this time, the silver brooch pinned to her collar like a thorn from one of Mama's roses. A man sat beside her in the forest room, his hair crisp like buttered toast, his gray shirt and trousers like fur.

When Lilly saw the uniform, her hands began to shake, then her legs and arms until she was shaking so hard the matron had to prop her up against a chair lest she fall into the trees.

Say *Ja*, the matron had commanded, to anything that was asked of her. *Ja. Ja. Ja.*

And remind the man that she was German.

Lilly wore the same blue dress as the last visit, her stains washed away, the same bow and shoes. The matron said she must look her best for those who came to shop for measured children.

But this time no other girls stepped into the room. Was this man going to adopt her? Or maybe he could take her back to her mama.

If she wet her dress, the matron swore she'd leave Lilly in the forest outside Sonnenwiese so the wolves could have her for supper.

The man and red lady didn't notice Lilly at first. They were laughing about something, petting each other on their arms. Perhaps they were going to adopt her together.

"Leave us," the red lady finally said, waving the matron away with her clipboard. Lilly clung to the armchair as the matron closed the doors, waiting for the questions.

The man stared at her a long time before speaking. "What is your name?"

This was one she'd practiced, the matron asking her before every meal. "Lilly."

"Where are you from, Lilly?"

"Ich bin Deutsche."

The man glanced at the red lady.

"Berlin," the woman said. "Her parents were killed in the bombing last month."

"Ja," Lilly said although she didn't understand all of the words.

He leaned forward now, his blue eyes flashing in the forest light like those of the wolves from her picture books. "Do you like dogs, Lilly?"

"Ja."

"Do you eat them for dinner?"

The red lady's eyes widened, but he'd asked a question. Lilly had to answer.

"Ja," she said, her fingers still curled around the chair.

"What are your favorite dogs to eat?"

So many questions at once, but she couldn't stop. The matron would take her to the woods. *"Ja."*

The lady lifted the clipboard, covering her face.

"Do you even know what I'm saying?" the man asked.

"Ja."

He and the red lady laughed as if she'd made a joke, but she hadn't meant to be funny. She'd done exactly what the matron told her to do.

She straightened her shoulders. *"Ich bin Deutsche!"*

They both stared at her, mouths open.

The man turned away, looking back at the red lady. "Do you have another girl this age?"

She shuffled through her papers. "No, but we have plenty of babies."

"My wife can't take care of a baby."

"I'm afraid Lilly's our oldest right now, but your men will bring us more. If you can wait a few months—"

He studied Lilly again, like she was one of the pastries her brothers used to bring home. "I suppose this one will do."

The red lady wrote on her paper. "She'll make a fine daughter."

"I'll return by the end of the year," the man said. "I hope she'll learn more German words by then."

"Our nurses will make sure she speaks fluently."

They were ignoring her again, a smile on the man's face. Something big just happened, but Lilly didn't know what it was.

The man stood and brushed his trousers. "It's been a much more enjoyable visit than I anticipated."

The lady's brooch sparked in the light when she nodded toward a side door, the toes on her shiny red shoes drumming on the ground. "You must sign some papers before you leave."

He smiled again. "Very good."

HANNA

25

"I have to visit the cobbler during lunch." Hanna pointed at the heel on her laced oxfords, the leather square flapping against the sole. It had taken some effort to loosen the piece without scuffing or breaking the side, but no one could question her need to repair it.

For the past month she'd been trying to connect with Frau Weber after work, but the driver that Kolman left behind was always waiting at the curb at five to transport her home, and lunch in the museum cafeteria had become mandatory for all the employees, to protect them in these tumultuous times, the director had said. And to protect the remaining artifacts, she suspected. Much of the collection had already been transported to the secret bunker, but Director Kohlhaussen didn't want anything leaving the building without an approved escort.

She had to find a new tactic to leave the museum before five.

Grete didn't even glance down at Hanna's shoe. "I'll tell the director."

"It may take a few hours."

Hanna stepped into a huddle of visitors who were exiting the lobby, walking carefully on her toes. If the driver was parked nearby, perhaps he wouldn't notice her in this crowd.

Lingering, looking around for the sedan, would only signal her irregular routine, so she moved quickly onto a path that wove through the buildings and crossed over a pedestrian bridge to the street where Frau Weber lived.

The cobbler loaned her a tight-fitting pair of Mary Janes while he repaired her heel, and she climbed the steps quickly to Frau Weber's apartment.

"It's Hanna," she whispered after the second knock, slipping inside when the door opened.

The roots of Frau Weber's hair had grayed considerably in the past two months as if this Reich were sucking the life out of her. Hanna glanced toward the kitchen door. Not only was it closed, it was partially obscured by Frau Weber's collection of plants.

Their time together would be short. No savoring conversation over coffee today.

"I love you like my own daughter, Hanna, but you are going to jeopardize us all by coming here."

"No one followed me."

"The Nazis have eyes in every corner of this city now."

Hanna sat on one of the chairs. "I read the biography on Paul."

"Did you burn it?"

"I can't burn his biography. We have to keep it as a record of what's happening in Nuremberg."

"Paul can share his own story when he returns," Frau Weber said.

Hanna considered her words. She'd jumped to her own conclusion that he wouldn't be returning. That his disappearance, the months that had gone by with no word, meant he'd met an ugly fate.

But Luisa must have understood the importance of keeping it or she would have never written it down.

Hanna glanced at the kitchen door, wondering if her cousin was behind it. "Do you think he'll return?"

Frau Weber didn't answer the question. "The Gestapo will kill you if they find it."

"I hid it in a safe place."

"North America is a safe place, Hanna. Great Britain, even. Unless you found a courier to ship it across the ocean, that story is not safe."

Places like America, Charlie once told her, had something called freedom of speech, but they knew no such freedom here. Speech was akin to marriage now. Only used in what was perceived to be the best interest of their government.

"Your father would have my head if he knew you were involved."

"I'd like to think he would be proud of me for helping."

Frau Weber nodded her head slowly. "Herr Tillich was a wounded man. Not just his leg, but his heart when he lost his son and then his wife."

"You and Luisa rescued me in that season."

"And I don't want you to get hurt now . . ."

But she couldn't step away, hiding in the lodge by herself while others like Frau Weber were hiding people. "There was a list of names with Paul's biography."

"You were supposed to burn that as well."

"A box from the Dreydel family came to me at the museum. They were one of the families on her list, and now they've been relocated, their things requisitioned as property of the German government," Hanna said. "Does Luisa know what happened to them?"

"Perhaps."

Exasperated, she nodded toward the kitchen. "Ask her."

"Luisa has relocated as well for a few days."

"She was sent east?" Hanna asked, alarmed.

"No. She simply moves around to protect all of us."

"I want to collect the stories," Hanna said. "When the war is over, we'll tell the world what happened in Nuremberg. What the Nazis have done."

"Only if Germany loses the war."

Frau Weber was right. If Hitler won, if the stories were found, they'd be killed, but if they didn't keep the stories, even if Germany won the war, no one would ever know the truth. Someone had to take a risk to hide the stories like the museum was doing with the artifacts. Someone without children or a family who needed her here.

"If some of the people on Luisa's list are still in the city, I'll find a way to speak with them."

"You married an SS officer, Hanna. They'll never trust you."

"I didn't have any other choice . . ."

"We always have a choice," Frau Weber said. "But sometimes it's better to go along with their demands in order to help whom we can. Wait here, please."

When she returned, Frau Weber carried a basket with fabric. "I fear my days in Nuremberg are numbered."

"Then you must hide like Luisa!"

"It's too late for me to leave," she said. "But these stories . . ."

Underneath the folds of material was a small stack of papers. A compilation of biographies chronicling what happened to Paul's sister and his parents and other families like the Dreydels who'd been taken away during the night. According to one of the papers, the morning after the Dreydels were removed from their home, taken away forcibly by soldiers in a truck, a separate van arrived for their things.

"Did you write these?" Hanna asked as she skimmed the stories.

"With Luisa's assistance. Many of these people are close friends of hers."

Hanna's stomach turned as she continued reading the accounts, at least twenty of them about Jewish people begging for food. A man who jumped out of a window. A woman who took the life of her child before the Nazis could take her away.

What was happening to her beautiful country? The strength of its people?

Germany's hourglass had turned upside down, and she'd only seen glimpses of the shifting sand while she was away. But newspapers like the local Der Stürmer, she'd discovered, were propagating the hatred of the Jewish people with their scathing articles and vulgar cartoons. The hatred seemed to be everywhere, filling up the papers and airwaves, some of the reporters urging fellow Germans to destroy the Jewish people like they were vermin.

But no one was reporting about those who'd already been destroyed.

No wonder the Gestapo was nervous. If they knew Luisa had been collecting these stories, they feared where she might send them. They controlled the information, the narrative of the German people, and Nazi leaders didn't want to provoke the world. No one, especially not a woman like Luisa, would ruin their plans.

Hanna lowered the stack of papers on her lap. "You said it's dangerous to have these."

"Terribly—"

"Then you can't hide them in your sewing basket."

"I don't have any place else to keep them."

If she couldn't gather the stories, Hanna would help Frau Weber hide them until the war was over, and then return dignity to those who had suffered by sharing them.

But she couldn't take the entire stack back to the museum with her. They wouldn't fit in her clutch bag, and Director Kohlhaussen or Grete would notice if she tried to hide a pile of papers in her clothes. Two or three papers, though, folded under her waistline . . . No one would see them on her way into the museum, but the director might notice the papers on the way back out, certainly if she was called aside for a personal search,

If she couldn't take the stories home to the labyrinth, she would find someplace else to hide them.

"Do you enjoy history?" Hanna asked.

"I much prefer sewing."

She returned the stack of papers. "Perhaps you might cultivate an interest."

"And what would I do with this newfound interest?" Frau Weber asked, her eyebrows raised.

"You could visit the National Museum. We still have some paintings on the walls and a collection of bells from the old abbeys."

Frau Weber tucked the pages back between her fabric.

"Visitors can take their purses into the museum, but employees aren't allowed to have any personal items inside," Hanna continued, developing the plan in her mind. "You could bring the papers when you visit. Two at a time."

"And you'd take them home?"

"No, we're monitored closely when we leave, but I could—

Frau Weber waved her hands. "Don't tell me."

"Could you visit the bells tomorrow? I'll shake your hand when I return from the cafeteria at noon."

Frau Weber thought for a moment. "I am quite interested in bells."

"You'll have to fold the pages small enough so no one can see."

Frau Weber smiled. "I've been tucking and folding for most of life."

For the next month Frau Weber came faithfully to the museum two or three times a week, passing along twenty-four of the stories, until Grete inquired about her interest in the abbey bells.

26

EMBER

"Why were you visiting Lilly Kiehl?" Alex asked, taking a swig of Irish beer from his mug, his trimmed beard gleaming in the light.

They were tucked back in a booth with enough license plates along the wall to outfit an army of tin men.

"I wanted to interview her for my dissertation."

"I'm proud of you, Ember. You are using the gifts God has given you to inspire others."

"Thank you." She couldn't stand the taste of beer, so she settled for something called an Irish Rose, a sparkling cherry lemonade that made her feel like a teenager again, drinking a strawberry milkshake to make the problems go away.

"Did you get what you needed from her?"

"I got more than I anticipated." She took a long sip of her drink. "Mrs. Kiehl started to talk about Lukas . . ."

Her brother leaned forward, his shoulder-length hair framing his drink. "What exactly did she say?"

"Nothing of significance, but the fact that she even knew him—I was shocked, Alex. I didn't think anyone on Martha's Vineyard knew about him, but then Dakota told me Lukas had lived on the island, back when Dad had his church there."

Alex nodded slowly. "That's when the real trouble began."

Frustration bubbled inside her. Sometimes her brother was like one of those stone walls around the Kiehls' farm. She'd read plenty of articles about the Aryan Council, watched the interviews and a documentary online, but those clips were only the shards that spilled after the story broke. Much had happened before and then after the fire. Things she didn't remember. Things from her childhood that she never knew.

The caseworker from Idaho had met with Alex before Ember had moved into his cottage, told him what happened on Eagle Lake, but Alex also knew more than she did about their father's church in those early years. Sometimes Ember felt like he'd spent the past twenty years withholding information from her even as she tried to pry back one ragged layer at a time, grabbling for the truth. While part of her wanted to forget what was behind her, knowing the truth about Lukas, at least, might help heal some of those wounds that festered whenever she heard his name.

"Why won't you tell me everything?" Her voice cracked. "Other people know more than me about my own family."

Alex studied the row of license plates as if da Vinci himself had painted them. The pause was fine with her. So much had happened in the past two days that she was still trying to sort it out in her own mind.

Dakota had taken her out for lobster and corn on the cob last night like he'd promised. In public. Where everyone in Oak Bluffs could see. Not that she knew very many people who still lived on the island, but he seemed to know almost everyone who passed by their patio table. After dinner, they'd combed the beach for treasures that the storm had recovered, a dozen beautiful shells for her to display in her condo to remind herself always that God still worked miracles.

Between the calm water and a Bonine tablet, her stomach had weathered the boat ride back to the mainland just fine. She'd said goodbye to Captain Kiehl at the train station, knowing she might never see the man again, but the reconciliation was a glimpse of what she'd imagined so many years ago. Redemption where she'd expected it the least. Her short trip had filled her with hope that she might be able to redeem more of her story.

"I don't like to think about those days, Ember."

"I don't like to think about them either," she said. "But the memories keep coming back."

"I wish I could have protected you—"

"You have been the best of brothers, Alex. It was our parents' job to protect both of us."

Joseph and Elaine Heywood had, in their own way, thought they were caring well for their children when they'd all lived on the island. The Aryan Council was supposed to incite a new Reich, and their father thought he was leaving a gift—a triumphant legacy—for his kids and the next generation. He'd been furious when Alex refused to join them in Idaho; then he'd disowned his eighteen-year-old son. Ember hadn't been allowed to communicate with her brother during the seven years she'd spent on Eagle Lake.

The Aryan blood, the hatred, running through her veins had terrified her when she'd first returned to Martha's Vineyard until Alex explained that blood replaces itself several times a year. Every red and white cell was uniquely hers.

But not her DNA, and that's what she was fighting against. The DNA and years of indoctrination that her father couched as sermons. The hours of being told who she was supposed to hate even as she knew, from her earliest years, that it was wrong. She'd never wanted to hate anyone.

"When the social worker first called me, I didn't know what to do," Alex said. "Titus swore never to tell anyone that we were the Heywood children, but I still worried someone from the council would come looking for you."

Not everyone in their group had been apprehended at Eagle Lake, but the FBI had arrested fifteen men and women and found homes for their children. The bodies of Joseph and Elaine and five other members were recovered from the rubble.

Ember changed her last name to Ellis like her brother, as if they'd both immigrated to this island in search of freedom. The first name was her choice, and she'd picked Ember, not even thinking about the flames she'd left behind. To her it was about starting over. A spark for new beginnings as her mind and body recovered from the shock. The initial E to remind her always of her baby.

Later, when her mind began to heal, Alex said the ember of her name was about starting a new fire, one to spread truth instead of destruction.

She twirled the cherry drink, watching it funnel inside her glass. "Titus must have told his mother about us."

"She already knew." Alex looked away from the license plates, refocusing on his beer. "I suspect he talked to others on the island as well, but no one ever asked me about the Aryan Council or any of its members."

"Lukas did something that disturbed Mrs. Kiehl."

"He arrived from Germany right before Dad moved the group to Idaho," Alex said. "I remember him bragging about being the grandson of an SS officer and showing off a Death's Head ring to prove it. For all I know, he bought the ring at a costume shop, but if Mrs. Kiehl heard him talking about his grandfather or the ring, it might have been traumatic for her."

Ember remembered the ring, but she didn't remember Lukas talking about the SS, not that she even knew in her early teens what the

SS was. By the time they'd married, Lukas was an officer of the Aryan Council and that usurped everything else until he lit the match to ward off the FBI.

She'd returned to Eagle Lake once after college and walked the perimeter, trying to remember what happened that horrific night in the fire and fog, but those hours blurred in her mind. Long ago Alex had told her Elsie drowned, that the social worker called months after that terrible night to say they found a body. But when Ember called the FBI, the agent said they had no record—at least not that they would share with her—of finding a baby girl, and none of the news stories she'd read ever mentioned a baby.

She watched Alex closely, daring to ask the question again. "Do you still think Elsie drowned in the lake?"

Instead of answering her question, her brother sipped on his beer as if it could give him the strength he needed to soldier on.

"The truth, Alex."

His eyes were focused on the mantle of foam. "I don't know what happened to her."

"But you said—"

"The social worker thought she drowned, but they never found her body."

Ember's back slammed into the wood, her heart almost erupting through her chest. "She might still be alive—"

"It's doubtful."

She had no pictures of Elsie, but the memories were stamped in her mind. Lukas had told her he had their baby, as they were running away, and then he was gone. If Elsie hadn't died in the lake or fire, someone had to know where he'd taken her.

Ember began the tapping again, palms slapping her jeans. Even after all these years, the weight of her guilt threatened to drown her as well. She'd loved her baby fiercely in their months together. "Why did you lie to me?"

"You wouldn't have been able to think about anything else except finding her, and you were too young, too wounded, to be a mother. You needed to figure out your life first."

"But when I was older—"

"Nothing either of us can do will bring her back, Ember." Another sip of the beer. "I only wanted the best for you. Still do . . ."

"I know." Her brother had given up three years of his life to care for her.

"Some of these white supremacist groups never stop looking for their people," he said. "If you start searching for information, I'm afraid someone from the council will find you."

The social worker had warned her of this, and yet she'd hoped that with the passage of twenty years, Sarah Heywood had been forgotten. "I've been getting strange letters at work," she said, a chill traveling across her skin.

"From who?"

"I don't know. Security thinks someone found my name on the museum's website, and they're trying to scare me so I'll stop my work. The letters are postmarked from Boise."

He reached for her hand. "You have to be careful, Ember."

"I've never received anything at home," she said, trying to assure them both. "They're empty threats."

"Is your picture on the website?"

"No, just my academic work, but Lukas is in prison and the rest of the council scattered after the raid. Who else would send me letters?'

"I don't know, but someone could be biding their time."

She paused, not wanting to worry him anymore. "What if Elsie is still alive?"

"She's not—"

"It's possible, Alex. She could be in college or have started a family of her own by now." A legitimate one.

"Or living as a neo-Nazi if Lukas managed to hand her off to someone else . . ."

She tapped her hands a little harder. Grounding herself. "I need to start looking again."

"It will be an endless journey, I'm afraid."

"But I think it might be a journey that I need to take," she said slowly. "Just one more time."

Searching for what was behind her now so she didn't spend a lifetime, like Mrs. Kiehl, wondering what happened to someone she'd loved.

If Elsie had survived, she'd be an adult with a new name and, Ember prayed, a new life outside the hate.

"I'll make a few calls," Alex said. "See if I can find anyone who left the council."

"Thank you."

"Will you come back to the mountains with me tonight?" he asked. "Maggie and Saul have been begging to see you, and Tracy said she needs some Ember time."

"I'd love to."

Her niece and nephew greeted their dad with hugs and then they wrapped their arms around her. Saul crouched like a lion, pretending to attack, and when he banged his elbow on the fancy baluster, Tracy chased away his pain with her motherhood magic. A kiss and a cookie to make it better.

As Tracy fetched a tray of snacks for all of them, Ember wondered again what it would have been like to have a mom who'd cared well for her.

And what it would have been like to mother her own child.

If Elsie was still out there, Ember would find her.

And she hoped Lilly Kiehl could find out what happened to her mom.

HANNA

27

A lioness lounged on a wedge of sandstone, the autumn sun splashing over the reddened leaves across the new Tiergarten. On the cliff above, a lion paced along the stone as if he were trying to decide whether to protect his mate or make certain that she didn't step out of line.

Hanna watched the animals through bars as she waited for Frau Weber to arrive, a flock of whip-poor-wills and other exotic birds clattering inside an aviary nearby. Most of the zoo had been sculpted into rock so the animals had natural shelter inside their cages. Hitler had wanted this place to demonstrate the mystery and power of the Reich like everything he'd built in Nuremberg. Even the straw rooftops shimmered in the light.

Juden Nicht Erlaubt—that was the sign beside the ticket booth at the entrance. Just like every other business in Nuremberg, Jews were no longer permitted to visit the zoo, but ever since Grete had inquired about Hanna's friend's interest in the bells, Frau Weber brought the stories here.

Hanna had collected almost fifty biographies now. An entire archive hidden to preserve the heritage of those who'd been taken away.

Kolman had been gone for three months, and she'd only received two short letters, both of them postmarked from Berlin. He couldn't say where their team was working—the archaeological digs were highly confidential—but each time he said that he'd be home soon.

Other women might have longed for their husbands to return, but Hanna wished hers would stay in the field. She didn't like the way Kolman watched over her as if she were the enemy. Nor how he'd begun to talk about children.

While he was traveling, the driver made sure that Hanna stayed firmly in her cage. He fetched her for work each day and delivered her home, took her into Nuremberg to shop on Saturday afternoon and attend church on Sunday. But every Saturday morning she pedaled her bicycle a full kilometer down to the zoo alone. No one bothered her here.

The zookeeper opened a slot and threw a slab of rotting meat onto the stone, the lioness pouncing on the meal before her mate. The stench of it transported Hanna back to a dump in Nepal last year where she and her team had searched for Aryan roots. Nothing in that rubbish pile had connected the ancestral heritage of Germans to a pure Aryan race, but the Ahnenerbe had sent cages of live animals back home to be studied. Some of them, perhaps, had ended up in this zoo.

She shook her head, refocusing. That world was no longer hers to embrace.

A woman with a burgundy scarf and matching coat stepped up to watch the lions, her purse clutched in both hands, but when Hanna walked over to speak with her friend, an SS officer moved between them, a man she didn't recognize.

Hanna looked back at the lions, her heart racing. Had this man come looking for her?

Then she saw that he wasn't alone. A woman—his wife, she assumed—and two young children stepped up beside him. The little girl took his hand, and they watched the lions devour their meal.

Hanna didn't dare leave, but Frau Weber moved across the footpath to look at the jungle of birds perched in the branches, as if these creatures didn't realize there was a whole sky above their heads.

Others gathered to watch the lions, crowding the fenced rim, and Hanna meandered down the treed path, stopping to look at the rhinoceroses as they bathed in the mud. Then she walked past an enclosure with deer who didn't even bother to look up. Every animal, it seemed, had their own obsession.

No one else was on the trail beyond the deer, but Hanna continued, casually strolling through the trees. The end of this path looped around a pond filled with ducks imported from America, several wooden chairs at the edge for visitors to feed them.

The woman, her hair covered with the burgundy scarf, was sitting in one of the chairs. When she looked up, Hanna almost squealed. Instead of Frau Weber, Luisa was sitting in front of her.

Hanna caught her breath as she slipped into the second chair. If only she could wrap her arms around her cousin.

But she'd embrace the relief in her heart instead, grateful the Gestapo hadn't found Luisa.

"I've missed you so," she whispered.

A sad smile swept across Luisa's face. "I'm glad you were gone these past years. I didn't want you to see . . ."

And Hanna knew. Her public humiliation must have been horrific. The scarf covered Luisa's sheared head, but most of her hair would still be gone. "They shouldn't have done that to you."

Her cousin looked back at the ducks swarming toward them as if they were about to enjoy a bounty of food, at the weeping willow draped over the edge of the pond. "It's only going to get worse."

"Have you received word from Paul?"

"One postcard," she said. "He wrote that he was taking a vacation, as if it was perfectly normal for my husband to be going on a holiday alone. At the time I was in prison for the crime of marrying him, so there was no vacation for me."

"Did the card say where he was going?"

Luisa shook her head, the lines in her forehead deep as if decades of worry had hollowed out her skin. "He said that he would send for me as soon as I was out, but at the bottom, he scribbled an X over his name, as if he'd made a mistake, then wrote out his name again. It was a signal between us, that I needed to hide the moment they released me from jail."

"They're still searching for you."

Luisa nodded. "Someone told them I was talking to the Jewish people, writing down their stories. The Nazis can't let anyone find out the truth of what they're doing."

One of the ducks lifted its wings, attempting to fly, but its wings were clipped.

"Another of Frau Weber's customers has been sent away," Luisa whispered. "They barely had time to pack their things."

Hanna leaned back against the wooden slats, her head pounding.

"The woman told Frau Weber there isn't enough work for her family in Nuremberg. The government has found a place for them to relocate."

"It's a lie," Hanna said, "about the work. With all the men being sent to the front, there are plenty of jobs in Nuremberg."

"Not if you're Jewish."

She closed her eyes, remembering the despondent men and

women she saw corralled together in Paris. "Where could they possibly be relocating them?"

"To a tent camp outside town at first, where Nazi Party members used to stay during the rallies. More trucks transport them away from there, but no one seems to know where they go next."

The stories they'd gathered were only part of the biographies. What happened to these people after they left Nuremberg?

"Where is Frau Weber?" she asked.

"Someone is watching her apartment. She can't meet you here anymore."

Hanna wanted to know every detail, where Luisa lived now and how Frau Weber knew she was being watched, but details seemed to be dangerous these days. "We'll have to find another way to exchange the stories."

"The walls feel as if they are closing in around us." Luisa checked the scarf on her head, pulling it close around her face. "Do you really think it matters, our collecting these stories?"

Hanna pondered the question. "I think it will matter very much to the families when this is over and perhaps to the rest of the world."

"The world doesn't care what happens to the people of Germany."

"They will once they know the truth," Hanna said. "We can't fight the Nazis now, but these stories will condemn them after the war."

Luisa unclasped her purse, and Hanna knew their time was coming to a close. Luisa's parents had died decades ago, before she came to live at the lodge, and the two of them had grown up together, the best of friends. Now the only family they had left was each other.

"Do you still have the key to the lodge?" Hanna asked.

"I do."

"It will always be your home."

"I can't return," Luisa said, shaking her head. "You're married to a member of the SS."

"It's the safest place of all when he's traveling."

Luisa pulled an envelope from her purse. "Here are the last of the stories."

"I'll make sure—"

Luisa's eyes grew wide before she looked back out at the weeping willow. The officer and his family had wandered up beside them, the wife holding a brown bag with bread for the ducks.

The girl tore a piece from the loaf and held out a portion of it for Hanna. "Would you like some?"

She took the bread, her hand trembling. Luisa was gone, but the envelope had fluttered to the ground, a flag waving between the chairs.

Hanna didn't dare reach out for it now, but she scooted her chair over as if she were trying to get closer to the ducks, covering the envelope when she reached forward with her offering of bread. The duck gobbled it, and the girl handed her another piece.

If she kept her gaze forward, her eyes on the ducks, she hoped the officer would keep his gaze focused on the water as well.

The wife sat in the chair that Luisa had just vacated, a young boy on her lap.

"Where did your friend go?" the girl asked.

"The elephant house. Her family is waiting for her there."

The officer turned to Hanna. "Are you alone?"

"Gunther!" his wife reprimanded, but he didn't rescind the question.

"My husband is traveling. He's also with the Schutzstaffel."

The man looked doubtful. "What is his name?"

"Standartenführer Strauss."

"I know your husband," he said. "I didn't realize his wife had moved to Nuremberg."

"I grew up here." Hanna tossed another piece of bread into the water. "But I've only been back since the spring."

"I suspect your husband is traveling as much as mine," the woman said, gazing over at her husband as if she might heil him. "We should have lunch together when our children are in school."

"I'm actually working at the museum," Hanna explained.

The woman looked at her as if she had the plague. "Your husband's making you work?"

She shrugged. "I like to stay busy."

"But what about your children?"

Why did everyone in this Reich think she should have a child? She'd thanked God almost every day that she hadn't gotten pregnant while Kolman was home.

"We don't have any children yet."

"You won't be able to work at the museum after your first one is born," the woman said. "I know we're supposed to have four, but I can barely keep up with my two."

"I'm not sure how I could possibly stop working."

The officer rounded up his family quickly as if Hanna might contaminate all of them with her progressive thoughts. When they continued down the path, Hanna secured the envelope inside her coat; then she hurried to the entrance before bicycling home. She'd hide those papers in the labyrinth at first light.

As Hanna neared the lodge, a silver Mercedes-Benz pulled up behind her, trailing her to the drive. Her heart pounded as she stepped off the bicycle, holding it close to her side as she waited for the door to open, her breath labored more from fear than bicycling up the hill.

Did the SS officer or his wife suspect her guilt? Or had the Gestapo finally returned?

The legs of a gray uniform exited the automobile first; then Kolman stepped out onto the gravel.

And her bicycle clattered to the ground.

"Hello, Hanna," he said, the visor on his cap slightly askew, an olive-colored scarf draped around his neck.

"Kolman—"

Someone else was in the back seat. A flash of blonde hair, the glimpse of an arm.

Kolman reached back into the vehicle and pulled out a girl who could be no more than four. Maybe just three.

"I've brought you a gift," he said as if this person were another bottle of French wine, as if Hanna would be pleased with his extravagance.

She stared down at the girl and saw the mutual terror in eyes as blue as the cornflowers that grew each summer in her meadow, their blossoms wilted now from the cold. "You can't just bring me a child."

"Her name is Lilly." Kolman released her hand and lifted a suitcase out of the trunk. "Lilly Strauss."

Hanna steadied herself against the truck. "You have a daughter?"

"*We* have a daughter." Kolman nodded at the child. "Lilly, meet your new mother."

In hindsight, she should have greeted the frightened girl, secured her in her arms.

Instead Hanna ran. All the way up to the abbey, to the labyrinth where her mother used to pray.

The Reich had made her a wife and now it was forcing her to become a mother.

As she dug her hands into the dirt, buried the stories in a tin, it felt as if she were burying the remnants of her life in this labyrinth as well.

28

EMBER

"So the Dakota Ban is over?" Brooke asked, pointing a fork at her cell phone like a spear.

"I suppose so."

This afternoon, like most Mondays when the sun was out, Brooke had called from a café in Minneapolis while Ember ate lunch on steps by the World War II Memorial, right in front of the fountain.

Brooke knew she'd grown up in Idaho, but Ember had never told her friend about the Aryan Council. About Lukas or Elsie. For the past twenty years, Brooke had been her normal on those days when the walls she'd built around her were crumbling.

"It's about time," Brooke said. "He's a good guy, you know."

Ember shook her head. "I don't know that. I only spent a few hours with him."

"You spent the night!"

She swirled lemon LaCroix in its can. "We slept in the same house. It's different."

"But he apologized."

"Indeed."

Brooke stopped to eat a bite of her salad. "And took you out for dinner."

"Lobster at the marina."

"And then he transported you on his *boat* to the bus station."

"I forgave him, Brooke. Really. But you know what a nice guy he pretended to be before he invited me to join him on that football field."

"No one, except you, thought he was nice back in high school. Even Alecia was wary."

A duck paddled along the perimeter of the pond. "So he's changed."

"I'd say. Have you heard from him since Boston?"

"He texted from Paris. Just making sure that I got home safely. And then . . ." She took a long sip of LaCroix, knowing that Brooke was about to freak out.

"Ember?"

"He has a long layover at Dulles this evening and asked if I wanted to get coffee before he takes off again." Actually he'd asked if she and Noah wanted to have coffee, but she told him that Noah already had plans.

"And his ulterior motive for a coffee date would be?"

"I don't know. My world's flipped upside down."

"Maybe he'll ask you out when he gets back. On a real date with white tablecloths and tiny forks and cocktails with fruit in them."

"He won't." She took another long drink. "He kind of thinks I have a boyfriend."

"Ember—"

"I couldn't help it. Noah texted, and . . ."

"You wanted Dakota to think you were taken by a ten-year-old?'

"It seemed like a good strategy at the time."

"Well, you'll have to unstrategize." A giant rolling of eyes followed Brooke's words lest the impact get lost in the transmission.

"I'm not interested in Dakota."

"Ember," Brooke said again, leaning closer to the screen. Her friend always flared her nostrils like a dragon when she was about to break down a lecture. "Would you like the man if you just met him? At church or work or something?"

She didn't want to admit it, but . . . "I suppose I'd be intrigued."

Brooke sighed. "Finally, some honesty."

"I'm not trying to be deceptive. Just avoiding a repeat."

"You think Dakota's going to be homecoming king again?"

"Hardly."

"Then give him an opportunity to redeem himself."

She thought of the sign hanging on the cottage door about second chances. "If I do, it will be the last one." Two was more than enough.

Brooke dug into her salad and took another bite. "So you're going to tell him that Noah is a kid?"

"Not yet."

"There's no one quite like you, Ember."

She smiled. "I'm taking that as a compliment."

"That's how it was intended."

Her phone buzzed from the alarm, and she turned it off. "I have to go dissert for a few more hours."

Brooke rolled her eyes again. "*Dissert* is not a word."

"It most certainly is."

"Right—"

"Look it up. And give those children of yours a hug from me."

She tossed her foam to-go container in a trash can and crossed back over Independence Avenue, weaving around tourists who nibbled on ice cream sandwiches and half-baked pizza slices from carts along the National Mall.

She and Alex had spent the past twenty years hiding in plain sight, the bond of their secrets gluing them together. Tracy knew their story—Alex had told her before they married—and the Kiehl family knew at least part of it.

Someday soon she would entrust Brooke with the entire version. *You're not that girl.*

That's what Brooke liked to tell her, about the insecure fifteen-year-old who'd stepped into her high school in 2000, shaking inside and out. The wounds were much deeper than a homecoming night prank. They'd started the day she was born.

Even though she'd promised herself to wait until after she completed her dissertation to search again for Elsie, she'd spent the weekend reading everything she could find about the Aryan Council, every interview from those who escaped, the FBI public files, the court records when Lukas was convicted. But they were all things she'd read before. The interviewees talked about Joseph Heywood and some talked about her mother, but no one mentioned their daughter, Sarah, or their son and certainly not a baby girl.

This time the archives and their detailed records didn't hold the truth.

So strange, this feeling of being erased. Her history gone except what she and Alex remembered together. Sometimes, she'd learned over the years, she had to be okay with the not knowing. Only a miracle would help her find a baby who'd never even been certified at birth.

Inside the museum, one of the few remaining Auschwitz survivors was sharing her story with a long line of students waiting to meet her. Words did matter, Ember thought, especially the stories. Stories could change the minds of their youth.

While she might never be able to find out what happened to Elsie, Mrs. Kiehl needed to know where her mom had gone. If the information was available, Ember would find it. To reunite a daughter with her mother by finding the truth.

Rebekah May was waiting when Ember returned to her office, sitting in Ember's chair, a cell phone in her hands.

Ember sighed as she dropped herself into the chair reserved for her officemate. "Another letter?"

The woman rotated her screen.

A picture of Ember was on it. Taken through the window of her condo, hovering over a giant bowl of ice cream at the kitchen counter, Noah with his golden spoon beside her.

Ember shook her head, her voice trembling when she spoke again. "He knows where I live."

"I'm afraid so." The woman lowered the phone. "Is that your son?"

"No, he lives across the hall with his dad."

"I need to call his father."

Ember gave her the phone number. What were they going to tell Noah? Routines like their daily ice cream date steadied him. Steadied both of them.

"Where was this postmarked?" she asked.

"Boise. He or she must have someone here in Washington, helping them."

Ember tapped her heels on the carpet. "How did he find my address?"

"He probably hired someone to tail you home." Rebekah nodded toward Ember's laptop. "But usually these kinds of people are trolling social media accounts instead of mailing letters."

"I avoid social media to the best of my ability," she said. "The only people I friend are those I know in real life."

"A wise choice." Rebekah clicked on her cell phone again. To a scan of the envelope, postmarked from Idaho, and a brief diatribe on lined paper.

Ember's heart sank when she looked down.

The envelope was addressed to Ember Ellis at the Holocaust Memorial Museum.

But the letter was addressed to Sarah.

HANNA

Hanna returned to the kitchen at dusk, her face streaked from the anger expunged with her tears. Kolman was still in his uniform, eating potato pancakes straight from their frying pan.

"Where's the girl?" she asked.

"Playing in the attic."

"How am I supposed to work at the museum and care for a child?"

"Restoring our Reich is the most important work we can do," he said. "We're raising the next generation for our country."

"You have to take her back," Hanna said. "To her family."

"There is no taking her back. We've already adopted her."

Was this what Kolman had planned all along? If she didn't conceive, he would begin bringing her *Kinder*? Four of them, according to the woman at the zoo, to solidify his position with the SS.

Hanna shook her head. "You can't adopt a child without my permission."

He stabbed a pancake with his fork and folded it. "Are you expecting a baby?"

"Not that I'm aware of."

"Himmler is requiring his officers who don't have children to adopt."

"But where are her parents?"

"She lost them both in a raid," he said sadly.

Hanna collapsed into a chair. No child should be without parents, but another woman would make a much better mother for Lilly. Like the SS wife at the zoo. "I'll find her a good home."

He pulled an envelope from the inside of his jacket, placed it on the table. "It's her medical certificate. I took the liberty of having a social worker sign all the adoption paperwork for you."

Hanna opened the envelope, hoping for more information about Lilly's family, but the certificate listed her name as Lilly Strauss. "What was her former surname?"

"I don't know."

"The adoption papers would have it."

"The agency kept most of the papers, but the social worker sent these along." He placed a manual beside the envelope. *The German Mother and Her First Child.*

As if she could learn motherhood from a book.

Then he tossed a copy of *NS-Frauen-Warte* on top of it, the magazine featuring a chubby blonde-haired girl in the loving arms of her mother.

Hanna looked back up at Kolman; his lips were pressed together, as stiff as his hair. This man she'd married had told her little about his past. It was entirely possible that this girl really was a Strauss. Kolman might have neglected to mention that he had a child.

"Where did you adopt her from?" she asked.

"A home near Berlin."

Hanna left the book and magazine on the counter and climbed up to the attic. Lilly was staring at the miniature tricycle, then at the hobbyhorse beside it.

Had she lost all of her toys during the raid?

She studied the girl's straw-blonde hair, a single braid that coiled across her crown, the rest pouring down her back. Pale eyes that changed between green and blue in the attic light. She was the perfect specimen of Nordic blood.

Something tugged inside Hanna, her own memories of childhood. And she saw herself in this girl's face, in the hours after Vater returned from the hospital alone. Eight years old, and the grief of it almost overwhelmed her.

With her mother's death, Hanna had been lost until Luisa arrived at the lodge. It was her cousin who'd held out a hand, offering friendship when she so desperately needed a friend. They'd spent a decade playing, working, and dreaming together until Hanna left for college.

No matter who fathered Lilly, she also needed someone to care for her.

"Your name is Lilly?" Hanna asked.

"Ja," the girl said quietly.

"What is your surname?"

"Strauss," she said as if she'd known no other name.

"How old are you, Lilly?"

"Four."

"And where is your Vater?"

"I don't know." The words seemed to wobble out of her mouth as if she wasn't quite sure of them. She was so young; she might not even know if Kolman was her father.

Lilly pointed at the tricycle before asking her own question. "What is this?"

Hanna eyed her curiously. "You don't know?"

"Nein."

"Ein Dreirad," Hanna said slowly. Perhaps the trauma of losing her mother made her forget some of her words.

"Dreirad," Lilly repeated.

"Very good." Hanna held out her hand. "Let's find you a place to sleep while we sort this out."

A full-size hobbyhorse stood at the end of Jonny's former bed, and Lilly climbed on it, tentative at first. Hanna pushed the girl slowly until Lilly began a steady rhythm on the wooden floor. Then she smiled as if the rockers transported her to another place, as if she'd ridden straight out of Germany, into a world where parents lived forever.

Hanna tied an apron over her blouse and boiled dumplings for the girl, frying them in butter. Lilly engulfed the dinner of melted cheese and *Spätzle* as if she hadn't eaten in days.

With Kolman busy at the desk, Hanna sprinkled salts into the warm bath upstairs and found a white nightie in Lilly's suitcase. Once the girl smelled like soap and chamomile, she climbed into bed. "Thank you for supper."

"You're quite welcome." Hanna eyed her from the doorway. She should probably read her a story or kiss her on the forehead or at least help her say prayers, but she couldn't pretend like Kolman that they'd suddenly become parents. If Kolman wasn't this girl's father, there must be family left in Berlin. Someone would be looking for her.

Kolman was in the great hall, transferring notes into a ledger. "You've taken well to her," he said, his eyes on the book.

She sat in the wingback chair beside him. "Was the team digging near Berlin?"

"The caseworker brought her to me after I put in the request."

"You can't collect children, Kolman. Not without my permission."

His eyebrows slid up. "You would have given permission?"

She didn't answer.

"You collect things, Hanna. It's what you do. Why not collect a family?"

"Because that's not how families are made."

"Who set the rules for how a family is formed?"

Himmler did, she wanted to say, with his mandate that SS officers needed to father at least four children.

But family, good or bad, was blood running through one's veins. If she and Kolman had a baby, God forbid, she would care for it. She just hadn't signed the papers to care for a four-year-old who wasn't hers, a girl who must have blood family someplace else.

"Are you sure you didn't fetch Lilly from Hanover?"

He turned slowly, the lightning bolt on his collar pointed toward her. "What are you asking?"

"Did you father this child?"

He swore. "Of course not."

"Then we need to look for Lilly's family. Someone must be searching for her. A sibling or grandparent or aunt . . ."

"The social worker already looked. It's not like the government wants to take children from their homes, Hanna, but either way, this is not about you or me or what we want. This is about caring for our own people. Building a new society."

She sank back into the upholstered chair, remembering the thousands who'd gathered on the rally grounds below this hill in 1934. The Cathedral of Light, the Nazis had called it, with columns of searchlights shooting upward into the night sky, as if taunting the Almighty with their power.

Kolman had probably been there with all the party's elite. The Nazi Party had made themselves into a family, canopied by this mission to step into the role of God and redeem what people had messed up—the purity of the human race.

She'd go to Berlin on her own, once Kolman left again. He couldn't argue with her if she found Lilly's family. The Nazis wanted to create the perfect family, not pull one apart.

She tapped her fingers against a filing cabinet. "Lilly needs things. Clothes and such."

"You can shop for her on Monday."

"But the museum—"

"You no longer need to work there."

All their months together in the field, Kolman had respected—valued—her and her work, but now he saw her as something different. Like one of the fixtures, it seemed, inside his new home.

She ripped the apron off, tossed it onto the floor. "I'm not resigning my position."

"Then find someone to watch her."

Hanna leaned forward again. "She seems to be struggling with some of her words."

"She'll be confused for a while," Kolman said. "She's been living in a foster home for the past year, but she comes from a strong family. Her father died in the Wehrmacht."

Hanna's eyes narrowed. "I thought her parents died in a bombing."

"The mother's body was found with Lilly in a bombed house. According to the social worker, she was a notable woman in their community."

"Do you know their last name?" she asked again.

"She's a Strauss now. That's all that matters. I know you'll take good care of her while I'm gone."

"You can't just come and go from this house whenever you please, Kolman. Bringing me children. You need to tell me where you are and when you are coming back."

His eyes narrowed. "So you can hide things from me?"

She stiffened. "So I'm not surprised to find someone here when I come home."

"Why are you hiding things, love?"

She glanced up at the portrait of Hitler, the unwavering gaze that unnerved her, then lowered her eyes back to meet her husband's. "I don't know what you're talking about."

"Your friend Marianne Weber is a Jew lover."

She shivered at the term, as if it were a crime to love their neighbor.

"Frau Weber is the best seamstress in Nuremberg. She has many customers in town."

"Stay away from her, Hanna, or you will get us both in trouble."

But he'd also told her to find help for Lilly, and Frau Weber needed the work. Perhaps she could step in as a nanny, just until Hanna was able to find Lilly's family. And it would give her a viable reason to visit every day and gather any remaining stories.

"Frau Weber was my mother's best friend," Hanna said. "You brought me a child, and she is the only one I trust to take care of her. Unless you want to watch Lilly while you're home . . ."

He looked back down at the ledger. "I am leaving again soon."

"You don't treat me like your wife, Kolman. You treat me like a mistress, not bothering to tell me where you are or when you will be home."

"Wife. Mistress. They are both the same really."

That smirk, she wanted to scrub it right off his face. This person before her was nothing like the man she'd worked with in the field.

"Why did you ask me to marry you?"

He shuffled through a stack of papers as if he had something of vast importance to find.

Since Himmler had united them in marriage, she hadn't spent much time reflecting back on the time in the vineyard when Kolman had proposed, but she saw it all again in the film of her mind, those moments after Kolman read the telegram from Himmler, when she'd run down the hill.

Somehow she'd convinced herself that he had proposed because he loved her. Or respected her, at least. But after their short honeymoon, he'd not only disappeared back into himself, he had disappeared almost completely from her life. It wouldn't be any different, she suspected, even now that he'd adopted a daughter.

Not that she minded his departures, but why had Himmler insisted they marry if Kolman didn't want her as his wife?

Her mind rolled back further on that fateful evening in France, to the telegram that Kolman had received right before he'd asked her to marry him. The telegram that stole her job away.

But perhaps it wasn't an impulsive offer. Perhaps this marriage was a direct command from above, like the fathering of children.

"Himmler ordered you to marry me," she said slowly. "He wanted me to leave the Ahnenerbe, but he didn't want me to go far."

"It wasn't an order," Kolman said, looking back over at her. "Himmler suggested that we marry."

"And you agreed."

"Of course."

Not only had she not wanted to marry Kolman, he hadn't wanted to marry her. The Reich had required it of him.

While she was simply biding her time, Kolman would do anything to further Himmler's plans, including marry an Aryan woman to build a family from the strongest of German stock. A woman who happened to own property outside this prized Nazi town, in a house that had recently been vacated.

"Did you know Luisa and Paul were gone before you proposed?"

"I am not privy to such things," he said.

But this marriage still bought him a house in the country. A wife to meet his needs whenever he liked. Another mother for the Reich.

Did Himmler have a further purpose for their union?

She stood up. "I'm an Aryan means to an end."

When she turned away, Kolman grabbed her arm, whirling her around. She felt as if her bone might snap. "There are things you don't understand, Hanna. Things much bigger than us."

Like a dictator who was misusing his people. She almost said the words, but Kolman's eyes were fierce, the gray in them clouding the blue.

Fear was her protector now, keeping her pride in check.

"You are doing a great service to our Reich," he said.

The first compliment he'd paid her since their wedding day.

Before she went to bed, Hanna checked on the girl who'd fallen asleep in Jonny's room. Like her own mother, she wanted to think, once checked on her.

During the night, she heard a cry. Kolman didn't move beside her, so she hopped out of bed and hurried down the hall. Lilly was sitting up, gazing straight ahead, staring in fright as if someone else were in the room.

Hanna turned on the light, hoping it would scare away the haunts like it had done when she was a girl.

"Nie," Lilly said, under her breath at first. Then she began to scream the word as if no one could hear, her eyes wide-open.

"It's all right," Hanna said, reaching out her arm.

Lilly fought back, kicking and screaming. Clawing at Hanna's sleeve. Sweat poured down her cheeks, her eyes wild as if no comfort could be found. Shouting more words that Hanna didn't understand.

Hanna looked down at the pricks of blood on her skin. How was she supposed to console this child now?

"Lilly," she whispered and then she said her name a bit louder. But whether the girl was awake or asleep, she couldn't tell. Whatever frightened her had settled deep into her mind. No comfort was to be had.

"You'll have to leave her be," Kolman said from the door.

Lilly was tossing off all the covers now, throwing them over the hobbyhorse, spilling blankets and pillows across the floor.

"I can't leave her like this."

"There's nothing you can do about it. She must be remembering the bombs."

"I will sit here then, until it passes."

Kolman reached for Hanna's arm again, tried to pull her away, but Hanna wouldn't leave her to face this torment alone.

When Kolman finally closed the door, she propped herself up on a pillow as Lilly screamed for her mama.

Eventually the girl quieted, falling back asleep on the tumbled mess of covers, and Hanna pulled a blanket off the bed, too tired to walk back up the hall.

She was awakened by footsteps in the morning. Minutes later, she crossed the corridor and looked out the window. Kolman was walking through the meadow again, this time with a messenger bag strapped over his shoulder, the olive scarf around his neck.

Lilly woke with bags under her eyes.

"How did you sleep?" Hanna asked as she made a breakfast of sausage and toast for her guest.

"Fine."

In her eyes, Hanna saw the frightened girl that she once was.

"You don't have to be afraid anymore," Hanna said.

Lilly stood up a bit taller. *"Ich bin Deutsche."*

As if she had to convince Hanna that she was German.

30

EMBER

Lawrence was a solid foot taller than Ember, his skin as dark as Noah's. A man who didn't mince words as he drove her home in a gray BMW and escorted her up to the condo so she could pack.

He'd worked in security for almost thirty years and didn't seem to be the least bit nervous about a stalker, but Ember was a wreck.

We must secure the existence of our people and a future for white children.

The author of the letter addressed to Sarah had repeated this familiar mantra in block letters. Fourteen words that had been ingrained in her when she was a girl.

The writer knew the slogan, and he knew both of her names, but it was the next sentence that did her in.

Stop playing with the—

Her lunch had ended up on Rebekah May's lap.

After she helped the woman clean up, she told their head of security everything. About her parents. The Aryan Council. The man who'd been sent to prison. Even the daughter she'd lost.

Someone from the Aryan Council might threaten her, but she wouldn't allow them to harm Noah.

Rebekah assured her that she would talk to law enforcement in Idaho and to Noah's father. Then she suggested that Ember leave for Nuremberg right away.

On the car ride home, Ember had called Noah's dad, and Jack said that he'd meet Noah at the bus stop. The airline hadn't been able to change her ticket, but Alex invited her to stay with his family in Pennsylvania, for as long as she needed to hide out.

How had the Aryan Council found her now? She'd been gone for twenty years with no communication and a completely different name.

Would someone follow her up to the Poconos if she went north for a few nights? Would they threaten her brother?

That thought sent another bolt of fear up her spine—she wouldn't do anything to jeopardize Alex or his family.

The doorbell rang, and she glanced at the clock in her bedroom. It was only 3:30. Jack had promised that he'd be at the bus stop, but the man didn't always keep track of his promises. If Noah's bus had come early, she had to get him out of the hallway.

Lawrence was looking through the peephole when she stepped out of her bedroom, a toiletries bag in her hand.

"Is it a boy?" she asked.

"A man." He pulled a gun out from under his jacket. "You recognize him?"

Her heart began to race again as she glanced tentatively through the hole, afraid of who might be looking back, but it wasn't a stranger from Idaho. It was Dakota, dressed in a pilot's uniform with a navy cap and gold wings on his jacket.

He wasn't supposed to meet her for coffee until five, but in all the confusion, she'd forgotten he was even flying in.

"It's a friend," she said, stepping back from the door.

Lawrence looked back into the hole. "Are you certain?"

"Yes." This time she was certain. "I've known him since high school."

Lawrence slipped the weapon back into its holster, but he stood nearby as she opened the door.

Dakota took off his cap before holding out his hand to Lawrence. "You must be Noah."

The security guard didn't shake it. "No."

Dakota glanced back and forth between them. "My flight got in early. I texted you."

"I didn't get your message yet," she said, waving Dakota across the threshold. "Lawrence is from my office. I'm afraid I can't have coffee. I have to leave for—"

She wasn't entirely certain where she was going, but she told him about the threatening letter, about needing to leave Washington while law enforcement tried to find out who'd been stalking her.

He raked his hand back through his curly hair, whiskers shadowing his face. "I thought you were going to Nuremberg this week."

"My flight is scheduled for Friday." She locked the door behind him. "The airline wasn't able to change my ticket."

"You mind if I make a call or two while you pack?" he asked, pointing at the bag in her hand. "I'll stay out of the way."

She directed Dakota up to the loft; then she tossed her bag into a chair and reached for the doorknob. If Jack didn't come home, she needed to meet Noah at the bus stop.

The doorbell rang again before she opened it.

"This time it should be a ten-year-old," she told Lawrence. "It's a regular party around here."

Noah held up his gold spoon on the other side of the door. "Surprise!"

She waved him quickly into the room. "What a pleasant surprise."

He stopped when he saw Lawrence. "Who are you?"

"I'm helping Ms. Ellis today."

Noah wielded his spoon at the guard. "I can help her."

Ember directed him toward the kitchen. "You can help me most by eating what's left of my ice cream."

Noah kept his eyes on Lawrence as he climbed onto a stool. She pulled the Phish Food out of the freezer and handed over the whole tub before texting Jack, telling him that he must come home right away.

The staircase creaked, and she braced herself at the sound of Dakota's steps, moving down toward the kitchen.

"If you can be at Dulles by 5:30," he said, "a friend can switch your flight to one headed to Frankfurt tonight. Then you can take a train from there to Nuremberg."

She blinked, processing yet another change, a much better one so she didn't endanger Alex or his family. "Thank you, Dakota."

"I'm glad it worked out."

It was a simple kindness, this willingness to help her once again when she hadn't even asked. And it disarmed her.

She glanced down at Noah, scooping the Phish Food into his mouth at a rapid pace, the gold spoon gleaming in the overhead light. Now to introduce Dakota to the only barrier left between them.

"I can leave here in about fifteen minutes," she said, "but first, I'd like you to meet one of my best friends."

Dakota smiled at Noah. "Hi there."

The boy didn't look up, his gaze focused solely on the caramel and fudge, and she lost the courage to say his name.

Dakota checked his watch, then sat down on the other stool. "What are you eating?"

"Phish Food." Noah's spoon dug back into the tub as if he were mining for treasure, his lips coated in chocolate.

"I'm Dakota." He drummed his hands on the counter, waiting for a moment before he asked, "What's your name?"

"Noah."

The word sank like an anchor between them before Dakota turned back. Even though he spoke to Noah, his eyes were on her. "Ember's told me a little about you."

Noah's eyes narrowed as if she'd betrayed him. "We're supposed to be remembering right now."

"You're right," she said, checking her phone. Jack had texted to say he was on his way. If she left in a half hour, she could still make it to the airport by 5:30.

She sat down on the third stool, focusing back on the youngest man in the room. "What did you remember today?"

He smiled. "After you divide a number, you can add it right back up again."

"That's a good thing to remember."

"And no matter how many times you divide, it can always go back together." He took another bite, his mouth full when he spoke again. "What did you remember today?"

She hesitated, avoiding Dakota's gaze. "I remembered that if you can forgive what happened in the past, it's possible to redeem the future."

"Second chances," Dakota whispered.

And in her heart, she agreed.

31

LILLY

NUREMBERG

SPRING 1941

The new mama picked up a gold piece and held it out to her. "What is this?"

"*Löffel,*" Lilly said, the word for "spoon" rolling across her tongue. She'd learned lots of new words as they played with the dollhouses.

Mami stood to reach for something in the tiny bedroom that looked a lot like Lilly's room downstairs. Along the wall were several small toys, and she held up a bat.

"*Der Schläger.*" Like the bat her brothers used to play with in *palant,* except she must call the game *Schlagball* now.

"My brother used to play *Schlagball,*" Mami said with a smile.

"Mine too."

When Mami's eyes grew big, Lilly realized she'd made a mistake.

This woman wasn't mean like the matron. She didn't whip Lilly when she said the wrong words or send doctors to measure her up.

Would she hit her now? Feed her to the wolves? Lilly braced herself for a slap that never came.

"You have a brother?" Mami asked.

Her stomach tightened like the metal of a nutcracker, crushing everything inside. How could she answer *Ja* to this question? She wasn't supposed to talk about her old family. The matron said someone would tell if Lilly talked, and the wolves were always waiting in the woods.

Mami set the bat along the wall again. "What was your brother's name?"

"I'm not supposed to . . ."

"Who told you not to speak about your brother?"

"The woman at the sunny home," Lilly said.

"You're safe to speak the truth here."

Lilly shook her head. The truth was never safe, even if she wrapped it up in cotton.

"What was your brother's name?" Mami asked.

Antoni, she wanted to say. *And Piotr.* "I don't have any brothers."

"But you just said—"

"No brothers."

"Do you remember anyone from your family?"

"No."

Mami peeled back a blue bedcovering as if she was waking up the doll who'd been tucked underneath. "I'm sorry, Lilly. It hurts very much to lose a family."

But she hadn't lost her family. They'd been taken away.

At least that's what she thought. Her old mama's face was a blur now; so were the smiles of her brothers. And no matter how hard she tried, she couldn't even remember what her papa looked like. Just the shine of his eagle buttons, the kiss on her cheek before he left for the war.

Sometimes she wondered if her other family was even real. Piotr and Antoni. Mama and Papa. What if they were pretend, like the figures in these dollhouses, wandering in and out of her strange dreams?

Her new father was gone most of the time. He polished the buttons on his uniform as well, but he never said goodbye, never kissed her head before he left.

And this mama never seemed happy to see him when he came home. They would go away together, letting Lilly play with the dollhouses on her own. Sometimes, after he left, she could hear Mami crying, but she never cried when Lilly was around.

The windows began to glow, and Mami looked at her watch. "It's time for our walk."

Later today Lilly would go to Frau Weber's apartment to help bake *Apfelkuchen* and play with her cat. Or she'd help Mami at the museum, putting things into boxes and covering them with scratchy sheets.

But each morning, before they rode into town, they walked up the hill to a broken church so Mami could pray while Lilly played with a collection of sticks and leaves.

Her old mama used to pray as well, except she knelt by her bed.

Was that mama still praying? Perhaps she had adopted another daughter. Perhaps, one day, another woman would adopt Lilly, but she liked it here for now with Mami and Frau Weber. It was much better than the sunny home.

A stuffed elephant under her arm, Lilly followed Mami down the front steps, out into the meadow and the trees. Something stirred the branches, and she reached for Mami's hand, hidden under a messenger bag.

They didn't have wolves here—that's what Mami had said—only in Poland. But that's not what the matron told her, and the matron was always right.

A German wolf would eat her for breakfast.

"Stay close." Mami wasn't worried about wolves, but the cliffs, she'd said, were dangerous. And there were holes in this forest that could swallow up a girl.

She clung to Mami so she wouldn't get swallowed.

"Will you tell me a story?" Lilly asked. Mami told the most wonderful stories about nuns who'd helped people during something called a plague. About artists and inventors and a woman named Katharine who died because she believed in Jesus.

"Of course," Mami said as they hiked around mossy stones and fallen branches. "Have I told you about the celestial war?"

Lilly shook her head.

"Four hundred years ago, the strangest thing happened right here above the trees."

"To the nuns?"

"No, the nuns were gone by then, but all the people in Nuremberg woke to a sky full of color."

Like the sun, Lilly imagined, when it didn't want to go to bed, spilling its paint across the blue.

"Different colors and all sorts of shapes," Mami continued. "There were spheres and wheels and smoke rolling in the air. And a giant black sword as if the heavenly beings were warring over Nuremberg."

Lilly didn't understand all the words, but she knew *sword*.

"Then the shapes disappeared," Mami said. "And all we have left to remember that battle is an engraving and the description of an artist who saw it. He believed that a merciful God was sending a warning to Nuremberg. That God would punish this town if they didn't repent and return to living as His children."

Lilly looked up at the sky, searching for a sword in the clouds.

Was God going to whip her for losing her parents?

"Wait inside for me," Mami said, pointing at the abbey walls.

Instead of building a house with branches, Lilly sat on a large rock, swinging her legs over the edge. She didn't like being by herself while Mami was praying. More than anything, she hated being alone.

A noise in the trees, a shuffle of leaves, and she jumped off the rock. Tiptoeing to the edge of the wall, she hid behind a tree so Mami could hear her if she screamed.

Her new mama moved in a circle as if she were playing a game. Then she knelt in the grass and opened her bag. Inside was a *Löffel*, much bigger than the one from the dollhouse. And she began to dig.

Why was Mami making another hole when there were already so many in this forest? Intrigued, Lilly began to step forward, but Mami had said she wasn't allowed to walk in these woods alone. So she waited behind the tree trunk with her elephant, peeking out as Mami placed a cookie tin in the soil.

When Mami finished, she put her spoon back into her bag and moved something over the hole. Then she began to circle through the grass again.

Lilly rushed back to the church.

Clouds as thick as pudding poured over the blue sky, the forest growing dark. Perhaps, if it rained hard enough, they could play with the dollhouses all day instead of going into town.

They hurried back down the hill. The car would come soon, and Mami wouldn't want to be in the forest when it arrived. She liked to wait inside the house, sometimes right beside the front window, watching the driver for ten or fifteen minutes before they opened the door. It was good for him to wait, she told Lilly.

But Lilly didn't like to wait. She was afraid that her potty would come in the front room or the car. She was afraid she wouldn't be able to stop it.

Something streaked across the meadow below, and Lilly's hand trembled as she clung to Mami's hand. If it was a wolf, could Mami scare it away?

Then she saw a yellow tail, a fuzzy head that popped up from the grass.

"Schatzi!" she shouted, letting go of Mami's hand, racing toward the cat.

Treasure. That's what the name meant. A word she'd never forget.

Lilly lifted the cat and cuddled it to her chest with her elephant. Schatzi must have been missing her.

Did Frau Weber know the cat had left the apartment? She must be worried.

Mami always held Schatzi when they visited Frau Weber, but this time she didn't even stop to pet her. Instead she raced toward the house, and Lilly followed, carrying the cat in her arms.

Lilly thought Mami would take off her coat, pour a glass of milk and cup of coffee like she always did after their walks, but she lifted the phone receiver instead.

"I need to speak with Frau Weber, on Weissgerbergasse."

Lilly opened the refrigerator and poured her own milk as Mami paced beside the pantry door. Then she put some milk in a bowl for the cat to lap up.

The line rang and rang until Lilly heard a woman's voice. "She doesn't seem to be home."

"Please try again."

Three times, Mami asked the woman to ring the same number. Where had Frau Weber gone?

Lilly snuck upstairs with her elephant and Schatzi to show off her dolls. The attic was her special place, like the stones for Mami in the woods. Neither matrons nor wolves were welcome here, and she could pretend to play with her brothers on the bicycles.

The door to the attic was open, and she thought this odd. Mami always closed it when they left for their walk. Had she forgotten this morning?

She climbed the steps and her heart broke at the sight. Her beautiful houses, the shiny furniture and spoons, the dolls that played alongside her. Someone had taken *der Schläger* to all of it, as if it were a game.

Now the pieces were scattered across the ground. Like the church on the hill.

She fell on the floor, buried her head in her lap. Schatzi cuddled in beside her, and she held the cat close.

Minutes passed before she heard footsteps shuffling up the stairs, the gasp on Mami's lips.

"The Gestapo was here," Mami said, and in that moment, she sounded just like the matron.

Lilly didn't know this person—Gestapo. Why would he want to break her beautiful houses? She'd never broken anyone else's things.

Mami swept her and her elephant off the ground, leaving Schatzi behind to guard the attic. The black car was waiting outside, and this time Mami didn't hesitate. They climbed inside, and the driver took them straight to Frau Weber's home.

32

EMBER

The flight was boarding when Ember and Dakota arrived at the gate. They stood together by the window, waiting for the agent to call her zone, and it felt as if everyone was staring, wondering if this classy uniformed man was going to fly their 767 to Frankfurt.

"You still have about ten minutes," Dakota said, glancing at his watch. "You want to be the last to board anyway, unless your backpack's going in the overhead."

"I'll keep it by my feet." Her larger suitcase, she'd already checked at the ticket counter. "Thank you for arranging this."

Kindness warmed his eyes when he spoke again. "I want you to be safe."

"No one except my brother knows where I'll be staying."

"Ember . . ." He took his cap off, brushed back his curly hair. "When exactly were you planning to tell me about Noah?"

She looked back out at the plane. "Never."

Two baggage handlers tossed the last pieces of luggage onto the conveyor belt. Soon they'd be shutting the door to the jet bridge.

"He seems like a great kid," Dakota said.

"The best."

"And he texts you every day?"

"He comes over every day after school. If I'm not home right at 3:40, he checks in."

"That's nice of you to hang out with him."

"I'm the lucky one," she said. "He's different from most kids his age, but I get him, and in some way, he gets me. I was different from the other kids too." Different and desperate.

"I think we're all created to embrace the world in a unique way."

Noah would grow into the kind of man who stood for what was right, no matter what people cared to think about him.

The agent called for final boarding.

"How about a rain check on coffee?" Dakota asked as he escorted her toward the door.

"I'd like that."

"I bet they have decent coffee in Nuremberg."

Her breath caught at the thought of spending time with him in Europe. "Seriously?"

Brooke's heart might fail when she found out. And the way her own heart was pounding, it might not make it either.

"My last flight arrives in Paris on Thursday, and then I'm off for a week. I thought it would be fun . . ." His voice faded out and not even a buttoned-up uniform could mask the insecurity.

As if what she thought actually mattered to him.

"I could help you search for Gram's labyrinth," he continued. "I won't get in the way of your work."

"I'd be grateful for your help."

The gate agent called her name over the intercom.

"Will you text me when you land?" Dakota asked.

She nodded as the agent scanned her phone.

An awkward moment passed between them, as if Dakota might embrace her with his gold-trimmed arms, but he just brushed his hand over her shoulder. "Have a good trip, Ember."

She wanted to look back before the Jetway curved, to see him one last time. She didn't turn, but her heart seemed to stretch as she crossed the Atlantic, all the way to Germany.

Maybe together they could find out what happened to Hanna Strauss.

PART THREE

The privilege of opening the first trial in history for crimes against the peace of the world imposes a grave responsibility.

The wrongs which we seek to condemn and punish have been so calculated, so malignant, and so devastating, that civilization cannot tolerate their being ignored, because it cannot survive their being repeated.

ROBERT JACKSON
UNITED STATES CHIEF OF COUNSEL
INTERNATIONAL MILITARY TRIBUNAL IN NUREMBERG
NOVEMBER 21, 1945

HANNA

33

Hanna peeled back the blackout curtains beside her bed and watched their meadow being transformed into a wonderland. The first snow used to mean that Advent would be soon upon them to celebrate the birth of the Christ child, but this winter held no hope of an Advent promise. She couldn't even take Lilly to the Christkindlesmarkt with its gingerbread stalls, spiced wine, and merry-go-round that circled on these cold winter evenings.

Light had been extinguished across their country, the Christmas markets and so many other things canceled. Even the light inside her, the hope for their future, had darkened in the past four years. The Germans continued to wait, but for what?

The Americans had entered the war three years ago, but *Völkischer Beobachter*, the Nazi newspaper, said Germany was continuing to win the war against the Allies and the Russians, their men fighting on both fronts. As if Hitler planned to extinguish the light in their entire world.

A picture of Charlie Ward swept into her mind, the memories of his short stay here. He'd been a light in her world, making her smile with the stack of books that he always carried around the university grounds, strapped together with a leather band. Fiercely handsome eyes that seemed to remember everything they saw. The long talks they'd had about religion and politics and the future of their world after the Treaty of Versailles.

Charlie had been a scholar though, not a warrior. Was he fighting with Allied soldiers now? Or had a German soldier, a fellow student from the university even, taken his life?

Lilly cried out, and Hanna rushed down the hallway to find blankets lumped on the floor again. Lilly's eyes were wide when Hanna turned on the bedside lamp, hands clenched around her pillowcase, muttering about her brothers and wolves hidden in the trees and the beautiful dollhouses the Gestapo had crushed three years ago as if they wanted to steal everything from this girl.

The terror had lessened over time, but with the change of seasons, the planes that sometimes rattled their ceiling, the nightmares returned with a startling strength as Lilly grew.

The end of this narrow bed was the best place for Hanna to avoid bruises from the thrashing as Lilly hit and kicked someone trying to hurt her, still speaking words that Hanna didn't understand. Words that Lilly didn't understand either when Hanna repeated them back the next morning.

She'd tried to waken Lilly once, but she had screamed and cried for the rest of the night, confused, it seemed, or overwhelmed. Hanna had never tried to waken her again.

If only she could step into these nightmares with her, see what had happened long ago so she could help Lilly navigate her way to the other side. Or at least fight off the monsters in her mind.

Lilly settled back on the mattress for a moment, and Hanna closed her eyes, knowing the respite might be brief.

In those first months after Lilly arrived, Hanna had sent letters to friends and agencies across Berlin, inquiring about this girl who'd lost her parents. They could offer no help without a surname, of course, and she'd intended to go to Berlin to search herself one day.

But the longer Lilly had stayed, the less Hanna wanted to search for her extended family.

More than a year had passed since she'd sent a letter. The terror from the past still tormented Lilly, but in the daylight, she no longer seemed to be afraid.

People across Nuremberg had continued to disappear until it seemed like anyone connected to the Jewish community had been sent away on trains. Rumors had drifted back from the east, scathing stories about people being killed in the Nazi camps. Her colleagues in the museum had whispered about extermination, fragments of information when the director wasn't around. She prayed the rumors weren't true, but on the nights like this, when she longed to hear news of friends like Frau Weber, she feared the worst.

Four years had passed since Frau Weber left Nuremberg. After the Gestapo destroyed Opa's dollhouses, the morning Schatzi arrived at the lodge, Hanna had visited her friend's apartment. Another woman answered the door, a star stitched on her sweater to distinguish her from Aryan neighbors.

Hanna had wanted to warn the lady back then. Tell her to leave this town before her family was swallowed up in the madness. Tell her to hide before the Nazis sent those she loved someplace else. But she suspected this woman might not really be one of the stars. The Gestapo, perhaps, was paying her to wear the emblem, to see who might show up at the door for refuge from the enemy.

No one, not even Kolman, spoke with Hanna about her last visit to Frau Weber's house or the dollhouses that she and Lilly had tried to restore with nails and glue. The driver no longer took her to work, but the Gestapo agents circled around her drive several days a week, watching the house as if they might pay another visit if she stepped out of line.

Lilly twitched several more times, calling out, and then her eyes began scanning the familiar leaves on her wallpaper, the vines twisted and stretched across a canvas of white.

"Mami," she gasped.

The word, even in dismay, sounded sweet to Hanna's ears. "I'll stay with you."

Lilly's voice trembled. "But I've wet the bed."

A deep breath, but Hanna didn't sigh. Not when she saw the lingering fear in the girl's eyes, the blue-striped pillow a shield against her chest. "It's okay."

"I'm sorry." Lilly's body shook as if she were still asleep. "So sorry."

"We'll clean it up."

Tears poured down her ruddy cheeks. Lilly was eight now but the pleading in her voice sounded like a toddler's. "I didn't mean to."

"It's not your fault," Hanna said. It was the fault of the demons who dared threaten her.

She changed the bedcovering and poured the last of her verbena-scented bubble bath that she'd been saving into the tub, but the warm water didn't stop Lilly's trembling. Hanna helped her into dry pajamas, and Lilly sank into her chest as they watched the snow fall across the meadow together, the moonlight burnishing the layers of white.

"Can the elephants see the snow?" Lilly asked, her stuffed animal tucked under an arm. Schatzi had curled up on the bed beside them.

The zookeeper would have coaxed the animals into cages so they had shelter for the night, but it was possible they could still see outside. "Perhaps."

"They'll be cold."

Hanna held her closer. "Not in their cages."

Lilly seemed satisfied with this knowledge as she nestled back into Hanna's side. The two of them together, mother and daughter snuggled in the cool of this night with the toy elephant between them, snubbing the chaos outside that was tearing families apart.

She'd do anything to protect this girl who'd become her daughter, taking care of her until the end of this war. After the fighting, she didn't know what would happen—no one did—but Lilly was her daughter for life.

Would Kolman—would Germany—expect the three of them to fold back into a family after the war? She'd thought Kolman might bring her additional children to adopt, but he'd brought no other *Kinder* and he rarely bothered to bring himself home, so she hadn't any fear of pregnancy.

He'd never sent many letters, but any correspondence stopped months ago. The last she'd known, he was digging in one of their newly occupied territories, but it seemed a strange time for the Nazis to be searching for the roots of their culture in the midst of this war, when those left in Germany were far from victorious Aryans with health and strength flowing through their veins.

They were cold, hungry, many of them sick now. And for what purpose? Hitler didn't need to take over the world. He needed to take care of their people.

Lilly pressed her nose up against the window. "Do you see a sword?"

Night and day, she watched the sky for a celestial display like the one in the Middle Ages, waiting with the unshakable faith that God would show up again to right all that had gone wrong.

Snowflakes stuck to her window now, piling up in the window box that once held flowers. And Lilly's breathing stilled.

Hanna laid her on the bed, sitting beside her in case she woke again. She began to nod off until she heard the creak of a door downstairs.

Sometimes a Gestapo agent would circle her driveway in the night, but no one except Luisa had attempted to come into her home and Luisa simply unlocked the front door with her key. The next morning, Hanna would find several biographies in the percolator, waiting to be hidden away. They'd collected about a hundred of them now, most of them buried on the hill.

She'd hoped her cousin was sleeping in the house as well, especially on these cold nights. Perhaps, if Luisa had returned, she could speak with her.

The only other person with a key was Kolman, and he never returned at this hour.

She hurried down the steps with her flashlight, hoping to find Luisa in the kitchen, but she stopped in the great hall. The chair was pushed away from the desk, papers scattered across the top.

Her breath quickened like Lilly's as she turned off the flashlight and shuffled toward the hall. Had she missed the sound of breaking glass, the Gestapo entering her home?

The front door had been locked, but it wasn't fully closed. Hanging on a peg beside it was an olive-colored scarf.

Her stomach rolled. Had Kolman finally come home? If so, why had he arrived during the night?

She opened the door and in the faint light, the canopy of snow, she could see a man's footprints leading around the side of the house but saw no tracks for a car. Closing the door, she relocked it, then dragged sandbags from the pantry to block the entrance.

All these months she thought Kolman was overseeing a dig in the expanded territory. Was it possible that he hadn't gone far at all? If so, did he often come to their lodge at night? Or, perhaps, while she was working in town?

Back at the desk, she flicked on the light and sat down. Utility bills had been dumped across the surface. Her father's records from the factory. Medical records that dated back to her mother's hospital stay.

She opened the top cabinet drawer and thumbed through the manila folders. More household records and inventories from the factory.

What was Kolman searching for during the night?

Not the stories, she prayed.

Near the back of the cabinet was an unlabeled folder and she pulled it out. Inside were the adoption papers for Lilly, a small stack of them stapled together.

The first was an adoption certificate with Hanna's forged signature and Kolman's name. Then a third signature, a woman named Inge Viermetz, who verified it. On a separate page was a state medical certificate issued from Berlin with the name of Lilly Strauss. The one she'd shown to the doctor a few weeks after Lilly arrived.

The last page was one she hadn't seen, an official form with a name she didn't recognize. Roza Nowak. Born March 7, 1936. Adopted from Sonnenwiese in October 1940.

Hanna looked up at Hitler's portrait, the face of all the mysteries that shrouded this Reich.

Was Lilly's name actually Roza? And this Sonnenwiese—was it the home near Berlin?

Outside, she heard a rumble of a motor and cringed. Either Kolman was leaving or he had returned to search for something among these papers.

She turned off the lamp and slipped back the curtain. No one was in her drive but in the sky—

A glint of silver in the moonlight. The wing of an enemy plane.

Was it too late to save Frau Weber and Paul Gruenewald and the other Jewish people that Himmler had sent away? To calm the fears of a girl being haunted by the past?

To stop the madness?

Perhaps it wasn't the enemy who flew over her home tonight.

Perhaps it might be a friend.

34

EMBER

On the two-hour train ride between Frankfurt and Nuremberg, Ember immersed herself in this country that had wrestled for centuries with the balance of protecting and caring for its people. A castle tower pierced through the treetops outside her window, a terra-cotta village tumbling around it like blocks, and she wondered who had built this fortress above town. Was it meant for a duke to defend his duchy or to detain prisoners in the old German Kingdom?

This history resonated deeply with her, the time capsule buildings that held secrets from entire centuries past. Much of it unchanged since the Middle Ages.

A cappuccino helped fight off her jet lag, her tablet propped up next to the broad window in the dining car. Patchwork, that's what she would be doing in Nuremberg. Collecting all the remaining pieces for her dissertation, stitching them together so she could put it on paper to defend. She would ask everyone she met about a man or woman who'd stood up against the Nazis, but sometimes, she knew, a hero was impossible to find. Sometimes they didn't even share their own story.

But adults didn't just disappear. Someone had to know where Hanna went after the war.

Tomorrow morning she was meeting with the director at the Jewish Museum of Franconia, near the courtroom where the world convened in 1945 to bring some sort of justice after the Holocaust. Dr. Graf, the assistant director of the Germanic National Museum, had also been able to reschedule their meeting. He would answer her questions on Thursday.

All her head knowledge about Nuremberg was about to merge with the realities of this place.

As the train sped east, she searched online for Mrs. Kiehl's labyrinth above the zoo. According to the map, there were miles upon miles of forest and cliffs layering these hills, extending east toward Czechia, and it felt a bit like Horton the elephant searching for his speck in a field of clover.

An abandoned church. Mrs. Kiehl had mentioned that as well. Germany was speckled with old monasteries and convents, but Ember found the ruins of an abbey within a mile of the Nuremberg Zoo, near where Mrs. Kiehl said she used to play. A fellow traveler had stumbled on the place, taking photographs of its ivy-clad walls when he was hiking.

Fascinated, Ember began reading about the convent named after Katharine of Alexandria, a princess in the third century who'd been well-schooled like her male counterparts. A woman who was grounded firmly in her faith, embracing who she was beyond her noble family, education, and potential marriage.

After receiving a vision, Katharine dedicated herself to becoming the bride of Christ, giving herself completely to Him. Unfortunately her beauty and intelligence captured the attention of Roman emperor

Maxentius, and that was the beginning of her earthly demise. The emperor appealed to her intellect first—employing fifty philosophers to dissuade her from her beliefs. Then he proposed marriage.

But this young woman refused to renounce her faith or marry the emperor. Angels cared for her in prison, and when Maxentius finally beheaded her, the angels escorted her home.

Katharine's story trickled down through centuries, Ember read, reminding sisters around the world that if they were faithful to Him, God would minister to them always, even in their pain.

Were the ruins of the abbey and its labyrinth on public property? She couldn't tell on Google, but when Dakota arrived, perhaps they could find it together.

Ember looked away from the screen as the train cruised past another red-roofed town. This country had mesmerized her for the past twenty years, but perhaps her interest was rooted in something deeper. Perhaps something inside her was trying to right the wrongs of what her family had done.

She wanted to return home with answers for Mrs. Kiehl and she wanted answers for herself.

Her phone chimed, and she saw a return text from Dakota.

Kayla and Gram found this in a shoebox.

It was a grainy photograph of a woman and a girl with braids, one of the child's arms wrapped around a stuffed animal, the other hand clinging to her mother. Or, perhaps, the older woman was clinging to her.

Charlie took this picture of Hanna and Lilly when they were in Germany.

She stared at the picture until the train pulled into Nuremberg's Central Station.

"What happened to you?" she whispered, tracing her finger around the woman's thin face, wondering why she looked so sad.

"She refuses to let the other children measure her," the principal said to Hanna, as if this infringement were worthy of the corporal punishment already inflicted on his second-grade pupil.

He'd phoned last night, asking for this morning meeting, and Lilly had gone to bed in tears, though she refused to tell Hanna what she'd done to warrant a spanking.

Insubordination, the principal reported. The worst possible quality in a Nazi maiden.

Lilly could quote from *Mein Kampf*, sing songs about their almighty Führer, but she wasn't allowed to return to school until her classmates could wrap their measuring tape around her head. Important training, the principal explained, to recognize racial impurities in their neighbors.

Perhaps it would be good for Lilly to spend a few days at home.

"Why won't you let your classmates measure you?" Hanna asked after they stepped out of the sedan.

"I don't want them to touch me."

"But you didn't mind the spanking?"

Lilly's lower lip trembled, and Hanna took the girl's hand as they walked toward the museum. She and the other children didn't know that most of the world didn't measure each other's heads. "Did one of the students hurt you?"

"No," Lilly said. "I was afraid."

It must have been a terrible fear if it was worth the strap. "Afraid of what?"

Lilly shook off her hand, wrapping her arms around her chest. Several people passed them on the slushy sidewalk, looking down at the girl who should be in school, but no one in Nuremberg greeted each other any longer on the streets, not even with a simple *Guten Morgen.*

It wasn't just the children who were afraid.

"You don't have to be scared of me, Lilly."

Her daughter released the tangle of arms, her hands back at her sides. "I was afraid that I wouldn't measure right."

Hanna slipped onto a bench outside the museum and held the girl tightly, knowing that something significant had shifted between them. If Lilly could trust her, they had hope for their future, no matter how they measured.

"What do you remember, Lilly? From before you came to the lodge."

Lilly shook her head. "I don't remember anything."

"You used to ask about your brothers." And she still asked about them when the night terrors struck.

"I don't have any brothers."

Hanna studied her face, and she didn't seem to be lying. Had she forgotten her years before Kolman brought her to Nuremberg?

The toy elephant was packed in Lilly's tote bag, the companion that always rode down with them to town. Hanna retrieved it, and

Lilly folded the animal into her arms. "You'll have to play quietly while I work."

The museum had been closed to the public for the past year, most of the exhibits stored away now. While *Völkischer Beobachter* continued to tout victory in its headlines, the few staff members left here were preparing for the worst.

She rang the bell by the entrance, and Grete answered.

"We've requisitioned another shipment," Grete said as she glanced down at Lilly. "Why aren't you in school?"

"She needs to stay with me today," Hanna said.

"The director won't care, as long as she's out of the way."

Her daughter knew well how to slip into the shadows.

Grete continued, "You'll probably need to work late tonight anyway. I will make sure you have something to eat."

Lilly tipped her head up. "Frau Cohn?"

"Yes."

"May I have something to eat too?"

Grete smiled, patting Lilly on her shoulder. "Of course."

Hanna moved toward the basement steps. "We'll get started right away."

"You'll need to work in the cloister," Grete said. "The boxes are too big to carry downstairs."

They followed Grete back through the empty museum to the renovated cloister that once held displays. Lined up along the walls were large crates, waiting for her to open and archive.

Lilly leaned toward one of the crates, trying to peek through a small hole. They'd catalog whatever was inside and then pack the crates back up again to ship off to Director Kohlhaussen's hiding place.

Hanna unscrewed the front, and Lilly helped her lower it. Masked in canvas wrappings was an elaborately sculpted panel of three wise men clothed in gold, one of them kneeling before the

Savior and His saintly mother. Lilly reached forward and petted the white horse that accompanied the men, its shiny red saddle crafted for royalty.

It was from an altarpiece, Hanna thought, carved during the Renaissance. She removed a second panel, this one a vivid portrayal of Christ dancing on His grave, a host of soldiers seemingly blinded from the shafts of light cast from His head.

"Jesus," Lilly whispered.

She turned back and saw the mixture of awe and terror in Lilly's eyes, as if something haunted her. "Have you seen this before?"

"At the church." Lilly's fingers smoothed over a beam of light. "You took me when I was little."

"I didn't—" She stopped. For a moment, she thought Lilly's mother had taken her to a church in Berlin before she'd died, but Hanna had spent four years at the university, visiting churches across that city. She wouldn't have forgotten this piece.

"Do you remember anything else about the church?"

But Lilly wasn't listening. She was introducing her elephant to the Christ child.

When Grete brought them steaming cups of chicory, Hanna pointed at the collection of panels now lined up against the cloister wall. "Were these taken from a German church?"

The secretary pressed her fingers together. "They were taken from a church."

"Please, Grete—"

She glanced back at the entrance, at Lilly rocking her elephant in front of the manger. "They're from Poland," she whispered.

The words sank into Hanna's gut.

She'd wanted Lilly to be from Berlin, wanted her to be German, but often the words that came out of her mouth, especially in her dreams, were a different language. And Kolman's stories about Berlin never rang true.

Was it possible that Lilly had been born across the border? That she wasn't even Aryan?

"But the pieces were carved by Veit Stoss," Grete said. A renowned sculptor from Nuremberg. "No one else except the director knows where they came from."

"What are we going to do with all these things after the war?" Hanna asked.

"We're only protecting them," she said. "But until it's time to return them, we can't tell anyone."

"Of course not." No one else could find out about these panels or the fact that Lilly recognized them.

That night, after she tucked Lilly under a pile of warm covers, several planes rattled the lodge. She collected supplies—a box of crackers and bag of dried apples, canteen of water, candles and matches, gloves and scarfs—and put them in a rucksack beside her bed, in case they needed to run in the night. Then she replaced the sandbags in front of the doors so Kolman couldn't steal inside the lodge without knocking.

She retrieved the adoption papers from the cabinet, reading through them one more time. Lilly was Polish; she had no doubt now. But how did she end up at an orphanage in Germany?

Grete said their country would return the altarpieces after this war was over. Would they also return the children?

That's why Lilly was so worried about her measurements. Someone might send her back.

Burn the papers. That was her first thought. It didn't matter if her daughter was Roza from Poland or Lilly from Berlin. Her heritage was now entwined with Hanna's. She was Aryan to the core.

But this was Lilly's story. What if her daughter needed these papers after the war? Hanna could always burn them later.

The medical card was the only thing that she'd keep, certified with the name Lilly Strauss to prove to any agent that her daughter was German. The rest of the papers she'd bury in the labyrinth, before the Gestapo found them and sent Lilly away to one of their camps. Or the war ended and she had to escort Lilly home.

The folded papers fit easily into a coffee tin. Her driver had stopped coming long ago, but sometimes one of the patrolling Gestapo agents would trail her when she left the house. On those mornings she and Lilly circled the meadow and returned home.

She couldn't wait until morning to bury this tin. Nor could she leave Lilly alone, in case Kolman returned or she had another night terror. They'd have to go now, in this midnight hour, hoping no one would follow them into the forest. And the airplanes wouldn't return.

"We need to go to the labyrinth," Hanna said, waking Lilly from her sleep.

Lilly rolled over. "It's too late."

"It's never too late to pray."

They bundled into their coats and boots before removing the mountain of sandbags by the front door. Then they stepped outside, the flashlight and coffee tin stored in her bag.

The mountain was dusted with snow, their feet crunching over the autumn leaves underneath. Thankfully the stars were bright enough to guide their steps. Hanna could lead them away from the cliffs, the opening to the mine, but she couldn't predict who might be in the trees.

"Stay close," she said.

"Frau Cohn says there are ghost rabbits in the forest."

"Grete likes to scare children with her stories, but it's only folklore."

"I'm more worried about the wolves," Lilly said. The same fear that had plagued her since she'd arrived at the lodge.

"The wolves are all in Poland," Hanna assured her, the branches around them shivering in the breeze. "And Poland is five hundred kilometers away."

No matter what happened, Hanna would never send her back to the wolves.

Lilly was old enough now to hear more of the labyrinth's story. Perhaps she, like Hanna, would find hope in the sadness. It was much better than the stories about frightening creatures in these woods.

"Have I told you the story about Emrich and Cristyne?" Hanna asked.

"No."

And so Hanna began to tell her about the young woman who'd wanted to become a nun, about the wealthy man who'd loved her. About how they'd labored together to rescue those who had been infected by the plague.

"The sisters rescued hundreds of people, but those they lost were never forgotten. They carved an initial on stones to remember their names."

Lilly moved closer to her. "What happened to Cristyne?"

"Sadly she died from the plague, but Emrich lived for many more years. He never forgot her."

"It's good that he remembered."

"It is good. According to the legend, he left something in the labyrinth to remember her always, like they'd remembered all who had died," Hanna said. "A pocket watch was a very rare thing back then, and they say Emrich buried his somewhere in the labyrinth. Because of it, time has stood still on this mountain for five hundred years."

"Has anyone found the watch?" Lilly asked.

"I don't believe so. According to the legend, the heart of whoever finds it will know love for a lifetime."

"I'm going to find it," Lilly said solemnly.

"I hope you do." Hanna lifted a branch, and they ducked under it. "The legend also says that whoever finds it must leave it in the ground. For timeless love to work, it must be shared with others."

Usually Lilly played at the abbey while Hanna buried her papers, but tonight she guided her daughter to the center of the labyrinth stones. "People have prayed here for centuries."

Lilly brushed her hands over the soil. "I'm going to look for the watch."

The girl wouldn't understand the significance of centuries, but one day the weight of the years would press on her, and she'd understand why Hanna couldn't tell her where she'd been born. The burial of these papers would save her life.

Hanna didn't have time to count stones, but she knew exactly where to hide the adoption papers. Under the initial *L*—Lael, they had named this one, from the book of Numbers. *Belonging to God.*

After moving the stone aside, taking care not to peel back any of the moss for others to suspect, she began to dig far into the ground so no one else would find these papers. Nor would anyone in the Nazi Party question Lilly's measurements.

She pounded the dirt firmly with her trowel and replaced the stone. "Let's go home."

Lilly stayed on her knees. "I haven't found the watch."

"Another day," Hanna replied. "You can search for it in the light."

The girl eyed Hanna's hands. "Where is your coffee tin?"

"I had to leave it behind."

"Like Emrich?" Lilly asked.

"Very much like him." She guided Lilly carefully through the trees with her gloved hands, but as they neared the tree line, Lilly stopped walking.

"What is it?" Hanna whispered.

Lilly didn't speak, only shaking her head as if she'd heard one of those wolves that she feared.

Then Hanna heard something too, the crunch of leaves. A deer, she thought at first, for the mythical creatures of Bavaria didn't make a sound.

Someone moved in the trees below them, and she saw a splash of light probing the ground. Who else was coming up the hill?

She pulled Lilly into a cleft of the sandstone, and they waited quietly together. Both of them in the shadows now.

36

EMBER

Dr. Franz Graf had a stack of papers waiting for Ember in his office and a trove of stories about their collection of artifacts from the years when the German Renaissance was centered in Nuremberg.

The first terrestrial globe, he explained, was wrought here in 1492, the globe that inspired Christopher Columbus to sail westward from Spain in search of a route to the Orient, stumbling on the Americas instead. In 1510 Peter Henlein invented the first portable watch in Nuremberg, made of copper and iron.

Ember had already told him via email about her dissertation and search for a hero during the Holocaust. They talked about the centuries of persecution and then that fateful day when a quarter of the Jewish population was massacred, the rest expelled from this town. Intellectual progress, ingenuity of their culture, contrasting with the fall of mankind.

"Do you have anything in your collection from Saint Katharine's abbey?" she asked.

The assistant director eyed her curiously. "We have the tower bell in storage."

Yesterday morning, she'd seen the intricately designed *Memorbücher* at the Jewish Museum, and she wished that she could see every piece in these museums, traveling back in time through their stories.

"I'm actually looking for information about a woman who used to live near the abbey church." She showed Dr. Graf the picture. "Her name was Hanna Strauss, and she worked as a curator in this museum during World War II."

He glanced at the photo, then typed something on his computer keyboard. "Unfortunately most of our records from the war were destroyed,"

"Anything you have would be most helpful," she said. "Her daughter wants to know where she went." And so did Ember, desperately.

The printer beside Dr. Graf began to hum, paper stacking up on top, but he didn't give any indication of what he'd found. When it finished, he swiped up the pile and waved his silver-studded fingers, a diamond on one hand catching a glint of light and casting it across the wall. "Walk with me please," he said, though it sounded like *valk vith me*.

Ember followed him under the lobby's bridge, into the cloister of a former monastery, Hebrew-inscribed gravestones from centuries past lined up against the plaster walls.

May her soul be bound in the Garden of Eden.

Ember scanned the translation from one of the stones as they moved through the tunnel.

Bound in the perfect Garden of beauty and peace and life.

Ember would bundle those words up in her heart as well, whenever she remembered her daughter.

They passed under the arches of a medieval church and a bronze sculpture of the archangel Michael, his wings spanning its stone wall.

She wanted to explore every inch of this place. Perhaps when Dakota arrived, they could return.

Dr. Graf stopped near a collection of wooden sculptures, several created by a local Renaissance artist named Veit Stoss. He pointed out one sculpture of a woman sitting on the ground, the wrinkles in her dress crisp, her eyes lifelike as she gazed beyond Ember, seeming to see something in the future.

"Gerhard Marcks sculpted this one," he said. "Do you know his work?"

"I don't."

"The Nazi Party said Marcks's art was unsuitable, so they confiscated all his sculptures and banned him from creating any additional material."

Ember studied the longing in the woman's face and wondered about the artist. Was he trying to demonstrate how he and others felt trapped under the regime?

"Hitler knew the power of art and entertainment. In 1937, the Nazis held their Great German Art Exhibition in Munich to display its value. Nearby, they also held an exhibition titled Degenerate Art to publicly shame Marcks and others for creating artwork that Hitler perceived to be about Jewish culture or something else contrary to his Reich. He redefined much for the German people, regulating what they could create and even the use of certain words."

Whoever owned the definitions, tweaking familiar words for their own use, could influence the morality of a people. The Nazis, she'd read, had tried to redefine the entire German society. Twisting their language. Writing fiction instead of fact. Re-creating their past and eliminating the hard truths for their future.

Purity meant prejudice. *Evacuation* meant murder. *Living space* meant stealing another's land.

And Hitler was supposed to be their savior.

What sounded good and right and true was really evil. Even the hooked cross, the swastika, was an ancient symbol of peace. The Boy Scouts once used it as a badge of kindness before the Nazis stole it for their propaganda.

Curious, Ember turned back to the assistant director. "Why are you showing me this?"

"National Socialists did terrible things in our country, but as you finish your dissertation, you must know that not all Germans were Nazis."

"I know," Ember assured him. "I've read many accounts of the German people who secretly conspired against Hitler or were part of a network to help the Jewish people." More than six hundred Germans had been honored for rescuing their Jewish countrymen during the Holocaust. "Just not in Nuremberg."

"The Nazis persecuted people in many different ways," Dr. Graf said. "Some they tortured terribly in the camps and I would never discount the horror those victims experienced, but they also stole away the livelihood from others who dissented. Their craft. Their families. They broke them down first and then they often took their lives."

She eyed the papers still clutched in his hand. "Did the Nazis kill Hanna Strauss?"

"I don't know what happened to her. The Americans wanted to try her husband here in Nuremberg, but he disappeared like his wife."

Ember wished she could read those papers. "What did her husband do during the war?"

"I'm afraid I don't have that specific information," he said. "Did you know Frau Strauss worked for the Ahnenerbe?"

"Yes, she was an archaeologist."

"Sadly the Ahnenerbe was doing much more than archaeology. You'll find it all in here." He lifted the papers but didn't hand them over yet. "Have you heard the German word *Vergangenheitsbewältigung*?"

She shook her head.

"It's what we call the process of overcoming the past. Our gov-

ernment doesn't tolerate fascism now, but there is a whole generation still trying to overcome our collective history. Hitler portrayed
himself as a father for the youth in the 1930s and an advocate for
the workingman. By the end of the war, there were more than eight
million members of the Nazi Party.

"Many of our parents and grandparents supported Hitler's regime,
but most Germans didn't know the extent of what was happening in
the concentration camps. Everyone knew that the Jews were being
persecuted, but few people spoke out. We bear the weight of this guilt
as a society, Ms. Ellis, even as we try to understand what went wrong."

He was testing her, the papers a carrot in his hand.

"We each make our own choice to bring good or evil into this
world," she said carefully. "I don't blame anyone in Germany for what
their parents did. Just as I pray my daughter won't blame me for what
I did when she was a baby . . ."

A sharp nod, then Dr. Graf directed her to a back door. "Frau
Strauss packed artifacts for the museum so they wouldn't be destroyed
in the war. Would you like to see where they were stored?"

Ember's heart raced. "Very much."

They walked out into the pleasant June morning, winding through
the cobbled streets of a city completely rebuilt from the rubble, the
medieval charm fully intact as they neared an open-air market.

A golden spike anchored one side of the plaza. The Beautiful
Fountain, it was called. She'd read about the dozens of historical figures displayed on this waterless sculpture, the brass rings along the
ornate fencing for good luck. Food and flower stalls were sandwiched
in the wide courtyard between the fountain and a Gothic church.

"Is this the Hauptmarkt?" she asked.

He nodded as they moved through the crowds with their shopping bags and cell phone cameras. Bells chimed in the church tower
and below the clock two trumpeters lifted their instruments to enter-
tain a sculpted Holy Roman Emperor figure, his electors, and all of

Nuremberg with their music like they'd done for centuries. In that moment, Ember realized that she was watching what Hanna and even Lilly would have watched. What those who visited Nuremberg five hundred years ago would have seen.

All of her reading, everything she'd learned about this town, centered right here in this marketplace where the Jewish community had gathered in centuries past.

The former Jewish synagogue was destroyed in 1349, and 150 years later—in 1498—the Jewish people living around the Hauptmarkt were expelled. Many of them returned to their homeland in Poland, but some went west to Fürth. Near the courthouse where the nations tried Nazi officials for their crimes against humanity.

The synagogue along the Hauptmarkt was destroyed again on the Night of Broken Glass in 1938, burned to the ground when the persecution against the Jewish people resurfaced.

The Nazi Party as a whole, not just Hitler, hated the Jews. The soldiers in their heavy jackboots had marched right through this square, probably rocking the ancient cobblestones. The rhythm of their power, shaking the buildings, would have beat deeply into the hearts of those who lived here.

Ember followed Dr. Graf across the Pegnitz and up a hill with Bavarian shops, museums, and restaurants on each side. At the top was the formidable Kaiserburg Castle, the crown of this imperial city in the Holy Roman Empire. Dr. Graf stopped in front of an unmarked door between shops and pulled a set of keys out of his pocket.

"We call this the art bunker." When he pushed open the door, a rush of cold air flooded into the street. He reached for a flashlight hanging on the rock wall and guided her down into a tunnel.

Inside the bunker were more doors, heavy ones that Dr. Graf unlocked along the way, the walls on both sides reinforced by wood.

"Frau Strauss and Director Kohlhaussen took great care in protecting the Holy Roman and German relics and items from the Jewish culture." He flipped a switch and an overhead light illuminated a stack of crates. "Ninety percent of the old city was destroyed in the bombing, but the museum staff was able to save most of our relics. Unfortunately the local government didn't prepare a bunker to save residents. Thousands of our citizens died."

Sadness washed over her. If only the Nazis had treasured their people as much as their artwork.

"I will tell Mrs. Kiehl what her mother did during the war."

He lifted the papers and handed them over. "She did something else, it seemed."

Ember glanced down at the typed papers, each of them with a name at the top. They appeared to be short biographies.

"Frau Strauss had been concealing these in crates with other artifacts before sending them off to this bunker. One of the museum secretaries found them after the war."

"She was keeping the stories . . ."

"It seems so. Collecting them would have been even more dangerous than those men and women who created the degenerate art."

Ember looked back at the man. "Is this secretary still alive?"

"She is."

"Do you think she would talk to me?" Ember asked, her heart racing at the thought of meeting someone who remembered Hanna.

Dr. Graf smiled for the first time since she'd entered his office. Then he handed her the last sheet of paper. "Frau Cohn is her name. You'll find her number here."

"Does she speak English?"

"A little," he said. "I took the liberty of calling ahead. She is expecting you tomorrow morning at eleven."

Ember glanced down at her watch. "I will be there."

And Dakota, she hoped, would arrive in time to join her.

37

HANNA

Knocking—that was the first sound Hanna heard when she woke. Like a woodpecker drumming against a tree. Then in the distance was an explosion, and she jumped to her feet, waking Lilly beside her.

Wings dipped in the moonlight outside her window, and Lilly screamed.

Airplanes, Hanna slowly realized. An angry swarm overhead. Neither sandbags nor gas masks would save them if a bomb dropped on the lodge.

"We have to run," she told Lilly, glad they were already dressed for the cold.

A screaming sound replaced the knocking, a boom and whistle like fireworks. They tied their boots quickly, and Hanna reached for the rucksack filled with supplies by her bed. The war, it seemed, had finally come to Nuremberg.

The museum's artifacts and artwork were supposedly safe, buried wherever the director had taken them. Now she and Lilly needed to find a place to hide.

"Schatzi?" Lilly called, her elephant safe under her arm.

"She's already hidden," Hanna said as she threw aside the sandbags blocking the front door. With this noise, the trembling of walls, they might not find the cat for days.

When no break came in the swarm, she tugged on Lilly's hand, ducking as they ran toward the meadow, trying to blend in with the tall grass. When they neared the forest, she pulled Lilly back into the cover of trees. Then she held her close to her chest, the two of them curled up at the base of the trees as if she could shield her daughter from the storm.

The last time they'd climbed this hill, someone else had been in the woods. Not a mythical creature. A man. He hadn't seen her and Lilly, but the encounter scared her enough that she hadn't returned to the labyrinth during the day or night. If Kolman was back in Nuremberg, if an agent was continuing to watch her, she didn't want to lead either man to her hiding place.

A racket of bombs released in the distance, and moments later, smoke began creeping up the mountain. Nuremberg blazed orange like a bed of coals in the blackened frame of night.

"The sky war," Lilly said in awe.

A bloodred glow. Black creatures that shifted in the moonlight. Perhaps this was exactly what the celestial war looked like in 1561.

Perhaps God had had enough.

Lilly waved her arms in front of her as if she could clear the smoke.

"Breathe," Hanna said, speaking to both of them.

The girl took another breath, poisoned by smoke, and coughed violently. Hanna dug a scarf out of her pack and masked Lilly's mouth, but she continued to cough.

A nearby crash shook the hill, flames breaking through the smoke.

Lilly pounded Hanna's arm. "The elephants!" she shouted over the roar.

Were the airplanes bombing the zoo? The animals must be going mad with the smoke and noise and the rattling of their cages.

If she were alone, she would try to help, but not with Lilly. Her priority was to protect this girl.

"The director's taking care of the animals," she said, praying it was true. "We have to go to the mine."

She guided Lilly up the hill, branches shaking as the planes dove over them. Perhaps it was finally the end of this war. The end of Hitler and Himmler and the lies from their regime.

But who would take their place? The land she loved, the strength of the German people, would they all be swallowed up by Communism now?

Another explosion and she heard the rattle of rocks on the cliffs. The Allied powers wouldn't care about one woman and a child. All Germans, they would assume, were the enemy.

Lilly tripped, and Hanna caught her before she fell into the quarry.

Ahead was the entrance to the old mine, and they stepped carefully over the iron grate. Inside, she pulled the flashlight out of her bag, flipping it on.

As a girl, she used to hide back in this tunnel when Luisa and Vater were distracted, playing among the rusted buckets and picks. She'd wanted to explore the different channels off the main path, but Vater's warning about the cave-ins and drop-offs and all who'd lost their lives had stopped her.

What if a bomb hit the hillside now? The ground would collapse, she feared, and then they would be trapped. But the outside seemed to be even more dangerous than in here.

A curtain of smoke hung low at the entrance, so she pulled Lilly around a corner, taking care not to trip over an old track embedded in the rock. When smoke began to creep around the corner, they followed the path down the corridor in search of clear air, the sandstone a vibrant red in her light. In France she had been searching for buried treasure, but here she was trying to hide the treasure in her care.

They walked until they could go no farther. Someone had installed another gate inside the mine, and this one they'd locked, just like the attic door.

Hanna fiddled with the latch, but it wouldn't open. Had her father built this before he passed away? If so, what was he trying to hide back here?

They fell to the ground, their backs to the door.

"I love you with all of my heart," she told Lilly.

The girl snuggled into her side. "Are we going to die?"

"I don't know," she replied. "Where's your elephant?"

Lilly reached inside her coat, removing the stuffed animal that had been more faithful than any friend, wrapping her arms around it.

How long they sat, she didn't know, but as the hours passed, they finished the water in the canteen. The box of crackers and dried pieces of fruit.

She'd lived at the apex of the unknown for almost five years now, at the tip of Hitler's sword, clenched in the talons of his regime. And once again there was nothing she could do except wait, hoping for a cushion near the bottom when they fell.

Help, she prayed, would come.

And she prayed that it would be the Allied soldiers, not the Russians, who marched into their town.

38

EMBER

Stormwater spilled over Fleisch Bridge, the river rumbling underneath. Ember rushed across it, window light carving a path for her in the rain. The stones were slippery beneath her feet, the castle above veiled in fog.

She seemed to be the only person outside in this deluge, as if locals were afraid of the storm. She'd blame it on the jet lag, but storms seemed to accost her without notice. Or perhaps she brought the storms with her.

At least this time, she didn't have far to run.

An old-world palace was her home for tonight, built for a bourgeois family at the base of the castle. In her attic room, she removed the papers that Dr. Graf had given her. Then she dried her backpack with a towel and hung it from the knob of a dormer window.

After settling on her bed, she began reading one of the biographies the museum had found hidden in the crates, a story about a wealthy

Jewish family who'd tried to leave Germany, but by the time they completed their paperwork, the borders had closed. They asked a neighbor to watch over their home when it was time for them to go east, but in days the government had requisitioned everything they owned. Their story didn't have an ending, but Ember suspected that none of these accounts ended well.

The second biography had been handwritten instead of typed, the story of a family with two sons, one of them handicapped. The parents sent the older son to Argentina, to prepare their new home, but then their youngest became ill and couldn't travel. At the time the parents thought it best to keep the rest of their family together in Germany. Even in the hardships, they thought they would have each other. When the paper began to describe what happened to the handicapped boy, Ember put it aside. Not because she didn't care. Because she cared deeply and nothing she could do now would stop their pain.

The third was about a woman named Marianne Weber, who had helped collect the stories with Hanna. A seamstress who hid some of her former Jewish customers in her apartment until the Gestapo found out and sent her away.

Ember read those lines again, her heart racing.

This was what she wanted to find for her dissertation. A woman like Frau Weber who had sacrificed everything to take a stand.

Her biography didn't have an ending either, so Ember logged into the Arolsen Archives—Germany's service that traced victims of Nazi persecution—and found a brief record of the woman's life and then death in Ravensbrück. A tragic hero.

Ember quietly grieved the loss.

Most everyone who stood up against the Nazis, it seemed, had been exterminated.

Five more biographies followed, and then the next set of papers was about the Ahnenerbe where Hanna had worked, the information based on transcripts during the Nuremberg military trials. The Nazis believed that as the most advanced people group in the world, it was their duty to expand into new lands and raise the next generation of an Aryan race. By removing those they believed to be racially inferior from their land—squatters—they were doing all of humanity a service.

Heinrich Himmler, a rumored member of the Thule Society, helped found this academic ancestral heritage organization to prove the Aryan heritage through archaeology and to build a master race. With fifty different research branches called institutes, his organization studied music, water, linguistics, and ancient Nordic runes. Like Indiana Jones, the Ahnenerbe archaeologists traveled the world, trying to find artifacts such as the Holy Grail, legends like Atlantis, the truth about the yeti. Secrets to unlock their ancestral heritage. They studied animals and used calipers to measure facial dimensions of people around the world, recording their findings for what they deemed science.

According to Dr. Graf's research, this pseudoscience organization became part of the feared SS in 1940, its work headquartered at a castle named Wewelsburg. Himmler and Hitler both used people who called themselves Christian to further their work, but the intention of the Nazi Party was to create their own Germanic religion, a new world order stocked by strong, pure Aryans, and in order to do this, their SS officers needed to populate the earth.

Monogamy, Himmler believed, was a diabolical invention of the Catholic church, holding his SS men back from their purpose. He wanted his men to marry, to uphold society's norms, but faithfulness to one's wife was not a value. In fact, the Nazis passed a law that allowed a man to divorce his wife if she already had four children so he could begin a new family with another woman.

Himmler didn't value the commitment of marriage nor did he value the lives of his test subjects. During World War II, the Ahnenerbe expanded their research duties by conducting medical experiments on prisoners, studying what they called a subhuman prototype. And the Nazi doctors justified it all by saying the experiments helped advance the superiority of their Nordic race.

Ember's stomach rolled at the thought of it. How could those doctors, the scientists, truly validate such horror? And how could Hanna Strauss have been a member of this organization?

Like Mrs. Kiehl, Ember wanted to find the good in Hanna's life. She desperately wanted her to stand up against the Nazis. Say what they were doing was horrific. Wrong. She wanted Mrs. Kiehl's mother to save someone's life, like Frau Weber had done, not just their stories.

But then again, she couldn't dare judge Hanna, judge anyone, when she hadn't even been able to save the life of the one who needed her most.

A friend to the Jewish people, that's what Mrs. Kiehl had said about her mother. And there was no greater honor in the Hebrew culture than to remember one's story.

She shoved the papers into a drawer and checked her phone.

I'm headed your way, Dakota had written.

This time she wanted to see him. Welcome him to this town like he'd welcomed her back to the island.

I'm glad, she typed and then erased her words. She *was* glad, but how she needed to guard this heart of hers that was spinning back out of control. **A friend of Hanna's has invited us over tomorrow at 11. You want to do breakfast before?**

She thought for a moment and then agreed to meet up with him in the hotel lobby.

One more text, this one to Noah, and then her eyes began to close, the jet lag catching up with her pace.

Some of the Ahnenerbe members had probably chosen this course for their life, but others might have been forced to comply with the Reich.

If she'd lived in Germany during the Holocaust, would she have doubled back under the tide like those who'd resisted the enemy? Thrown one of her stones at Goliath?

Neither her parents nor Lukas had been forced into following the neo-Nazi code like the people of Germany. They chose to impound this hatred in their hearts. If it hadn't been for the fire, the raid, it was entirely possibly that she would have succumbed to the madness around her instead of resisted. That she would have chosen to hate as well.

She began tapping her legs as she lay down on the narrow bed.

She was tired of trying to forget the first fifteen years of her life, stuffing it away in a shoebox at the back of her mental closet. She couldn't just forget it. She needed to pray that in some way, God would heal it instead. Redeem what happened even as she moved forward.

When Dakota arrived, she would tell him exactly what happened in Idaho. Perhaps she would even tell him about Elsie.

If, by a miracle, Elsie was still alive, she prayed that her daughter had chosen to love instead of hate. That she had stood up against evil.

And Ember prayed that she could find out what happened to her daughter and that somehow she was still alive.

Her heart stirred at the thought, her hands resting at her sides.

Just once, she wished, Elsie would call her Mom.

39

HANNA

SPRING 1945

The medieval city of Nuremberg, a millennium of history, had been crushed in hours by the Allied bombs. Even though she'd tried to forget, that night kept replaying in Hanna's head, the terror as she and Lilly had huddled together in the mine, the smoke coiling around them. She'd spent those hours making peace with her Maker, thinking they would never survive, but God didn't take them home.

After the sky finally quieted, the air clear enough to breathe, she and Lilly had crept back down the hill, the thunderclouds raining ashes. They'd coaxed Schatzi out from under a sofa in the great hall, and Lilly had fallen asleep with the cat in her arms.

The Communists never arrived, thank God, and Kolman didn't return home. But the Nazi agents and soldiers were replaced by a swarm of American soldiers—*Amis*—who arrived via truck. They'd picked through mountains of rubble, searching for members of the Nazi Party. Enemy combatants. SS officers. Werewolves, as the remaining fighters called themselves. Men who were preparing to fight for the Fourth Reich.

The Americans fought among the smolder until they'd taken over the enemy's hive. Then some of the soldiers stayed behind in German homes to restore order to the chaos.

Stunde Null. That's what Germans called it. Their zero hour. They wanted to forget the past decade, begin rebuilding, but Hanna suspected that the world would remember.

Most of the museum had been destroyed in the bombing, and she didn't know where Director Kohlhaussen had gone . . . or if he was still alive. But those crates of artifacts that he'd carried out at night, she wondered if they were hidden in the abandoned mine. Perhaps that was why Himmler had sent her home to work at the museum. He wanted to use her and her property to protect all they'd plundered.

If the mine was being used for storage, it would explain why she'd seen someone walking in the forest at night. Why she'd been assigned a chauffeur to escort her into town and make sure that she stayed at the museum, why the driver and later the Gestapo agents often waited in the car while she was at home. They were guarding this land.

Both the fighting in Nuremberg and the fear of roaming lions kept her and Lilly close to the lodge. They'd seen smaller animals from the windows, freed from their cages, and exotic birds in the trees. She still didn't know what happened to the zoo's predators, but if they'd escaped, she hoped they'd wandered far into the wilderness where no one would ever find them.

Finally today, while Lilly was consoled by her make-believe world in the attic, Hanna felt safe in returning to the mine. She rattled the locked grate again, her flashlight beam breaking through the iron barrier. The light exposed another curve in the tunnel ahead, but she couldn't see any crates.

If only she could get past the gate. See what was inside. But she'd wait to tell the Americans what she suspected so these artifacts wouldn't be plundered again.

As she walked out of the tunnel, down to the meadow, she thought back to the Holy Grail she'd tried to uncover in France. To the artifacts they'd brought home from places like Sweden, Iceland, and Nepal. She'd been part of the plundering, from the stolen altarpieces to children from the east.

It was zero hour for her too.

Did Lilly have a mother waiting for her? If so, how would they find her in all of this mess?

The stolen artifacts, she thought, should be returned to their homes right away, but Lilly needed to stay in Germany where she was safe. Later, they would search for any survivors of her family. When order was restored.

And when the time was right, Hanna would honor those who'd been transported east by sharing their biographies and educate the world in hopes that the Nazis would never be able to persecute the Jewish people again.

A giraffe wandered out of the trees in front of her, stopping to eat the grass in her meadow. She waited by the edge, mesmerized by the animal who didn't seem to notice her, the breeze strumming the spring flowers. Then she heard a rumble in the distance, the crunch of gravel making her jump before a dusty Jeep circled her drive.

Hanna rushed out toward the vehicle, wanting to deter whoever had arrived before they tried to enter her house.

A man in a tailored blue suit and skewed tie stepped out, an American with hair shaved close to his head. "I've never seen a giraffe in the wild," he said, quite friendly, but she didn't trust him any more than she'd trusted the Gestapo agent who searched her house five years ago.

"A number of animals escaped from the zoo," she replied in English, thanks to the university and all the American and British friends she'd made in Berlin.

The giraffe turned its back to eat another clump of grass, and she wished that she could do the same with this agent.

The man flashed his identification card, but she didn't bother to look at it. "Surely you didn't come here to visit the giraffes."

He glanced at the flashlight in her hand, the mud on the hem of her trousers. "I've come to inquire about your husband."

She cringed. "I haven't seen my husband in two years."

He pulled a pocket-size memo pad from his coat and scribbled something on it. "Any children?"

"One daughter."

He scanned the forest behind her as if Lilly were among the trees.

"Visitors scare her," she said. Especially all the soldiers who'd congregated recently in Nuremberg, celebrating their victory over the Nazi empire.

She didn't tell this agent that she was celebrating as well.

He eyed the large house. "It's just you and your daughter living here?"

Her groan folded into the wind, remembering well the Gestapo agent who'd followed her to her bedroom. The knife was back in its proper place in the kitchen, but perhaps it was even more important for her to carry it now. "I don't have to answer that question."

The man looked back at her, and she expected him to demand an answer, a tour of her house even. "If you are hiding your husband, you will be held responsible for collaborating with the enemy."

She almost scoffed at this. Just weeks ago, this man in front of her was supposed to be the enemy.

He tapped the pen on the writing pad. "Kolman Strauss is his name?"

"Yes."

"Do you know what your husband has been doing the past five years?"

"He was in charge of an archaeological team. They were digging for German artifacts."

"During a war?"

"It was important to Himmler . . . ," she began, but the words, her lingering loyalty to a man who'd deceived them all, sounded absurd. The former Reichsführer had since taken his own life, swallowing a cyanide pill after he was apprehended by the British.

Kolman's digging, she suspected, had stopped years ago. Maybe even before the war.

The agent studied her face before slipping the pad back into his pocket and handing her a card with a telephone number. "You will alert me if Kolman returns."

"I have no telephone line," she said. "Nor electricity."

The man was generous enough to look concerned. "How about water?"

"We have a well."

"One of my men will check on you soon to make sure you have supplies."

"There's no need." She'd had men checking on her for the past five years, and the oversight had exhausted her. Now she just wanted to be left alone as she waited for news about Luisa and Frau Weber and the many others who'd disappeared.

40

EMBER

"Where does Frau Cohn live?" Dakota asked as they traversed a narrow winding lane.

Ember checked her phone. "Two blocks over."

The clouds had rained themselves dry during the night, the cobbles as shiny as the polished stone that Mrs. Kiehl wore around her neck.

"I need to take a picture for your grandmother." She snapped a photo of him standing beside a medieval arch. Later she'd text it to Kayla.

"And how are we supposed to ask questions about Hanna if Frau Cohn only speaks German?"

"I downloaded an app."

Dakota smiled. "I have a half dozen of those apps and I've yet to find one to replace a human."

"We'll figure it out," she said, mustering up much more confidence than she felt.

Frau Cohn was more prepared for the visit than Ember and Dakota. A woman in her thirties, wearing a summer dress and Birkenstocks, answered the door. And she greeted them in English.

"I hope it was a good trip," she said, inviting them into an Ikea-inspired apartment, modern pieces of art crowning the walls.

Ember wanted to hug the woman, but she extended her hand instead. "Your English is perfect."

"My grandmother insisted that I learn."

"Frau Cohn is your grandmother?" Ember asked.

"No, but she's like a grandmother to me."

The woman's name was Christine, and she introduced them to Frau Cohn, a slight woman whose stern-looking face broke into a smile when she welcomed them into her home. She was 103, Christine told them, and her mind was as sharp as it had been when she first secured her secretary job at the museum.

Over coffee and pastries, Christine seamlessly moderated the discussion between them.

"You're Lilly's grandson?" she asked, translating Frau Cohn's question for Dakota.

"I am."

"So many threads were left dangling in the aftermath of war. One day Lilly was here, and the next, it seemed, she was gone. Like so many during that time." Frau Cohn smoothed her hand over her thin hair. "I always wondered what happened to her."

Dakota inched forward on his seat. "She moved to Massachusetts with my great-grandfather, Charlie Ward."

"The investigator?"

He nodded. "He was only in Nuremberg for a few months . . ."

"I remember Herr Ward," Frau Cohn said through Christine. "He came back years later to look for Hanna."

"Do you know where Hanna went?" Ember asked.

Frau Cohn drew her fingers in a small circle on the evergreen-colored upholstery beside her. "Those years were a lifetime ago, I'm afraid."

History had a way of repeating itself, as if it were serving penance. The truth was a delicate line to navigate alongside the lingering guilt from those who survived the regime. The older generation suffered the weight of guilt from following a man like Hitler into the Holocaust, and their children and grandchildren now suffered from the wondering of how it could have happened.

Ember tried to soften her tone, tried not to press too hard. "Did you see Hanna before she left?"

"Everything was in shambles after the war. Old friends didn't even recognize each other in the streets." She took a slim bite of her pastry, Christine continuing to translate her words. "Is Lilly well?"

"Yes, but her childhood memories are confusing. She'd like to know what happened to her mother."

"Hanna adored her," Frau Cohn said. "I've never seen a better mother, especially one who'd adopted a child."

Ember looked over at Dakota, but his eyes were glued to the woman. He didn't seem surprised by this information. "Do you know where Lilly's biological family was from?"

"Berlin, I believe. Someplace up north." Frau Cohn sipped her black coffee before redirecting the conversation. "Hanna collected stories during the war, including the story of Christine's grandmother. It was remarkable really. She kept evidence for the investigators to use after the war, but they were only a glimpse of the atrocities that happened. Many things we didn't find out about until the trials.

"During the war, Jewish families were sent to a camp at the edge of town, just below the zoo," she explained. "They waited there with their mounds of things, anxious to begin their new life in the east. They thought it would be much better there."

"I didn't know there was a camp in Nuremberg," Ember said.

"Langwasser, they called it. On the old rally grounds. At first the Nazis used it for the Jewish people and others whom they considered to be enemies of the state. Then it was a camp for prisoners of war from Poland and France and other countries. After the war, the Allies used it to contain thousands of SS members."

"When did you see Hanna last?" Dakota asked.

"During the military trials," Christine translated. "When she brought her daughter over for a visit. Soldiers were being billeted at her lodge at the time, so Lilly came here to play."

Ember leaned forward. "I thought Hanna lived in an old convent."

"She did. The convent had been renovated into a hunting lodge long ago."

A piece—one of many, she feared—that she'd missed earlier.

"Do you know who lives there now?" she asked. "We would like to visit the labyrinth and church on the hill."

Christine translated the words, and Frau Cohn replied with a nod.

"You may visit," Christine said. "Tomorrow would be best for the owner."

Ember glanced over at Dakota. Neither of them would endanger the offer by asking who exactly owned the property.

They thanked Frau Cohn for her help; then Christine stood, escorting them back toward the door.

"Was your grandmother Jewish?" Ember asked Christine, wondering why Hanna had kept her story.

"No, but she didn't play by the Nazi rules."

"What exactly did she do?"

Christine stepped outside with them, the aroma of wood-fired sausage streaming up the lane. "She helped Hanna collect the stories at first and then she managed to get food and other supplies to the prisoners through the barbed wire at Langwasser. The Nazis captured her several months before Liberation, and the British found her later at Bergen-Belsen. Eventually she made her way home."

Another hero, Ember thought, in the midst.

"How did your grandmother know Hanna?"

"They were cousins." Christine smiled. "After the war, Oma distributed these stories to the people who came home or to those who had loved them."

41

HANNA

Charlie knocked on Hanna's door after a rainstorm had turned her drive into a lake. She opened the door, expecting another agent, and fell back against the post when he took off his hat.

The handsome grin from Charlie's youth had been sculpted into the mature smile of one who'd experienced much after their university years. They were the same age, but he looked a decade older than thirty in his suit and tie, as if the war had hewed away any glimpse of boyhood, replacing it with a man.

How she'd loved him when they were in Berlin, thought him to be the Emrich to her Cristyne. And this man, for a season, had seemed to love her back.

White blossoms dangled from the edge of her basket, the wild carrots on their ends robed in fresh dirt. She probably bore two extra decades on her face. The war had stolen years from all of them.

He slapped the doorpost, speaking to her in German. "I was hoping you still lived in this old house."

"The war forced me home," she said, closing the door behind him.

"It's nice to see you, Hanna."

Emotions washed over her like the rain. Memories of his visit ten years ago, of the many times she'd wondered about him since. She'd never imagined that he would return to Germany. Especially not to Nuremberg.

How different her life would have looked if he had proposed marriage. And if she'd been willing to give up her pursuit of archaeology to travel to America with him.

"I can speak English just fine."

"But my German is rusty," he replied. "I need the practice."

They'd spent hours together at the university, practicing both English and German and discussing the peculiarities of German law since Charlie had wanted to become a lawyer. She'd grown to care deeply for this man during their year together.

He studied her face as if she were on display. "Sadly, this war forced me far from my family."

"Martha's Vineyard," she said, remembering his description of the beaches. This man she'd loved with all her heart had returned to his island, a place far from the rubble. "You have a family?"

"I married a classmate from college."

Of course he'd married. Girls were probably lined up back home, waiting for a proposal after he graduated. "Why are you here?"

"The zoo is in shambles," he said.

She glanced out at the meadow, but the giraffe wasn't there today. "The United States government sent you here for a zoo?"

"People are living in the cages," he said. "My superior wants us to put the place back into order and protect the animals who remain."

The Americans, she'd heard, were still searching for members of the SS. Those they'd apprehended were being interned on the old rally grounds, but many more were hiding out so they wouldn't have to face the consequences of their actions. Perhaps their occupiers thought party members had found shelter in the zoo.

"I've wondered about the lions," she said.

"Those predators who didn't die in the bombing were shot."

"What about the elephants?" a quiet voice asked behind them.

They both turned to see Lilly standing in the kitchen entry, her stuffed animal tucked firmly under an arm, her lower lip trembling.

Charlie's eyes grew as wide as sunflowers before he responded. "The elephants are just fine."

"There's a baby—" Lilly started.

"The baby is with her mother." Whether Charlie was telling the truth or not, Hanna didn't know, but the words seemed to comfort her daughter. "Now we must make sure the rest of the animals are safe."

Lilly glanced up at her. "The mothers of the other animals must be worried."

"We're here to return all of them home."

Questions raged through Charlie's eyes when Hanna introduced him to her daughter.

Charlie knelt beside the girl. "How old are you, Lilly?"

"Nine."

Charlie looked back up, his brown eyes flickering as he seemed calculate the numbers. "Nine?"

"You must be hungry," Hanna said, stepping away. "I have fresh berries in the kitchen."

He rose again, studying Hanna as if she'd wiped some of the dirt from the wild carrots across her face, his easy smile fading away. "She's nine years old . . ."

She didn't want to explain to this man how she'd raised a daughter who would have been born the year after she and Charlie had been together.

"You are always welcome to visit us." She turned toward the

kitchen, her head spinning. "Dinner, perhaps, when we receive our next rations."

"Hanna—"

But she didn't want to hear what else he had to say. He followed her and Lilly into the kitchen, and when she looked out the window, she saw a canvassed army truck wading through the pool on her drive, the kind of truck that transported soldiers.

She turned slowly back to him, knowing the truth but wanting to avoid it for as long as possible. "You're not just here for a visit."

He shook his head, speaking in English now. "Our commander is billeting six of us in your house to be close to the zoo."

"You were sent ahead to calm the storm," she said.

"No storms, Hanna. Simply to visit an old friend."

Friends. That's what she had been to him. Only a friend.

She placed the carrots into a colander and turned on the faucet, the water washing away the dirt. "The zookeeper has a large house. It's right outside the entrance."

"Most of it was destroyed in the bombing." He took the colander from her shaking hands, put it on the counter before turning off the water. "You'll have electricity soon, and we'll be hiring a housekeeper. I'll share our rations with you and Lilly."

"You're not supposed to be fraternizing with Germans."

Fraternizing—even those who didn't speak English were well-versed in that word. Fraternizing and denazification.

"We're rooming with you. Not fraternizing."

"I don't want soldiers in my house." Nor did she want Charlie here with his questions.

"I'm afraid this isn't a choice either of us get to make, but George Patton has mandated these men be on their very best behavior. If not, they'll face stiff consequences."

She nodded as if she had a choice in the matter. Then she decided to claim her space before the soldiers took over every room. "Lilly and I will sleep together in my bedroom."

"That would be fine."

Hanna wiped a puddle of water off the counter as she spoke to her daughter. "Go pack up your things."

Lilly nodded, her blue eyes tinted gray in this light, before hurrying out of the kitchen.

Charlie didn't move. "Is she mine?"

"I'm not going to talk about her." She wouldn't lie to him, but she wouldn't tell him where Lilly had come from either. If he drew conclusions, so be it. He was the one who'd shown up at her door uninvited this afternoon, without any time for her to prepare. Now she had to protect her daughter from him and all the men still inside that truck.

"I have a right to—"

"You have a right to my house perhaps, but you have no right to my family."

Except for the man she'd married. Charlie could have him.

42

EMBER

White lights were strung along Nuremberg's ancient limbs, the castle glowing like a Christmas angel on its throne of pine. Dakota and Ember strolled through town on this warm night, into the Hobbit-like hole of a restaurant with waxed tables and a row of beer steins displayed like porcelain on the wall.

"It's not exactly a coffee date," Dakota said after they ordered sauerkraut and local sausages, charred over a grill.

"It's better."

"I doubt there's anything left in that labyrinth," he said as if he needed to soften the blow from Mrs. Kiehl's memory of Hanna digging in that place.

"We can always pray while we're there."

He took a sip of dark beer. "Have you ever prayed in a labyrinth?"

She nodded, her mind wandering to the riverside labyrinth in Georgetown. "It's like a prayer pilgrimage," she explained. "You draw closer to God as you circle; then you drop your burdens in the middle. On the way out, you thank God for His blessings."

"There's no one quite like you, Ember."

She studied his face to see if he was teasing her, but he seemed serious. "Every day, I think, should be a pilgrimage."

Christine had told them about Luisa Gruenewald and her first husband, Paul. The stumbling stone that her family had designed for his childhood home after he'd been killed at Auschwitz. While the biographies had been used during the Nuremberg trials, it turned out they were even more important for those who'd lost loved ones and for those who returned from concentration camps. They validated what each person had experienced when so many were trying to forget.

The autobiography of Christine's grandmother had told the story of Luisa's humiliation in front of the entire town of Nuremberg. But she didn't let the shame of it keep her from doing good. She'd loved her husband fiercely, being faithful even when the government demanded a divorce. She'd cared for the hungry and sick and oppressed when the authorities saw them as problems instead of people.

Courage like that, Ember thought, could change the world.

She would use Luisa's story in her dissertation.

A server dressed in a tan-and-white dirndl, teal earrings dangling an inch above her shoulders, delivered their steaming plates of food. As they ate, Ember was transported back to high school, to their junior year when Dakota had sat across from her in the library to discuss *The Odyssey*. They'd been assigned to write a speech together about secrets and identity. About what makes a hero.

She'd done the writing, of course. Neither of them had really considered that he might contribute. At the time, it hadn't even mattered to her that he didn't offer to help, and that was the problem. She'd elevated—or lowered—Dakota to the level of a god she must serve.

Whichever, she'd seen Dakota as someone who was better than

her. Someone she didn't deserve. All she had wanted was to be a normal teenager who liked music and movies and boys. A teenager who hadn't lost her parents or child. But normal had slipped through her grasp long ago. Nothing about her past, it seemed, could be summed up as ordinary.

"Do you remember when Mrs. Smith selected us to be partners to read *The Odyssey*?" she asked.

The blank look on his face proved her point.

"Of course you don't remember." The highlight of her year hadn't even blipped his Richter scale. "I read the poem and wrote the speech. You only had to read it to the class."

"I thought I wrote that speech."

She shook her head.

"I always thought you were talented, Ember. A lousy way to show it, I know. I didn't deserve an ounce of your admiration."

She tried to force a smile onto her lips, embrace the normal. "You really didn't."

"If we could go back, I'd do everything differently."

"Starting with . . ."

"*Odyssey*, I suppose. That speech would have taken weeks to write because I would have wanted to spend hours upon hours with you."

If only they could have a do-over.

"And I would have gone to your brother," he continued. "Asked him if I could take you out on a real date to get seafood in Oak Bluffs."

She looped a finger around the mug handle. "I would have done just about anything for you back then. It would have been a lousy relationship. No relationship, really." Just hero worship that he would have tired of quickly.

"Well, if I had my personal *Groundhog Day*, I'd do it all again. The right way."

He waited for her to speak, as if her words might encourage this endeavor, but he wasn't the weatherman in some nineties comedy. Nor was she going to spill her heart out on a redo.

Her phone chimed—it was 9:40 local time.

She sent her favorite ten-year-old a text, and he replied right back. Noah didn't understand why she had to be gone so long, but his father had filled their freezer with Phish Food. And he'd been able to rework his schedule so he could meet his son at the bus stop every day.

"Why is your father angry with your grandmother?" she asked tentatively, a skater testing out the ice.

Dakota motioned for the server and paid their bill. "You want to walk a bit more?"

"Sure."

Last night's rainstorm had chased Nurembergers inside, but this evening people huddled around outdoor tables, eating dinner and sipping their wine. Laughter drifted through the buildings, bringing life to the old stones as Dakota and Ember climbed up to the castle. The steep hill flattened into a plateau, an open courtyard beside the locked castle doors.

"You're hiding something," she said softly as she looked out over the city lights, marveling at the restoration after this town had been destroyed by bombs.

"Something I'm ashamed of . . ."

"Shame, I think, shuts us off from those who care most." At least, that's what her counselor once said.

He turned to lean back against the wall. "Dad decided to take a DNA test this spring to prove the purity of his genes, but the results were not what he anticipated. He sent in new samples, multiple times, but they all came back the same. He's half-Jewish, on his maternal side."

She blinked. "You're ashamed of being Jewish?"

"Of course not." He looked wounded by her question. "But my dad is furious at Gram for 'ruining' his genes. He thinks she lied to him."

"Did she know she was partially Jewish?"

"No. She doesn't remember much before Charlie brought her to the island, but she's always been proud of her German heritage."

"Perhaps Hanna was able to hide her Jewish background during the war."

"It would have been hard to do that in Nuremberg, wouldn't it?"

"Extremely," Ember said. "Does your grandmother want to know the truth?"

"I think she might be afraid of it."

"I understand." Both their families were messy, it seemed. "People might lie, but genetics never do."

"I want to find out what happened to my grandmother, for our family's sake," he said. "I want my children one day to know exactly where they came from."

"You'll be a good dad, Dakota." So different from his father. "Like Charlie."

"I pray so."

The past might not define her—define either of them—but others created their own definition from the little they knew. Conclusion jumping, like she'd done so often herself.

If Dakota was going to run, now was the time. Once she told him the truth of her past.

"Have you heard of the Aryan Council?" she asked.

"It was in Idaho—"

She nodded. "After my father left Martha's Vineyard, he decided it was his mandate to strengthen the white race and destroy anyone he perceived to threaten it. He founded this hostile group in a former Christian camp near Coeur d'Alene and stocked the commune with guns for the millennium. The FBI tore it apart at the end of 1999 before they could attempt their new world order. But it's how I was raised. Me and my baby."

She couldn't blame Dakota for running now, but he didn't move. "You had a baby?"

She nodded again, drumming the damp wall. "Her name was Elsie. We think she drowned in the lake, when the FBI raided."

"Oh, Ember . . ."

"In the aftermath I felt like I was drowning as well, but returning to Martha's Vineyard was a new start. A place for me to learn how to live."

His gaze dropped to the cobblestones. "My dad began to embrace the religion of white supremacy when I was a child."

"Did my father convert him?" she asked, alarmed.

"He was already well on the way, I'm told, before your dad arrived. Mom wouldn't let him go to your father's church, but they met secretly. Hiring Alex was a way for him to stay connected, I think."

Guilt—*Vergangenheitsbewältigung*—rushed over her. As if this were somehow her fault.

"Now I'm the one sorry."

"You didn't do anything wrong," he said, his voice strong. "At some point, Dad decided that the trouble with the world, all of his problems, boiled down to the race issue. He moved west to where, I'm told, he found others equally devoted to the Aryan cause."

She leaned forward. "Is your dad still in Idaho?"

"That's what Gram says. I haven't talked to him in years."

She looked back out at the lights. Titus Kiehl had known for many years where she and Alex lived. He'd never made any attempt to harass either of them, but perhaps Ember became a threat when she started her fellowship at the Holocaust museum.

"Dakota—" She took a deep breath. "The letters I've been getting are from Idaho. I wonder if members of the Aryan Council are still working there."

He reached for her hand, squeezing it gently. "You have to tell someone about my dad."

"I'll call the head of security at the museum. She's working with the Boise police."

It was a few minutes before five in Washington, so she placed the call, giving Rebekah the information.

She and Dakota walked quietly back down the hill, hand in hand, as if nothing else mattered in that moment except being together. They were much different from the two teenagers who'd failed as friends in their high school years. Both of them knew who they were now, beyond their DNA.

"Good night, Em," he said, looking like how she'd felt in all her awkwardness at seventeen. As if he wasn't sure if he should give her a hug or even kiss her on the cheek.

This time, she didn't correct him for the nickname. Instead she patted his shoulder, like he'd done to her at the Jetway. "Good night."

And she slipped quickly up to her room.

43

HANNA

SUMMER 1945

Hanna spent her summer with a team of women carting mounds of rubble from Old Town to a towering debris hill called Silberbuck on the Nazi Party Rally Grounds. Lilly returned to school during the morning hours, in a building outside the wall where the teacher didn't require her to measure fellow students. Afternoons Lilly often spent with Grete Cohn.

How ironic, she thought, to be digging haphazardly through piles of destruction when she used to dig with great care in her profession. Now she was shoveling up pieces of broken buildings and artifacts alike in order to survive, throwing it all into wheelbarrows, the income providing for their most basic needs.

The summer garden and forest at home had given her and Lilly a full bounty, but autumn was coming and food was strictly rationed. She didn't want to rely on the Americans to feed them.

Daily she went to the Red Cross, checking for information about

Luisa Gruenewald and Marianne Weber. She'd pinned their names to the bulletin boards, along with a picture of Luisa, but neither woman had been found.

Her work at the museum seemed like a lifetime ago. She didn't know what happened to all the crates she'd packed and neither did Grete, but no amount of wrappings, no cellar, could have withstood this bombing in Old Town. The director had used the mine, she hoped, to store it all away.

The zoo reopened in May and new animals arrived almost daily from zoos across Europe that had suffered irreparable damage. American troops continued to oversee the Tiergarten, so the soldiers remained in her home. And Charlie. She made certain she was never alone with him, and he didn't push the issue. He was rarely at the lodge anyway.

This afternoon, though, she was shocked to see him walking through the market square with Director Kohlhaussen and several American officers. The director didn't see her, didn't even seem to look at any of the workers he passed. His mind, she guessed, was focused on trying to recover any remaining artifacts.

But what was Charlie doing with him?

An orphan, one of hundreds who lived among the wreckage on these streets, stopped Charlie. Guttersnipes, the soldiers called them. Some of them had lived at the zoo. Others built their own little rooms out of the rubble. They all stole coal from the trains to exchange for food.

Charlie took out a silver case from his pocket, gave him a Chesterfield. Americans weren't supposed to give gifts to any German, young or old, but this one cigarette would buy the boy food for a week.

If something happened to her, God forbid, Lilly would be on the streets with these orphans. They'd survived the war, but Lilly, she feared, would never make it trying to live among the brokenness of their city.

"No time to linger," the supervisor said, and Hanna scooped another pile of rubble in her shovel, one of thousands necessary to relocate the remains of Lorenzkirche.

When she turned back, Charlie and the other men were gone.

That night, she slipped out of her room after Lilly slept. Charlie was downstairs at the desk, eight other soldiers smoking their cigarettes in the great hall, playing cards in the glow of electric light, drinking their schnapps.

She sat down beside him. "You're not really here for the zoo, are you?"

His eyes flashed in response; then he motioned to the other men. They crushed their cigarettes in an ashtray and stomped up to beds scattered in the three remaining bedrooms and between dollhouses they'd helped restore.

"The soldiers are working at the zoo," he said.

"But not you," she persisted. "What exactly are you doing here?"

"I have another assignment in Nuremberg."

She studied the empty space behind the desk where Hitler's portrait had hung. Kindling, she'd used it for over the winter. One day she would put Saint Katharine back on the wall.

"I saw you today," she said, "walking through the Hauptmarkt."

He nodded but didn't say anything.

"I helped Director Kohlhaussen pack crates to store the museum's artwork and other artifacts during the war, but no one has told me if these crates have been found."

"They've been located," he said. "We are working with the director to safely retrieve it all."

"The crates survived the bombing?"

He nodded again, but he didn't tell her where they were. The information, she thought, must be kept secret to stop looters, but if they'd found the museum's cache on her property, wouldn't she have seen their trucks?

Then again, she never saw German soldiers bringing crates up to the mine.

Was this the reason that Charlie decided to billet at her home? To find all the artifacts? But if the crates were on her property, why was he with the director in Old Town?

Charlie, like her husband, was keeping secrets. She wouldn't ask again, nor would she tell him about the locked grate until he was honest with her. Or she found out what was inside.

A picture reappeared in her mind of Kolman on those early mornings before she rose, walking through the meadow.

"Have your men located Kolman?" she asked.

He watched her carefully before responding. "We have not."

"But you are continuing to look for him."

"Intently," he said. "We are searching for everyone who persecuted the Jewish people."

Kolman had tormented her in his own way, but persecuting others? What had her husband done?

"Kolman is an archaeologist . . ."

"*Was* an archaeologist," he said. "We've found camps of people in the east, and terrible things happened there . . . Kolman, we believe, was an integral part of it."

Nausea rippled up from her stomach, and she took several deep breaths to calm it. As much as she wanted to contradict this possibility, as most wives would do, she wondered if Kolman had murdered some of the Jewish people.

"We have to find the truth, Hanna."

She straightened the ashtray on the coffee table, wanting to right in some way what Kolman—*who* Kolman—had wronged.

"During the war," she said slowly, "I kept the stories of what happened to some of the Jews in Nuremberg. Of what the Nazis did—"

He inched forward. "Do you still have them?"

"Yes." She turned toward the window. "They are hidden away."

"We have to convict these beasts," he said, his eyes flashing. "I need the stories, and I need evidence to prove what they did."

She turned the ashtray one more time before speaking again. "Are you here to convict me as well?"

"Have you done something wrong?" he asked quietly as if he was afraid of her answer.

She glanced up at the ceiling, to the space below where Lilly slept. "I cared for things taken from fellow Germans and other countries. I protected them so they wouldn't be harmed. At first I didn't know they were stolen, but eventually I found out."

He sighed. "It was an impossible situation."

"What have you heard from Poland?" she asked. "Some of those artifacts . . ."

"Poland is in a terrible state. The Russians have taken over."

"So nothing will be returned?"

"Eventually, I hope, but not now."

"What about the people?" she asked.

"We are working to bring everyone home."

Bringing the Germans home from Poland, but what about returning the Polish children? She didn't dare ask. Didn't even want to know, really. Lilly would be sent into a broken state, she had no doubt. Her beautiful daughter would be a target for those who preyed on children.

She had to protect Lilly, at least until the world began to make sense again.

At first light she walked out to the mine, but the grate was still locked and didn't appear to be disturbed. She continued her walk to the labyrinth and dug up the stories, dozens of them, she'd buried under the rocks. But she left Lilly's paperwork under the soil. Charlie was here to return things, to right what had gone wrong. To bring justice back to Germany.

It wouldn't be justice to send Lilly back to Poland. Not yet.

One day she would go with her daughter and see if the Nowak family survived the war.

44

EMBER

"You can't go back."

Ember woke in the middle of the night, the fog clearing as those words rattled in her head. The night of the fire, in those moments when Ember was fighting to save Elsie's life, Aimee had told her that she couldn't go back to the cabin.

A latch flipped inside her. A quaking that shifted the fragments of memories even as she hammered the mattress with her fists. She couldn't go back, didn't want to go . . . unless she could recall the missing pieces in the fog. That was the only reason she'd return.

Her hands began to slow, her mind drifting.

For years, the tapping had calmed the memories, but she decided to stop for just this moment, allow herself to step back into that dark place one more time.

So she could remember.

She had kissed Elsie's head before walking down to the lake that night, like she always did. And she'd tiptoed out of their room so Lukas wouldn't hear.

Her heart had been wrecked, the turmoil overwhelming. The lake had called to her, but God's call was stronger. A call to live.

Aimee was about five years older than she was, the daughter of another elder. While Ember hadn't really called her a friend—they'd all been raised to be suspicious of one another—she knew her well enough to know her greatest secret.

Joseph didn't allow anyone to deliver things to the compound, so Aimee was one of the few who drove into Coeur d'Alene for supplies. And Aimee had fallen head over heels for the young man who'd bagged their groceries.

Jim. Tim. Something like that. The son of the store's owner. And he seemed to be quite enamored with Aimee as well.

It had been Aimee who'd yelled at her that fateful night, Aimee who'd pushed her into the boat. Aimee who'd said they had to go.

But in all of the chaos, where had Aimee gone?

People had crowded onto the pontoon boat that took Ember across Eagle Lake, but she didn't remember seeing Aimee onboard. Had she ridden over with Lukas?

If so, perhaps she would remember what happened to Elsie.

Few of the Aryan Council members had been identified in the news stories, but Aimee had been quoted once, a year or so after the fire, in an article about Lukas and his conviction.

Ember opened her tablet and began sifting back through the hundreds of files and interviews that she'd stored online, searching until she found the quote.

"God saved my life that night," Aimee had said. "Rescued me from the fire and set me on higher ground."

The details were sparse, Aimee's last name withheld, but the reporter said she had married and wanted nothing else to do with the council.

What if she did remember what happened on the lake? Her memories might be as fragmented as Ember's, but if she had seen Lukas, Elsie . . .

A miracle, that's what she had prayed for. And in order for a miracle to happen, she would have to first throw one of her stones.

She found a listing for the grocery in Coeur d'Alene, but it had since been bought out by a conglomerate, so she began searching for the owners of grocery stores across northern Idaho, hoping the son might have pursued his father's work.

When she didn't find anything, she expanded her search until she located a Timothy and Aimee Lane, owners of several grocery stores in Montana. And a corporate photograph that matched the face of the woman who'd broken free the same night as Ember.

She called the grocery in Kalispell, asked for Aimee Lane, and the manager said he'd tell her that Sarah called.

Her name had been hidden for so long, but the letter writer knew the truth and probably others like him. It was time to use her old name for good.

with the other mothers and some of the children. Why couldn't she leave with them?

Gunshots rumbled in the distance and the sound silenced her cries, but the women in the trucks only cried louder.

Where were her brothers? They'd promised Mami not to let the soldiers take her away.

An airplane slashed through the sky, raining down fire on their heads. Charlie tossed her into a different truck than Mami, the bed filled with dozens of children. Then he climbed in beside her.

Agony ripped through Lilly when the truck rolled away, leaving her mother behind in the smoke. Digging in the dirt. Burying tins under rocks. Alone.

She flung her arm out again, trying to get away from Charlie and the other soldiers, but they laughed at her pain. Laughed when she wet her pants.

A crash, and Lilly sat up in the darkness, her heart racing as she scanned the bedroom that she'd shared with Albert Kiehl for almost fifty years, before he'd gone out on a wintry night two years back to fill the sheep's trough.

A patch of ice. A hip injury. And his body failed him.

How she missed that man who used to wake with her in the night, talk her through these nightmares. Remind her that dreams rarely made sense, like the brothers that she dreamed about as often as Charlie Ward taking her away.

Why had Charlie, the man who was supposed to love her, stolen her away from her mother? She wished she could have asked him, but her nightmares had started long after this man she'd called father was gone.

She'd been young, nine years old when she left Germany with him. She couldn't remember much before this island. Almost as if she had to forget the past in order to embrace her new life here.

Forgetting was what she needed to push forward.

Forgetting, in a sense, kept her alive.

But she had begun to remember more about Hanna. About her mother kneeling in the forest to pray, near the abbey. By the stones.

Her mother had always been digging in those stones.

Her memories were so scattered, shifting with the passing of time. And the memory that she wished to erase, the one of her being taken away, was the one that preyed upon her sleep.

She had no brothers, not even through Charlie and her American mother. But Charlie told her often, when she was younger, that he loved her as his own. Still, what kind of loving person separates a mother and child? Surely Charlie could have found a way to bring both Hanna and Lilly back to the States. Mami could have done her digging on this island.

Lilly leaned back against the pillows, trying to coerce memories out of the caverns in her head. They were important, she thought. Important, even, to what Ember was trying to find now.

What had Hanna buried in the forest?

Frau Weber was the one who'd said Hanna had been a friend to the Jewish people, and she'd clung to those words. Hanna had worked for the Nazis, but she hadn't been one of the bad ones.

A good Nazi.

That wasn't right. A good German.

There were good and bad members of every people group. Her German father had been one of the bad ones, but not her mother. Mami had been good to Lilly, every year they spent together.

If only Ember could find out the good that her mother had done. Find if she had indeed been the hero that Frau Weber believed her to be.

She needed to call Dakota, tell him everything she knew. Tell him about her crazy dreams. Perhaps it would help them find out where Hanna had gone.

Her clock, she'd knocked to the floor, but it was still night, darkness blinding the view from her window. Sleep never returned after these dreams, so she put on her slippers, padded into the kitchen for tea.

The house had become eerily quiet after Albert's death. She welcomed Kayla's company during the day, but her housekeeper had a family of her own to care for at night.

The clock in the kitchen read 2:23. She flipped on the lights and turned on the electric kettle. A cup of black tea always helped chase these nightmares away.

On the dining room wall were pictures of the Ward and Kiehl families. One of Charlie and her when she was about twelve, carrying fishing poles down to the pond. As his only heir, Charlie had taught her everything about the farm and this island.

Albert had no experience in farming, but he'd caught on quickly and Titus had pitched in. Their son didn't have any long-term interest in the farm, but she'd thought he would stay on the island, for the money if nothing else. Instead he'd moved to Idaho.

Hotheaded, that was the demeanor of their son. Way too proud of being white in this diverse country. And he'd gotten it from her; that's what she feared. He'd grown up hearing her stories about Germany along with the ones that Albert liked to tell about his family before they'd immigrated to the United States. His parents left in the 1930s when the Nazis began vying for power.

She was proud of her German heritage, and she'd never tried to hide that. But she also didn't want others, her own son especially, to believe that she thought Germans were somehow an elite race.

God help her, she hoped that she'd never given the impression to anyone that she thought she deserved to sit on some sort of throne. What many of the German people had done during the war was horrific. Still, to this day, she couldn't watch movies, read books about World War II. She had enough of a war in her mind, battling the memories. And on nights like this, it felt like the memories had captured her in their scope.

The telephone rang, and she knew exactly who it was.

"Hello, Kayla."

"Why is your light on?"

"I used to be able to get up in the middle of the night for a cup of tea, and nobody bothered me."

The woman ignored her testiness. "Are you okay?"

"I—" A gunshot blasted through her mind. The rattling of plane engines. Crackle of fire. And with the crackle came the heat that flooded up her skin, her lungs heaving from the smoke. She collapsed onto a kitchen chair, the mug shattering on the floor.

She'd forgotten to fill it with water.

"Lilly?"

Her voice shook. "I don't know what's wrong."

"I'll be right over."

She was being pulled away to a place she didn't want to go.

Charlie had tried to be a good father to her, in the decades he had left on the earth, but when she'd asked about Hanna, he would only say she'd been lost like so many in the chaos after the war.

But Hanna hadn't disappeared. Charlie had taken Lilly away from her, all the way across the Atlantic. And she still wanted to find her mother.

Her legs felt wet, and she remembered sitting in a hard chair, the longing for her family so deep. She'd called out for Mami and someone had whipped her for it.

A wolf.

Her head ached, her hands shook, trying to sort it all out.

It wasn't a wolf. It was the matron.

But why was a matron chasing her through the forest?

None of it made sense.

She reached out again in the darkness, searching for her mother until she found arms to hold her.

"I'm right here," Mami said. "The ambulance is on its way."

But she didn't need an ambulance. She only needed to go home.

46

EMBER

Cliffs had been carved into the stone walls above the hunting lodge, just like Mrs. Kiehl had described, and at the top of the hill, she and Dakota found a moss-covered wall from the abbey, leaning against the trees.

On the opposite side of the ruins was the labyrinth, barely noticeable with each stone pressed into the ground, the mossy tops circling like an aisle runner to the center. They never would have found this place without Mrs. Kiehl's direction, but Ember could see it clearly now, hundreds of stones curling around themselves, the never-ending circle of time.

She knelt by one of the stones, brushing her hands over the moss, and saw a letter carved underneath. She clawed at the moss, scraping it away until the letter *M* appeared. "There are initials on these."

"Remarkable." Dakota knelt beside her and scraped off more moss until they saw the letter *P*. "They're like the memorial stones in the Bible."

She looked up. "From where in the Bible?"

"Joshua, I think." He tapped his phone. "When God told the Israelites to collect twelve stones so they'd never forget what He did."

He showed her his phone, the passage from Joshua.

"In the future your children will ask you, 'What do these stones mean?' Then you can tell them . . ."

That the Jordan River stopped flowing as the Ark of the Lord's Covenant crossed, drying up like the Red Sea. Memorial stones so the world would forever remember that God's hand is powerful. Holy. That evil cannot stand in His midst.

Ember studied the swirl of stones. The tangle of memories.

Which of these many stones had Hanna been digging under?

All they'd brought were two trowels, purchased from a merchant near the zoo. But even with these tools, it would take days to mine this dirt.

She sighed. "Where should we begin?"

It was early in Martha's Vineyard, a little after five, but Dakota said Kayla might already be at the house, helping Gram prepare for the day. He'd ask her.

But his face flushed after Kayla answered the phone. Whatever she said seemed to frighten him.

"Where is she?" Dakota demanded, his cell phone fixed against his shoulder.

Fear captured his gaze, and she marveled at how this man had changed. She didn't doubt it now. He cared more about Mrs. Kiehl at least than she'd ever imagined him being able to care about anyone.

"Is she okay?" Ember whispered.

He nodded, but the worry lingered in his eyes as he stepped away.

She began to pray for Mrs. Kiehl as she stepped between the stones, circling slowly like nuns would have done centuries ago. And she prayed for Elsie, if she was still alive, that she would know the true love of a father and it would wash away any hatred from her heart, capturing her soul.

Then Ember prayed for whoever was stalking her, that the authorities would find him or her before they hurt anyone. And that God would heal the animosity in the Kiehl family.

Her burden grew heavier as if she carried the weight of it all. Like each rock, about two hundred of them, had latched themselves to her ankles, the wide path narrowing as she drew closer to the middle.

She couldn't carry it any longer.

As she neared the center of the labyrinth, her steps slowed. The path stopped at a stump, at this place of surrender, and she must stop as well.

Collapsing on her denimed knees, crushing the leaves, she laid it all right there at the foot of a cross she couldn't see. A cross that could bear every pound of her burden. Shoulders that could balance the weight of her past, every ounce of her pain.

Love, overwhelming, swallowed her as she sank back into the leaves, the center stump steady beneath her hands.

Beloved.

Her soul stirred at the word. She was loved, deeply loved, not because of what she did or said or pretended to be. She was loved because God had chosen to love her when she was still in her mother's womb. Not because of her blood. Because she was His daughter.

She couldn't force people to stop hating. They had to choose it for themselves. God hadn't sent His Son as a narrow-minded dictator who demanded they follow Him. He'd sent His Son as a gift. Because there was no other way. Out of His deep love, this outpouring free to everyone He'd created, God paved a pathway on the back of His Son.

No matter what she'd done, what anyone had done, it wasn't beyond the width across Christ's arms. The two nails that staked boundaries from the east to west, a giant crevice between them that dropped into the endless depth of His love.

He'd loved her in the darkness of that chasm. Even when she'd turned her back, run away, He was waiting there all along.

The hatred slipped off her own shoulders, falling into that chasm, lost forever. And she never wanted to see it again.

She dug her trowel into the soil, inches from where a cross might have stood, wondering if Hanna might have done her digging here too. A chain appeared in the dirt, and she reached for it carefully.

Had Hanna buried this?

It was a cylinder piece made of copper and iron, Roman numerals displayed on its face. A watch from an era long past, like the one invented by Peter Henlein in Nuremberg. Centuries before Hanna would have visited this place.

Ember stared at it for a moment, thinking about the abbey bells that were stored away in a museum cellar, preserving them for the next generation. But they were far from where they were meant to be. The earth had done a good job preserving this watch, she thought. She might never know its story, but the labyrinth, she decided, was its home.

She took a picture of the watch to show Dakota, then scooped dirt back over it before retracing her steps. With each stone she passed, she thanked God for one of His many gifts. For the brother who'd cared for her. For the niece and nephew she loved. For the man who waited for her in the trees. And for the woman on Martha's Vineyard who'd reopened her heart to the truth.

How she wanted to give this gift of truth to Mrs. Kiehl.

The worries on this mountain must have been staggering at one time, but also the gratefulness. A grateful heart, she'd read, was better than medicine for healing one on the inside.

The path grew wider, the center far behind, and she felt lighter as she stepped out of the stone circle, breathing in the forest air, wiping her face dry from the tears. It was perhaps the greatest blessing of all, being able to lay down that hatred she'd carried for so long. Lay it down and leave it here.

Her soul sang in response, like a meadowlark in the trees.

Dakota hiked back toward the labyrinth, pocketing his phone.

"What happened to your grandmother?" Ember asked.

"She collapsed on the kitchen floor during the night."

Her heart sank.

"She's awake now, and my mom is with her at the hospital. The doctor believes it's a form of PTSD. Delayed onset. Apparently a memory is trying to elbow its way out, and her body isn't able to take the load of it. She keeps calling out for her mother, as if Hanna might still be alive."

Ember shook her head. "I've triggered something terrible, haven't I?"

"She's been having nightmares for several years," Dakota said.

"If only we could find out what happened to Hanna . . ."

"Kayla said Gram's been talking about the stones again. About her mother digging here. Mom is worried, and she said that my dad is angry again."

"Because your grandmother is in the hospital?"

"No, because he doesn't want us to find anything that might validate the results of his genetic test. My mom, on the other hand, doesn't want me to stop searching."

"I found an old watch," Ember told him, showing him the picture. "In the center of the labyrinth."

"Gram said that Hanna buried a coffee can here."

Ember tucked her phone back into her pocket and knelt down with her trowel beside the entrance. Then she slowly turned the first mossy stone over, pressing into the earth for whatever it was that Hanna left behind.

Nothing appeared underneath.

"We might be here for a week," Dakota said as he edged the second stone back across a hole.

"Not if you have shovels." They turned to see Christine, carrying three of them under her arm. "I thought these might help."

Ember hugged the woman. She couldn't help herself.

Christine handed her a shovel, and Ember rolled the handle between her palms. "This is so much better than a trowel."

"Are we allowed to dig like this on private property?" Dakota asked.

Christine held one of the shovels out to him. "You can if the owner gives you permission."

"Who is the owner?" Ember asked as he took it.

"Me." The young woman smiled. "I inherited this place from my grandmother."

"Luisa?"

Christine nodded. "Hanna left the house and land to her."

"I wonder what else Hanna left behind . . ." Ember gently turned over the next stone with her foot and inched the blade into the sandy soil. Nothing appeared in the hole, so she refilled the dirt and moved on to the next rock. And the next.

Every stone bore the burdens of those who had prayed here over the centuries. Burdens and then the spill of their grateful hearts, collecting blessings like raindrops, growing the moss, it seemed, from the tears.

"I'm going to move to the center," Ember said as Dakota and Christine began to dig near the front.

She stepped over the loop of stones, making a straight path to the stump. Then she stopped. One of the stones in her path was missing part of its stole, as if an animal had clawed the moss away.

Kneeling down beside it, she saw the letter carved into the top.

L, for Lilly.

"Dakota," she whispered, and both he and Christine joined her.

She rolled the stone away; then Dakota dug his blade into the dirt. It clanked against tin.

He nodded for Ember to retrieve it, but this was his family's story. "It's yours," she said.

The can was round, any exterior printing erased with time.

Inside were several official-looking sheets of paper, each one typed in German and signed.

Dakota handed them over to Christine and she quickly perused them.

"These are adoption papers." Christine lowered them to her side. "Hanna must have hidden them before she disappeared."

Dakota looked up. "Adoption paperwork for who?"

"A girl named Roza Nowak," she said.

"Hanna adopted another child?" Dakota dumped dirt back into the hole, patting it down with his blade.

"No." Christine hesitated, looking back at the document. "Only one. The girl that Hanna's husband supposedly brought her from Berlin."

He shook his head. "I don't understand."

"Have you ever heard of Lebensborn?" she asked. "The Fount of Life."

Dakota hadn't, but Ember had read about the Nazi program in her research. Lebensborn was developed to grow the size of the Aryan population. Young women from across Germany gave birth in designated homes, the children sired by prominent men in the Nazi party.

Did Kolman and Hanna adopt a child who'd been engineered Aryan? Or had Hanna adopted someone already fathered by her husband? That would make Titus happy. Character didn't matter when one was trying to play God.

Then again, God didn't allow anyone to impersonate Him for long.

"Was Mrs. Kiehl born in one of the Lebensborn homes?" Ember asked slowly.

"I don't believe so." Christine scanned the paper again. "Some of these children were brought to Lebensborn homes during the war."

Dakota leaned forward. "What do you mean?"

"The Nazis lost many of their men on the field and not enough women were giving birth for their Third Reich. To compensate, SS officers kidnapped thousands of Nordic-looking children from eastern countries. If these children passed rigorous measurement and medical tests, they would be adopted by upstanding Nazi families."

"They were fabricating the Aryan race."

Christine nodded. "They were desperate. It says that Roza Nowak was from Poland."

"Lilly is Polish," Ember said, her eyes on Dakota.

He leaned back against a tree and planted the shovel blade into the ground, a smile playing on his lips. "So my family is Polish and Jewish . . ."

"And German," Ember said.

47

HANNA

Reels of film were discovered behind the mine's locked door, boxes and boxes of them. What was on these films, Hanna didn't know, but after Charlie handled the damning biographies with care, returning the originals to her, she told him about the iron grate.

A team of Americans showed up the next day and picked the lock, lugging these reels of film down from the mine, through her front door. The boxes hadn't remained at the lodge for long. A truck arrived the next morning and carried them away.

She remembered Kolman in the grotto, on all of their digs, with his lights and camera, capturing every key moment on his motion-picture camera. And then his frequent journeys into the forest when he came to Nuremberg. What had he kept on these reels? And why were they stored in the mine, behind this locked gate?

The soldiers were still billeted in her home, using her rooms and eating the food their hired housekeeper cooked for them. Charlie was rarely there, but he came home late on a Friday and knocked on her bedroom door.

Lilly was already asleep when Hanna slipped out of the room, back down into the great hall. Charlie sat across from her on a couch, his golden wedding band catching a glint of light. He'd been faithful to his wife, not even hinting at their former relationship. For that she was grateful.

"Have you heard from Kolman?" he asked.

"Not a word."

He leaned forward, pressing his hands together. "If you are lying, there will be penalties that I can't control."

"I'm not lying. I would like to know, perhaps even more than you, where my husband went." The nightmares had returned, the ones with the monster hunting her, and she wanted him imprisoned like many of the Nazi leaders. "He used me for this property and for—"

She almost said to raise a child, but that would give everything away that she needed to hold close to her heart.

"Did he adopt Lilly?" Charlie asked.

"Yes." That much was true.

"Is she my daughter, Hanna?"

How could she tell him the truth about this? The penalties might be just as stiff for lying if he found out, except she'd hang her heart on the gallows and no rope would end the pain.

But she wasn't doing this for her heart; that's what she tried to tell herself. She was doing this to protect her girl.

"I'll tell you everything you want to know about Kolman, but I'm not talking about Lilly. She is my daughter, and I have raised her well."

Charlie looked like he was going to probe further, but he stopped. He could believe whatever he wanted. She didn't owe him an explanation.

"Why did you marry a man like Kolman Strauss?" he asked.

"The Nazi Party didn't give me a choice. He was an SS officer in need of a wife and children for the Reich, and I happened to own a property that the party wanted to use. They requisitioned me."

"Did you know he was married before you?"

"They divorced . . ."

"Not according to Elsie."

"Who is Elsie?" she asked slowly.

"Kolman's first wife. She doesn't know where he went either."

The news about his marriage should have surprised her, but it didn't. She'd known for years that Kolman was deceiving her, but she didn't know the depths of it. Nor did she care anymore except for curiosity's sake.

"This Elsie, is she in Hanover?"

Charlie nodded. "She's raising three of his kids."

So Kolman was able to offer the Reich four children after all.

"If it's true," he continued, "your marriage to him wasn't legal."

Part of her was angry at Charlie's revelation, but mostly she was relieved. She'd been misled into becoming Kolman's mistress, and he no longer had any right to her bed or her daughter.

Nor had he any reason to return to the lodge, except to retrieve his film.

Hanna rubbed her hand up her cheek, trying to press the thought away. "If this film is incriminating—"

"It is."

"Then he might do something desperate. He will fight for the Reich until the end."

Charlie offered her a cigarette from his case. When she shook her head, he took one out and lit it. "There is no Reich left."

"His devotion to Hitler was about more than being a party member, Charlie. It was a rite of passage. A belief stronger than religion. Just because this war is over, Kolman won't give up willingly."

He took a long drag on the cigarette. "We'll be having a military trial soon to convict him and the other officers for what they did."

After all the fighting, the swift justice they'd once had in Germany without a judge, it felt strange to talk about a trial.

"It will be an international tribunal," he explained. "First time in history."

"That's why you've come to Nuremberg."

He nodded. "It's my job to compile the evidence against them. The film . . ."

The details of the trial he would need to keep secret, she understood. Just like the secrets her team had to keep when they were on an expedition.

"We're painting a picture for the jury, and it's very dark."

She'd seen the photographs in the *Regensburger Post*, the only newspaper permitted by their American occupiers. The people in camps who looked as if they'd been starved and beaten. As if most of the world had forgotten them. "It's terrible, what happened."

"I don't understand." He leaned forward. "Why didn't the citizens of Germany stop it?"

She reached for one of the cigarettes, and he lit it for her. "Because we were proud on one hand. We wanted our country to be victors after losing the First World War, and nothing brings people together like a common enemy. Once the Nazis started to kill the Jews—" Her voice broke. "Most of us didn't know the entirety of what was happening in those camps; I suspect we still don't know."

"I suspect that you don't," he said. "I'll be leaving soon to move closer to the courthouse."

"And the other soldiers?"

"I don't know how long they will stay here," he replied. "I would like it if you could attend the trial for a day as my guest. To watch the films you helped us find."

"I could do that." Silence settled between them. "Tell me about your wife."

He smiled, taking another drag. "Her name is Arlene. We met at Columbia after—"

She didn't want to talk about their time together in Germany. "Do you have children?"

The smile fell. "Arlene is desperate for them, but she's not able to have kids."

"I'm sorry . . ."

"But I can still fight for children," he said, grinding his cigarette butt into the tray. "Bring justice to those men and women who hurt thousands of kids during the war."

She stood, rubbing off the chill on her arms. "Charlie—"

"What is it?"

"If something happens to me before you leave, will you make sure that Lilly is cared for?"

"Our soldiers will keep you safe."

"Please," she begged. "Promise me you'll take care of her."

His gaze traveled to the ceiling as if he could see Lilly through the plaster. "I promise."

She placed her hand on the banister, a crutch to help her move forward when these minutes felt as if they were standing still. "I need all the sleep I can get before I start digging again."

"You don't have to work, Hanna," he said. "When we leave, I can send others to stay in our place."

Other Americans to pay for her utilities and food.

"I need to do this for myself."

Once they cleared out the rubble, perhaps this country she loved could start over again.

48

EMBER

Hundreds of Japanese lanterns bubbled from the Campground cottages, the pathway between them washed with light. The Grand Illumination, locals had called it for a hundred and fifty years.

Ember and Dakota strolled through the grove on this warm evening as a symphony of music spilled out of the Tabernacle. They'd landed in Boston yesterday, and he didn't want her to miss this illumination or the opportunity to give Mrs. Kiehl the adoption papers.

"You're smiling," Dakota said as they passed under another string of lights.

"I've been plagued by shame for my entire life, and I left it back in that labyrinth. I no longer have to carry it around . . ."

He lifted his arm slowly, tentatively, and then he wrapped it around her waist. She folded into his chest, and he held her there, steadying her as if she might fly away without the stones, the shame, weighing her down. This place, it seemed, was exactly where she was meant to be.

"Is that you, Dakota?" someone called.

He released her. "Hello, Mr. Hawkins."

An elderly man stepped up to the porch railing, pointed his cane at them. "Are you with a girl?"

"Indeed I am," he said. "This is Ember Ellis."

The man squinted. "Umbrellas?"

"No, her name is—"

"It's okay," Ember whispered. She sort of liked being an umbrella, holding off the rain.

"Should be some sort of law about names," the man muttered as they walked away.

"We're home," Dakota said as he stepped up onto the porch of the Second Chance cottage. Lanterns dripped from the ceiling like jewels on a necklace, one commissioned for the lovely queen who was rocking on a patio chair.

Dakota greeted his grandmother with a kiss on her cheek, and Mrs. Kiehl smiled at both of them. "Welcome back."

Mrs. Kiehl would stay here for the week, Dakota had explained, with his mother. Even if they weren't fond of the crowds, they were minutes from the hospital, and they both enjoyed the music and the lights.

"Anything else from the doctor?" he asked, pulling up two chairs beside his grandmother.

"He says my brain has gone haywire."

Dakota sat beside her. "Your brain has been through a lot."

It remembered, Ember thought, even when Mrs. Kiehl struggled to put all the pieces into their proper place.

"Where's Mom?" he asked.

"Right here." The younger Mrs. Kiehl, her chestnut hair tied back in a scarf, pushed the screen door open with her hip, a pitcher of lemonade in her hand. "It's supposed to be cooler on this island than Boston, but it sure doesn't feel like it tonight."

"Ember, you remember my mom."

"I do," she said, helping with the pitcher. "I never got to thank you, Mrs. Kiehl, for your gift back in high school." The flowers and verse from 1 John.

"Call me Julie, please. I'm glad you received it."

"What gift?" Dakota asked.

Julie patted his arm. "Something between girls."

End of discussion, those words.

"I'm sorry for what I said about Lukas," Mrs. Kiehl told her.

"I'm glad you did. Until then, I didn't know he used to live on the island."

"He came here on vacation at first and then decided to stay," Mrs. Kiehl said. "Showed off his grandfather's death ring like it was a trophy and then hounded Albert and me when we didn't agree with his sentiments."

Dakota glanced over at Ember before speaking again. "I think we might have some answers for you, Gram, if you want to hear them. But they may only lead to more questions."

"Perhaps they will answer some of the questions in my mind."

The band across the plaza struck up "America the Beautiful," trumpets leading the charge. Their small group stopped to listen before speaking again.

Dakota unfolded the papers from his pocket, smoothing them out on the patio table. It was almost impossible to read the worn type in this light, but he'd wanted to show his grandmother what they found.

"These are adoption papers," he said. "They were buried in that coffee tin."

"Adoption?" she asked, her voice shaking.

He nodded slowly. "Hanna and Kolman signed them when they adopted a girl."

She sat for a moment, her gaze on a group who'd stopped to look at their lights.

"Adoption," she said again after the tourists left, as if the word was a missing link to the confusion in her head. "Where did they adopt me from?"

"A home called Sun Meadow, although I suspect it wasn't a very sunny place to live."

The music stopped in the Tabernacle, an intermission.

"That's where the matron lived," Mrs. Kiehl said slowly. "She told me about the wolves in the forest, the ones hungry for children."

"Oh, Mom—" Julie took hold of her arm.

"I kept asking for my mama until . . ."

Julie patted her arm. "You don't have to talk about it."

Dakota refolded the papers. "The Nazis kidnapped Aryan-looking children from countries like Poland and then Germanized them for new parents to raise."

"And Hanna knew?" Mrs. Kiehl whispered before answering her own question. "She must have known."

"Frau Cohn said she was a good mother to you."

"I always thought Charlie was the one who kidnapped me, but it was the Germans . . ."

"Nazis," Ember corrected her. "Few Germans knew about this program during the war."

Mrs. Kiehl looked out at the people streaming across the plaza. "Do you know my birth name?"

"Roza," Dakota said. "Roza Nowak."

"Roza," she repeated as if the name was exhuming something inside her. "How can I find the Nowak family?"

"You'd start with the Arolsen Archives." Ember pulled out her phone. "They have a tracing service for victims of World War II. I can help if you'd like."

"I would like that." Mrs. Kiehl reached for Dakota's hand. "Thank you for finding this."

"It's all of our story, Gram."

"Where did Hanna go after the war?" she asked, her voice soft like a child's.

"We don't know yet," he said, but they told her about the dozens of biographies that Luisa and Frau Weber had collected. About Hanna hiding these stories and then recovering them as a gift for families of the victims and evidence used in the Nuremberg trials.

As Mrs. Kiehl began to remember, a notification blinked on Ember's screen. She ignored the message, but later, when she finally checked, she almost dropped her phone.

"My name's Aimee," the recording said. "I'm looking for a woman named Sarah."

49

HANNA

Hanna's world shattered the day she sat in the upper gallery of Courtroom 600. It was unprecedented, this international trial of a nation and its crimes against humanity. The people who'd crammed into the benches and tables below, the rooms behind filled with members of the press from around the world—they were paying attention now.

This Palace of Justice was built during the last World War, but the courtroom below had been remodeled to accommodate the attorneys, translators, and select reporters—all of them wearing headphones—along with a row of cameras. At the left of the room were uniformed sentries who stood guard along a paneled wall so the twenty-four men lined up in the defendants' box wouldn't flee.

Charlie sat at the prosecution table alongside six other investigators and attorneys, across from the defendant seats. Four judges presided over the trials from the raised bench to her right, each representing a different country—Soviet Union, Great Britain, France, and the United States. Forced labor, the prosecutors had talked about this morning. Death camps and extermination.

At the thought of Frau Weber and Luisa, imprisoned in one of these camps, the bitterness in her stomach raged again. It was one thing to focus on the heritage of the Aryan people. Another to create a master race by killing off an entire people group and those who loved them.

"I really do have the intention to gather Germanic blood from the whole world, to rob it, to steal it wherever I can."

Himmler was dead, but the attorney still read these words of their former Reichsführer. An unsuccessful chicken farmer, he said, who'd decided to apply his breeding practices to the human race, replenishing their society with children like Lilly, stealing her away from her family in what seemed righteous to him.

The process of examining each defendant was excruciatingly slow. Every question asked by the American attorney would be translated into German, Russian, and French along with every response. One of the judges, she noticed, had begun nodding off in the heat.

Not only was the room warm, it was almost void of decor. Sage curtains blocked any sunlight from entering the windows, the overhead lights casting a dull glow across the spectators. Marble pillars braided a side door with the bronze sculpture of Eve overhead, handing Adam an apple. The nations hadn't been able to remove those pieces, but the chandeliers were gone from the ceiling along with the carved paneling. The spartan design, Charlie had told her, was intentional. The prosecution wanted the Nazi officials to be treated like common criminals instead of celebrities.

As far as she knew, the Americans had yet to locate Kolman, and she wondered again—what was his part in this tragic scenario that Charlie and the other men were unveiling for the press corps and judges alike?

Commander Donovan, one of the American attorneys, called

Wilhelm Frick to the stand—the man who'd enforced the policy against Jewish people. The lights on a row of television cameras blinked red as the commander began to ask him about concentration camps. Herr Frick denied the existence of any such camps.

Commander Donovan leaned forward on his podium. "You never heard about any prisoner camps in Germany or Poland?"

The question hung between the men like a barrage balloon, forming a net to snare whichever one crossed the line.

The translator repeated the question, but Herr Frick refused to be trapped. "I know nothing about these camps," he said again, his stoic gaze focused on the prosecutor, defiance in his eyes.

"And you were the—" Commander Donovan referred to a paper—"minister of the interior."

Until Himmler replaced him in 1943. Then he served as a Reich protector in their newly acquired Lebensraum.

"I have already stated my position, Herr Donovan."

"Indeed. You have stated several times that you never heard of these camps."

Herr Frick glanced at the row of justices, arms folded over his chest. "Why must we waste everyone's time?"

Commander Donovan motioned at the table behind him, and Charlie stood, straightening his black tie. With permission from the court, Charlie pulled down a screen beside Herr Frick so both the justices and the media could see his evidence.

Someone dimmed the lights, and Charlie began to project the film he'd found in the mine. Films that Kolman had taken for Herr Frick and other leaders in the Reich.

Silence swept across the noisy courtroom as they watched shaky frames of this film together.

Nothing could shock her anymore, that's what Hanna had thought, not after what happened to Luisa and the others and the devastation in her town, but these images were horrific.

Instead of excavating in Poland, Kolman had been working in these death camps, filming the experiments that Himmler had conducted in order to create a genetically pure race. The man she'd once called husband had watched others die under the Ahnenerbe's purported research, and he'd done nothing to help them.

A sound began to swell from the courtroom floor, a rustling at first and then whispering among the defendants and the press. None of the justices were nodding off now.

She clenched the sides of her chair, tried to stop the shaking. She'd done the same thing as Kolman, watched people taken from her town, transported to these camps. And she'd done nothing except keep their stories safe.

Charlie had read the stories, but he didn't really need them, not with these films. All the Nazis had been done in secret was being exposed to the world.

Kolman would kill her if he returned to the lodge now. Not only had these films indicted him, his work indicted every man in the box below. None of them could fly back again to the safety of their eagle's nest.

The Nazi officers ultimately hung themselves with their own pride.

Charlie started another film, from a camp in Poland, one that appeared to have Herr Frick in a frame. The woman beside her began to sob at the desperation, the horror of it all. Hanna closed her eyes, but she'd already seen too much, the images flickering on the screen of her mind. Her stomach would hold no longer.

She ran out of the gallery, down the steps, throwing up by the front gate.

How could anyone do these things to another person? Nothing could justify this evil.

The tram took her back east from this palace, toward the rubble of Old Town. She stepped off near Central Station, looking up at the smokestack where the Tillich Toy Factory once stood, one of a hundred toy factories from decades past that had operated in Nuremburg. When parents across Germany were clamoring to buy steam engines and magic lanterns and dolls for their children.

What would her father think of all this?

She was glad, in a sense, that he was gone so he didn't have to see his country in ruins. Didn't have to watch the children who'd once played with his toys turn into adults who experimented on their former classmates and teachers. On their country's bankers and grocers and seamstresses.

Had Herr Frick and the other defendants done things to Paul and Luisa, to Frau Weber for helping? To Lilly's brothers in Poland? She'd hoped Luisa would return home by now, but she hadn't heard a word from her cousin.

She rushed toward Lilly's primary school, straight into her daughter's class. Once they were outside, she squeezed Lilly tight. "I'm so sorry."

"For what?" Lilly asked.

"For not doing enough."

That evening, after Lilly was asleep and the soldiers were playing craps around the dining room table, she climbed up to the labyrinth with her lamp. She didn't care if Kolman found her. Or the creatures in the night. Charlie would take care of Lilly if something happened to her.

Kneeling before the stump in the center, where the cross had once stood, she repented for the cowardice in her heart. The crimes of her people. None of them were pure without embracing the love—the blood—of the One who had washed their sin away.

Would Jesus forgive them? Perhaps because of those who had helped, who had sacrificed their lives, He would share His love with all of them.

She stayed out among the rocks for hours, tears watering the cold ground. She prayed for Lilly, that she would never know such guilt. For Charlie, that he would bring justice on those who'd orchestrated the killings. For Luisa and Frau Weber and Paul, wherever they were, that they could find their way back home.

Charlie said he would keep searching for Kolman, but she suspected Kolman Strauss would never be found. And that, when the Americans stopped looking, his Hanover family might disappear with him.

50

EMBER

Hope was her name.

The oldest of five children. Blue eyes with the prettiest of smiles, long hair more brown than blonde. She was a dancer. Cello player. An accident, she'd been told when she asked about her parents' wedding date. An accident they adored.

After all these years, Ember had found Elsie, except she was someone else's daughter now.

She looked at the photograph as Aimee, tears streaming down her face, told her about the girl who had grown up as part of the Lane family. A young woman who'd been loved dearly for the past twenty-one years.

Timothy sat beside his wife, a strong presence next to her tears.

Hope was traveling with a group from their church for the week, on a mission trip to Puerto Rico, and the four other Lane children were scattered throughout the beautiful home that overlooked a river and the ribboning Glacier National Park in the distance.

"Hope's heart is as big as our sky," Aimee said. "That, she got from you."

Ember should have said something, a thank-you even, but she couldn't take her eyes off the picture.

Alex shifted in his seat. "What happened that night on Eagle Lake?"

It was just the two of them who'd come. Dakota had volunteered and so had Tracy, but it had been her and her brother grieving alone in the aftermath. This was something she and Alex needed to do together now.

"He tried to kill Hope," Aimee said, her eyes on Ember. "After you got on the boat."

"Lukas wouldn't kill our daughter—" It was the weakest of protests. She knew, like the rest of them, that he was capable of killing anyone, especially if the authorities might take his child away and give her to a non-Aryan family. Better that she was gone, he'd think, than grow up without the council.

"She started crying," Aimee continued. "I suspect it scared him."

Ember looked back down at a photograph of Hope when she was about five or six. Lukas, who was never scared of anyone, had been frightened by a three-month-old girl.

"So you grabbed her?" Alex asked.

"I dove in after her when Lukas threw her into the water. I don't think he ever intended to follow you and the others. He was headed back up the mountain."

Where they'd stored enough food for ten years, a millennial opportunity when others were terrified about Y2K.

Ember traced her fingers along the edge of the album. "You saved her life . . ."

"I didn't even think about it at the time." Aimee stared down at a picture of her and Hope together, celebrating a birthday with cake and balloons. "After we got out of the lake, I just ran and then crawled through that hole in the fence where I used to sneak out at night."

Ember slowly turned the album page, studying each picture. "I was waiting for her and Lukas on the opposite shore that night. The FBI didn't know where either of them went."

"I told the police in town she was my daughter," Aimee said. "No one questioned me except Timothy, and I told him the truth. The next day, he put a ring on my finger and a week later we were husband and wife."

"And parents."

Aimee nodded slowly. "I tried to look for you, as Sarah Heywood, but I didn't look very hard. At first, I worried that Lukas would get custody of her, and then, after he was sent to prison, I thought you might return to the group. I couldn't bear to have her . . ." Tears fell again, dripping on the album page.

"You wouldn't have found me," Ember said, "even if you'd scoured the entire state."

"I'm still sorry—"

Alex put his arm around her shoulders, and Ember leaned into him. What would have happened if she'd stayed behind, rescued Elsie from the water? If only she'd known . . .

"I want to meet her," Ember said.

Timothy leaned forward. "Can we wait until she returns from Puerto Rico?"

"Of course."

The days would give her time to process what she'd say to this beautiful girl. She hadn't meant to abandon her, but would Hope be angry that Ember hadn't searched until she found her?

When they finished meeting with the Lanes, Ember and Alex drove down to Eagle Lake. As they circled the shore, she cried happy tears followed by sad ones. The cabins in the old camp were long gone, replaced by a grassy park, but the bark on some of the trees was still charred.

The trees remembered what happened here. They still bore the scars.

"Lukas intended to kill her," she whispered as they stood along the bank.

"He would have killed anyone in his way."

"Thank God Aimee jumped into the water."

A turtle wriggled up onto a log, catching the sun on its face.

"Ember . . . ," Alex started.

"What is it?"

"There's something else I haven't told you."

A chill swept through her skin. She'd told Alex that she wanted to know everything, but she wasn't certain now.

"The whole reason for Lukas coming to Martha's Vineyard was to kill someone."

Her hands began shaking. "Did he succeed?"

"No." Alex picked a rock off the grass and threw it into the lake. "He wanted to kill the man who tried to prosecute his grandfather after the war. The man who, he thought, tried to ruin his family."

"Charlie Ward?"

Alex nodded, his eyes focused on the mountains where Lukas and the others had planned to hide.

Jonny Tillich—that was the name of Lukas's grandfather. The former SS officer who ignited hatred in his heart, then passed along the mandate with his skull ring to revive the Aryan race.

Ember took a deep breath. "But Charlie was already gone when Lukas arrived—"

"Exactly." Alex threw another rock into the water. "So he befriended Charlie's grandson instead."

HANNA

51

Hanna and Lilly hadn't been alone in the lodge for months, but their guests had relocated yesterday to assist with the trials, taking the housekeeper with them.

Tonight Hanna planned to take a long bath, wash the rubble off her skin. If only she could wash away the film images that had been seared into her mind, the bruised bodies of those killed in the camps. They haunted her wherever she went.

"Go play in the attic," she said, kissing Lilly on the forehead. The hobbyhorse had lost its draw once Lilly was tall enough to rock herself in a chair, but she still loved Opa's dollhouses. Each piece they'd restored over the years came alive in her hands.

"But the soldiers?"

"Are away for now, and I have it on good account that those dolls have been missing you."

Lilly giggled. "Where are you going?"

"To forage." She reached for a basket to collect onion grass and nettles and chickweed—autumn greens for a dinner salad. "I won't be long."

Lilly scrambled toward the steps, and Hanna opened the front door, her basket in hand, Schatzi on her heels.

A man in worn civilian clothes was outside her door, pacing beside the front window. She should have slammed the door shut that moment, bolted it and every window in her house, but she stood there in shock as if a bomb had been dropped on her doorstep, a crater swallowing her whole.

Kolman's trousers were torn in one knee, shirt stained with mud as if he had escaped from one of the camps. Or just returned, like so many of the men, from fighting a war. "I feared you wouldn't be home," he said.

She stepped onto the stoop. "And I feared that you would come back."

The lock clicked when she shut the door behind her, the key buried in her pocket. She prayed that Lilly would stay up in the attic. That she would hide, like she used to do, when a man came to the door.

"My key stopped working," Kolman said.

"The Americans changed our locks when they moved in."

"They aren't home now," he said. "And I need your help to find something."

Did he know about the film reels the Americans had already found? If so, he'd kill her for what she'd done.

"What are you searching for, Kolman?"

He didn't answer, but she saw the glimmer of metal under his sleeve, the gun that had been outlawed.

How many of these officers were still hiding out in the wilderness? Flinging around bullets when the world had already crushed them with bombs?

If only she'd brought one of the kitchen knives in her basket, instead of these dull scissors, to protect her from the predators.

"Inside, please," he said, motioning toward the door.

When she hesitated, he picked up a rock and threw it into the window. Glass shattered on the ground.

Schatzi hissed as Kolman picked up a second stone, but there was nothing a house cat could do in the face of a lion.

Hanna stood tall, her shoulders square, as she unlocked the door. She couldn't ignore what was happening this time. Not with Lilly inside.

Kolman followed her into the great room, and they sat together as if they were about to conduct a meeting, except he placed his pistol on the desk, the barrel facing her.

But he didn't need a weapon. She would do anything to protect her daughter.

"Where are they, Hanna?"

"Where are what?" she asked, forcing herself not to look at the ceiling. The stairs. Lilly would surely hide if she heard Kolman's voice.

"My boxes of film."

"I didn't take your film."

"All my reels are missing from the mine."

And if he knew they were being watched by the entire world, he would kill her now. "A lot has happened since you left, Kolman. Mainly you lost the war."

"Our war," he said. "They haven't taken this country yet."

Was he delusional or were he and the other missing officers really planning to continue their fight?

She pressed her fingers together, trying to calm the tremor in her voice. "It's too late."

"We're not giving up, Hanna," he said, shaking his head. "Not any of us."

"Himmler is dead. The papers say he killed himself."

His eye twitched. "We don't need either him or Hitler to carry on this Reich."

She saw it now. The loss of these Nazi leaders wasn't a defeat. It was an opportunity for Kolman and the other officers to step up in the ranks.

He glanced to the side as if he was just now realizing that something was missing. "Where's Lilly?"

"Out playing with friends, but you don't need to worry about her," she replied. "I'm told you have three other children in Hanover that call you Vater."

"They are hiding now, and I can take Lilly away as well." He snapped his fingers. "In an instant."

"You would kill your daughter?"

"She's not mine," he said. "But I'd drive her to the eastern border and tell her to find her way back home."

How had Kolman, who'd once seemed kind, who had searched for artifacts alongside her, turned so cruel? The war had changed all of them, but it had hardened the very soul of this man. He'd used her and Lilly both.

"You are a smart woman, Hanna. You will do what is right for the greater good." He opened the filing cabinet and began rifling through the papers. Was he planning to show officials that Lilly's adoption had been a farce?

But he didn't say anything more about Lilly. Instead he lifted out a manila folder and stuffed it under his shirt. "Burn that film, Hanna."

"I don't know where it is."

He glanced up at the rafters, at the portraits of the Tillich family. "I think I will spend the night, since the Yanks are occupied at the moment."

Her stomach rolled again, like it had at the trial, but she couldn't run away now. She had to protect Lilly from this man, hide her until Charlie returned.

But in order to protect Lilly, she'd have to give up the Holy Grail.

"The cave," she said quietly.

He leaned closer. "What is it, Hanna?"

"In France. I found something buried in the Cathars' grotto. The cup, I think."

"You think?"

She swallowed. "I know. I was planning to return after the war so I could keep it for myself."

That, Kolman understood.

His gaze darted between her and the filing cabinet. "Why would you tell me now?"

"So you can whisk your Hanover family away with the money you earn from it and leave my family alone."

He reached back into the cabinet and took a second folder, combining the contents with the first. "We'll have to steal a car."

"I'm sure you can manage."

"And we'd need to leave right away."

That was exactly what she wanted to hear.

She packed quickly, tossing her trousers and an extra blouse and her hiking shoes in a canvas bag. *Find Charlie*, she wanted to scribble on a memo pad, but she had none in her bedroom.

Instead she kissed her hand and lifted it toward the ceiling, praying that all would be well for Lilly.

"Hanna," Kolman said from the door, his gaze trailing up to where she'd raised her hand. "If you don't find the Grail, I'm coming back for her."

She strung the bag over her shoulder and rushed out of the room.

The Americans wouldn't let them drive at night, out of the city. For that matter, she doubted they would get past the first checkpoint. Guards across Germany were looking for those who'd been employed by the SS, especially the officer beside her.

But she shouldn't have doubted.

Twenty hours—that's how long it took them to travel from Nuremberg. They stopped only for gasoline and food and the roadblocks, Kolman charming every gatekeeper along the way.

"Jonny Tillich," he said when they reached the French Zone, to the soldier asking for his papers. "This is my wife, Hanna. Our children lived with an aunt in France during the war, and we are anxious to reunite with them."

Kolman handed over Hanna's identification card with her maiden name and then the paperwork for her brother.

A man who'd never been a member of the Nazi Party.

A man who would be free to go almost anywhere he liked.

Because Jonny Tillich hadn't done anything wrong.

52

EMBER

A train trestle stretched across the canyon below, bridging two of Virginia's spruce-clad mountains. They sat together, Ember and Hope, on a bench under the pine trees, the faint smell of diesel in the air.

Her daughter was a senior in college just three hours west of Georgetown. And Hope had wanted to meet with her on campus. Alone.

Both of them, it seemed, were equally bewildered at this twist in their stories, but as surprised as Ember felt, the sweet joy of it all was . . . there were no words to describe the depth of gratefulness for this truth. Another gift from God.

Dakota was waiting at the student center nearby, and she suspected that Aimee and Timothy were also close. But for now it was just her and Hope, beginning where they'd left off except there was no crib or lake or threat of fire.

She wanted to embrace this beautiful young woman, hold her

tight, but she was afraid to scare her away. So she shook her hand, introduced herself like they were meeting for the first time.

Hope pressed the toes of her sandals together, her skin tan from Puerto Rico. "I'm not sure what to say."

"Me either," Ember replied, lifting a small gift bag off the ground. "I brought you this."

She handed Hope her present. The perfect gift that she'd found in Pennsylvania while she worked and waited for Rebekah and the police to find Titus Kiehl. They had a lead, Rebekah said, but the police hadn't been able to locate him yet. Whether it was Titus or someone else who'd been harassing her, the letters had stopped while Ember was away from the museum.

Hope peeled back the silver paper and lifted out a white polished stone, like the one Mrs. Kiehl wore around her neck. Like the one Ember had purchased for herself.

Ember tucked the stone she owned under her blouse even as Hope held up her gift. "It's pretty."

"There's a story behind it," she said. "I'll tell you one day if you'd like."

"What should I call you?" Hope asked, lowering the chain. It dangled over the rips in her jeans.

Perhaps it was too late for Mother or even Mom, but maybe friend. "Ember is fine."

"I like your name."

"Thank you." She gently drummed the sides of her legs, the roll of each finger calming her mind. "I've been looking at some of your pictures online." The ones of her daughter digging in the Puerto Rican soil to help locals plant a garden, dancing with a whole troupe of children. "I'm immensely proud of the confident, loving woman that you've become."

Hope smiled.

"You have a million stories, I know. And I want to hear every one."

"I'm a music major," Hope told her. "And I teach ballet at a nearby studio."

"I'd love to see you dance."

Hope lifted the chain and clipped the stone around her neck. "I didn't know anything about this, about you, until last week."

Several students waved as they hiked by, greeting Hope by name. Ember waited until they were on the other side. "I thought you died more than twenty years ago."

"Tell me what it was like," Hope said. "Caring for me on that compound."

Ember stopped tapping her legs this time, wanting to remember the good and bad. "It was a dark place, but you brought hope in the midst of it. When I held you at night, I knew that I—that we—would somehow make it through."

"I was supposed to be a Nazi—that's what my mom said. The people in this cult were trying to have lots of white babies."

Ember's phone chimed, and she quickly muted it. "You are uniquely you, Hope. What runs through your heart is most important, not your blood type."

"I used to have these dreams." Hope looked down at a train as it crossed the bridge. "I was twirling on a dock someplace and fell into this terribly cold water. Even though I tried to swim, I could never get out on my own, until—"

Ember leaned closer, encouraging her.

"A presence, that's the only way that I can describe it. A light swept under me like a net and lifted me out of the darkness."

She'd had the same dream as her daughter. "You almost drowned when you were a baby; did Aimee tell you that?"

"A few days ago, and then my dream began to make sense."

"Aimee was your angel," Ember said. "God sent her, I think, to rescue you."

Hope lifted her face to the sky, like the turtle on Eagle Lake who'd come out to sun. "They've been good parents to me. I never would have known I wasn't their biological child until . . ."

"I didn't know if I should search for you. If you were still alive, I didn't know if you'd want to be found."

Two more students passed, nodding toward them.

"I'm glad to know the truth," Hope said.

"You are Timothy and Aimee's daughter." Ember swallowed the bitter sweetness of those words. "I'm not here to break your relationship apart, but someday, perhaps, you'll be a little of mine too."

The sound of feet pounding, running up the hill. She thought another student was hiking along this path, but when she looked up again, it was a full-grown man. And in his eyes—

Titus Kiehl was in these woods, wearing an overcoat on this warm day, his head shaved clean. But it wasn't his face that she recognized first. It was the evil that poured from him, the familiar hatred in his gaze. She'd seen it over the years among the council members, but until she'd stood on the sidewalk during the march, it had never before been directed at her.

Titus clearly hated her.

"What are you doing here?" she asked, trying to calm her voice.

"You left Washington."

"I had to leave," Ember said.

Titus stepped closer. "So I followed you here."

One hand was in his pocket and on the other she saw a flash of steel, the Death's Head forged for members of the SS.

"Where did you get Lukas's ring?" she asked, reaching for Hope's shaky hand.

"He let me borrow it."

With Lukas in the penitentiary, this man, Dakota's father, seemed to be bearing the torch for the Aryan Council. Another disciple, like the ones her own father had made, who would do anything to usher in an Aryan nation.

And he knew her name, past and present.

"Did you send letters?" she asked. "To the Holocaust museum?"

"I was trying to help you, Sarah. Bring you back for your family's sake, but you chose to ignore the warnings." He fiddled with the pocket. Was it a gun inside or a knife?

Ember squeezed Hope's hand and then stood up so she'd be looking straight into the man's eyes. "Go home to your family, Titus. If you do something stupid here, you'll lose everything."

"It's Lukas who needs my help."

"Lukas can have me." Ember moved away from the bench, hoping he would follow. "I'll visit him in prison. Ask what he needs."

"Lukas doesn't want you anymore," Titus said, his eyes on the bench. "He wants his daughter."

Ember's stomach churned. That's what Lukas had been searching for all along, through Titus. And Ember had led these men right to her.

But this time she wouldn't be getting on the boat.

This time she stepped right in front of her daughter.

"Neither you nor Lukas can have her."

"It's not up to you."

The knife plunged toward her heart, but it barely nicked her shoulder. Dakota might not play football anymore, but he remembered how to tackle. And he took out his father in seconds, the knife clattering to the ground.

Then Hope was by her side, kneeling on the sidewalk. "Are you okay, Mom?"

Those words, the best of music to her ears.

She was much more than okay.

Her heart felt whole again.

53

HANNA

MONTSÉGUR, FRANCE

Hanna's rucksack was still resting against the wall, in the narrow tunnel off the cathedral room. She didn't lead Kolman back to the cupboard chamber, to the blood-tipped arrow that she'd discovered five years ago. Instead she knelt by her abandoned things, searching for her trowel.

"The Grail was here," she said, pointing at the ground. "I reburied it where I left my pack."

Kolman would never take her back home, even if she led him straight to the treasure. Her job now was to protect Lilly, extend the hours so Charlie could find her. Give him time to steal Lilly away before Kolman returned.

She'd kept her daughter's secret from everyone. The girl, a child of God, was more precious than a grail. Only Kolman knew about her past, and she prayed that he'd never find Lilly now.

Hanna held out the trowel, but he didn't touch the tool. "You dig it up," he said.

She moved slowly, deliberately, taking care not to harm any artifact under the soil. When she found nothing, she began digging nearby.

An hour passed. Maybe two. Locked up in this cage with a lion. She had no reason to hurry, but her body was failing, her eyes drooping in the darkness no matter how hard she worked to keep them open.

But in her weariness, in the depths of exhaustion and despair, God stepped into her sorrow. No matter what happened tonight, she was in His care.

"You lied," Kolman said, his eyes as fierce as the monster in her dreams, glowing yellow in the lantern light.

"It's here someplace," she insisted.

"Then I'll have to search alone."

"No—" Had enough time passed? More than a day since they'd left Nuremberg. Kolman would need to sleep, a few hours at least, and another full day to return if he could charm his way through the checkpoints. Would Charlie whisk Lilly away in three days or would he linger at the lodge, waiting for Hanna to come home?

But Charlie had seen Kolman's film. He knew what the man was capable of. Surely he would remember his promise to keep Lilly safe.

Kolman swung his gun in Hanna's face, and she pressed her trowel back into the soil, digging faster as if she might find the Grail here. Every moment that he believed her ploy, every minute she could continue deceiving him as he had done to her, she was buying time for Charlie Ward.

The gun exploded in the cavern, burning her ears.

"I have more ammunition," Kolman said, the sound echoing around them, her ears pounding with her heart.

As she looked up at him, an unexpected peace settled in the cool air like snowflakes on her meadow back home.

"That's a good way to start a cave-in." She sifted another layer of dirt off the ground, her gaze focused on the sweat that poured down Kolman's face, the wildness in his eyes. "You'll bury us both here."

He swore. "Show me where you found the Grail."

But it was a secret that she planned to keep. Like the Cathars.

"Show me, Hanna."

Her time was short. She whispered a prayer again for Lilly and Charlie. That God would care well for both of them. Her fear was secondary now to a greater hope. If Charlie didn't come to the lodge, she prayed that God would still rescue her daughter.

"I'm leaving." She picked up the rucksack that she'd left behind long ago, the journal with all her notes, and began walking toward the entrance. Not for a moment did she believe Kolman would let her live, but she wasn't going to wait here any longer, pretending to lead him to the treasure. If she could rappel down the cliff, send a telegram to Charlie, he could tell Lilly what happened. That she would see her daughter again soon.

Hanna rushed through the cathedral room, light filtering in from the entrance, the threads of sunset weaving together a carpet rolled out just for her.

She'd almost made it to the ropes when Kolman grabbed her arm, whirling her around. Hate raged again in his eyes, vile words spewing from his lips, but she was no longer afraid. Nor did she hear his rant. The words, they seemed to dissipate into the colors.

"God forgive you," she said. As God had forgiven her.

She fell when he pushed her out of this cage, but only for a moment.

Then she flew.

Frau Weber, she saw first, among the colors of the sky. Vater, then her mother at his side. And a glorious King who welcomed anyone who asked into His Kingdom.

All was at peace—restored—in this beautiful new world.

54

EMBER

Coolness washed over Ember's face as Brooke led her out of the rented car, the sweetness of autumn clematis accompanying her steps this evening. She listened for the rustle of waves near the pavement, but the only sound she heard was whispering. And the clanking of keys.

"Wait here." Brooke sat Ember in a dark room, a bandanna wrapped around her eyes. "You don't want to peek until it's ready."

"Until what's ready?"

If Brooke heard her, she ignored the question. Her friend had been acting strange since they'd arrived on the island yesterday to celebrate the successful defense of Ember's dissertation. A girls' weekend, they'd planned. A redeemed homecoming of sorts.

A weekend where she finally told this dear friend of hers the whole story.

But a blindfold? It was a good surprise, Brooke had assured her, but Ember felt as if she were back in high school, a pawn in another game that couldn't possibly end well.

She stuffed her hands in her jacket, trying to play along, but she'd reached her capacity for the unexpected in the past three months. Her stitches were gone, her shoulder healed, and she was more than willing to forgo anything that began with *Surprise!*

Thankfully, there'd been no surprises when she presented her dissertation. The committee had been fascinated with the stories about Nuremberg, both from centuries ago and then the documented accounts of three women who'd worked together to record Jewish biographies during the Holocaust. Two of these women had helped to hide people, and the third one ultimately discovered the film footage that convicted men like Albert Speer, Alfred Rosenberg, and Hermann Göring during the military tribunals. It had been the first time that film was used as evidence in a trial.

Ember's dissertation had been focused on the past, but her gaze was on the future now. On the importance, the simplicity, of looking someone of a different nationality, a different background, in the eye. Talking with instead of at them, hearing their story. Replacing an identity of hatred with one steeped in God's love.

The concept looked good on paper, at least. It was harder to implement in real life. Harder to love without getting wounded in the process.

When men like Lukas refused this love, when they rallied people around a perceived enemy of their race, murdered and destroyed, she prayed that justice would continue to prevail. That others would rally together to stop the slow dripping of prejudice before it drowned them all.

She and Dakota had celebrated the completion of her doctoral degree, the beginning of a new journey, with dinner at the Four Seasons in Georgetown. After a three-month break, she was scheduled to begin teaching in January.

Thank God, the board had not only denied Lukas's request for parole, but they'd banned him from applying again, so life in jail, it seemed, really would be life. Titus was currently in prison as well, awaiting trial for aggravated assault with a deadly weapon. Mrs. Kiehl was sad but relieved to have him in a place where he couldn't threaten anyone else.

Dakota had returned this afternoon to coach a game at the high school. He'd invited her along, but that was one invitation she declined. They'd meet in the morning to have brunch with Mrs. Kiehl and her fifty-seven-year-old niece Lidia, who was visiting from Poland. One of Mrs. Kiehl's brothers, Piotr, had survived the war, hiding for most of it in a friend's potato cellar. He had three children, and while he'd died in the 1970s, the Nowak family welcomed Mrs. Kiehl back into their fold.

Charlie had found her back in 1945; Mrs. Kiehl remembered it soon after she realized that Charlie hadn't stolen her away from her biological family. Then the tangle of her traumatic memories began to unravel.

Her family in Poland, she remembered them next. Two brothers and parents who'd loved her. The German soldiers who ripped her from her mother's arms. Then her mind had flashed to the attic where Charlie found her in Nuremberg, curled up behind one of the doll-houses, as if no one could snatch her out of her make-believe world.

More memories followed. Of her last night in the lodge. Hanna walking out to the meadow before dinner, and then Mrs. Kiehl—Lilly— had seen a man outside. A man who'd escorted her mother away.

Kolman Strauss, they all assumed. Where he had taken her, they might never know unless Lukas decided to tell the Kiehl family, but it seemed that Hanna's marriage to him had been her demise.

Days later, Lilly had boarded a ship with Charlie for the United States. She was his biological daughter—that's what Charlie had told the immigration officer. He had plenty of clout by that time as one of the chief investigators of the Nuremberg trials and the valid excuse that Lilly's paperwork had been destroyed in the bombing.

After Charlie told the officer that he'd attended college in Germany, that he'd reunited with his former girlfriend in Nuremberg, the man had no reason to doubt his story.

A long letter home to Arlene had softened the blow before they arrived, and this new mother—her third one—told her that she'd never have to leave this home. And she never had.

Light trickled under the edges of Ember's bandanna.

"Brooke?" she called out. "This is silly."

She trusted this woman with her life, but if Brooke made her wait one minute longer, the blindfold was coming off.

"It's time." Brooke's hand was under Ember's elbow, helping her stand.

"I have to know what—"

"Good," Brooke interrupted, urging her forward. Cool air gusted over them as they stepped back outside.

Were they in the Tabernacle? A surprise concert maybe. A reunion of some of their high school friends. A celebration for Lidia's arrival.

But why would Ember need a blindfold for a concert or reunion?

Pavement no longer pressed against the soles of her ankle boots, the ground soft now with the padding of grass. Metal clanged around her, then a cacophony of voices. Sounds that transported her right back to high school.

Surely Brooke hadn't brought her back to the football field.

"You can take it off," her friend said.

But Ember no longer wanted to comply. It was the thinnest protection between her and the outside world. A shell that she didn't want to shed.

When she didn't move, Brooke unknotted the blindfold. It slipped over her eyes, her mouth, dropping to the ground.

Pockets of light sparked in the darkness like stars in a distant galaxy. It was impossible to focus, clouds masking the skylights.

A loud whoosh startled her, a wave of light breaking overhead, and she felt as if she'd been plunged into the ocean. Complete submersion in this spotlight.

And it was much too cold to swim.

Stadium bleachers were to her left, the benches packed with people waving flags of purple and white. Like the spectators on homecoming night.

Her lungs begged for air as she tried to calm the racing in her heart.

Football players lined the field, cheerleaders with pom-poms glistening at their sides.

Did Brooke want her to confront this fear? Somehow break through the panic that was engulfing her? Step into her nightmare and remember that night in order to overcome?

This was a lousy way to do it. She and Dakota were in a good place, the past between them finally healed.

Turning, she prepared to run away from this game, back to the ferry before it left for the night. But then a speaker crackled on the field. A voice bellowing across the stadium.

"A warm welcome tonight to Dr. Ember Ellis."

The man's words were followed by applause, and she glanced up at the box above the stands, to the place where Glen Hammond had called Alecia's name to accompany the homecoming king.

The crowd was cheering as if she'd just made the winning touchdown. But why were they clapping for her?

A quick scan across the crowd, and she saw a familiar face in the bleachers. Her brother was seated in the front row, along with Tracy and their two kids, a smiling Maggie waving at her.

Then she saw another face between them.

Hope.

The young woman who'd stolen her heart had stolen those of her cousins as well. Both Maggie and Saul were cuddled up close, her arms around their shoulders, and Noah, he was there with them. He and his father.

Below them all, looking like royalty on their sideline chairs, were Lilly and her niece Lidia, clinging to each other's hand.

A white Bentley convertible rolled onto the field, and Ember covered her eyes to block the bright lights, squinting to see who was inside. The driver was Beatty, Dakota's friend, wearing a cap like a Boston cabbie. He hopped out to open the back door.

Dakota stepped onto the field, dressed in jeans and a purple-and-white football jacket, number 15 stitched onto the sleeve.

She shivered in the autumn air, old fears threatening her again. What was she supposed to do now?

Dakota stood in the middle of the field, hands hidden in his pockets. Instead of the proud homecoming king from long ago, he looked like a terrified pauper. As if this moment could break him, like it had broken her.

"To escort Dr. Ellis on the field tonight is Coach Kiehl." The speaker popped twice as Dakota lifted his head. *"If she'll have him."*

With those words, the rustle behind her quieted. And warmth flooded over her skin.

Dakota wasn't humiliating her. This time around, he was giving her the opportunity to humiliate him. She could turn away, leave him standing in front of an entire stadium of spectators. Friends. Family. His football team.

No one on Martha's Vineyard would ever forget if she left him now.

He was walking toward her, one of his hands outstretched, and everything else began to fade away.

"Will you come with me?" he asked, motioning toward the center line.

"You don't need me on the field."

"I want to replace the old memories with something new."

She shook her head. "This is crazy."

"Please, Em."

She slowly took his hand.

It was a dream, this walking across the field beside Dakota Kiehl. A dream that she'd never forget.

When they reached the middle, two students joined them. One with a plush golden crown. The other carrying a pillow with a tiara, the rim lined with costume jewels.

The crowd cheered when Dakota and Ember were coronated king and queen. She didn't need this, the attention from the crowds, but something deep inside her seared back together as they clapped. The lie that she wasn't good enough, that she was a fool to care for this man, began to disappear.

Love poured through her as she glanced back at her family in the stadium. At Noah's golden spoon waving in the air to remember this day always with her.

Only a God of redemption could bring this all together. Replacing animosity with hope. Hatred with healing.

But Dakota wasn't finished yet. From his pocket, he took out an antique-looking watch, the hands ticking to record each second that passed by. She no longer heard the cheering from the crowd, only the gentle voice of the man in front of her.

"It's like the one in the labyrinth," she said as he slipped the watch into her palm, the chain dangling from her hand, their initials carved on the back.

"I want to start again, Ember, beginning right now. I want to treasure every minute, every second with you."

She closed her fingers over the watch as if she could make this moment stand still. Then she tapped her legs one last time before reaching for Dakota's hand.

No one could ever take this memory from her.

It was one that she'd cling to like a rock for the rest of her life.

DISCOVER MORE GREAT FICTION
FROM MELANIE DOBSON.

"A tale you won't be able to put down—and won't want to."

—*ROSEANNA M. WHITE,*
bestselling author of
the Codebreakers series

"An unforgettable story. . . . This is a must-read."

—*PUBLISHERS WEEKLY,*
starred review

"Exquisitely penned . . . *Hidden Among the Stars* is Dobson at her best."

—*CATHY GOHLKE,*
Christy Award–winning author

Brilliant color flickered across her canvas of wall. Sunflower yellow and luster of orange. Violet folded into crimson. A shimmer like the North Sea with its greens and blues.

Most of the walls in her bungalow were filled with treasures of artwork and photographs and books, but this pale-cream plaster was reserved solely for the light, a grand display cast through the prisms of antique bottles that once held perfume or bitters or medicine from long ago.

The colors reminded her of the tulip fields back home, their magnificent hues blossoming in sunlight, filling the depths of her soul with the brilliance of the artist's brush. Spring sunshine was rare in Oregon, but when it came, she slipped quietly into this room to watch the dance of light.

Sixty-eight bottles glowed light from shelves around her den, their glass stained emerald or amber or Holland's Delft blue. Or transparent with tiny cuts detailing the crystal.

These wounds of an engraver—the master of all craftsmen with his diamond tools—made the prettiest colors of all.

Only one of the bottles was crimson. She lifted it carefully off the shelf and traced the initials etched on the silver lid, the ridges molded down each side, as she lowered herself back into her upholstered chair.

All of them she treasured, but this one . . .

This bottle held a special place in her heart.

Her fingers no longer worked like they used to. They were stiff and curled and sore. But her mind was as sharp as a burnishing tool. Perhaps even sharper than when she was a girl.

She held this bottle to her heart, leaning her head back against the pillow.

No matter what happened, she wouldn't forget.

Couldn't forget.

A cloud passed over the sun, darkening the room for a moment, and she felt the keen coldness of the shadow. The memories.

Some memories she clung to, but others she wished she could lock away in one of the vaults under Amsterdam's banks. Or a tunnel carved into the depths of the old country.

Closing her eyes, she remembered the darkness, the chill of air deep underground seeping back into her skin. The memory of it—of all she'd lost in Holland, of the terrible mistakes she'd made—had haunted her for more than seventy years.

Shivering, she pulled the afghan above her chest.

Seconds ticked past, time lost in the cold, before sunlight crossed over her face again, color glittering in the gaps of darkness. When she opened her eyes, the light returned to illuminate the wall.

Slowly she stood, balancing against the lip of wainscoting that rounded the room until she placed the bottle back on the shelf. Her legs felt as if they might give way, just for a moment, but she regained her balance long enough to find the sturdy legs of her chair. A front-row seat for her memories.

"Oma?" her great-granddaughter called from the hallway, on the other side of the door.

Her children and their children all worried about her, but they needn't worry. Even in her heart sadness, even when her body tripped over itself, all was well with her soul.

Her family, they knew about her Savior, but they didn't know all she had done. No one who remained in this world knew. It was her secret to harbor, for the safety of them all.

"Come in," she said softly, her gaze back on the glass.

Even if her mind began to slip like her feet, this room would always remind her of the ones she'd lost.

And the one she had to leave behind.

* * *

AMSTERDAM
MAY 1942

"Dinner, Jozefien, that's all I ask." Klaas dug his hands into the pockets of his trousers, wagging his head as if she'd wounded him with her refusal. "I'll take you to Café Royale."

Schutterijweg 265.

Each letter, number, clicked like a typewriter key in her brain, making an imprint before she forgot the address.

"I can't," Josie said, trying to focus on the man standing beside her, the woven handle of the basket seeming to burn her hand. "At least, not tomorrow night."

It seemed innocent enough, this basket. A bouquet of purple and orange tulips, two glass jars, and a lining of gingham napkins. But her brother had hidden an envelope in the bottom, under the gingham. And no one, including Klaas, could find out what she was delivering to Maastricht tomorrow.

Schutterijweg 265.

Klaas fingered the tulip petals. "Orange is supposed to be banned."

"Fortunately no one told the flowers."

Klaas leaned against a marble column of the expansive lobby, his blond hair combed neatly back, the knot of his plum-colored tie bunched up above his waistcoat. He wrapped his arms across the breast of his gray-striped coat. "What's more important than dinner?"

"I'm helping Keet with her children."

His eyebrows arched up, his handsome blue eyes studying her. "She only has two *kinderen*."

"She's had another since you visited," Josie said. "And now there's a fourth on the way."

An older couple scooted past them, and the yellow stars stitched to their clothing seemed to glimmer in the chandelier light and ripple across the long marble countertop in the lobby, trying to penetrate the milky glass that separated the bank tellers and managers from their Jewish patrons. The woman clutched the man's arm with one hand and the other was gripped around the strap of a fashionable shoulder bag. He carried a tan attaché case that, Josie assumed, was filled with money and jewelry and perhaps the title to their house. Everything valuable they owned.

The bank of Lippmann, Rosenthal & Co. had been formed almost a hundred years ago by two Jewish men and had been well-respected until the occupation. This new branch, called Liro by Amsterdammers, was designed by the Germans to secure all the valuables of Dutch Jewry. The securing of property became mandatory with yet another regulation by occupiers who'd vehemently promised they wouldn't persecute the Jewish people in Holland.

Then again, the Germans had promised they would never bomb the Dutch, hours before they crushed the grand city of Rotterdam into dust. Now Holland was being assaulted from inside and out. An onslaught of German soldiers, Gestapo, local police, and NSB—Dutch Nazis—who were all implementing what Hitler demanded of them.

Josie switched the basket to her other hand. "Samuel will go to dinner with you tomorrow."

He eyed the basket. "Did he bring you another gift?"

"Jam." She lifted the flowers to show him the two amber-colored jars. "Golden raspberry from home."

She was fairly certain that her brother had purchased it at the market—he hadn't been back to Giethoorn in weeks—but Samuel often called her from the bank these days, saying he had a gift from home. Better, he'd once told her, for them to make their exchanges in public than attempt to do so in secret.

Klaas reached for one of the jars, and she held her breath as he examined it, hoping he wouldn't find the envelope.

Schutterijweg 265.

She couldn't allow him to blur a single one of these letters or numbers in her mind. The smallest of details meant life or death in their work.

Klaas placed the jar back onto the napkin, and she swung the basket casually to her side. "How's Sylvia?"

"Sylvia and I are no longer together." He gave her that sly smile he liked to use when they were children. "She said I was much too interested in someone else."

Josie hugged the basket to her chest, not certain how to reply. Klaas had never treated her as anything more than Samuel's little sister. Someone he had to tolerate even when she annoyed him, a responsibility she'd taken quite seriously until Eliese arrived in Giethoorn.

They were all grown up now, Eliese safe in England while Josie, Samuel, and Klaas had moved to Amsterdam. It was her first year in the city, studying at the Reformed Teacher Training College, but Samuel had worked for several years at the Holland Trade Bank before transferring to Liro, and Klaas was employed at an architectural firm. Unlike her, Klaas managed to pretend that nothing in Holland had changed in the past two years, that their future was as promising as it had ever been.

He glanced at his watch. "I must return to the office or my boss might decide to lock the door." He tweaked her chin like she was a child again and they were skating along the canals back home. "I wish I could go back to Maastricht with you."

"Perhaps one day . . ."

"Perhaps." He smiled again before he left.

Josie glanced at the partially caged window where her brother sat, helping another Jewish customer entrust his worldly goods into the care of the regime. A *roofbank*—that's what this new branch of the respected institution was called. A pirate ship ready to plunder. The Nazis never planned to return anything they stole, but her brother kept pretending that all the gold and diamonds and certificates of stock were simply being stored here.

If only Samuel could have remained at the Holland Trade Bank with Eliese's father and their investors. Instead, the occupiers shuttered the bank's door months ago because of Mr. Linden's Jewish heritage. Last she had heard, Eliese's father was cooperating with the Germans.

The rain had stopped, but Josie still tied her red scarf under her chin, wishing it were a brilliant orange. Klaas didn't think she knew much, but she was well aware of the ban on her favorite color.

In the early weeks of the occupation, she had worn her orange sweater—the color of Dutch royalty—to classes each day until Dr. van Hulst, the headmaster at her college, quietly pulled her aside and handed her a blue cardigan, saying there were much more productive ways for her to rebel against the unwelcome guests who'd taken up residence in their city.

She'd found a bracelet in the pocket of that cardigan, and she'd worn it every day since, hiding the silver links and orange lion under her sleeve.

A row of green-uniformed guards stood outside the rain-soaked windows; their honey-brown hair reminded her of the yellow pollen produced from ragweed, infiltrating every inch of this bank's plaza. She rushed out past them, toward the bike rack, before someone stopped to search the contents of her basket more thoroughly than Klaas had done.

The road followed the river back toward the college, located at the edge of Amsterdam's Jewish Quarter. The handle of the basket looped over one arm, the glass jars jostled as she bumped along the cobbles, trying to avoid the puddles. On a normal day, she would slow down to protect her wares, but today she wanted to deliver this envelope back to the safety of her room.

In a year, she hoped she would be ready to teach on her own. In a year . . . if the Allied troops prevailed and the Jewish children in their country were once again allowed to attend school.

She hated this feeling of being caught in the enemy's web. Stuck. Of only being a courier for her brother with letters he said were making a difference, yet she didn't know if they were doing anything at all. People whispered about resisting this enemy, as her country had done so long ago with Spain, but they needed—she needed—to do more.

Someone cried out nearby, and her heels dropped to the ground. It was a little girl, standing on the stoop of one of the row houses, a stuffed bunny clutched to her chest.

Josie pedaled beside the parked automobiles in the alley and leaned her bicycle against the stoop. In the windows she could see faces of other people, watching the child, but no one came outside to help.

She rushed up three steps with her basket and knelt beside the girl, her heart sinking when she saw the yellow star on her cardigan. She must be at least seven. The younger children weren't set apart by the stars.

"What's wrong?" Josie spoke quietly lest she frighten the child even more.

"They're taking us away."

"Who is taking you away?" she asked.

The girl pointed toward a blue automobile that waited at the opposite end of the narrow lane, a capped driver inside. "The police."

Something rumbled inside the house, thunder echoing between the walls, the sound of heavy boots pounding down the steps.

Would this girl's parents want Josie to steal her away before the police did? Surely one of the neighbors would open up their door if she knocked, hide the girl inside.

But when Josie reached out her arm to take the girl's hand, she shrieked in terror. A woman rushed out the door and held her close, glaring as if Josie were the one threatening their family.

Two Dutch policemen stomped out behind her, grim shadows in their black shirts and boots like the fabled Ossaert, a clawed monster who searched for innocent victims in the night. The agents were gripping the arms of a disheveled man wearing a tailored suit coat with a torn star and a swollen bump on his head.

Had they beaten this poor man in front of his wife?

"What are you doing?" Josie demanded.

The sergeant's gray eyes, dual blades, pierced through her. She took a deep breath, the blaze of her anger dying down into embers of fear.

"Are you a neighbor?" He scrutinized her skirt and jacket as if searching for a star.

She shook her head. "I was worried about the girl."

"You needn't worry," he said stiffly. "We're relocating her and her parents to a safer place."

The terror in the girl's face shredded Josie's heart. If only she could still steal her away . . .

"Please let the woman take her!" the father pleaded.

"*Stilte!*" the sergeant barked.

Silence.

The second policeman, the one who refused to look at Josie, shoved the father toward the car. The look in the mother's eyes had changed, pleading now for Josie to help.

"Please . . . ," Josie begged the sergeant.

He grasped Josie's wrist, and the teeth of the orange lion bored into her skin. If he pushed back her sleeve and saw the bracelet, he'd arrest her right there.

Then again, he might arrest her anyway.

"I didn't realize you were taking her to safety," she said, relenting under the pain. And she hated herself for letting him bully her, cowering while this family was dragged away.

"Go home, Fräulein." He pointed. "Is that your bicycle?"

She reached for the handlebars. "It is."

Several people had stopped along the sidewalk, gazing at the family as if they were a parade of animals being led to the Artis Royal Zoo.

"What do you have in your basket?" He swept it out of her hands and threw her tulips on the wet sidewalk, the purple and orange petals wilting in the puddled raindrops.

"Diederik!" he called before tossing a jar of jam. The other officer tried to catch it, but the glass shattered against the cobblestone, spraying shards and raspberries across the pavers. The sergeant lifted the second jar, studying it as Klaas had done earlier. Then he turned over her basket, and the two cloth napkins slipped to the ground, red-and-white checkers bleeding on the ground.

She held her breath, waiting for the envelope to fall out, but no envelope appeared.

Had Samuel forgotten to hide it in the basket?

The sergeant ground his heel into the orange flower petals before turning to leave.

She slid down to the ground, wrapping her arms around her knees. Her entire body was trembling. She reached for the crushed flowers first, as if she could somehow recover their beauty, as if the brilliant color of their petals could soak up the darkness suffocating her.

As if the flowers could help her breathe again.

Then she picked up the napkins.

The bottom napkin felt stiff. Someone had stitched the fabric of two napkins together, concealing what must be Samuel's envelope.

Schutterijweg 265.

The face of the little girl haunted her as she clutched the napkin to her chest, tears welling in her eyes. She'd deliver this message to Maastricht for this girl and her parents and all who were being tormented by the Nazis.

An elderly gentleman seemed to appear out of nowhere, wearing a black raincoat and hat.

She stood beside him. "Do you know this family?"

"As well as any of us can know each other these days."

"Do you know where the police are taking them?"

"To one of the camps, I fear."

"What happens at the camps?" she asked.

He took a step away as if he'd already stayed too long. "None of us know for certain."

She glanced back toward the end of the alley. "What are their names?"

"Van Gelder," he said. "Werner, Hanneke, and Esther van Gelder."

"I only wanted to help," she whispered.

"It's too late to help them. Too late for any of us now."

AUTHOR'S NOTE

"My mom lived in Nuremberg, right after the war."

These simple words from a friend sparked *The Curator's Daughter*. Suzanne and Bing Ng occupied a home near the Nuremberg airport in 1945, the owner becoming their servant and friend. Suzanne saw the rubble, attended the Nuremberg trials, and took photographs of soldiers sledding with the local children.

This book wasn't based on Suzanne's life, but the foundation was inspired by her memories. The story of Nuremberg—a free imperial city—stretches back almost a thousand years. As I began to write, I realized that if I focused solely on World War II, I'd miss the rich history of this beautiful place and its centuries of innovation, art, and religious reformation through the German Renaissance. And I'd miss the cyclical integration, persecution, and then expulsion or murder of its Jewish citizens. A pattern that began long before the Holocaust.

Writing about gender or race evokes many emotions. We all have a story about victimization, some of them tragic. As I researched, I met with Anne LeVant Prahl, the curator of collections at the Oregon Jewish Museum, and was shocked by her stories about the growing anti-Semitism near our home. About those in Portland who troll for young men, in particular, offering them a brotherhood founded in hate.

My dear Jewish friend, Gerrie Mills, told me the same thing. So did Kevin Bates, a friend and pastor who shared his experiences from earlier years in Idaho.

Sadly, the news concurs with these personal accounts. CNN recently reported about the rise in domestic terrorism:

> Americans are being killed. Murdered not for what they
> have done or being in the wrong place at the wrong time.
> Slaughtered again and again because, whether Jewish
> or black or simply not "pure" white, they are seen as a
> pestilence to be purged.

History is circling back around one more time, and I can't ignore the revival of hatred around our world. Nor do I want to forget the hope of God's redemption and love for all. That a spirit of fear does not come from Him (2 Timothy 1:7).

I've written six novels inspired by events that happened during World War II, and each time I have learned something new. Until I started this book, I didn't know about the Nazis' obsession with archaeology or the horrific kidnapping of thousands of children (some say more than 200,000) from countries like Poland, Czechoslovakia, and Yugoslavia. After the war, all four leaders of Lebensborn, including Inge Viermetz, were found not guilty of any crime during the Nuremberg Trials.

My research for *The Curator's Daughter* took me on a grand adventure up the East Coast with my daughter Kiki before heading across the ocean to explore Germany. I've uploaded pictures on my website of the places and people that inspired this story, but one of my highlights was visiting the baroque Lutheran church in the German village of Pfungstadt, built in 1746. Several of my greats worshiped in the sanctuary, and my double great-grandfather Peter Wacker was baptized there in 1845 before he immigrated to the United States.

Another baby was being christened the morning of my visit, and during the baptism, Pastor Dienst spoke about my ancestors' legacy. About how the Christian heritage of Johann and Wilhelmine Wacker, through the life of their son Peter, had passed down through the generations. As I sat there steeped in the history, blessed by his words, I thought about identity, how we can embrace the good parts of our story and adopt new ones to replace the evil.

The writing of this story was a personal journey for me as I sought answers as to how so many of the German people, my ancestors, rallied behind the cruelty and oppression of Hitler's Third Reich. Some of them, I discovered, knew well what was happening in the east. Others suspected but didn't know the extent. Many felt helpless with no way to stop this tsunami from hitting their land. When it was over, they didn't want to talk about it.

While I had to tweak a few dates and places for the sake of story, I tried to keep the key historical events in place. The abandoned church was inspired by the ruins of an abbey near Schmausenbuck and named after Katharinenkirche, a medieval Nuremberg church destroyed during World War II. While the SS began kidnapping Eastern European children in 1939, Sonnenwiese (Sun Meadow) didn't begin "Germanizing" abducted children until 1942. Another date to note—the Nuremberg Military Tribunals were a series of trials that lasted until 1949, but it was the first international trial in November 1945, with its shocking film footage, that awoke and horrified the world.

Countless people answered my questions as I wrote this book. I am grateful to each one and also for those who courageously recorded all that happened during the war, including Emanuel Ringelblum and his group of scholars who chronicled the suffering in the Warsaw ghetto, burying their archive of documents so the truth would be discovered later. Some of these biographies have been found while others remain hidden. And Ingrid von Oelhafen and Tim Tate who coauthored *Hitler's Forgotten Children*, a firsthand account from a girl stolen away from her family and then adopted through Lebensborn. *Word-smelters*, they called the Nazis who twisted and distorted the best of words.

While *The Curator's Daughter* stemmed from my faith as a Christian, not everyone who contributed so kindly to this book has these same beliefs.

A special thank-you to:

Joy Ng for entrusting her mother-in-law's story to me. My agent, Natasha Kern, and editors Stephanie Broene and Kathryn Olson for helping me weave together this fictional account based on the frightening truth of what happened in Germany during World War II. I'm grateful to the entire staff at Tyndale House for using the many gifts that God has given them to create, edit, and spread the word about faith-based books. It's a joy to partner with all of you!

Sandra Byrd and Michele Heath—my fabulous first readers who helped me close the gaps and stay on track. Corinna Doty and Gerrie Mills for offering me your invaluable perspectives on both heritage and history. And my own Inklings—Julie Zander, Nicole Miller, Tracie Heskett, Dawn Shipman, and Ann Menke—for your laughter and logic and for pushing me back up into the writing saddle whenever I begin to slide. Each of you ladies were instrumental in molding the shape of this story.

Family friends Gabi, Freya, and Andreas for welcoming me to Germany and sharing your many stories, past and present. *Wacker*, Gabi says, is the name of a stone. In Germany, if you've done something *Wacker*, you've done it brave and strong. A beautiful tribute to my courageous aunt Janet and all of my Wacker (and sometimes *wacky*) family.

Maria Evers—it was an absolute delight to celebrate your birthday at the Frankenstein Castle above Pfungstadt. You and your family made my day!

Curator Anne LeVant Prahl and the staff at the Oregon Jewish Museum and Center for Holocaust Education for answering my questions and collecting the stories of many who experienced first-hand the horrors of the Holocaust. Mary Ann Hake for all of your encouragement and sharing the interview with a Jewish man from Nuremberg who survived the war.

The research scholars at the United States Holocaust Memorial Museum who helped me understand their fellowships-in-residence program and provided the resources necessary to make this story as factually accurate as possible. It was a sobering honor for me to research in your library and then read the Nuremberg trial transcripts about Lebensborn at the National Archives. (Any errors in this story are my fault.)

Ruth Cohen—an elegant Holocaust survivor who graciously thanked me for writing these stories. She's a beautiful reminder of why it's important to never, ever forget. To teach our children and grandchildren the truth before the evil in this world circles back around.

Jim and Lyn Beroth for blessing me with your daily prayers and encouragement. I am grateful to have parents like you.

Jon, Karlyn, and Kiki for laughing with me when my mind was so lost in this story that I forgot things and bumped into things and left other seemingly important things in the oddest of places. I love each of you with all my heart!

To our three-in-one God of redemption, creativity, and holiness. I pray for ears to hear Your voice, eyes to seek the truth, and a willing heart to tell Your story.

DISCUSSION
QUESTIONS

1. At the beginning of *The Curator's Daughter*, Hanna admires anyone who could protect an important secret like the location of the Holy Grail. How does this desire to protect secrets alter the course of her life?

2. What is the significance of Hanna and Ember collecting the stories of Jewish people before and during the Holocaust? How can remembering a past story change the future for an individual or family?

3. The medieval buildings in Nuremberg were destroyed and then completely restored after the bombing in World War II. How does Ember have a similar journey of restoration in her life?

4. Lilly Kiehl says, "All King David needed was the stone that God gave him to kill Goliath, and I need to use whatever gifts that God gives me to defeat the giants in my world." What unique gifts do you have to defeat the giants in your world?

5. Ember has a choice in this story between reconciliation and retribution. Have you ever had to forgive someone who meant to harm you? Did this process end in restoration as it did for

Ember and Dakota or more like Ember's confrontation with Titus Kiehl?

6. During the Nuremberg Trials, the atrocity of war crimes comes to light, and Hanna is overwhelmed with horror. In the labyrinth, she repents of her sin and the sin of her people, but she still wonders if Jesus will forgive them. What does the Bible say about God's mercy? What do we need to do to be forgiven?

7. Lilly believes several significant lies about herself, instilled in her when she was a child. Have you ever believed a lie like this? What did you do to free yourself from it?

8. In this story, Ember keeps trying to forget what happened in her past, but she eventually has to remember in order to heal. What is the best way to balance one's memories without letting them influence contemporary reactions and relationships?

9. The Nazis were adamant about controlling both entertainment and language as they tried to manipulate their culture. Often what sounded good—*purity* and *heritage* and *living space*—was really propaganda for evil. How do the definitions of a language influence the morality of its people? And how does a society fight against intellectual manipulation?

10. In the end, Hanna exchanges her fear for hope and her shame for forgiveness. What choices do the other characters make in regard to their own fears and shame? How do past choices impact the characters today?

ABOUT THE AUTHOR

Melanie Dobson is the award-winning author of more than twenty historical romance, suspense, and time-slip novels, including *Memories of Glass*, *Hidden Among the Stars*, *Catching the Wind*, *Chateau of Secrets*, and *Shadows of Ladenbrooke Manor*. Five of her novels have won Carol Awards; *Catching the Wind* and *Memories of Glass* were nominated for Christy Awards in the historical fiction category; *Catching the Wind* won an Audie Award in the inspirational fiction category; and *The Black Cloister* won the *Foreword* magazine Religious Fiction Book of the Year.

Melanie is the former corporate publicity manager at Focus on the Family and owner of the publicity firm Dobson Media Group. When she isn't writing, Melanie enjoys teaching both writing and public relations classes.

Melanie and her husband, Jon, have two daughters. After moving numerous times with work, the Dobson family has settled near Portland, Oregon, and they love to hike and camp in the mountains of the Pacific Northwest and along the Pacific Coast. Melanie also enjoys exploring ghost towns and abandoned homes, helping care for kids in her community, and reading stories with her girls.

Visit Melanie online at melaniedobson.com.